Jewels of Ursus

ELYSSA EDWARDS

ELLORA'S CAVE
ROMANTICA PUBLISHING

An Ellora's Cave Romantica Publication

www.ellorascave.com

Jewels of Ursus

ISBN 9781419959486
ALL RIGHTS RESERVED.
Mating Stone Copyright © 2008 Elyssa Edwards
Lovers' Stone Copyright © 2008 Elyssa Edwards
Soul Stone Copyright © 2008 Elyssa Edwards
Edited by Helen Woodall.
Photography and cover art by Syneca, Les Byerley.

This book printed in the U.S.A. by Jasmine–Jade Enterprises, LLC.

Trade paperback Publication August 2009

JEWELS OF URSUS

℘

MATING STONE
~11~

LOVERS' STONE
~77~

SOUL STONE
~155~

MATING STONE

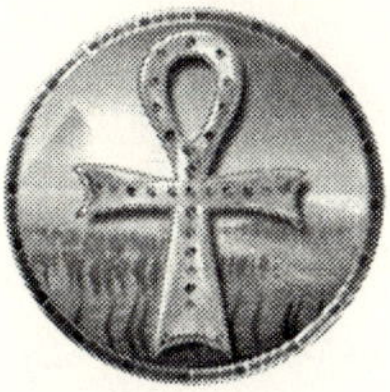

Trademarks Acknowledgement

ഇ

Chapter One

∞

Sarah smoothed her straight blonde hair as she examined her reflection. Her hair was pulled back into a loose knot at the base of her head that left tendrils of dark gold falling in a disorderly frame about her face. She brushed the strands back out of her eyes and smiled. She could almost feel Mark's hands cupping her cheeks as he gazed into her eyes. He'd smile that sweet smile of his and tenderly tuck the errant strands behind an ear. By the time he kissed her she'd have already begun to tremble.

He almost seemed to enjoy when her hair fell into her face, as if he were secretly pleased to be able to offer such a tender and loving gesture. Tonight she wanted to give him what he seemed to enjoy. He had something special to talk to her about, or so he'd said two nights before when he'd left her at her door. He hadn't come into her small townhouse as he had so many evenings before over the past three weeks they'd been dating.

Somehow it didn't seem that it could possibly have been only three weeks. No, it seemed more as if Mark Ursine had been in her life forever. The days when she couldn't pick up her ringing cell phone and hear his voice, when she didn't look up from her book in the quiet of her living room to see him, feel him holding her against his side as he watched the evening news or listened to the music that played softly in the background seemed a lifetime away.

She smoothed down the dark emerald dress she wore. The halter bodice was not one she'd normally have worn but her sister had been with her the day they saw it and had insisted she try it on. Once she'd felt the soft fabric against her skin and caught sight of her reflection in the mirror it had been a sale. This was something else about Mark. Since he'd entered her life she heard the negative voices in her head less and less often. The green of the soft silk pulled the green from her green-gray eyes, making them seem more than just the murky shade of in-between that had always disappointed her when she looked in the mirror. Her Nordic heritage should have given her sunny blonde hair and bright blue eyes. Instead she described her hair as "dirty blonde" and her eyes as "washed-out, foggy green".

A smile lit her face. No one had ever corrected her until Mark. She'd groaned at her appearance and repeated her litany of complaints at the end of their first week together as she hurriedly pulled her hair back into a tail while quickly glancing in the mirror on the visor of her car. Sitting in the passenger's seat, Mark had frowned seriously. "Is that what that mirror shows you?"

Sarah had arched a surprised brow at him and dryly observed that that was what all mirrors showed her. Mark had snorted angrily, put his hands on her shoulders turned her to face him and informed her she needed to get her eyes checked. "You're the most beautiful woman I've ever known, Sarah-mine." It had been the first time he'd spoken the endearment to her and it had touched her so deeply she felt the tears burn the backs of her eyes. He'd pulled the clip from her hair and tangled his fingers in it. "Your hair is like golden honey and your eyes, oh my sweet, your eyes are like the greenest sea at sunrise before the harsh sun burns away the mist." He'd kissed her then. Kissed her as they sat in the driveway of her parents' home. When she opened her eyes she'd seen first his dark brown gaze burning into her, then her sister standing on the front porch with wide eyes and an odd smile. She'd only been supposed to drop something off but it had ended up entirely different. It had ended with Mark meeting her family and charming them even more than he had charmed her. Which was saying something.

Now the green dress seemed to help her see what Mark said he saw in her. At least she could concede her eyes were passably pretty. And the empire waist was certainly forgiving of what her mother insisted on calling baby fat, what she called proof of her addiction to all forms of chocolate and what Mark insisted on referring to as her "lush and tantalizing curves". The man was mad. No doubt about it, he was mad. Only it seemed that mostly he was mad about her. She didn't understand it but she'd spent many a night lately, lying in the warmth of his arms, thanking God for it.

The doorbell rang right on time, or rather it rang fifteen minutes early, which Sarah had learned constituted on time for Mark. She'd once asked him if he was ever late anywhere. He'd flashed her that devastating smile of his and admitted that yes, he was occasionally late. "But never for you, love. If I'm late some other male might come along and steal you away from me." He'd lifted her hand to his lips and kissed the knuckles. "And that would be my undoing. I've survived a great deal in this world but never could I survive losing you." The lines should have seemed cheesy and rehearsed but they flowed from him with such conviction and sincerity that he either deserved an Academy Award or he really meant the lyrical things he said.

Sarah hurried to the front door and pulled it open. He turned as she did and her breath caught in her throat. Seeing him, especially if they'd been apart for a bit as they had been the last two days, always had this effect on her. Hell, he stole her breath so often it was a wonder she hadn't died of asphyxiation.

And tonight was certainly no exception. He stood there on her stoop, his dark brown hair combed back from his face and curling slightly at his collar. The sable eyes swept over her body and returned to meet hers with a hunger that made the heat pool in the pit of her stomach. "Sarah," he whispered softly. He didn't need to say anything else. The soft baritone of his voice was deepened even further by the same something that made his sudden intake of breath audible to her.

And the sight of him robbed her of her ability to do so much as utter his name. He was dressed in a black Armani suit. She knew nothing of fashion. She was a scholar, a biblioanthropologist, who knew more about the binding of ancient texts than designers. "Such a useful profession," her mother often remarked just before she asked how things were going for Sarah working at the local bookstore. No she didn't understand fashion or glitz but she'd seen the labels in his jackets enough to know he turned to the designer almost exclusively for formal and semi-formal wear. His tie hung untied around his neck, giving him a rakish air, and the jacket contrasted sharply with the crisp white shirt, open enough at the neck to reveal the tanned skin that beckoned her fingertips now even more so than when she lay with her head on his shoulder and her palm pressed to his bare chest.

A flush filled her face and she felt the heat grow in her cheeks. She'd never been one to move quickly but with Mark everything had moved at supersonic speed. By this point in a relationship, the few she'd had, she would still be hesitating about sleeping with the man and would feel guilty for having allowed him to reach second base.

She watched the smile sweep over those full lips and reveal the dimples that turned the perfect face into that of a naughty boy. There was only one word for him when he smiled. Cute. Yes he was sexy, yes he was virile and masculine. But when those brown eyes shone over the sweet dimpled cheeks, her heart wanted to hold him tight and make sure nothing ever removed that smile. He was definitely adorable.

"For you," he almost whispered and Sarah noted for the first time the flowers in his right hand. She smiled broadly and stepped back from the door.

"Thank you," she turned to him after shutting the door and reached for the flowers. They were lovely. The bouquet was not exactly what the rule books said a man should bring on a date. He'd brought her those on Valentine's Day. As she'd arranged them they'd talked about flowers. He told her about the Victorian traditions of flower language, that each flower had a meaning that could be deciphered by an attentive admirer. It seemed not only the flower and the color that were important but even how the bloom was displayed held importance. He'd apologized for not asking before and inquired as to her favorites, telling her a lot could be deciphered about a person based on their favorite flowers. Mark regularly amazed her with the tidbits of information he knew. History, culture, languages, so many things about him put him so far out of her league.

This cluster of calla lilies, chrysanthemums and gladiolas, all in a purest white, showed without a doubt that he listened to her when she talked and that he cared about doing things that pleased her. Her flushing deepened and pleasing her was something he was very good at. She'd never known a man who seemed so...er...devoted to pleasing a woman.

Holding the bouquet to her chest to hide the increase in her breathing from his penetrating gaze, Sarah walked to the kitchen to retrieve a vase. She filled it with water and arranged the flowers without a word. She could feel his presence in the room but he too chose not to speak. When the last bloom was in place she turned to find him leaned back against the small café table that sat in the bay window. He was watching her and for the first time since she'd known him his gaze seemed almost guarded, as if he didn't want her to see what he was thinking.

Wanting to wipe away the look that almost frightened her, she boldly crossed to him and wrapped her arms around his chest, laying her cheek on his shoulder. He was tall, at least three inches over six feet she guessed since her own average height tucked her up under his chin. He often lowered that chin to rest it on the top of her head, as he did now, his arms enfolding her. The embrace was one that made her feel completely encompassed by him, as if he held all of her cocooned in his protection and warmth. "I did say thank you, didn't I? They're beautiful," she whispered against his throat.

"Yes, Sarah-mine, you said thank you," his voice rumbled over her ears and down her nerve endings, causing her to shiver slightly. He pulled her tighter and laid his cheek against her hair.

"Should we be going?" she asked softly, feeling the heat of his body warming her. She turned her face slightly and pressed her lips to his throat and felt the vibration as he murmured against her skin.

"No, we have time." He placed one finger beneath her chin and guided her to look up at him. His smile made her heart race, accompanied as it was by the dark look in his eyes. She loved that look. Something in her thrilled each time she saw this tell-tale sign of hunger in his face. A hunger for her.

She pulled away, suddenly feeling shy, and lifted the crystal vase from the counter. He followed her into the small dining room of the townhouse. She set the flowers on the buffet and opened one of the drawers to pull out a small doily. She'd purchased it at an estate auction, as she had the dining suite in this room. She loved old things, things that had a history. It was almost as if each item in the room had a story to tell.

Mark said nothing but watched her closely as she placed both in the center of the dining table. Sarah turned around to find him running his hand over the surface of the sideboard. "Things like this were made to last," he muttered softly. "It's important, you know, Sarah. Creating things that are meant to last a lifetime," he paused, "or beyond." She clung to the back of the chair behind her and waited. Something was definitely off.

He turned his gaze to her and held out his hand. She went to him and he pulled her back into his arms. She tipped her face up to his and heard him whisper softly against her lips, "I've missed you so," before he claimed them with a passion that made her melt against him. She had missed him too. Missed his touch. Missed the sound of his voice. And she'd especially missed the way his hand molded to her breast as his tongue pushed deep into her mouth. Just when she was sure she could no longer breathe, he pulled his lips from hers and brushed them along her cheek to her neck.

He licked and nipped at her skin as if he were starving. As if he wanted to devour her. Sarah slid her hands over his back and felt the roll of the muscles there as his hands moved over her body. The man knew how to touch her, knew how to make her incoherent with need for him. His hands started to gather the fabric of her dress and lift it over her hips. His faintly roughened palms stroked her curves through the soft silk of her panties. Strong fingers kneaded the flesh with an urgency that made her feel needed in a way that only served to increase her arousal.

She whispered his name as he kissed her neck and teased her ear. "I've missed you," he murmured. "Never so long again, Sarah-mine."

"You were only gone two days." Her chuckle changed to a gasp as he slid his hand into the bodice of her dress and brushed against her breast. His fingers stroked the nipple until all she could do was hold onto him and groan with delight. No one had ever made her feel like this. No man had ever had the power to turn her into a complete wanton in his arms.

Mark turned them slightly and she felt the sideboard press into her hips. "Too long. Too long to go without tasting you," he spoke the words as he grasped the edges of her panties and pulled them down over her hips with a sudden jerk. She felt the silk slip down her legs and drop to the floor. In an instant he'd cupped his hands under her backside and lifted her onto the sideboard. She felt the cool wood against her skin. Skin that was already swollen, wet and ready for him.

She started to protest but his mouth cut off her voice as he kissed her again. His hands pushed aside the fabric of her dress and she felt the cool air against her breasts as the bodice separated to expose her. "God, I love this dress," he muttered as he lowered his head and sucked the hard nipple into his mouth. His touch was deliberate and hungry. There was nothing teasing or sweet about it. He licked and sucked at the nipple, biting into the taut peak as she squirmed and moaned. He dropped to his knees and met her eyes. The look on his face was almost feral. Keeping his eyes on hers, he moved closer to her. His breath was hot and tickled against the lips of her pussy. She moaned his name softly and saw him smile up at her.

"Too long to go without tasting you," he repeated and ran his tongue in a long, broad stroke up the slit in her folds before pressing into her and finding her opening.

"Mmmm," was the only sound she found she was capable of making. Mark pressed deep into her while he slid his hands under her hips, pulling her closer to the edge. Sarah leaned back and heard the clatter of falling knick-knacks. Not that she cared about that or anything else at the moment as Mark teased her entrance with his probing tongue. He licked up the wetness and pressed as deep into her as he could. She could feel him suck softly as if drinking in her essence.

When he withdrew his tongue he replaced it with two long fingers that pressed into her and stroked her with a curving come-hither motion. His lips moved up to fasten on her clitoris. His tongue swirled over the sensitive flesh and she gripped the ledge of the sideboard, pressing herself up to him. Mark groaned against her and swirled his tongue faster. He alternated the motion with sharp, short flicks and a gentle sucking that had her bucking up against his face nearly as much as the deepening thrusts of his fingers. It was as if he was feasting on her and was nowhere near to having eaten his fill.

Sarah wound her fingers through his soft silky hair and tried to push him deeper. He chuckled and she felt him smile. He worked her body harder and harder. Pushing her desire higher and higher until she cried out as she arched her back and her body clenched wildly around his fingers. The release was sweet and her heart pounded in her chest.

God she'd missed him.

Mark rose from between her thighs, licking his lips wickedly and smiling in a very smug, self-satisfied way. And with damn good reason. He kissed her and helped her slip down off the sideboard before holding her against his chest. "So passionate, my love."

Passionate was not a word anyone had used to describe Sarah in the past. But with Mark it was true and even she knew it. She moved her hand down to stroke him. He was hard and ready for her and she was shocked when he grabbed her hand and stilled her movements.

"My family will be waiting," he said softly. This was the second reason for splurging on the green dress. Tonight she'd meet Mark's family. She had to admit this was moving very fast yet it seemed right. So exactly right. He kissed her again and smiled. "After tonight, we will have all the time in the world."

She readjusted the bodice of her dress as he lifted her panties from the floor and knelt. He held them out for her as she stepped back into them. He kissed her again as he slid the fabric almost reluctantly back up over her hips. She tried to smooth down the skirt of her dress, just certain it was wrinkled beyond help. He caught her chin and tilted her head up. "You look beautiful. But before we go, there is something I want to give you." Mark smoothed his hands over her hair and tucked a wayward strand behind an ear. Sarah couldn't help but smile. He stepped back slightly and closed the last buttons on his shirt and quickly tied his tie. He brushed at his jacket and drew in a deep breath. Looking even more incredible than before, he reached into the pocket of his jacket and pulled out a large, flat, dark blue box. Sarah's eyes widened. Mark was always giving her little things, whether they'd been apart minutes, hours or not at all, but that was a jeweler's box and it looked more than a bit expensive.

He put the box in her hands and gestured for her to open it. When she did, her jaw dropped. Lying on a bed of black velvet was a large amethyst. The stone was simply set and hung from a delicate box chain. She looked up at Mark. "Mark, this is..."

He cut her off. "A gift, Sarah." Something about his voice was thick and odd. "It is something I want you to have, something I hope you will accept." His eyes gazed deep into hers. "Darling, my family...our traditions are different from most. A lot about us is different from what you're used to. We don't give rings, my love. When a man in my family asks a woman to join her life to his, he gives her a stone like this, her birthstone. And this stone," he drew in a deep breath, "this is my promise to you. My pledge, Sarah-mine."

"Mark, are you saying... Are you asking..." She couldn't finish the sentence. Was he asking her to marry him?

"It can't be a surprise to you that I love you, Sarah. I know that you feel strongly for me. I can see it in your eyes when you look at me, feel it in your touch. I want you to be mine, to be my wife, my partner, my mate. I want you by my side, my love. This is what I had to go away to do, I had to find the stone and have it set for you." He caressed her cheek softly.

"This is so fast," she murmured. She wanted to scream yes with all that was in her but it was so fast. And Sarah never did anything fast. Her whole life had been about slow and easy. The word "impulsive" just wasn't in her vocabulary. Not until she'd met Mark.

The night they met had been her birthday. She'd let her sister and some friends talk her into going to a club to celebrate. "Come on, Sarah, it's February 2. It's your twenty-eighth birthday, so do what all good little groundhogs do and get out. Even if you see your shadow, at least you had fun before you run back and hibernate some more," her sister had teased until she'd agreed.

She'd not met Mark at the club but afterwards on her way home. Hitting a pothole had blown her tire and while she could change a tire herself—hell, like any good ol' Minnesota girl she could change a tire, put on her own snow chains and use the jumper cables in her trunk—she just didn't relish doing it in the short skirt her sister had talked her into wearing.

Resigning herself to ruining her stockings and probably the new skirt, she'd been hauling the jack and donut from the trunk when a motorcycle had roared up behind her. The headlight had almost blinded her but not as much as what stepped out into the light. Pulling a black helmet from his head, the man had been devastating. His black jeans and leather jacket completed a monochromatic feast for the eyes.

Flashing her a smile almost as bright as his headlight, he'd insisted he couldn't let a lady like her change the tire. He'd made short work of the flat even if she did stand there like an idiot and chatter away. By the time he was done he knew it was her birthday and where she'd been. If it had taken any longer she'd hated to think what else would have come bubbling out of her mouth.

He packed her jack back into her trunk and asked her to allow him to follow her home since he didn't have much confidence in the small rubber tire. When she'd hesitated he'd pulled out his driver's license and a credit card. He put them in her hands. "Hold on to these. If you get spooked at all you know who I am, where I live and can either call the police or charge a fortune for yourself in compensation."

When they'd arrived at her place she handed them over and smiled nervously. "Thank you just doesn't seem like enough," she nodded down to the damp patches on his knees where he'd knelt in the wet snow alongside the road.

"Then have dinner with me tomorrow." He'd flashed an encouraging smile and she felt as if her bones melted. "That's all the thanks I need."

She agreed and had started to walk away when he called out to her. He was pulling something from the storage compartment under the seat and walked quickly up to her. His long-legged strides held her so transfixed she didn't see what he had in his hands. He stopped in front of her and hesitated. She looked up at him. He suddenly seemed shy and uncertain, grinning up at her through the hair that had fallen over his forehead.

"Happy birthday, Sarah." He placed a single red rose in her hand. His quick kiss to her cheek was so soft and so fast that she almost missed it. By the time her fingers rose up to touch where he had pressed his lips to her skin, he was back on his bike, turning it and roaring away. Odd but only now did it occur to her to question where on earth he'd gotten the rose.

His voice pulled her back to the present. "Sarah, I know this is fast for you. I know that you... Sarah, for me this is much simpler. I know exactly what I want and I know it will never change. But I want you to be sure. I don't want you to answer me yet. It's not fair to ask you to make up your mind when you haven't even met my family. I only want you to think about it and I wanted to give you this so there is no question in your mind or anyone else's where we stand. I want you and my family to know I am yours and you are mine. No gray areas."

She looked up at him. She loved him. She really did love him and for some stupid reason, not a part of her believed he didn't love her. She wanted to marry him. She wanted to raise a family with him, grow old with him. She wanted every silly romantic cliché and she wanted it with Mark. She swallowed hard before speaking. "But doesn't my not answering you leave a lot of gray area?"

"You've answered." He kissed her softly on the lips and then on the forehead. "With your eyes, Sarah-mine, you've answered." He smiled down at her. "But I want to give you the option to change your mind once you've seen the true level of insanity that spawned me."

"Everyone thinks their family is weird, Mark," she reassured him.

"Mine isn't weird, Sarah. They're… well, you'll see."

Chapter Two

ଈ୬

Mark helped her into her car and they left his motorcycle sitting in the drive. She still couldn't figure why he rode it in the cold weather. His answer had been that as long as it wasn't icing up, he preferred it to the SUV alternative. As he started her car she asked, "Is Mardi Gras a big holiday for your family? I don't know of anyone else who actually celebrates it outside of places like New Orleans, certainly not as far north as Minnesota."

His hand hesitated as he slipped the key into the ignition. "Some years February is one big celebration for my family. You might say we all look forward to shaking off the chill of winter."

"Mark, February is hardly the end of winter," Sarah frowned in confusion.

"For us it is, sort of a reawakening you might say."

She began to wonder if her question had somehow affected his mood as Mark became uncharacteristically quiet for several minutes as he navigated through the streets of St. Paul. Just when she thought she'd ask if she'd said something wrong, he reached out and took her hand in his. He lifted her fingers and pressed his lips to the back of her hand. "I'm sorry if I'm not the best of companions tonight, Sarah. Seeing my family isn't something I look forward to. I especially don't look forward to subjecting you to them. At least when I met your folks you knew they wouldn't be openly hostile. I can't promise the same thing." He grew silent for a moment. "They know you're coming but there are some things about you that will surprise them."

"Surprise them how?" *Openly hostile?* The nervousness made her stomach flip.

Mark sighed. "You might say you're not my usual type, or more accurately you're not the type my family thinks should be my usual type."

Sarah suddenly felt self-conscious and pulled her wrap tighter. She was glaringly aware she wasn't the kind of woman a man like Mark would normally date. Mark was gorgeous. His perfectly sculpted good looks, his dark hair and eyes, these were only the beginning. The tawny skin covered one hell of a ripped body, one that had stunned her the first time she'd seen him in all his glory. She'd never believed a real man looked like that under his clothes. He was incredibly strong as well, evidenced by the fact he had lifted her effortlessly that first night and carried her to the bed. Of course his family would expect him to bring home a woman equally as beautiful.

Her insecurities won the silent battle in her head against the words of adoration Mark had whispered these past weeks. Her brow drew tight in a frown, "Mark, if you'd rather not introduce me, it's okay."

He sighed. "It's not that, sweetheart. My family is not what you're used to. They're...a bit odd and..." His voice trailed away for a moment. Then he turned those incredible eyes to her and grinned somewhat sheepishly. "It's just that the house is big, there are a lot of people and I don't want to lose you."

Mark still held her hand in his when he turned into the circular drive of an obscenely large home filled with lights, people and music and brought the car to a halt. He turned in his seat. "Stay close to me, Sarah." He reached out and brushed his fingers along her cheek, "Unless I tell you to stay with someone, stick close and don't get separated from me."

She couldn't help but smile back at him, the anxiety starting to slip away. "Stick close, got it."

He slid his fingers down her face to cup her chin before leaning in to kiss her. *Damn, could this man kiss.* His lips pressed to hers and she forgot in the warm, soft feel of them that there were actually people about, people who could see them. When he pulled back, his dark eyes were bright. "I wish this wasn't necessary," he muttered as he turned away. He slid out of the car and walked around to open her door. That had taken some getting used to. Even when she drove, Mark opened her door. Sarah had honestly believed such behavior was archaic and long dead in men today, at least the men in St. Paul. But Mark was the epitome of good manners and chivalry. He opened her door, held her chair and offered his arm when they walked. A blast of cold air chilled her when she slipped out of the car. Mark pulled her wrap around her shoulders tighter and slipped her hand in the crook of his elbow before he walked her toward the house. "It's all right," he whispered softly in her ear as he reached around her to push open the front door. Sarah couldn't help but wonder who he was reassuring, her or himself.

The foyer had a high ceiling but was surprisingly small. She wasn't sure what she'd expected but it hadn't been this. The walls were all paneled in dark rich woods or painted in deep earth tones. The floors were polished wood with numerous thick braided or woven rugs of natural fibers. Large potted plants and trees were everywhere. She almost felt as if she had walked into a forest. The few people who stood in the entry turned to look at them curiously and she felt Mark stiffen. Each of them was beautifully dressed and the men wore masks while most of the women carried theirs.

Mark didn't take her wrap but guided her over to a long, low table against one wall. It was spread with a variety of Mardi Gras masks, each more elaborate and beautiful than the next. He reached for one. It had dark brown feathers trimmed with gold accents including golden beads on the leather ties. He placed the mask, which covered his eyes and most of his forehead, on his face and quickly tied it in place.

"You need a new one," a soft voice said behind them. "You've been using that same mask for far too many Mardi Gras." Sarah turned to see a small smiling face. The woman was quite old with lines around her eyes and lips. Her hair was a lovely silver gray. Around the woman's neck was a large ruby set in an intricate gold setting that reminded Sarah of the stone she now wore around her own neck. Sarah glanced about her and saw two more women in the foyer who wore large colored stones, each in a unique setting.

She was relieved when Mark smiled. He bent down and took the offered hand and kissed it gently. "You, Grandmother, look even more ravishing than ever." As he folded both his hands over the gray gloved fingers, his grin broadened into the heart-stopping smile that sent shivers down Sarah's spine. "It really isn't fair to the other women here for you always to look more beautiful than them."

The woman giggled girlishly and batted his hands away with the porcelain mask attached to a gilded stick that she carried. "Imp." She turned to Sarah. "He's always been positively incorrigible." Her eyes softened. "You must be Sarah," she offered her hand and Sarah found she had to repress the urge to curtsey to the grand old dame. "You are welcome in my home, dear.

"Come here, child. I had a feeling from Mark's description of you that you'd wear green tonight." She took Sarah's hand and led her to the table. Her fingers gingerly lifted a white mask mounted, as hers was, on a slender gold rod. Feather brushed swirls in green and purple spread over each cheek and up the sides. Feathers in a purple-edged black and gold fanned out from its edges. "I was saving this one for you."

"Thank you," Sarah fingered the beautiful mask. "It seems almost too fine to wear."

The woman laughed. "Be glad that we don't have to wear them on our faces as the men do. I promise you," the old woman met her eyes. "You will be much more comfortable in this mask than you would be in one of these itchy feather monstrosities we make the gentlemen wear. They're a bit warm and once you start to sweat," she gave a mock shudder and smiled. The smile was very much the same wicked grin she'd seen on Mark's face from time to time. "Nothing worse than damp molting feathers sticking to your skin."

"If they're so uncomfortable why do the men wear them?" Sarah asked the question as much to Mark as to his grandmother.

"Tradition, my dear," she replied. Sarah saw Mark roll his eyes behind his mask as his grandmother continued. "You will find a great deal in this family is dictated by tradition."

"Tradition," Mark muttered. "The fool's excuse for refusing to accept that all things change."

"Do not start that argument tonight." Her face was stern. "Your grandfather is under enough strain at the moment without you getting everyone all fired up—any more than will be necessary." She patted Sarah's hand. "Don't worry, my dear. We must all have our first Mardi Gras with the Ursines. It won't be boring, it may be a bit intimidating even but the moment you feel out of your depth, or if you need anything, come to me. I decide who is welcome in this house and you, my dear, are welcome."

Her words did little to still Sarah's butterflies. In fact, they seemed to turn them into full-fledged swallows flapping madly.

Mark reached out and again took the tiny hand. His eyes seemed to shine. "Thank you, Giselle."

"That's Grandmother to you, scamp. I've earned every one of these gray hairs and I'll not be denied them." She touched his cheek with her free hand. "She's beautiful, my boy. Take care of her."

"I will," Mark promised solemnly.

She turned and smiled at Sarah before reaching out to touch the amethyst that hung from her neck. "Enjoy yourself, child. Our family may not be ideal but there are advantages to membership."

Sarah stared after the old woman as she walked away much more nimbly than Sarah thought a woman of her age should be able to manage.

"Ready?" Mark sighed as he looked down at her. When she gave a nervous nod, he slipped his hand around hers and pulled it to his arm. "Whatever they say, Sarah, whatever they do, remember this is about you and me. They aren't what's important to me. You are."

He led her through the archway into a large room that seemed overflowing with people. Sarah thought that she would be introduced to one after another family member but nothing could have been further from what transpired. She and Mark seemed to move through the crowd as if it parted for them. No one approached them and Mark approached no one. In fact, it was almost as if they were being actively avoided. She tried to fathom a reason for the odd reception. Giselle had been so sweet and welcoming. Mark seemed not to notice as he handed her a glass of wine and steered her from room to room on a grand tour of the large home.

No one even seemed to see them. Not until Mark was walking her down a long hallway decorated by paintings of his ancestors. They were halfway when a man stepped out of a room at the far end and walked toward them with a long, easy stride. Sarah felt Mark stiffen beside her and his grip tightened almost painfully on her hand. The newcomer wore a gray mask trimmed in gold that matched his charcoal suit. Eyes that looked remarkably like Mark's looked out of the openings and the full-lipped mouth that seemed to mirror the man beside her was stretched in an insolent smile. His hair was the same dark brown as Mark's. He moved toward them slowly. He seemed to wait for Mark to speak.

"What do you want, Luke?" There was no mistaking the edge in Mark's voice.

"The same thing everyone here wants." The man swept his gaze over Sarah and she felt herself shiver slightly at the look that settled in those chocolate eyes. "To see with my own eyes if it's true."

Mark stood silently as Luke walked in a circle around them. He was whistling a tune under his breath that was more confusing than the uncomfortable appraisal. Was he really whistling "The Teddy Bear's Picnic"? Sarah's stomach fluttered and she had no idea what to think. Mark's acceptance of the way he was looking them over was more than she could even begin to understand. His gaze fell to the stone that hung around her neck and he stared at it pointedly. "I see it is true." Luke swept his eyes over her once more before meeting Mark's. "Beautiful, she is beautiful, my brother."

Of course, she'd known in the back of her mind they must be brothers. The resemblance was too much for them not to be. "Aren't you going to introduce us?" Luke asked as his smile again fixed on her.

Mark's sigh indicated plainly he'd rather not but he made a quick introduction that made a knot form in her stomach. He released her hand and moved to wrap one arm around her waist. "Sarah, this is my brother Luke. Luke, this is Sarah."

This is Sarah, not *this is my fiancée Sarah*, simply *This is Sarah*. But then again she'd not exactly said yes yet, she reasoned with herself.

Luke extended his hand and she gave him hers. He turned it palm down and lowered his head, making a sort of half bow. She heard him softly start to sing, "It's lovely down in the woods today but safer to stay at home."

"Luke, stop it." Mark's voice sounded bored and flat.

"I can't believe you'd really give it all up." Luke shook his head and turned as if to walk away from them. He paused, standing very close to Sarah, and swept that assessing look over her again. "Of course for something like her, I almost think a man would be a fool not to."

"Luke," Mark spoke softly. The oh-so-similar eyes met over her head. "I'm taking her to meet Tarris."

A wicked smile broke the handsome face. "Are you? How *generous* of you."

"I need to talk to you. Later."

"I'll try to squeeze you in." He started to walk away.

"Luke, I mean it. You and I need to talk." Mark's words stopped his brother. He looked back at Mark and Luke opened his mouth as if to automatically refuse, then closed it and simply nodded and left, again whistling the children's tune. Mark stood perfectly still, his hand still on her waist. It wasn't until Luke disappeared that he seemed to breathe. Mark stepped away from her to stand next to the bust of some long-dead relative. His breathing was heavy and, with his finger, he drew a line down the marble face.

Sarah watched him, confused. Give it all up? What on earth had Luke been talking about? What was Mark giving up and why would his brother think he was giving it up for her? She'd certainly not asked him to surrender or sacrifice anything for her. She walked over to where he stood and reached out her hand to lay it on his shoulder. She felt the muscles flex under her hand and then droop wearily.

"Mark?" Sarah swallowed hard. Her voice sounded so small, almost swallowed up by the large room. "Mark, what does your brother think you're giving up?"

He was silent for a moment, then turned and pulled her into his arms and held her tightly. His breath was warm against her temples where he pressed his lips. Mark tilted her chin up and pressed his mouth to hers. The kiss grew passionate with a speed that made her dizzy. His hand was tangled in her hair and his tongue pushed demandingly into her mouth.

He shuddered slightly and pulled back from her, nuzzling his face in her hair. He'd not answered her. "Mark, what does your brother think you're giving up?"

His voice was a hot breathless whisper as it brushed across her ear. "Everything."

Sarah struggled to understand his words. "Mark, I don't understand…"

He took her hand in his and led her to the stairs. "Not now, Sarah. Not here. I promise I'll explain it to you tonight but not now. Come, there's someone I want you to meet."

She followed him. His mood, his silence was frightening. She scrambled for something to say to break it. Her voice sounded so small, almost swallowed up by the large room. "Why was your brother singing 'The Teddy Bear's Picnic'?"

"He thinks it's funny. He's just weird that way," he answered her question. He was leading her toward the door that Luke had come out.

"Isn't your friend at the party?" Sarah asked.

"No. Tarris will not be at the party. He gets on very well with most of my family. He's practically a part of the family. We've taken care of him all of his life and he's given back to us more than you can imagine. But he won't be there. He doesn't like crowds. He's solitary by nature." Mark seemed to hesitate. "My father found him when he was only a boy. His mother had been killed. Father brought him home and he's been more than a brother to Luke and me all of our lives."

Her head began to feel funny. Thick and heavy, it almost ached but not quite. It was a feeling she couldn't articulate. She suddenly felt as if she'd had too much to drink. Her footing stumbled and she grabbed Mark tighter to steady herself.

Mark paused when they reached the door and looked into her eyes. "Are you all right?"

"I suddenly feel as if I have a headache," she admitted. "Suddenly I'm very sleepy."

Mark nodded curtly, opened the door and led her into a large bedroom with an enormous comfortable bed and a fire burning in the fireplace. Two armchairs faced a television set.

An old kung-fu movie was playing and she was fairly sure the guy kicking major butt was Bruce Lee.

Her eyes widened as a man stood up and looked at them. *Holy hell!* Mark was gorgeous. She adored Mark. Mark made her toes curl and her insides melt. But this man was beyond anything she'd ever seen before. He was desire, he was sex.

His long blond hair hung almost to his waist, flowing loosely around his shoulders. It wasn't a brash platinum blond but shone like polished gold in the reflected firelight. His eyes were the most blue she'd ever seen, they almost glowed. No one had eyes like that unless they were retouched by special effects experts. *It must be a trick of the light,* she decided.

He was inches taller than Mark and wore only a neat pair of black slacks. His feet and chest were bare. Sarah felt something very warm begin deep inside her as she looked at that chest. It was tanned and smooth. The way the flickering firelight cast shadows highlighted the definition of the abs and tempted Sarah. The sharply etched muscles seemed to demand she trace them. With hands, lips, tongue, whatever was handy. He didn't speak but watched her for a minute before smiling. Her body reacted to that smile shamelessly. He broke eye contact and shifted his gaze to Mark.

Sara drew in a sharp breath. *What is wrong with you? Mark is standing right behind you and you're ogling some strange guy.* She groaned inwardly. *You're ogling his friend, a guy he called more than a brother.*

Mark's hands came up to rest on her shoulders. She turned to steal a glance at him and saw him smiling down at her. "It's okay, Sarah. Tarris often has that effect on people, men and women. He's one of the most beautiful beings you'll ever see."

She flushed bright red and covered her face with her hands. Mark's voice came from close to her ear. "He says you are beautiful too."

Looking up, she saw the smile had widened on Tarris' face. He nodded his agreement with Mark's words. "But you didn't speak." Sarah frowned.

Tarris shook his head, his lips parting to show her straight white teeth. A shiver ran through her and sank deep into the pit of her stomach.

Mark stepped around her. He grabbed his friend in a firm embrace and the two exchanged the manliest hug Sarah had ever seen. Arm still draped around Tarris, Mark turned to her. "Tarris doesn't speak like you or me."

"You're mute?" she asked and he nodded in reply. "But you can hear?"

Tarris nodded again.

"Do you use sign language?" Sarah had learned a bit of finger spelling at summer camp.

The long hair caught the firelight and shimmered as the handsome head shook, the blue eyes crinkling with amusement.

"Don't worry, he gets his point across," Mark said wryly, tightening his arm around his friend's shoulders. A silent laugh shook the blond man's shoulders. Mark turned to him. "Sarah's head is feeling funny." The tone of his voice was as odd as the look he gave his friend. The blue eyes opened wide as if in innocent surprise but his grin twisted up his face, revealing a single dimpled cheek. "Right," Mark said. "Sarah, why don't you lie down? Tarris and I will have a little talk while you rest."

"Mark, it's okay, My head will be fine."

Tarris looked at her intently and gestured toward the bed. She didn't need Mark to interpret. He too thought she should lie down.

"I can't just take a nap," she reasoned with them. "In the middle of your family's party."

"Sarah, this 'party' will go on for hours. No one will notice. Lie down, my love, and rest."

I don't..." She was halted by Tarris coming toward her quickly. He reached out and touched her hand. The world swayed and she found herself being swept up into two strong arms. The scent of his skin swirled in her head. He smelled overwhelmingly masculine. An indistinct combination of sandalwood, odd spices, a burning fire and the musky smell of a man's neck as a woman curled her face into it in the afterglow of hot, passionate sex.

"Showoff," Mark snorted from where he'd already taken a seat in one of the chairs. "It's probably the heat of the room, Sarah. Tarzan here thinks it should feel like Miami in August. Thankfully it's winter or he'd be wearing even less." Tarris smiled down at her gently and shook his head. His expression was playful and said clearly that Mark was positively silly and was not to be believed. He laid her carefully on the bed and slipped off her shoes before pulling a soft blanket from the foot of the bed over her. A charming curve to his lips, he reached out to brush a strand of hair from her forehead. His touch corresponded inexplicably with the thickening of the fogginess in her brain and her eyes felt heavy.

"Sweet dreams, Sarah-mine," Mark's voice sounded far away as she drifted off to sleep.

At first she thought she'd awoken. But there was something about the feeling and the scene that made her certain she was dreaming. Everything up close was clear but the edges of her vision were glassy, blurry. And there was the fact that she was lying there wearing only the white silk slip she'd put on under her dress. Only the slip and she definitely had not gotten undressed before going to sleep.

She felt the mattress give and looked to her left. Mark was stretching out on the bed beside her. The feel of his body told her he wore only his pants, his arm sliding under her neck to cradle her to his chest. His head lowered and he kissed her tenderly. His mouth was soft, almost playful in its exploration of hers. When he lifted his head, his eyes were again filled with that dark hunger that never failed to cause a physical response. She felt the aching begin between her thighs. Her body was readying itself for him, desperate to feel his touch. She explored his mouth with her tongue and he responded by palming her breast and beginning to squeeze gently. His hand ran down her body, smoothing over the silk until he reached the edge where it lay across her mid-thigh. He lifted his head slightly and brushed his lips across her cheek to her neck. As she turned her head to allow him access she realized they were not alone.

She should have been shocked. She should have been horrified. But she wasn't. There was an almost disturbing sense of calmness as she looked into Tarris' blue eyes. His eyes were soft, like falling into a warm, soothing pool. He stood at the edge of the bed watching them, a soft smile just curling up the edges of his lips. There was a seductive, needful look in his eyes but his face didn't seem hungry or in the remotest way predatory. Mark's kiss, his tongue stroking her neck, made her gasp and she couldn't look away from the voyeur.

Mark's hand caressed her shoulder. "It's only a dream, Sarah. Only a dream."

"A dream," she murmured, lost in the feel of Mark's touch and the beautiful blue gaze of the man who stood beside the bed watching them.

"Look," Mark pointed toward the chairs. She lifted her head. She saw Mark sitting there, his head tipped back and his eyes closed. She couldn't see Tarris but then she hadn't seen him sitting in the chair when she entered the room. "It's only a dream, Sarah. Tarris wants to join us. He wants to share this with us. But it is your choice."

She hesitated. A rather vociferous part of her was yelling, *Hell yes!* But another part of her dreaming mind — *and damn this had to be a dream* — was still rational. She looked into his dark eyes searchingly. What would he feel if she said yes? Would he hate her for it? Would she hate her for it?

"Sarah," he smiled gently. "If you want to feel his touch, if you want to share our passion with Tarris, it is all right. It's his way. He's not like us, Sarah. Tarris is an incubus. He needs this, the energy our bodies radiate as we touch and are touched, to survive. This is part of who we are, my family. We take care of him and he gives back to us more than you could understand until you feel it. Think about it, Sarah. Would you deny your sister food if she were starving?" The dark eyes lifted for a moment and met his friend's. "I want to share this with him. To give him what he needs. It would not be the first time between him and me but this is not a world you are used to. So the choice is yours."

An incubus? Her gorgeous, sexy boyfriend wanted her to help him feed Tarris, the incubus? Damn but her mind had pulled out all the stops to justify this erotic little dream. An incubus was the very symbol of forbidden and decadent sexuality. Dark spirit beings, they came in dreams to indulge the darkest and most hidden of fantasies within a woman. And they fed off her reactions, they fed from her passion. Her release, her pleasure was the very food of life to them. Some lore painted them devils tempting women — or it seemed in this case men too — into the sin of lustfulness.

Sarah swallowed hard. God, she'd never done anything like this before, even in a dream. But there was no denying she wanted it as well and if Mark was okay with it… It was only a dream after all. She turned to look at the beautiful face hovering over her. Slowly she reached out her hand to him. His smile brightened and he took it. Within seconds, the warm heat of his body was pressed against her right side and he had sandwiched her between them. A warm glow seemed to encompass their bodies and she watched Mark tip back his head and sigh. She felt it too, this sense of being wrapped inside sexuality, in the arms of need and desire.

Sarah suddenly felt out of her depth. She had no idea what was supposed to happen now. As if he read her mind, Mark was speaking tenderly. "Relax. All you have to do is relax. Let us please you. We are here for your pleasure, my darling."

A shudder ran through her when, as if choreographed, the two men placed their fingers gently against her cheeks. They moved them down over her jaw, down her neck and across her collarbone. The two hands slipped down over the curves of her breasts, down her ribs and came to rest on either pelvic bone.

Mark unfastened the halter of the slip. Working in perfect harmony, their hands moved up and pulled down either side of the silk covering. Pausing, the men's next actions stunned and delighted her. They kissed. Mark's head met Tarris' over hers and their lips brushed. The kiss deepened and she saw two tongues slide against each other. A tremor ran through her. She'd never seen anything so erotic as these two beautiful men in a soft and sultry kiss.

Tarris looked down at her, his hand still curled in Mark's hair. The blue eyes met hers and she saw his lips move. He spoke and the vibration of his voice reverberated off her skin as if she were a tightly stretched drum. "Does this please you? Do you find it exciting?" He seemed certain of her answer, as if the question were a courtesy.

"Yes," she whispered almost breathlessly. "Kiss him again," she practically commanded with an uncharacteristic boldness.

Tarris laughed and Mark raised an eyebrow at her before he fell into the kiss with obvious enjoyment and passion. But she was not forgotten. Quite the opposite. As their lips touched and their tongues danced the men slid the slip from her body.

Mark stroked her breast gently as Tarris turned his head toward her. "May I taste your lips?" *Damn but the mute guy had one hell of a voice in this dream.* She nodded, not trusting herself to speak.

The blond man lowered his mouth to hers and kissed her. He tasted unlike anything she'd ever known. There was a sweetness, a heady drunkenness to the feeling the kiss was pushing through her. She felt as if sweet wine was being poured directly into her veins. His mouth swallowed her gasp as Mark's covered her nipple and sucked gently.

Two sets of hands slid over her skin as Tarris continued his exploration of the warm wetness of her mouth. When his head pulled back from her he closed his eyes, arched his neck and gasped for air, a triumphant smile of delight on his lips. When he opened his eyes and looked at her they had changed. They really were glowing. It wasn't a trick of the firelight. He kissed her neck while Mark continued to tease the point of her breast, both men stroking the softness of her stomach just above the juncture of her thighs.

Tarris' kiss moved down over her skin until he claimed her other breast. Again in unison the two men brushed their hands down her legs and hooked her behind her knees. They lifted her legs, spreading them, bringing them to rest over their own. She sighed as the tickle of fine hairs and the heat of male flesh sent flames of desire through her. The pants that both had worn were now gone. *Of course they're naked,* she reasoned. *This is my dream, I want them naked, so they're naked.*

The air of the room blasted against the lips that were now so damp and wet she knew she'd never be able to hide from them just how turned on she was by their joint touch. Tongues flickered over hard nipples and teeth grazed the tender peaks as two strong hands moved up her inner thighs to meet in the moist curls. She moaned as those hands slid up either side of her folds, not quite touching her where she most wanted their caress but tormenting her even as the sucking and nibbling were making her writhe between them. Mark lifted his head and watched her eyes as he pressed open the soft flesh between her thighs and stroked her slit. His eyes burned into hers and she saw them blazing even hotter than ever before.

"Mark," she whispered softly and he covered her lips with his, kissing her deeply. His hand was joined in her warmth by another hand. Together they traced a line over her skin and pressed her clit between them. She felt their hands enfold as they gently rubbed the hard sensitive nub between their fingers, making her cry out. Mark chuckled against her lips.

"Like that, do you?" He turned to nuzzle her ear. "Let go, Sarah. It's a dream, only a dream. Let go and feel." Mark was her id, she decided. He was the part of her that wanted this dream to start with. *What the hell?* she thought. *Why not?*

Mark shifted her leg off his and turned her to face him. Arms tight around her, he rolled and pulled her on top of him. She came up on her knees and straddled him. The same challenging smile that always lit his face when she pressed him back on the bed and rode him filled his eyes.

"Let go, Sarah." This time the voice was spoken in her ear as she felt the warm hard chest press against her back. "I won't touch you any way you don't want me to." His hands slid over the curves of her hips as Mark's hands spanned her waist and the two men lifted her gently. Together they positioned her and eased her down over Mark's erection until it was buried deep inside her. Sarah leaned back against Tarris' chest. His hands came around her body and he cupped her breasts as she began to move over the man she loved. There was no accusation, no jealousy and no regret in the dark brown eyes. There was only want and passion.

Mark's face wore a look of pure pleasure. His eyes were only partially open as he watched her. His hands slid up to toy with the breasts Tarris had abandoned so he could stroke her clit. The incubus eased her to lean farther back against him, surrendering herself into his arms. Almost sitting in his lap, she felt one strong arm hold her tightly against him. He moved for her. He used his body to dictate her movements. Rocking her as she rode Mark, he controlled the passion, the pleasure for both of them. *He* determined whether her movements were fast or slow, deep or shallow, hard or easy. He controlled how far and hard she pushed Mark's need, how fast it rose in him. Something about his touch prolonged the wondrous sensations raging in both of them.

Tarris' thick hardness pressed into her. She felt suddenly guilty. Not about being with him but about his giving both of them such pleasure and yet his own need was being ignored. Aside from the energy they were generating, which Sarah could now actually see shimmering around them, he seemed to be foregoing his own fulfillment. Sarah reached behind her and grasped the long, thick cock that was pressed against her. Gently she caressed him, somewhat awkwardly at first but he shifted, putting a small amount of distance between them to allow her to reach him. Tarris pushed aside Mark's hands and teased her nipples. The shockwaves ripped through her only to increase as Mark moved his hand between them and began to rub the hard, wet nub of flesh where their bodies met.

This change of position forced Tarris to surrender control of their movements and she set the pace now herself. Mark was meeting her, thrusting upward in time to her downward strokes. The wicked tension was building in her to an overwhelming level and the feel of the men's hands, the feel of Mark's body within her own, the feel of Tarris in her hand, his breath coming more quickly in her ear, brought a soft cry from her.

"I want..." She lost her voice as Tarris tweaked at her nipples, twisting them in his fingers. Mark's hand seemed to follow him as it squeezed gently at her clitoris. The way the two worked in tandem was more, she suspected, than just Tarris' influence on them. It was from their strong familiarity.

She looked down at him, uncertain for a moment. His jaw was tight and he growled out through clenched teeth, "Tell him, Sarah. He won't until you tell him." His dark eyes weren't on her but over her shoulder, looking intently at the other man.

Sarah twisted her hips slightly and Mark groaned. She looked over her shoulder at the beautiful creature her mind had created an incubus. "I want to taste you."

The blue eyes closed for a second. "You do not have to please me. I do not have to reach climax for me to feed, Sarah."

"It's what I want." She marveled that she felt no embarrassment. "You both said this was about my pleasure. This is what I want."

"It's not the way of things," his voice shook. "I'm here to enhance your pleasure, Mark's pleasure and to feed. I... It isn't what I need."

His face was almost blank. He was hiding what he felt from her and she could see it in the tense line of his jaw. Sarah reached up and touched his face. "It's what you deserve. You're not a toy, Tarris. Let us please you."

The eyes opened and he gave her a dark look. She knew that she'd hit on a nerve but he said nothing, just nodded to her and moved. He knelt at Mark's head. The man beneath her took over the driving movements of his cock inside her and she moaned, burying her face for a moment in the bend of his neck. His strength astonished her. The desire, the need, was building in her and she knew it wouldn't be long before she reached release.

Lifting up her head, she felt two warm hands come to rest on her cheeks. Tarris was looking down at her, his hands brushing her hair back from her face tenderly. His blond hair hung around his face like a mantle of gold and his eyes were no longer a sweet, gentle blue. They were flames of desire as she moved her hand over the warm, hard evidence of his arousal. He pushed his hips forward and her lips parted for him. The feel of his cock as it slid into her mouth made her moan around him. Bracing one hand against Mark's shoulder, she cupped the soft sac between Tarris' legs and massaged it gently.

Mark's hand stroked over Tarris' thigh while his own pace quickened and his thrusts grew unbelievably hard and fast. She lost the ability to wonder at his endurance and strength in the feeling of him slamming into her again and again as Tarris filled her mouth. *Oh God, this is good.* So forbidden in her strait-laced little world and so good.

She felt the crest of the orgasm hit her and her body seemed to implode. She sucked at the cock in her mouth as Mark continued to thrust into her pussy, gripping her waist tightly. She felt the wave begin again. *Oh God,* she was going to come again. The vibration of her cries was more than Tarris could bear and she felt him release deep into her throat with a moan that sounded otherworldly, almost as if it were sung instead of spoken. The taste of him, as had been his kiss, was different. It wasn't salty but sweet honey as he burst against her tongue. He dropped forward, bracing his hands on her, gasping. As he pulled from her lips, she licked the rounded tip and he shuddered.

Beneath her Mark's breathing had turned ragged. The soft primal noises deep in his throat told Sarah he was close. She lifted back over him and started to rock her hips, fast and hard, matching his rhythm as he plunged into her wetness. When she reached down and stroked the hard nipples, her fingers brushed Tarris' as he moved his hands over the hard, smooth planes of Mark's chest and abs. Mark tipped back his head and she felt him explode inside her. A single word mixing with the almost animalistic cries that escaped him—"Sarah!"

She settled against Mark's chest and he held her there. After a moment, he rolled her onto her side and she found herself pressed between the men. Tarris was stroking her hair. She felt the overwhelming sleepiness as she had once before. "Thank you," he whispered to her. She smiled softly and snuggled deeper between the two warm bodies that held her close.

Chapter Three

❧

"Sarah."

A hand was shaking her. She woke slowly, feeling fuzzy at first, then jerking awake. Her hands moved to her chest. The feel of the green silk dress met her touch. She looked down to reassure herself and yes, she was not only still wearing her dress but the blanket was still in place over her legs.

Mark was watching her face. She blushed furiously, her cheeks feeling as if they'd been set aflame. She had a moment of panic when she thought he actually knew. That he actually knew what had taken place in her dream. Shyly she lifted her gaze and looked for Tarris. The blond man was gone.

"Sarah," Mark's voice was soft and his touch on her shoulder was warm. "You need to wake up. We should be getting back downstairs."

She nodded and pushed back the blanket. *Good grief, Sarah*, she thought, *that was one hell of a dream.* It seemed as if her body didn't realize it had been only a dream. Her legs shook as she slipped her feet into her shoes and tried to stand. She had that weak, sated feeling she always had after she and Mark made love.

Mark took her hand and led her to the door. Before opening it, he pulled her against his chest. He held her for a long moment in silence before easing away from her and leading her down the backstairs. She couldn't have been more shocked when he headed straight for Luke. His brother stood in the middle of a cluster of family members deep in conversation. The hushed tones betrayed that this was no light and friendly chat. The truth of this observation was confirmed for Sarah when the group immediately pulled back and dispersed as they approached.

Luke's mask hid any reaction to his brother except for a narrowing of his eyes. The lazy smile that had curved his lips upstairs in the gallery was missing as he watched Mark guide her closer.

"Exactly what are you doing?" Luke's calm voice belied a subtle sense of urgency hidden beneath his casual tone. Sarah was a bit surprised by how easily she could tell the man was distinctly not happy. She didn't see the typical signs of displeasure. His lower jaw was relaxed and his lips were not compressed tight. Yet still she could tell he was unhappy. Even more than this, she could almost taste the distrust and dislike between the two brothers.

"I'm tired of waiting," Mark said in a low voice that held a deadly calm that chilled Sarah more than a bit. "It's time to get this over with."

Luke looked at his brother almost blankly for a moment then a strange realization seemed to dawn in his eyes. "You're asking me to..."

"Take Sarah out of here and watch her for a few minutes, will you?" Mark turned to her and looked into her eyes. "Stay with Luke. It's okay. I promise."

"Isn't this a bit like asking the fox to watch the hen house?" The amusement was back on the other man's face.

Mark's lips twisted into a smirk. "Actually, it seems obvious and quite practical. After all, you stand to gain or lose the most. You know perfectly well it's in your best interest to keep her safe."

The two men watched each other intently. Luke broke the eye contact first and Sarah could see him relax. "True. Your happiness in this matter means the world to me."

Mark extended his hand to his brother. "Swear to me you'll keep her safe."

After a moment, Luke took the hand and clasped it firmly. "I swear it." The smile he gave his brother before turning his gaze to her was not warm or pleasant.

Mark didn't reply but held his brother's gaze. Luke's eyes seemed to soften slightly. There was a tone to his voice that seemed uncharacteristic, almost sad. "Are you sure you want to do this? Walk away into the night, just like that? There is another way. Look at Grandfather and Giselle."

"Exactly," Mark said flatly. "Look at them and the struggling, constantly justifying themselves. Do you really think that's the life I'd want? For myself or Sarah? I want this clean, definitive and easy, Luke, and we both know you'd never allow it to be any of those things."

Luke said nothing but the gentler look was gone. "As you say, big brother."

Mark took her hand and lifted it to his lips. "Go with Luke. Stay with him until Giselle or I come for you." She wanted to protest. She didn't like the indolent amusement in the other man's eyes. He didn't feel safe. "Go on, Sarah," Mark squeezed her hand. "Trust me. Luke's given his word. He won't break it." Without so much as a glance at his brother, Mark slipped away from her and was soon lost in the crowd of people.

"Come on." Luke's grip on her arm was firm. "Let's get you out of the way."

"Out of the way of what?" Sarah tried to pull herself loose but Luke tightened his hold and led her out of the room. As they crossed the entry hall a high-pitched chittering noise crept over the sounds of the house and was followed by absolute silence. The murmuring started again and Sarah noticed that everyone but them seemed to be hurrying into the main room.

Luke ignored the curious and confused looks thrown at them as he led her through a large dining area that was filled with bustling servants laying out a large buffet.

"Through here." Luke's voice was eerily similar to Mark's except for the hard, dry edge it held.

"Where are we going?" Sarah dug in her heels and forced Luke to choose between dragging her and stopping. Fortunately he chose to stop.

"To Grandmother's private solarium," he said, his voice edgy and irritated.

"Why are we going there?" she insisted.

He blew out an exaggerated breath that caused the feathers on his mask to flutter. "Woman, there is nothing sinister here beyond the normal bullshit of this family and that's a lot in and of itself. Fortunately for you it's not something you'll have to deal with after tonight. I promised Mark I'd take care of you and I will. Relax. Trust Mark if you won't trust me. He'd not leave you with me if he thought you were in danger. Just a few minutes and the yelling will be over and you and Mark walk out of here and into happily-ever-after." He tugged on her arm and she allowed him to pull her into the small room at the back of the house.

Happily-ever-after? Nothing she had heard tonight made her think of happily-ever-after. Doubts began to filter into her chest. Mark was a great guy, he was incredible and so wonderful to her but the tension and stress she could feel in these people made her wonder if something darker, something more frightening, lay beneath the surface. There had been a chilling sensation of fear hanging over the interactions between Mark and his brother, especially when he made him swear to take care of her. She was certain she was missing something.

Luke released her arm once they stood inside the solarium. He closed the glass doors to the house and locked them. The sound of the clinking metal sent a shiver down Sarah's spine. He turned around and, ignoring her completely, settled himself on a small Victorian settee. He stretched out, feet up on one arm and his back against the other arm resting on a small cushion he'd stuffed behind him. He pulled off his mask and Sarah was stunned by what she saw. Brothers? The face that stared back at her was identical to Mark's. Not brothers but twins.

Luke sighed with comfort and then seemed ready to acknowledge her. "Sit down, little Sarah." He jerked his chin in the direction of a winged-back chair. "So tell me, did you *enjoy* meeting Tarris?"

Sarah felt her face flush and she looked away. He couldn't know about her dream, yet his words had carried a heavy sexual innuendo. She tried to focus. She was locked in a room with a man who was feeling more and more dangerous to her by the minute. Her heart was fluttering and she willed her overly vivid imagination to stop before it got carried away imagining all sorts of bizarre scenarios. "What is going on here? Why did you lock that door?"

The brown eyes rolled and he gave an amused snort. "Woman, believe me, this is where you want to be right now."

"Why? What's happening out there?"

Luke closed his eyes, boredom pouring from him. "Don't play stupid with me. You know what's happening."

"I'm sorry but I don't." The fear was growing and starting to fuel a flame of anger. "What is Mark doing and why do I need you to protect me?" Her heart was pounding so hard she could hear it thud, especially when her own ears heard just how frightened she sounded.

One eye opened and looked at her. Luke sat up, swinging his long legs back to the floor, and stared at her as if she had a puzzle written across her face. "It's not possible," he muttered softly. "Mark isn't this stupid."

"What are you talking about?" she demanded.

Luke stood and began to pace the room. He paused. "She's wearing the pendant. He has to have told her. He wouldn't hide this from his mate." Luke shook his head slowly. "Would he?" He seemed to be talking to himself so she stood silently watching him as he began to pace again. After several minutes he stopped at the far end of the room and turned to look straight at her. Faster than she had ever seen anyone move, he closed the distance between them, grasped her left hand and turned it palm up. The oath he uttered was loud and coarse.

She tried to control the tremble of fear that was making her knees weak and shaky. She bit down to keep her lip from quivering noticeably. Luke stared into her eyes for a long moment. "You really don't know what's happening, do you?" The awe in his voice gave way to a flash of fury as he thrust her hand away and dropped back down onto the sofa. "By all that's holy, you really don't know." Sarah watched him shake his head. "Oh my brother, you're not only a fool, you're an unmitigated ass to boot."

"Mark isn't a fool or an ass."

She was rewarded by a derisive snort of angry mirth. "Little Sarah, you have no idea who or what my brother is or you'd already have run away screaming."

The remark made no sense and she decided he was trying to confuse and frighten her. "So now that we've decided I don't know, would you please answer my question? What is happening out there? What is Mark doing?"

The anger seemed to vanish as if he squelched it deliberately. The lazy smile was back. "What's he doing out there? Being the noble, idiotic, idealistic fool he has always been."

Sarah felt her jaw clench. He was the most infuriating man. He was deliberately wicked and argumentative not to mention he seemed to have mood swings that made any woman's PMS seem tame. No wonder Mark disliked him. He shook his head in disbelief at his own thoughts and muttered so softly she almost missed the words, "Giving it up and he hasn't even mated to her, hasn't told her…"

He wanted to be difficult, she could be difficult too. She'd keep at it until he answered. "All I'm asking for is a straight answer. There's something you think I should know but don't. What don't I know?"

"More than you can imagine." Sarah gave a high-pitched grunt of frustration. A soft chuckle escaped the man's throat and he held his hands up in concession. "Okay, little Sarah, you win. I'm going to answer your questions but don't blame me if you don't like what you hear. Mark is out there right now surrendering his birthright because he's been fool enough to fall in love period and with your kind on top of it. He's giving up his place as head of this family—the money, the prestige, the power that goes with it—because he's too weak to fight for it." Luke leaned forward, putting his hands on his knees, elbows turned outward.

"Giving up his..." She couldn't make the words form coherently in her mind. Mark was giving up some kind of inheritance. "Why would he have to give up anything?" The tiny flicker of anger that had ignited earlier burst into a full flame. "What's wrong with me?"

"Nothing, my dear. I quite see why my brother is drawn to you." His lips parted to show a glimpse of perfect white teeth. The smile was different from the one she'd seen from him 'til now. It didn't seem mocking or derisive. "But you are what you are. You're not one of us. And he doesn't have to give up anything. He's *choosing* to rather than fight to keep all that he wants, all that should be his." The broad shoulders shrugged. "But what the hell, it's all good for me in the end."

Stupid Sarah, she thought. *Stupid.* "Because you'll inherit what he's giving away."

"Because I will accept what he's throwing away." Luke's eyes were suddenly frighteningly fierce as his fist came down hard on his thigh. "For Giselle's sake I'd have let it pass to him as long as his actions didn't endanger the family. But Mark knew that bringing you here would force this. Either he'd have to give up everything," his eyes narrowed, "and I do mean everything, Sarah, or face my challenge. I'm here with you at this moment because I swore to protect you in case anyone out there decides getting rid of you would be an excellent way of avoiding this entire mess. Or at least I'm sure that's what he's telling himself. More likely he didn't want to face this delicious little humiliation in front of me."

The picture Luke was painting sounded barbaric, savage and primitive. What kind of people were these? "How could I endanger your family? What do you mean challenge?"

"I'd have argued him unfit to lead our family, my little Sarah, and you are only the tip of the iceberg, only the final pebble that sends the entire mountain crumbling. And it would have fallen on my dear brother. And he'd have deserved it." The dark eyes were hard and cold. "I'm going to hate to have missed seeing dear saintly Marcus taken down a peg or two but it will be worth it in the end."

"Why do you hate him so?" She had siblings. She and her sister had had some nasty fights in their days but this was different. This felt like a cold, slow-burning hate.

"Because he turned his back on his responsibilities." Luke's face was as impassive as a smooth, blank slab of marble. "Because he turned his back on his family."

"Mark wouldn't do that..."

"You have no idea what Mark would or wouldn't do." His voice was low and soft and it was the most terrifying thing she'd ever heard. "You barely know him, in fact you don't know him at all or you wouldn't be asking these questions. He's always hidden from the inconvenient truths. The truths of who he is, the truth of his duty, the truth that it was he who got our younger brother killed."

Sarah's head was pounding. "Killed?"

Luke faltered. "It was a long time ago. But yes, Jonas' death was his fault. But his crimes don't stop there." He met her eyes and held them. The fathomless brown depths no longer seemed hard or scary. She wasn't sure what was happening but something about the way Luke was looking at her was softer, less frightening.

"Poor little Sarah," Luke said softly. He stood and walked toward her. She fought the urge to take a step back. "There is so much my brother hasn't told you. How unfair he's being to you, you deserved to know the truth before it was too late."

"Too late?" Sarah pulled her head away as Luke reached for a strand of hair that hung loose around her face in a gesture that was achingly similar to his brother.

"So lovely," Luke whispered. He pushed the strands back behind her ear. A flash of what seemed remarkably like compassion filled the chocolate eyes as they looked at her. His palm rested against her cheek tenderly and his head tilted slightly. "So much he's kept from you and he's supposed to be the honorable one."

Sarah's eyes widened. He was moving toward her. *He's going to kiss me,* she thought.

He leaned closer until his face was just millimeters from hers. Then he stopped. The dark eyes closed. "Lucky for you, little Sarah, I too have something left of honor." He turned abruptly away from her.

"I don't understand this." Sarah gripped the edge of the chair tightly and Luke put even more space between them.

"Of course you don't. But look around you, Sarah. Go on. Look. What do you see?"

She glanced about her in confusion. "I don't understand what you're asking."

Luke sighed impatiently. He started to make a circuit around the room, whistling the child's song he'd been humming earlier. Every few steps he paused to touch a carving, a photo, an engraving, a painting. Sarah slowly saw the pattern. Bears. There were bears everywhere. In the patterns on the cushions, in the wood carvings of the woodworking, figurines, all around her were bears.

"Put it all together, Sarah. You're a clever girl." Luke picked up a large gilded frame from the shelf of a hutch. "Our last name, the pretties in this room." Luke stopped before a large object that had been covered with a curtain. "Come here, little Sarah."

She hesitated and then remembered the flash of tenderness she'd seen and his words about honor. Suddenly she knew Luke wouldn't hurt her. Frighten the hell out of her, yes but not hurt her. She moved to stand before the curtain. Luke's voice was in her ear. "Giselle must have covered this for your benefit. Odd, I never thought she'd help Mark deceive one of her own kind."

"Her own kind?" Sarah tried to ask what he meant but he continued.

"This mirror shows us as we truly are. It's enchanted, Sarah." He grinned. "Magic. It shows our true nature." Luke moved to stand beside it. "Shall we see who we really are?" Without waiting for her to respond he pulled the cover from the mirror. Sarah's words about there being no such thing as magic or enchantments died on her lips as she looked at her reflection in awe. Gone was the woman she thought she knew. The figure who stared back at her was beautiful. Her eyes were a brilliant sea green, her hair the color of honey. The face of the woman in the mirror was smiling back at her. Her hand was touching the amethyst that hung around her neck. There was a glow in her skin that Sarah had never before seen in a mirror. She looked like a woman in love.

"You see now," Luke's voice was low and rumbled over her nerves. "My brother found himself a very beautiful mate." Sarah pulled her eyes away from her reflection and looked at Luke puzzled. He wore an ugly smile for all the sweetness of his words. "Now, dear Sarah, I think it's time you saw what I see — what Mark sees — in this little mirror." He walked around behind her and her gaze followed him. He stopped and she let her eyes move back up to the polished surface of the looking glass.

Horror froze the blood in her veins. She looked into the hideous and distorted face. The face of a creature that was not quite man, not quite bear. Her lungs struggled for air, she tried to scream. "This is who we are, little Sarah." Luke was snarling at her as their eyes met in the reflecting glass. "This is who your precious Mark is. This is who I am. Part beast, part something more than mere man, the soul of a superior life form bound to that of an animal."

Before stepping back he shoved the frame he'd been holding into her hands. Sarah turned slowly, her eyes rising to meet his. The voice in her head screaming that this was foolish, this was a joke, a trick, a scary story created by a man who hated her fiancé to try to frighten her. But when she looked up at the face before her the voice fell silent.

"Go ahead. Look at the painting." He gestured to the miniature in her hands. "Tarris painted it. He's quite gifted in a number of ways. He really managed to capture Mark."

Slowly she looked down. The antiqued frame held a painted miniature of a creature almost identical to the face she'd seen in the mirror. Mark's face, only it was twisted and distorted on one side as it morphed into the snarling, fanged face of a bear. Mark. Her Mark.

"Think about it, my dear," Luke's eyes narrowed. "The wicked beasts that go bump in the night are real. Werewolves and much, much more really howl at the moon in a world that exists outside of nightmares." His smile terrified her. "And you walked right into our den. And just after hibernation too. When we're all very, very," he licked his lips suggestively, "hungry."

Her heart felt as if it would explode within her chest. This couldn't be happening. It couldn't be real. The brown eyes danced with angry, hateful glee. He walked around her, circling her while singing as he had done in the hall. The child's rhyme mocked her fear. "For today's the day the teddy bears have their picnic."

He stepped back and watched her face for a long moment. Sarah could find no words, none of it seemed as if it could possibly be real but she was finding it harder and harder to convince herself it wasn't. "Do you wanna see, little Sarah? Do you want to see what animal lies inside this skin? Do you want to see what beast it is that holds you in the night?" Luke reached for the collar of his shirt and pulled his tie loose.

"Stop it," her voice and her knees were weak and shaking.

"Yes, do stop it, Luke." The voice that came from the doorway was gruff and slightly labored.

Sarah looked up to see Mark standing in the doorway. His mask was gone as was his jacket and his tie. His shirt was open, torn open she realized, halfway to his waist. His hair was tousled and a small bruise was forming on his jaw.

Sarah started to run to him but stopped. She looked back at Luke, as incredible as it all sounded, she believed him. She turned her gaze back to Mark. She searched his dark chocolate eyes. "Is it true?" she whispered, terrified to hear his answer but needing to hear him confirm the story.

Mark frowned. "Is what true?" He looked up at Luke who let his own gaze fall meaningfully on the mirror. An expression of horror crossed the handsome face. "What have you told her?"

"What you should have told her long ago," Luke snapped. "I told her the truth. Exactly what you should have done. At least you haven't bound her to you yet. She still has a chance."

Sarah pushed past what the two men were saying. "Is it true?" she said, her voice stronger this time and she held out the portrait. "Are you a…a…"

"I believe monster, demon from hell or abomination have all worked well in the past," Luke snorted.

Sarah finally got the words out. "Are you some kind of werewolf?"

Mark looked at her for a long moment then shifted his eyes to Luke. "You bastard."

"Marcus!" a shocked female voice spoke from the door. Giselle glided into the room and looked at the two men. "You know perfectly well your parents were ma— married." The sweet voice faltered slightly. She froze and the half smile slipped from her face as she read the tension.

"Is it true?" Sarah insisted. "Is it?"

Mark sighed. "Not a werewolf, no. But yes, I am a Were. We are Bears, Sarah. All of my family, except Giselle. Like you, she is human."

"You're an animal," Sarah breathed the words. Her eyes rose and locked on Mark's. Blackness swirled in front of Sarah's eyes and she thought for a moment she might succumb to the worst of female stereotypes and faint. The ground seemed ready to rush up to meet her. She was brought rushing back to reality by a hard, loud slap across her cheek.

Chapter Four

ഌ

"Don't you dare faint!" The sharp old voice steadied her and the pain in her face brought her vision back to startling clarity. "You do not show weakness in this family. Do you understand me?"

Sarah met the narrowed gray eyes with their soft fan of wrinkles. Giselle held her gaze with a hardness that the younger woman had not expected to find. "This is important, Sarah, important for your survival and Mark's. You do not show weakness of any kind. Even lying on your death bed you must never show fear."

Sarah shook her head to clear her thoughts. She backed away from the woman and stood there trying to make sense of the impossible that was happening around her.

"I'm sorry, dear, but you must understand. It's a life and death matter." She watched her face for a moment before stepping toward her. "Are you all right, child?" The wrinkled hand reached for hers. Just as she would have jerked her hand away from the grasp Sarah's brain clutched at one important thought. *She's human. She's like me.*

"I don't think I am all right. I don't know what... I mean I never dreamed..." She stopped trying to answer and put her hand to her forehead. No one moved. Mark stood there looking at her, his eyes pleading for her understanding.

As the silence stretched, Luke affected a bored look and sighed. "Can we get on with this? Come on now, little Sarah, either throw yourself in his arms and declare you love him no matter what so you two can disappear into mindless oblivion together or, and if I have a vote I'd prefer it, run screaming from the room shouting how he lied to you and betrayed you.

Come now, let us hear how you could never love a monster like him." He looked expectantly at her. When she didn't immediately respond he grunted with impatience and rolled his eyes.

She felt Mark's hand reach out and touch her arm. For a moment she saw only the sweet, loving man who had been a constant at her side the past weeks. The man who had made her feel more confident and happy with herself and her life than she had ever dreamed she would feel. In his eyes she saw his feelings for her there. Love and an urgent want burned in the brown depths but so did a deep regret.

"Get on with it. I have things to do that don't involve standing here." Luke gave them a bored roll of his eyes.

"Behave," Giselle admonished him. Luke shrugged and turned away, giving the impression he was suddenly interested in studying the night sky through the windows.

"For what it's worth," Mark's voice carried an almost hopeless tone, "I do love you." He lifted his hand to touch her face and she caught sight of what looked remarkably like a bite mark on his forearm. It wasn't deep but it was pronounced and starting to purple.

"Is that...?" She reached out to touch it.

"It's nothing." Mark pulled at his rolled-up sleeve to cover the darkening bruise.

"It's a bite mark." Sarah looked at him as sympathy and compassion twisted inextricably with repulsion and disgust inside her. Someone had bitten him? No, *something* had bitten him, this wasn't a human bite mark.

"It's nothing, Sarah." Mark unrolled his sleeve and started to button his cuff, hiding the wound.

Luke was suddenly no longer bored. "A bite?" His face became an angry, stony mask. "Why would they bite you? Biting isn't part of the gantlet."

"Gantlet?" Sarah's mind conjured up the images from Greek, Roman and Native American lore of those who had been disgraced being forced to run between two rows of warriors armed with clubs and spears. The runner would be beaten, jabbed and spat upon as he tried to make it to the end and to some semblance of safety.

"Yes," Luke spoke quietly. His eyes were fixed on his brother's face. The two men held eye contact without flinching or blinking. "He'd have had to run a gantlet to be permitted to leave the family, or so tradition says. And in this family tradition is law." Suspicion was written clearly on the man's face. "Now that I think of it, you do look a bit too good. Not even you should have come through *this* lightly."

"That's because there was no gantlet," Giselle said firmly. She walked over and seated herself calmly in a large comfortable chair. "Come over here with me, child," she said to Sarah. Not really sure why she did it, Sarah moved over and stood beside her. "Why on earth would Mark need to run a gantlet?"

"What happened out there?" Luke ground through his clenched teeth. "You said you were going to give it all up."

Mark shrugged. "I never said I was giving up anything. You did."

Luke's expression hardened as understanding dawned in his dark eyes. Sarah was wishing he'd share that understanding with her as she felt more confused by the minute.

"You issued the challenge, didn't you?" The anger that was quickly reaching boiling point was apparent from the flush that was spreading across Luke's chiseled features.

"I did." Mark held the gaze steady, his voice betraying nothing.

Sarah looked down at Giselle, hoping she would explain what had happened. Whatever had transpired had definitely pushed the tension between the brothers to a whole new level. The older woman looked at her calmly. "Mark has claimed his inheritance. He issued a challenge to his grandfather, claiming his right to lead the family."

"Challenge?" Sarah shook her head in irritation. "Everyone keeps using that word, would someone please explain what the hell it means." Mark's eyes widened at her words and Giselle gave a small exhalation that might have been a laugh.

But it was clear Luke found nothing funny. "It means he finally questioned our grandfather's fitness to lead." His voice was thick and raspy. He turned to face Giselle with what Sarah thought might be more than a bit of hurt in his eyes. "And you can sit there so calmly as if nothing's happened. I guess you've become more Bear than human after all. I guess the clan needn't have worried all this time about humans weakening us. It certainly seems your blood has made some of us quite the animal."

"And it has made some of you a bit too dramatic," the old woman snorted.

"Your mate is lying dead and you can tell me I'm being too dramatic?" Luke spat the words at her.

"Dead?" The sharp gray eyes narrowed in on him. "We are not wolves, Luke. No one is dead." The wrinkled face turned to look into startled and horrified green eyes. "No one is dead," she repeated.

"Sarah," Mark's voice drew her attention back to him. "Do you really think me capable of killing my own grandfather just to gain his position?"

She looked into his soft brown velvet eyes and knew the truth. Mark may be what Luke said, he may be a…whatever he was, but he was not a cold-blooded killer. "No," she said softly, "I don't think you would."

"But I do," Luke snarled and took a step toward his brother. "You lied to me to get me out of the way so you could do this without having to face me."

"Grandfather is not dead," Mark spoke to Sarah, ignoring Luke. "He will no doubt be dead very soon but that is not my doing. That is simply the inevitability of time catching up with him finally. He's over eight hundred years old. He can now spend his last days, weeks or however long he has without the burden of leadership." He glared at Luke, "Without everyone pulling on him and demanding things of him."

"Eight hundred?" The words came out of Sarah in a squeak. It was impossible. No one lived that long. Without thinking about why she would trust her word, she turned to Giselle for confirmation.

"Yes," the woman spoke with a smile. "I met him late in his life after his first mate had died without giving him an heir. He'd not yet ascended to the position as *Amar* of our people."

"How old are you?" Sarah blurted out the question.

Giselle laughed, the sound ringing out like a small bell. "I'm not so very old. I am only three hundred and eighty years old."

Sarah stared at her in amazement. "But Mark said you were human."

"I am," the elderly woman nodded. "Our rapid aging is one reason that so few of the Weres choose to mate with humans. It is sad for them to see us age and die. And in the case of those species who mate for life, like the wolves, it ends the Were's life as well." Her hand touched a large ruby pendant that hung around her neck. "Our aging can be slowed. When the life forces, the spirits, of the mates are joined in the mating stone, the pendants you see all of our mated women wear, the Were spirit nurtures and elongates the life of the human. It can even heal us."

"Yes, it's wonderful, it's lovely," Luke sneered. "Lover-boy can't catch even a simple cold and neither will you once you're mated, let alone any nastier little human diseases. A get out of jail free card on all colds, viruses and STDs."

"Hush, Lucas." Giselle turned back to Sarah. "We are unlike Wolves, divorce is possible for Bears and comes when the stone is destroyed, freeing the two spirits. But it must be by mutual choice." She stroked the red stone. "When my mate dies, the stone will break and release his spirit. I will age normally again until death finds me."

"You know this is all lovely and delightful but it doesn't change the fact that you lied and cheated your way into the role of *Amar*, brother of mine." Luke's eyes were burning with hate. "And it doesn't change the fact that I have no intention of letting you get by with it."

"Exactly how have I lied?" Mark's eyes held a sliver of amusement.

"You cannot lead us, Marcus. You are not mated." Luke's voice held a note of triumph.

"No," Mark conceded. "I am not."

"Then the oath is a lie. It is not binding." Luke's smile spread wider.

"I didn't take the oath," Mark responded with a quietness that shook his brother.

"Then you are not *Amar*." Luke stared at him for a moment then slid off his jacket and began to unbutton his shirt. "Then there is still time to challenge you."

"You would disrupt all of our lives, split the family?" Mark looked at his brother with a sneer of distain. "You would make me hurt, possibly kill, my own brother?"

"You can try," Luke's eyes were filled with a deep hate. "It wouldn't be the first time you caused the death of one of us."

Mark's eyes blazed with anger. "Fine. Have it your way. Let's go." He pulled the remnants of his shirt over his head, turned and headed out the glass door that opened into a large lawn. Luke was right behind them.

Sarah turned to face Giselle. "Stop them. You can't let them…"

"I cannot stop them." The woman's face looked twenty years older than it had seconds ago. "It is Luke's right by tradition. We thought we could prevent it. We thought he would accept you as Mark's mate without question."

"We?"

"Mark's challenge was no surprise." Giselle stood and moved to follow her grandsons. "Mark, his grandfather and I discussed it before he went to find the stone." Sarah followed her out into the cold. She took her own wrap and placed it around the thin shoulders of the older woman before turning to look at the brothers who were circling one another.

The whole situation became terrifyingly real as Luke tilted back his head and let out an inhuman roar. They were really going to fight. It wasn't a game. "Giselle, how far will this go? They won't hurt each other, not really. Tell me this is just sibling rivalry."

The gray eyes were dull and pained. "Sarah child, in this family sibling rivalry can mean something much more horrible than you can imagine. Gaston was forced to kill his brother because of a challenge." Tears slid down the lined face. "Because of me."

Sarah turned a horrified face to the brothers. "Mark! You can't seriously do this."

"I don't want this either, Sarah, but he's not leaving me a choice."

"Stay out of this, Sarah," Luke's lips curled and two large fangs were suddenly visible.

"Luke, don't." Sarah's own tears were starting to burn.

"Don't worry, little one. I'll try not to kill him and if you still want him, you can have what's left."

"I'll leave. I'll go away. I won't be a danger to you," Sarah pleaded.

Both brothers looked at her in shock. Mark's face was dazed, Luke frowned deeply. It was he who spoke. "This is not about you, little Sarah." The soft look she'd seen earlier flashed for a moment though his eyes. "This is not about you." He turned back to his brother who was still watching her.

Luke used Mark's distraction to attack. As he slammed into him, there was a brilliant flash of light and she was no longer watching two men but two enormous brown bears. They came together hard, the force sending them rolling onto the ground. As alike in this form as in human form, it was impossible for Sarah to tell who was who.

They were well matched. The one she thought was Mark, if she'd followed their movements right, managed a swipe of his large paw that sent the other bear scrambling away, shaking its large furry head and roaring in rage. She could see three gouges on the large hump over the creature's shoulder. The bears circled and both screamed out their challenge. She closed her eyes and turned her face away as the two started toward each other again.

Giselle gasped.

Sarah turned in time to witness an unseen force shove them both back. The bears flew several feet in opposite directions, landing hard. In the center of the circle of combat, a golden light illuminated the night. From it stepped a man whose presence made her blush furiously. Tarris.

The same sexy voice she'd heard in her dream filled her head. *You will stop.*

"Thank God," Giselle whispered softly. Sarah stared at him. Her mind struggled to find a reason, an explanation, any explanation but the one that seemed all too clear. That all this was real and that there, standing in the middle of two Werebears, was a *bona fide* incubus.

"Oh God," she groaned. If Tarris really were an incubus then...

Two smaller flashes of light and Mark and Luke sat on their backsides in the snow, both glaring up at the man who showed no sign of knowing it was the middle of winter despite being half naked. He ignored them and walked toward her. "You really are..." She looked into those blue eyes.

He smiled broadly. *Yes. Mark told you what I was.*

He reached out a hand and touched Giselle. The pale skin flushed warmly and she murmured a thank you. His hands moved to rest on Sarah's bare shoulders. She'd almost forgotten the cold until a sweet, delicious warmth flooded through her.

"Thank you." After hesitating a moment she asked, "Why can I hear you now?"

Because I've been in your dreams, touched your soul and your passion, sweet Sarah. And for that I thank you.

"It was real then?" Sarah wasn't sure what she felt. She should be embarrassed, horrified but when she looked into the gentle face before her, she couldn't feel any shame.

It was a dream, Sarah, just as Mark said. You did not really touch me. Mark did not really touch me. An incubus cannot feel sexuality beyond dreams because we have no true soul with which to reach another. It is our curse. I simply created a place that exists only in dreams where we could be together.

His words made her heart ache but his face told her he didn't want to discuss the matter. Not when there were more important things to deal with. He stroked his hand down her arm tenderly then turned and passed a not so gentle look to the two men behind him. *As to you two, I'm getting tired of playing mediator.*

"Then butt out," Luke grumbled. Both he and Mark had gotten themselves off the ground and were covering the short distance to where she stood with identical movements.

When you grow up, maybe I will. He turned a frown on Mark. *You're supposed to be a leader.*

"He challenged me, I..." But Tarris cut him off with a dismissive wave of his hand. Mark glared at him.

Don't go all big and bad on me, little Marky, I'm not a Bear and I don't care if you're Amar or not. Don't make me embarrass you in front of your mate. And you, he rounded on Luke. *Perhaps we should just open the gate to those who hunt us? Have you forgotten what it feels like to lose a brother? Was Jonas' death so unimportant to you that you would think nothing of losing another?*

"And whose fault is it he's dead? Who was supposed to be protecting him?" Luke shouted.

Sarah watched the pain fill Mark's face. "I was. I know my blame, Luke. I've never denied it. But you seem to forget I left him to go find you. Because you couldn't follow directions."

"You know why I went back," Luke's rage was far from being tamed.

"You know you were told to stay put," Mark's voice rose to a yell.

"I was supposed to let Mother die alone?" Luke was looking at Sarah. "Let her face the hunters while we hid?"

"You were boys," Giselle reminded him. "You were only boys."

"We were old enough to fight. So I risked my own life. It was mine to risk. Mark was supposed to…"

Enough! Tarris' voice was so loud in her mind she winced and saw the others do the same. *Jonas was not only your brother, he was part of this family. We all mourned for your mother, Jonas and for others lost that night. Your grandfather, Giselle, the entire clan mourned them. Mourned Jonas. Do their feelings count less to you? Do you think they want to lose one of you as well?* The eyes were once again blue flames and Sarah wondered if this was a sign of deep emotion in the incubus. *He was important to me.* Even in her mind the voice carried a pain so deep it made her ache. *As you are important to me. Do you care nothing for me? Am I to lose you, not as I lost him but to each other?*

His eyes were still fixed on Luke. *Is being* Amar *worth your brother's life?*

Luke was looking down at the ground shaking his head. "None of you have ever understood. I don't want to be *Amar,*

I've never wanted it." At Mark's disbelieving grunt, Luke lifted wounded and angry eyes to meet his brother's. "What do you know? Of me, of what I want? You left this family long before tonight. You left us the night Jonas died even if it took you another twenty years to move out. So yes, it was easy for me to believe you would leave it now for good. You know nothing of us and who we are anymore. You have lived away from us so long I don't believe you know who you are or how to be *Amar*. I don't want it. But you didn't want it either, brother, and I wasn't going to let it pass to someone who hadn't the balls to do the job. Someone who was too busy playing at being human to care about us."

"That's how you see me?" Mark's voice was filled with incredulity.

"How often have you been home since you came of age, Mark? In the hundred years since you came of age, how many times?" The fight in Luke's voice had given way to pain.

"Not often enough," Mark admitted.

"So you will let this pass?" Giselle asked Luke. "You will withdraw your challenge?"

Luke looked over at Sarah and held her eye. The tenderness she'd seen earlier was back. "There is only one person who seems to know who you are beyond this family. One person who knows what type of man you've become. I leave it in her hands." The face he turned to his brother was unreadable. "Fine, I was a fool. I made the mistake of believing I still knew how you thought. I was wrong and you won. But you challenged tonight under false pretenses. You are not mated. You have only until sunrise to take the oath. If by then you can convince Sarah to become your mate, then I will be a good little boy. I will stand at your side and be the first on my knee to acknowledge you."

Chapter Five

ഌ

Tarris brought them back to the room where she had first seen him. His ability to shift through space, he'd explained briefly. Mark had moved away from them and sank onto the edge of the bed she had slept on earlier. Tarris held on to her for a moment until the wave of dizziness passed.

It has been a very frightening and overwhelming night for some of us, Tarris spoke to her. *Many of us have choices we must now make, things to be considered. But remember, Sarah, that as we make them, we must be true to ourselves and to our hearts.*

"I'm not sure what that means," she said quietly.

No one can explain it to another or even know what is right for someone else. But when you do know, Sarah, don't be afraid to act. Whatever your choices, make them and don't look back. He squeezed her hand and the soft flash of light that had announced his appearance marked his departure.

She looked over at the man she had been certain she was going to marry just a few hours ago. Mark rested his face in his hands, no longer the strong, proud figure he'd been when he faced down his brother's challenge. "Sarah," the voice was muffled, "I know there is no way… I should have told you…"

"Yes, you should have."

"I loved you so much, Sarah-mine," he whispered. "I kept telling myself I needed time for you to love me enough it wouldn't matter. Can you understand? I was so afraid of losing you."

"I understand and I do love you," she spoke the words that were just as true now as they had been at the onset of this insane night.

"You love me?" The hope in those words tore at her heart. "Even if I'm a monster?" His eyes closed and he seemed to hold his breath.

"Those weren't my words." His eyes opened and he looked at her. She crossed to him and knelt. Never in her life had she acted on impulse until this man had come barreling into that life. "I don't understand all of this. But if I agree, what do we have to do to mate?"

"We make love holding the mating stone between our hands. When we climax, which a mating couple does very quickly, it will bind our spirits in the stone." Mark shook his head. "Sarah, you can't want to do this."

She reached up and ran her hands down his bare chest and felt him shudder. She looked into the brown eyes. Now, here in this room with no one else, she could see him. She could see Mark.

Mark, whose eyes had burned bright as he told her she was beautiful. Mark, who spoke softly as she'd lie back against his chest sitting on the patio lounge chair wrapped in layers of blankets because he wanted to look at the stars with her. Mark, who was infinitely patient as he tried to teach her how to ride his motorcycle just for fun. Mark, whose breathing lulled her to sleep at night as his arms held her to him.

She touched his face and then folded her hands over his. "I'm crazy, I know. But you said, before all this began, that this was about you and me—not them." He nodded, watching her face. Sarah swallowed the lump in her throat and the fear and uncertainty went down with it. "I love you. I've been the happiest I've ever been these past weeks with you." She leaned in and kissed him. His hands clung to her as if he was terrified she was going to disappear. His kiss was fevered and almost desperate.

Sarah pulled away from him and stood. Slowly she removed her clothes and lifted the large amethyst from her neck. He watched her clutch it in one hand as she crawled up onto the bed. "Are you coming?" She settled onto her back and waited.

Mark stood, his eyes never leaving hers. "You're sure?"

"I'm sure. Don't tell me you've changed your mind? Don't want to be mated to me after all?" She smiled up at him. "I love you. Nothing I've seen or heard has changed that, Mark."

"Sarah..."

"Mark?"

"Yes, my love."

"Get up here."

He quickly slid out of his clothes. "The stone will make this different," he whispered as he joined her, watching her eyes. She already knew this. She could feel her body vibrating, pulsating from just the feel of him next to her. She was wet and the need for him was starting to throb. "It will magnify what we feel. It is said to burn at the moment..."

"Mark," Sarah placed her finger to his lips. "Shut up and kiss me."

He wasted no time complying. His tongue ravaging her mouth, he moved over her, his left hand reaching across their bodies to grasp hers, pressing the stone between their palms. He lifted their hands over her head and held them there as he stroked her skin. The energy radiating from the stone was buzzing through her like a supercharged vibrator. Her nipples ached as if they were being sucked. Her clitoris was shooting tremors through her body as if a voracious tongue was teasing it mercilessly. Mark was moaning against her lips and she could feel his hardness pushing at her, wondrously ready for her.

He lifted up and she reached between them to help guide him inside her. A cry erupted from both of them. Sarah felt the sensation explode through her. It was as if he was buried impossibly deep inside her, stretching her. A dozen hands seemed to be roaming over the most sensitive parts of her body as he moved, thrusting into her. He was right. This was going to happen quickly. Mark's voice growled in her ear. "Sarah-mine, I'm gonna come fast." He began to drive into her hard and fast.

An erotic vortex was swirling, pulling her down until it closed over her head. As the feelings ripped at her, pulling the height of sensation from each nerve of her body. All she could do was cry out for him in desperate words she'd never uttered in her life. "Fuck me," she moaned. "Oh God, Mark, please, hard." The power of the stone raged through her body. Time seemed to stand still as they moved, hovering on the brink, hanging there indefinitely as they both begged for release. When it came, it drowned out the burning heat that seared their joined hands. All Sarah could feel was wave after wave of orgasm passing through her. All she could hear was Mark's cries sounding in her ears.

As he held her against his chest only Mark's words of love sounded over the beat of her heart as he poured them out into the darkness punctuated by soft kisses to the left hand he held tight in his. A left hand that held a painless burn in the exact shape of the stone that again hung around her neck.

She snuggled closer and held him tightly. "Mated?" she giggled. "It sounds strange. Nice but strange."

"Sarah." His voice was suddenly strained. "If you decide that you can't do this. That you can't be bound to one such as me, just tell me and…"

"You'll destroy the stone and release me?" she whispered softly.

"Hell no!" He sat up and looked down at her. "I'll pull you back into this bed and remind you why you said yes in the first place."

* * * * *

Sarah was more than a bit nervous standing at Mark's side. She understood none of what was being said as it was being spoken in a language that did not exist any longer in the human world. She'd have been completely alienated and lost if not for Tarris' running translation courtesy of the thoughts he shared with Mark and Luke. He wasn't in the room—that was not permitted. No matter his ties to this family, he was not one of them. She was only permitted because she was Mark's mate. She'd felt horrible when she'd learned that Giselle would be banished from the ceremony. Since she was no longer the mate of the *Amar* she was only another human and could not stand and see her grandson take his rightful role.

"Tradition," Mark had all but spat the word when he tried to explain it to her. "Sarah, this family has tradition so far up its collective—" He took a deep breath and censored himself.

"My child," Giselle had smiled sadly. "I told you, tradition was very important in this family."

Now she heard Tarris, who stood just beyond a doorway behind them explaining what Mark was doing and saying.

He's pledging his life, his wisdom and his body to the clan. Tarris summarized the words her mate was speaking. His voice was hypnotic as he spoke the words and she couldn't take her eyes from his face. *He has to seal that promise with his blood, Sarah. Just a drop or two.*

She winced as Mark drew a line across his palm with a ceremonial dagger. It cut deep into his skin. *You think this is bad,* Tarris chuckled in her brain, *it's a good thing that they didn't let you watch the challenge.*

Sarah was quite glad of that fact.

Okay, this part may be a bit scary but it's okay. Tarris warned her. There was a brilliant flash of light in the room and suddenly she was the only person standing on two legs. Mark and all the Bears present had transformed. The new *Amar* stood up on his hind legs, towering over her. Seeing all those massively powerful creatures was more than a bit intimidating when you considered the smallest of the females had to weigh a good three or four hundred pounds. She remembered Giselle's words and tried to force her face to look calm. As a group those who stood before them stretched their heads low in show of respect.

Her heart slowed its pounding when they transitioned back into human form. The rest of the ceremony she understood. They all knelt. True to his word, Luke's knee was the first to bend but his eyes were not on Mark. They were on Sarah, who detected a tiny glimmer of a smile in their depths.

One by one the clan stepped before them and bowed, first to Mark and then to her. That this gesture did not go down well for all of them was apparent by the varying depths of their bows. As each person paid homage, they left. After what seemed forever, the only person still standing before them was Luke.

He moved forward and bowed before Mark. "*Amar*," he spoke evenly, almost blandly, as if the events of the night had not occurred. Turning to face her, he bowed low over the hand she offered. "My *Amari*." He stood and looked into her face for a long moment. "Do not worry, little Sarah. I will always stand his second and I will defend him with my life if need be. I told you I was not without honor."

"I know you're not," she smiled at him. "I am grateful to you and proud to call you brother and you are always welcome in our home." She leaned forward and placed a chaste kiss on his cheek. He smiled back only with his eyes.

Luke turned and walked away from them. She watched him go, feeling sad for him. He seemed so alone. When he reached the door she saw Tarris appear at his side. The taller man put his arm around Luke's shoulder as they walked away.

"That was good of you," Mark said softly, his arms wrapping around her. "It will take me longer, Sarah, but I will try. And oddly enough, I think Luke will too."

"Family stands together, Mark," she answered firmly.

"You sound like Giselle," he laughed. Mark tipped back his head and closed his eyes and sighed contentedly. "Thank God that's over."

"It's not over yet," she looked up at him.

He raised one eyebrow. "It's not?"

She laughed happily, "You know this doesn't get you out of a wedding, right?"

"Make a girl a Princess and she's still not satisfied." Mark smiled down at her wickedly. "As long as I get a honeymoon, Sarah-mine, you're on."

LOVERS' STONE

൭

Acknowledgements

I owe a thank you to several people for helping me on this series of stories. Jenny and Britannia who have supported me as a writer for several years by reading my ramblings and helping me find worth in them. And to Kari and Alison who have been wonderfully supportive of this series. To Anny Cook, whose brilliance helped me find such a perfect title for this story. And to my wonderful editor, Helen Woodall for reminding me always this is supposed to be fun.

Chapter One

80

"Thanks Luke," the young man looked at him seriously. "I appreciate this."

"We're family," the tall dark-haired man answered with equal sobriety. "Not many in our clan would believe it, Rand but that does mean something to me." The dark brown eyes frowned as they examined the light blue ones before him. "Our fathers were brothers. I have to say this or I'd not be doing my duty here. Are you sure you want to do this? Are you really ready to present Bethany with a mating stone?"

The younger man smiled at him. "Yes Luke, I'm ready. Besides there's always a chance I won't find my stone. There's still a chance to change my mind after I find it. Besides, we may be Weres but we're not wolves. We're bears. We don't mate for life. If Bethany and I find out we've made a mistake, we can simply destroy the stone and move on."

Luke suppressed the urge to slap the kid in front of him. "Rand, if you're walking into a mating already planning how to get out then you're not ready. Promise me you'll really think about this before you do it. Let's go and come back in a week, in a month."

The handsome face of the young man frowned at him. "It's now, Luke. I'm ready now and you promised Father that since I have no brothers you'd come with me, watch my back. The hunters are getting bolder. No one thinks they know about this place but what if they do?"

"Then I'll kick their asses while you find your mating stone," Luke sighed. "Go on in but don't ask me to wish you luck." The kid smiles too easily, Luke thought. He should be a hell of a lot more nervous.

"If I don't find it, then it's not meant to be, right?" Rand shrugged, turned and headed down one of the tunnels to the left.

"Good luck," Luke whispered, "whatever that means." He moved over to a smooth, worn ledge on one side of the small cave and sat down. The gray walls domed over his head. It was dark and the only light was the flashlight he held in his hands. Farther inside, down the corridors, the way was lit by the glow of torches. Torches that would light and extinguish as a man walked past them. Or at least that was what he'd been told happened. Luke had come to this place only once before with his friend Wade. Wade had come seeking his own mating stone. One he never had a chance to use because a group of hunters cornered him alone the next night and killed him. They had pumped him so full of silver nitrate almost nothing was left of him but the blood red stone that was still in the pocket of his jacket. Either the hunters hadn't recognized the large garnet as having any value or they hadn't even bothered to check.

Only the male seeking his mating stone entered the lower chambers. There were thirteen that branched off this main room. Down each were the precious and semiprecious stones that were capable of binding the spirit of a male Were to his mate's spirit. Rand wouldn't need him while he searched, not even for protection. No one who wasn't of their clan could enter this cave. The door had been enchanted. It was hidden from view and none who did not bear the blood of their people could enter even if they did manage to find it. Luke leaned back against the wall. The stone was uncomfortable. He sat up and peered into the darkness into which his cousin had disappeared. It sounded so simple. Go into the correct cave, find the mating stone and come out. It had taken Wade ten hours to find the right damned stone. *Screw it*, he thought and snatched a small pillow from midair before stretching out on the bench to wait. Truth be told he hoped Rand took his time. He'd been dragged from his bed at an ungodly early hour the last couple of days and was exhausted. What the hell had possessed him to volunteer to look after his nephews while his brother, Mark and his mate got away for a weekend? When he figured out what weakness had prompted it, he was damned well going to rip it out and kill it.

How hard can it be to keep reins on two boys? They've got a nanny. The famous last words of a fool. He'd actually volunteered mostly to see the shock on his brother's face but also to test out the limits of the forgive and forget scenario his sister-in-law, Sarah, had forced on the two of them. Sweet Sarah. The night Mark had sworn the oath as *Amar*, leader of their people, Sarah, the new *Amari*, had kissed his cheek and called him brother despite over a century of animosity and unfriendly competition between the twins. She'd reached past the anger and hate inside him and made him want to be... Gods, he couldn't even say it...good.

Yeah, there was one person in the world who could touch anything inside Luke and it was Sarah. Okay, more than one. The boys, Nicky and Jake, gave him one hell of a warm feeling inside. He fucking hated it but they did. And he and Mark were under strict orders to provide a good example of fraternal bonding for the two.

And for Sarah's sake he would try. The human woman had changed everything when she'd mated his brother. She'd brought gentleness and tenderness into their lives that they hadn't known before. And despite what others may mumble quietly when he and Mark could not hear, her compassion only seemed to make them stronger. He never would have believed Mark would have become the leader he'd shown himself to be the last two years. And he knew that part of what made the *Amar* impressive was the whispers of the *Amari* in his ear.

Luke closed his eyes. He'd almost dozed off when he heard a voice calling. He sat up slowly. A glowing gold mist covered the floor of the cave and it was coming from the central passage. He rose and walked slowly to the archway and stopped. Each of the other twelve corridors led to rooms that held stones. A male picked the path whose stones corresponded to the birth stone of the female he hoped to mate with. Only one stone in the tens of thousands that filled this mountain would support the mating of a particular couple. Supposedly if the mating was not meant to be, he would not find the stone. Wade had searched through hundreds of gems to find the right one. He'd told Luke it had sung to him the minute he touched it. Wade said it had glowed and the face of his future mate had appeared in its depths. More, it had vibrated in such a way that he'd become instantly aroused and his need to join with his mate had burned like a fire in his body.

But this center corridor, this thirteenth passage was one that was never used. It could not be entered except by those who were called. And to Luke's knowledge no one had been called down this path in so long what lay at its end had become legend. An oasis of lovers' stones the lore said. A collection of stones from each of the caves but they were more than just simple mating stones. These stones were for those Weres who were tied to another by destiny. The two bound by a lovers' stone were destined for more than mating bliss. Theirs was to be a great lifelong love. To Luke it sounded like more than legend. It sounded like bullshit.

The mist swirled around him and Luke's legs carried him of their own volition through the arch and down the narrow tunnel. There were no torches here, only the glow of the golden fog lit his way. He heard the voice call again. "Where are you? I can't see you." It was a woman's voice.

He heard nothing but the voice. Not even his inexplicably bare feet made a sound on the stone floor. He took turn after turn following the light that pulled him along. Abruptly the fog rose to the ceiling just in front of him taking the shape of a doorway through which he could not see. He heard her calling again. She was looking for someone. She was looking for him. The realization lifted something inside him. He stepped through a large bank of the golden mist and found himself in a vaulted chamber. In the center of the room was a shimmering pool surrounded by large low pallets filled with cushions and pillows. Directly across from him an identical doorway had formed. Before it, watching him with large frightened eyes was a woman. Her long black hair was loose and flowed down her back. The blue eyes glowed so brightly for a moment he considered that she might be a succubus but dismissed the thought. No creature could have gained entrance here except those who were like him. Only another Were could have entered the cave, let alone this most sacred place. Or that was what they'd always been told.

The woman was dressed in a long, red satin nightgown with thin straps that barely contained the full breasts that threatened to overflow the bodice. Her hips curved in a way that made a man long to run his hands over them, to hold tightly to them as he thrust inside her. The pull she seemed to be exerting over him was stronger than any desire he'd ever felt. Screw mating stones, just looking at this woman was making him hard.

* * * * *

The man who stepped through the shimmering golden door was heart-stopping. His shoulder length dark brown hair and equally dark eyes gave the finely chiseled face a brooding, sexy look that just screamed out, "Baby, I'm exactly what your lonely little body has been waiting for." Every time she'd had this dream, followed the mist from her own bed, down the hall and into this room, she had found herself alone in this place that looked like something from Westerners' fantasies about the decadence of a sheik's harem. She'd known he was there, out of sight, out of reach but he had never appeared until now. He was finally here and God was he worth waiting for. The sight of him sent a rush of desire through her until it swirled in the pit of her stomach.

She knew his name. She'd known it the moment she looked into his eyes. "Lucas?" she whispered softly. A smile so bright it nearly blinded her and so seductive she felt her body scream out its readiness for him, stretched his full lips across perfect white teeth. Well, almost perfect. His incisors were a bit longer and sharper than the norm. *Oh yes,* a voice in her cried out, *I'm going to have one of those dreams were the heroine is ravaged by the sexy vampire.* Just like in the novels by her favorite author, she was going to get down and dirty with vamp-boy.

"Annie," his voice was a rich baritone that sent a shiver down her spine. Annie. No one had called her that in almost ten years, not since her mother had died. Her name was Anna. She hated being called Annie. Correction. She hated it when anyone else called her that but when he said it her body jolted as if he'd touched her.

He crossed the room quickly and she found herself in his arms, his hands wrapped around her. The dark eyes held hers as he lowered his head. When their lips met it was as if a blast of pure want shot through her body. Her nipples hardened and she whimpered softly. She brought her hands up to wrap around his neck as his tongue pressed its way into her mouth. His long hair, where it brushed the backs of her hands, felt so soft. Tangling her fingers in it she found it thicker and lusher than any hair she'd ever known. It was almost like sinking her hands into the softest of fur.

His hands were strong and demanding as they moved down her back to cup over her ass. He pulled her against him and she was momentarily shocked at how blatant his arousal was. That he was a truly gifted man was obvious even through his clothes. His fingers kneaded the curves of her ass as if he couldn't quite believe what he was feeling before one broke away and moved up to her breast. As strong and almost harsh as his grip on her buttocks had been, the hand that closed over the satin covered breast was gentle. It massaged her making her nipples even harder, making her breasts swell and ache.

He broke the kiss long enough to lift her into his arms. He carried her to the soft bank of cushions near the small reservoir of water in the middle of the room. The pool was surrounded by gemstones in all colors that seemed to glow from within adding a kaleidoscope effect to the walls and ceiling. He knelt next to her and she reached up, placing her hands on his chest, pushing him back slightly. The expression that washed over his face blended confusion, impatience and more than a bit of hurt. "I want to know something." She forced the words out through her rapid breathing.

"Anything, my darling," he moved closer to her again and she didn't stop him when he brushed his lips against her neck.

She moaned softly at the feel of the kiss against the sensitive skin and blurted out her question before she could chicken out. "Are you a vampire?"

He froze for a moment and lifted his head. One eyebrow was raised and an amused smirk was growing on his lips. "Vampire?" He laughed at her softly but she didn't feel the pained rejection she would have expected. The laugh was sweet not mocking. "No, Annie. I'm not one of the undead. I'm very much alive. Would you like me to prove it to you?" There was a wicked glint in his eyes. "Vampire? No my sweet, I'm no blood-sucker."

He kissed her again and her head swam. Okay, scratch the vamp-boy fantasy. He wasn't a vampire but this was as sure as hell one amazing dream anyway. He trailed his kiss down her shoulder as he pushed the strap of her gown down. She slid her arms free and tugged at the t-shirt he wore. He helped her pull it over his head. *Holy hell*, she thought as she looked at his bare torso. Forget vampires. Who needs vampires when she has a sex god leaning over her looking as if he can't wait to show her pleasures she didn't know existed.

She watched his eyes as he slid down her body. He pulled the bodice of the gown as he went and bared her breasts, her stomach and the soft triangle of hair at the top of her thighs then on down until he slid it completely off. The look in his eyes as he raked his gaze over her body made something in her begin to burn. No man had ever looked at her like this. She didn't think of herself as beautiful. She was average, nothing special. But the look in her dark angel's eyes as he examined every curve made her feel sexy. It made her feel brazen and bold.

Anna pushed herself up onto her knees. She reached for him and slid her hands over the skin of his chest following the touch of her fingers with the touch of her lips. She explored and traced the lines of his pectorals and abs pushing him back. His hands toyed with her breasts as she tasted his skin, moving lower. He didn't try to stop her, didn't even pause in the delight he was spreading through her as she opened his jeans and slid them down his hips. Commando. Fine by her, that was one less layer to remove. As soon as she'd freed him from the denim confines she realized her imagination had not begun to do him justice. She let him kick away the jeans and crawled back up to wrap her hand around the thick, hard cock that stood begging for her attention.

The sound he made was low in his throat and so primitive it touched a place inside Anna she didn't know existed. Lovers in the past had asked, begged and even threatened for what her mind now desperately wanted. In the past she'd sometimes given in, but now the feel of him in her mouth was something *she* wanted. She leaned down and drew her tongue up the length of him, from the broad thick base to the smooth rounded head. He moaned her name and the sound of it made the taste of him even sweeter.

"Turn for me, beautiful," his hands were on her hips and he was pulling her toward his head. She twisted around, keeping her lips around him and her hand caressing him. He guided her until she was straddling his face. His tongue touched first the soft inner thigh and she jerked at the feel. He blew a soft breath over her wetness before pulling her down to his mouth and tasting her.

The feel of his hardness sliding against her tongue as his ran long searching strokes through the folds of her wet skin made tremors shoot through her. The man had one hell of a talented tongue. Slowly he fucked her with that tongue, pushing it into her entrance. She moaned as she sucked at his cock, loving how it filled her mouth, loving how he didn't try to thrust up deeper than she was taking him. His tongue moved from her opening to torment her clit. Rapid hard flicks against the tender nodule made her legs tremble. Her groans of pleasure vibrating against his cock were causing him to answer her with deep grunts that assaulted her clitoris as delightfully as his tongue.

As if by a signal they pulled away from the oral pleasures in unison and each sought the others lips, the taste of their passion mingling on their tongues. He eased her onto her back, never ceasing the relentless plundering of her mouth. His knee urged her legs apart and she opened for him willingly. As he lay between her thighs she brought her legs up, wrapping them around him. The pressure of his erection pressed against her swollen lower lips and made her want to scream for him to be inside her. As if he heard her, never breaking the probing beauty of their kiss, he pressed into her.

He filled her completely. She cried out into his mouth. It was then he broke the kiss. Holding himself still inside her he reached down and teased her nipple. Pinching it gently, tugging on it softly. As he tormented her breasts he started to move slowly. Long, deep thrusts that took him to the limit within her body and then out again withdrawing almost totally from her wetness. She could see the fierce concentration in his face as he fought for control. His strokes increased in speed and power. Anna closed her eyes and arched her body to hurry his pace. Her head began to twist and the hands that had been moving over his chest flung out and grabbed at something, anything. Her right hand twisted in the fabric covering the pallet but her left hand struck something hard and wet.

She was only vaguely aware she must have touched the small pool but as he began to drive into her harder, his groans becoming more erotic, more desperate in the pleasure he was finding in her body, she closed her hand around the hard, uneven protrusion on the edge of the pond. The reaction was immediate. Something charged through her body causing her to scream with pleasure. Each motion, each move of his cock inside her seemed a thousand times more stimulating, more tantalizing. Her hands clenched harder. She heard and felt the cloth in her right hand rip. She felt the piece of the pool in her left hand start to give. When he reached between them and stroked her clitoris something erupted inside her more powerful than any adrenaline burst she'd ever felt.

The lip of the pool to which she clung broke free. Her body curled in on itself, her legs wrapping tighter around him. She pressed her hand to his chest, unmindful of the hot glassy object she held clutched in her fist. He jerked violently as if the same power was suddenly running through him and she heard him cry out. He was moaning her name and pounding away at her flesh. Nothing existed for her in that moment, nothing but the tidal wave of sexual pleasure that soared through her. Then with her hand frozen in a fist around the stone, the world exploded and both of their screams rang out loudly, bouncing off the high ceiling. The stone slipped from her fingers as her body went limp in the wake of the orgasm. Anna clung to him and heard him murmur something that sounded like, "I love you," just as the world went black.

* * * * *

Luke could hear someone calling his name. Rand must have finished. He opened his eyes slowly and they focused on a large vaulted ceiling painted with gold and silver celestial patterns. He was instantly awake. He wasn't in the outer room. He wasn't sleeping on the bench. He remembered in a flash of panic. He was in the inner chamber lying on a soft pallet of cushions. The forbidden inner chamber. He lay there listening to Rand's voice but not hearing it. Because beyond the inconvenience of being in a chamber that was supposed to be off limits, beyond the fact that he was lying there naked was the fact that he could feel something cool and hard clenched in his left hand.

Luke sat up slowly and lifted his hand. He opened his palm. In the center lay a rough cut, bright red stone. It glowed and vibrated in his hand. The pulse that moved through him made his body stir. He heard a voice in the back of his mind whisper his name. Lifting the roughly heart-shaped gem he looked into it and saw a raven-haired siren with bright blue eyes gazing back at him.

"Oh shit," Luke closed his eyes. This was not happening. This could not happen. That stone. He'd not come here seeking it but there was no mistaking it. He felt her somewhere in the back of his mind, he felt her body against him though she wasn't there. He smelled her on his skin. The woman had been real and in his hand lay the proof of it. In his hand lay his mating stone.

Him? The man his own brother referred to as Lucas "screw the whole world and everyone in it" Ursine? And that was when he wasn't pissed at him. But how? To whom? He had to see the Oracle. The Oracle would know. He looked at the stone again. A ruby? He searched his mind for an explanation. Why was he holding a July stone? Bears didn't give birth in July. As Weres—shapeshifters whose bodies were tied to the animal whose spirit they shared, in their case the bear—they too had "seasons". Late fall and winter were the birthing months. Spring and early summer the months of conception.

This meant only one thing. She wasn't one of his people. There were few species in this world with whom a Were could mate. They could mate with the angelus, winged creatures humans often mistook for divine beings. Though rare, they could also join to the fey, a varied group of little creatures that humans called faeries or gnomes. And humans. And since the woman who had just given him the most intense orgasm of his life didn't have wings and she had full, lush, mouthwatering curves it could mean only one thing. His destined mate was a human.

Luke glared angrily at the red stone. "Just my fucking luck."

Chapter Two

ॐ

"Jack you can't be serious," Anna sighed. She smoothed a hand over her black hair, pressing back the strands that had escaped the tail. "Hasn't this family suffered enough?"

"I don't happen to see taking my place as a hunter, being one of hundreds of generations of this family dedicated to protecting the uninitiated among us from the monsters out there as adding to anyone's suffering. We are why they can sleep nights. We are what chase away the boogeyman." His hazel eyes flashed angrily.

"You're not a *see'er*, Jack. You can't tell the monsters from the paperboy," she huffed.

"No," his lips were compressed into an angry line. "You're the *see'er* in this family, Anna. But the fates didn't exactly leave you prepared to take up the duty we owe to humanity."

"Do you hear yourself? Good gods, Jack you sound like..." she stopped herself before she said it.

"Like Dad," he finished standing abruptly. "Yeah, I do Anna and I'm not sure when that became a bad thing around here."

"How about when he was sentenced to life in prison because he killed the wrong man? He killed a *man*, Jack. Did you learn anything from that? Didn't it show you how stupid an idea it is for someone who's not a *see'er*, who can't see the monster's true form, to undertake this..." Her breath fled from her and she began to cough. The hacking came from deep in her lungs and lasted for almost a full minute. Her face was a strangled shade of purple by the time her brother pushed the glass of water into her hands and she'd stopped coughing enough to sip from it. He pulled the glass away and handed her an inhaler.

"Easy Anna," his voice was soothing now. His dark brows were furrowed deeply as he stroked the side of her face. "I shouldn't have told you. I shouldn't have come here. It's my fault. I've gotten you all worked up."

"Don't...you dare...go...all big...brother...on me," she rasped out. She put the plastic mouthpiece between her lips and tried to breathe deeply as she compressed the top. The bitter tasting medication was sucked into her lungs. After a pause during which he pushed the water glass back into her grip and patted her knee, she spoke again, "Don't do it, Jack."

"The hunters are our family, Anna. I trust them. Someone has to stop the werewolves, the demons and the other dark ones from preying on the defenseless. I'm not a *see'er*, true but I won't be picking the targets. I'll be matched with a *see'er* for patrols."

"Like the genius they paired with Dad?" she couldn't stop herself. He had to see reason. "He told Dad that guy was a Were. Dad killed him only to find out he was an insurance salesman with three kids."

Jack stood up and frowned down at her. "I've made my decision, Anna. You can't step into Dad's place, I can."

"Great, so it'll be my fault," she closed her eyes. "Because I have the bad gene. Because I developed the sickness, my brother becomes a killer. Nice."

He stroked her hair like he used to do when she was small and would climb into his bed during thunderstorms. Lying curled to him, a very grown-up five years older than her, he'd soothe them both back to sleep with a song, a story or the tender brush of his hand on her hair. "Get some rest, Sis." He kissed the top of her head. "Do you want me to help you lie down?"

She shook her head. She was exhausted and it wasn't even noon. "I can do it."

Jack nodded, squeezed her shoulder and left.

She kept her eyes down on the table until she heard the door close. Damn it. What was he thinking? At thirty-two he was too old to decide to play cowboy. Wasn't he? Anna pulled back on the small black lever in her left hand and the soft whir of a motor could be heard. The wheelchair reversed, taking her away from the table where she and Jack had been having coffee. Pushing the lever forward she maneuvered the electric wheelchair into her bedroom. Jack was right about only one thing. She needed to rest.

* * * * *

Luke rubbed his fingers over the stone in his jacket pocket. He watched the reactions of the four faces as he finished his story. No surprises. Sarah looked thoughtful and a bit pensive. Tarris looked sadly amused. The Oracle's face was blank. And Mark looked pissed.

"You entered the thirteenth chamber?" he said it again for the third time.

"Dear, I think we've established that," Sarah said quietly and laid her hand on his.

"It's forbidden to enter the thirteenth chamber," the *Amar* glared at his brother.

"Not precisely," the Oracle spoke for the first time. The figure was old. So old it had lost all hint of gender. The head was bald, the face lined, the hands that folded in the robed lap were gnarled. The voice sat on the indefinable line between male and female. "It is forbidden to enter unless called. From what Lucas has described, I think we can safely determine he was called."

"So there's no crime here?" Sarah sighed and sat back. "He hasn't broken any rules." Being human she was struggling hard to adjust to the brutal rules of conduct, tradition and punishment the clan clung to. She'd only learned of the existence of the shapeshifting Weres two years ago

91

when she'd fallen in love with the man destined to lead their clan. Luke had to give her credit, she was adapting admirably.

The Oracle smiled for the first time. "No child, our Lucas has done nothing to warrant punishment." The smile faded. "But there is a great deal here that I do not understand."

"Like why the chamber called Luke of all people," Mark muttered.

"What's that supposed to mean?" Luke protested before reminding himself he was actually getting off pretty lucky here. At least Mark wasn't doing something that would make him have to forget he wasn't just his pain in the ass big brother anymore and was actually *Amar*. Kicking Mark's ass would be satisfying. Kicking the *Amar's* ass could land him before tribunal. He shuddered slightly. That was not something he wanted.

It called Luke because it was tired of waiting for him to come to it. Tarris, an incubus and unable to speak as either human or Were except in the world of dreams, sent his thoughts into the heads of the others.

Mark rolled his eyes but the Oracle nodded. "According to legends when a male enters the cave he awakens a chamber, the chamber where his mating stone lies. The thirteenth chamber is said only to awaken to those with a special destiny. Those who have a soul mate that they have not yet found."

"A soul mate?" Sarah asked curiously. She was learning that even simple terms she might be familiar with in the human world held a different meaning for the Weres.

Luke answered. "This stone isn't just a mating stone, Sarah, it's a lovers' stone. Some of us mate in the normal way. There is no one true mate. Those who were born with soul mates, however, find that they cannot mate to anyone else. Only that one lover will ever light the stone for them. It is more than an exaggerated feeling of intimacy, it is a real and lasting connection to that one soul that will survive even death."

"But why Luke?" Mark insisted.

Why Luke? Tarris stood and looked down at the older twin. *Why you?*

Both brothers stiffened. Mark looked down and Luke stared at him, anger building. "You?"

Mark sighed. "Sometimes I hate telepaths. Yes, me. I entered to find my stone. I had searched all through the amethyst caves. I'd been there an entire day when I heard Sarah calling me. I followed her voice into the entrance and down to the thirteenth chamber. There I found our stone."

"And you didn't tell me?" Luke snapped. "If everyone had known Sarah was your soul mate they'd have known that she was the only one to whom you could mate.

"First of all, we weren't exactly buddies at the time, Luke. Secondly, I figured it wasn't a very good idea to give anyone any more impetus to try to kill Sarah to get at me."

The Oracle cleared its throat. The light gray eyes pierced through Luke as if they could look inside his mind, forcing him to set aside his anger at Mark. "You believe the woman called to the chamber was human?"

Mark shook his head. "Why on earth would the chamber call a human?"

"I'm starting to feel a little insulted," Sarah glared at her mate. "He's your brother, your twin. You found your soul mate to be a human. This is our lovers' stone around my neck, dear."

"The *Amari* is correct. Twins are often tied together whether they like it or not," a faint curl tickled the ancient one's lips.

So now Luke just has to find this woman and convince her to mate with him. Tarris' words in Luke's head carried a sorrowful tone. It went beyond sympathy to something more. *That may not be easy.*

"I don't think convincing is the problem. She didn't need a lot of convincing," Luke admitted with an arrogant grin. "Finding her will be the hard part."

No, Tarris was looking off over their heads at the two little boys toddling and crawling about in the garden under the watchful eye of their nurse. Sarah stood and walked over to stand beside him as he watched her sons at play. Her hand tucked in his arm. *I can find her easily. Her spirit clings to you and to your lovers' stone. Convincing her will be the hard part.* Though all heard his projection, he directed these last words to Luke.

"That part I can handle," Luke grinned.

"Luke," Sarah warned, "what if she doesn't realize it was anything more than a dream? We often do things in dreams that we would never allow ourselves to do in the waking world and vice versa." She rested her cheek on Tarris' arm and Luke was puzzled by the sudden melancholy that had descended on this man who was closer to him than any mere friend could ever be. Tarris was more than friend.

"So it won't be easy. But if she's my soul mate, if the lovers' stone chose her for me, then I'll do what it takes." Luke stated firmly. "If not now, then I have a lifetime to do it. She's the woman I'm destined to love and she will love me. She just doesn't know it yet."

Tarris moved away from the windows and toward the door. *I'll be in my room when you're ready to begin searching.*

The Oracle excused himself and Luke turned his attention to his *Amar* and *Amari*. "What's wrong with Tarris?"

"That's for him to tell, if he chooses," Mark stopped Sarah from replying. "You should go to him. He'll help you find your mystery woman. He needs to feed, Luke."

Luke looked from one to the other, a bit confused. Tarris was an incubus, a creature whose very life depended upon its feeding on the sexual energies of others. Found orphaned by their father, he'd grown up with the two brothers. When he reached sexual maturity they'd happily been the source of nourishment for him. Both brothers had shared willing partners with him, allowing him to enhance the experience and to guide them, to a degree. This allowed him to feed. He'd been lover and friend to both. The heightened sexual appetite of the Weres had been enough to sustain him. He'd never known hunger and because of it had never crossed over to the dark life of an incubus. Luke knew, though no one ever spoke of it, that Sarah and Mark had shared their passions with him on the night Mark had introduced them.

"If Annie doesn't mind, I sure as hell don't." Luke stood and left the room. "And if she'd mind I can't see how the lovers' stone could have bound us together."

Tarris was sitting beside the fire as always. His kind craved heat and the Minnesota summers just didn't cut it. The air vents had been blocked in this room and the temperature was roughly that of Miami Beach on the hottest day in August. Luke stripped off his shirt as soon as he entered and dropped into the opposite chair. Within seconds sweat started to shine on the broad muscled chest. This place was better than a sauna.

You're ready? Tarris asked without looking at him.

"Let's do this," Luke nodded and reached for Tarris' hand. The touch of the incubus wrapped around his brain and he was asleep, head leaned against the back of the chair before he drew his next breath.

* * * * *

Anna was swimming. The Olympic-sized pool in the housing community's clubhouse was just perfect. She felt the cool water slide over her skin as she kicked and pulled, skimming through it in what was sure to be a record time. She hit the side, stopping the timer and smiled at the results. Her best yet. Pulling herself out of the pool she grabbed her towel and dried her arms and shoulders before pulling the cap from her hair. As she bent to dry her legs, an eerie feeling swept over her. A part of her woke up. She froze suddenly aware she was dreaming. She looked down at the pool. She'd not been able to swim as much as a lap in almost a year now. She was barely able to stand long enough to dress herself.

"Why couldn't I have stayed asleep," she muttered.

"You are mostly," the voice sent a wave of goose bumps across her flesh. "Only one part of you is awake. And I think you might want to be at least a little awake for this."

She smiled and turned toward the voice. He was back. She'd never forget that voice as long as she lived, dreaming or waking. The man who had been part of the most intense sex dream she'd ever had was back. Her sex god had returned to her. His dark eyes were shining as he watched her. His chest was bare and she could almost taste the golden skin that stretched across his pecs, almost feel the darker circles of flesh that marked his male nipples tickle her tongue. The cargo shorts rode low on his hips and she could see the dip just below his hipbone. Strong legs were sprinkled with dark hair. Good God, even this man's feet were sexy. She realized in that moment she was wetter now than she had been while submerged in the pool.

Lucas. His name was Lucas she remembered as he walked to her. His hands reached for her and cupped her face. "Annie," he whispered softly before lowering his lips to hers. The kiss was just as delicious as she remembered. His tongue was bold and his arms slid around her pulling her close. He began to move his hands over her body, slipping them over the wet swimsuit that clung to her. He broke the kiss and held her for a moment, his hands resting now on her hips. He lowered his head to touch his forehead to hers. His eyes were closed and a smug little grin was curling his lips.

"I think we can do better than this," he lifted his head and jerked it in a gesture to the pool. "Tarris? What do you say?"

The scene melted around her until it seemed as if they had fallen onto a blank canvas awaiting an artist's brush.

Suddenly the new vista burst forth around them. She was no longer standing in the clubhouse. Eyes wide, she surveyed the changes that had been wrought. The pool had been replaced by a small pond being fed by waterfall. The water was so clear she could see straight through to the sandy bottom. Several large rocks jutted out as if nature had placed them for diving boards and stairs. Trees formed a lush green canopy above them and brilliant flowers the like of which she'd never seen blazed in patches of explosive color.

"Lucas, it's beautiful," she breathed in astonishment. "But if this is my dream, how did you..."

"Luke, my dearest." He corrected her. "No one calls me Lucas unless I'm in deep trouble and I didn't do this." He moved closer to her, his chest against her back and placed his hands on her shoulders, his fingers brushing the skin and making her almost forget her question, almost forget everything but the need that was starting to build inside her. The sight and scent of him were enough to make her surrender any pretense of playing hard to get but his touch drove such foolishness from her mind. He lifted her hair from her neck and pressed his lips to the column of fair, white flesh. His lips were warm, scorching hot as they moved from the lobe of her ear down to her shoulder. One arm stole around her waist and pulled her back against the hard wall of his body.

Her modest one-piece suit was gone and replaced by a bikini top she would never have had the nerve to wear. Her breasts spilled over its bright tropical print edges as if threatening to render it moot. Around her waist was a sarong over a pair of cute bottoms with the smallest bit of flounce. No way she'd have ever had the nerve to try this thing on in the store, let alone actually wear it. But the way Luke was kissing her, touching her, he didn't seem to notice this wasn't exactly the sort of suit a woman like her should be wearing.

"He did." The words bounced in her brain for a moment before she realized he was answering her question.

She opened her eyes and saw him. "Mother of all that's holy," she exclaimed softly. Standing in the shade of a tree on the opposite side of the pond was the most beautiful man she'd ever seen. If the man holding her was a sex god, what the hell did that make the blond man watching her with the most intense blue eyes she'd ever seen? His golden hair hung around him like the mane of a wild lion. His bare chest was smooth and broad, his torso tapering to narrow hips that were clothed only in a soft pair of what looked like buckskin pants. One hand was braced against a tree trunk and she could see the definition in the muscles of his arm, accentuated by the play of light through the leaves overhead.

Luke's chuckle sounded in her ear. "He is beautiful, isn't he?" His hands moved over her rib cage and stopped, splayed just under her breasts as if he'd halted just before cupping them. "He created this."

Anna's eyes widened. She looked hard at the blond man. The rational part of her mind started putting pieces together and she didn't like what she was seeing. She pulled away from Luke and looked at him sharply. Her *see'er's* vision worked in dreams for only one type of dark creature—only the incubus— but even for her they were difficult to identify. She examined Luke's features. There was no shimmer or change in him. There was a small scar above one eye. Handsome and dead sexy yes but not perfect. The incubus would be perfect. "Tell him to step into the light."

Luke was frowning at her, confusion and apprehension written on his face. He looked over at Tarris who nodded and stepped into the full sunlight. Anna looked at him. It flashed for only a second but there was the waver of his skin, shifting darker then lighter. If he were an incubus the shift should have been more dramatic, she should have seen him as he was, if only for a split second. What exactly was he?

"Annie? Tarris won't harm you." She felt the touch of his hand on her arm. "He won't even touch you if you don't wish him to." He moved to stand behind her, his hands on her again, his lips on her skin. "I hope you will want him to, but he only came to help me find you. I had to find you, my darling."

She tried to stay focused on the man who might or might not be a dangerous creature but the feel of Luke's hands made it impossible. She heard a second voice speak, its deep sultry vibration swimming over her senses and her skin.

"I'll remove myself," the blond man spoke. "I cannot leave, or Luke would have to leave with me, but I'll remove myself."

"Don't," Luke stopped him. "Let him stay, Annie." The voice was soft and coaxing in her ear. "He is my friend, my lover, let him stay. He won't harm you. He'll stay over there."

"He'll just stay there? Watching us?" Anna felt the pull of the blond man's aura and the intoxication of Luke's touch assaulting her ability to think rationally.

"He needs this, he needs to feed off our energies but he won't touch if you don't want him to." So he was an incubus. The question was, was he real or an illusion? She'd played with the idea of Luke's being a vampire the first time he appeared. Perhaps she was seeking out an even more dangerous creature this time.

Luke turned her to face him, his smile was wickedly sexy. "Besides, imagine it, Annie. Him watching us. Him watching me take you, caress your body and fill you so deeply you cry for mercy."

Something in her trembled violently. A sense of excitement stirred in her and joined the vortex of feeling that was spinning in that place just at the juncture of her thighs, making her body tingle and vibrate with need. She looked back over her shoulder in time to catch a sad look pass over the beautiful face before he turned and walked back into the shade of the tree. He sat down and pulled his knees up, his forearms crossing over them. His eyes met hers and there was no reproach, only a poignant longing.

Luke's finger under her chin guided her gaze back to him. He kissed her and she pushed aside her worry. It was just her dream. If the blond man had really been an incubus he'd have shown himself dark and evil to her eye. She'd have seen the red eyes, the leathery wings, the horns. She'd have seen one of the dark ones. Luke's tongue brushed hers and she wrapped her arms around his neck and pressed against him. She had mistaken Luke for a vampire in the first dream and he wasn't. Surely his friend was not one of the dark ones. *Besides,* a small fragment of logic burst through her brain as Luke swept his hand down to cup the curve of her ass, *neither of them is real. Nope, none of this is real, Anna, so shut up and enjoy your sex god while you can.*

She felt a soft hint of amusement brush her mind but it was gone as Luke took her hand and led her toward the water. Walking backward he pulled her after him into the pond at the base of the waterfall. Releasing her hand he turned and struck out with powerful strokes toward the falling water whose roar was the only sound in the clearing. She followed him to where he'd stopped, treading water at the base of the waterfall in front of large rocks that formed a platform. The spray from the falling water was a light mist around them. He lifted himself from the water and went to stand under the cascade that fell from the ledge of stone above them.

She watched him push his long mahogany-colored hair back off his face as the water pounded over his shoulders and ran down his chest. He turned his back to her and faced the stone wall. Watching him carefully she pulled up onto the rocks. The fabric of the sarong now clung to her legs. She realized what he was doing only a split second before he slid the cargo shorts down his hips and tossed them off to the grass beside the pond.

She was sure some sort of exclamation was in order, an expression of approval, a statement of admiration but the sight of that tight, toned ass stole all words from her vocabulary. The skin was perfect except for another scar that puckered the flesh over one shoulder blade. It looked terrifyingly like a bullet wound. She moved in close as he stood there, letting the water wash over his body. Why would her mind produce a lover who bore such a mark? Her hand lifted of its own volition and touched the scar. He stiffened for a moment, then turned and looked into her eyes.

"How?" she barely got the word out before his lips claimed hers again. He swallowed her question and along with it any hesitation she felt about the man sitting several yards away. With Luke's tongue invading her mouth she forgot about him altogether. He pulled her to him and the water from the waterfall fell down over her. The sensation was sweetly erotic. The pounding water was just the perfect temperature and it made a delightful line of pressure across her shoulders and her back.

"This is not fair," he breathed against her ear as he brushed it with his lips. His hands moved over her skin and smoothed along the wet flesh until he held her breast in his hand. "One of us has on far too many clothes."

He eased her back to pull them out of the direct fall of water and turned her away from him. The mist rose up around them, wrapping them in a cool vapor that didn't chill but kept their bodies coated with a fine layer of beading moisture. She closed her eyes and leaned back against his chest. The warm flesh pressed to her made her moan softly, as his arms slid around her.

"Too many clothes," he repeated and his hands found the wet knot of the sarong and struggled to free it. It gave way and he tossed the cloth aside. His hands moved to massage her breasts. She opened her eyes slightly and saw the blond man sitting exactly as he'd been. He was watching them, his face unreadable. He was watching Luke massage her breasts, watching as his thumbs moved over the hardened tips making her breath catch. The blue eyes followed Luke's hands as they moved up over her shoulders to untie the neck of her suit.

The wet straps slid deliciously along her skin, tickling her as Luke pulled them free. He let the top fall and her eyes locked on the face of the voyeur as he looked at her bare breasts. The look was no longer blank. The blue eyes now moved over her with apparent hunger as Luke untied the final strap of her top. It fell to the rocks before her and her lovers' hands were again on her breasts, rubbing his knuckles in a synchronous and tormenting motion over her nipples. She saw the other man's jaw clench tight. Suddenly his eyes locked on hers and she could see in them that he was aroused by her body, by watching Luke touch her.

It shocked her that she would find herself so willing to do this, so willing to stand before this strange man and allow her lovers' hands to expose her. Even more shocking was just how excited she was by his watching. Luke's fingers were pulling at the edges of her bottoms and she reached down to help him ease them over her hips and down her legs. She kicked them aside and leaned back, eyes still on the other man. What had Luke called him?

Tarris.

The word was in her head as if the man had spoken. Tarris. Luke's friend. His lover. As Luke slid one hand down to play with the soft dark hair, she groaned. He teased her. One hand rubbed her outer lips while the other tweaked and rolled her nipple between his forefinger and thumb. God she was turned on. More than she ever had been.

Luke circled her and reached for her hand. She longed for his fingers to return to their torment but his smile promised even greater delights if she complied. He walked her to the side of the ledge of rocks. A series of stones rose up as if they had been created to be steps. She stepped down into the pond and felt the water rise up to sooth the heat that was burning in her pussy. The cool water did nothing to ease her need but rather lapped at her, just the right height to ripple against her but not to cover her.

Luke put his hands on her shoulders and turned her. "I want him to see this ass," he murmured against her ear. She wanted it too, or she must have, because in response to his words she found herself wiggling her hips and bending slightly to thrust the curve of her buttocks out toward Tarris. Luke chuckled and his hands smoothed over her back, moving lower until they cupped her backside, squeezing the mounds. His finger slid down the crevice between her cheeks and followed it until he found her opening and farther up, until he found her clitoris. Rubbing slowly with one hand he lifted hers and placed it on the stone ledge in front of her.

"So wet," he groaned softly, "You're ready for me, my love."

"Yes," she reached back and stroked his thigh as it pressed against hers. She wriggled her ass feeling the length of his cock brushing against her skin. She wanted him. She was on fire for him and needed him inside her.

"You don't care that he's watching?" Luke's voice was playful as he continued to stroke her clit with one hand, the other returning to play with her nipples.

"No," she muttered. "I don't care."

"You want him to see, don't you?" Luke pressed a kiss to her neck.

"Yes," she moaned. And she did. She wanted the blond man to watch Luke inside her. She wanted...

Luke moved beneath her and in a single slow thrust buried himself inside her pussy. She grabbed at the ledge as she cried out. His movements were slow and powerful as he withdrew and plunged into her again. She had both hands on the ledge now, holding on as his thick, long cock moved inside her. The water splashed around her, teasing the sensitive skin as he took her. She rocked back against him, meeting his movements. When his arm wrapped around her and pulled her up to lean against his chest she moaned softly. God he felt so good. Her upright position limited the movements he could produce but each shift, each tiny thrust sent shock waves through her.

When he pulled out of her, she whimpered in protest. He pulled her tight against him and kissed her neck. "I'm not done, darling, don't worry." He hoisted himself back onto the rock and reached for her hand. She clambered up and he pulled her to lie down beside him. "Turn away from me," he kissed her, his mouth claiming hers hotly before releasing her so she could do as he asked.

It felt awkward at first when he lifted her leg up and draped it over his own but when he slid between her thighs and slipped the hard shaft back into her she felt as if she had suddenly become complete. Something was missing from her life and she now knew what that was. Luke. This dream man filled places inside her that no man in the real world ever had. She wondered for a moment if she might be going mad but lost all sense of the thought as he rolled them until she was lying on top of him.

His knees spread her legs wide and he braced his heels against the rock to anchor the thrusts that had her crying out in abandon. She pushed up into a sitting position. Faced away from him she could see the blond man again. She let her eyes lock with his. He was no longer sitting quietly but was standing against the tree with a pained expression on his face. The bulge in the tan pants made it obvious he was aroused by their display. She held his gaze as she added her own motions. She rode Luke hard and fast, rising up and coming down as if she wanted to drive him all the way through her body. Tarris' blue eyes were soft and gentle but there was no denying the hunger in them.

"Tarris," she whispered the name.

He moved instantly. His pants disappeared in a flash and she saw him stand, pausing for a moment so she could look at him. Oh God, he was perfect. Then he dove into the pool and swam the distance. He launched himself out of the water and reached for her. His hand hesitated and he waited. His scent made her head spin. His eyes seemed to make the sensations that were raging through her multiply. She saw his gaze slip to

Luke. Luke's hand reached for him and Tarris bent down to him. The hand touched Tarris' face and Anna watched over her shoulder in fascination as the men's lips met. She watched Luke's hand fist in the blond hair and pull his lover's head down, deepening the kiss. When Luke released him, Tarris pulled away to look at her, he was asking her permission with that look.

She repeated his name and was rewarded by a kiss like none she'd ever experienced. His mouth was sweet. She could feast on this mouth forever. His hands were busy. One caressed Luke's chest while the other cupped her breast and began to stroke her nipple. Beneath her, her lover resumed his movements and was pushing up into her. Her sigh of pleasure was lost in the kiss that ravaged her lips.

Tarris pushed on her shoulders and eased her back. Luke's movements were harder and faster than she'd have imagined given the position. She wasn't prepared for what happened next. Tarris slid off the rock ledge and reappeared between her knees. Luke widened his to push her legs apart even more. Moving up between them Tarris stroked both lovers gently before lowering his head. She had expected to feel his mouth but then realized it had gone first to Luke. The long pink tongue stroked up Luke's soft sac, then flickered against them both where he moved in and out of her. Finally it reached her clitoris and swirled around the hard nub. He repeated this motion again and again, adding the feel of his mouth to the pleasure they were both experiencing.

"Annie," Luke moaned. "Annie, Tarris."

She was confused at first until she saw Tarris lift his head and smile. She heard his voice as she felt his breath blow across her where she lay exposed, held open to him by Luke's legs. "Control freak. You always have to play the Dom don't you?" He winked at her before causing all breath to leave her body by closing his mouth around her clit and sucking softly. Tarris' hands rested on her legs and he matched the thrusting movements of the man beneath, bobbing his head in time to them so he could keep his tongue tormenting her.

The hard cock sliding in and out of her pussy, the tongue licking at her clit, Luke's hands pinching, tugging and teasing her nipples relentlessly drove her passions to a point she didn't recognize. She'd never been this high, never wanted release this much. The sounds coming from Luke's throat were turning into rumbling groans that shook his entire chest. She could just see Tarris' head between her legs, see the movement of his arm and knew he must be massaging the sensitive pouch of flesh between Luke's legs.

Her body felt as if it were whirling faster and churning harder than the whirlpool at the base of the waterfall that fell around them. "Don't stop," she cried out to both men, "Oh God, please don't stop."

She felt the moan of satisfaction that erupted from Tarris' throat. Felt it vibrate through her tormented nub and radiate out through her body. "Come Annie," she heard Luke growl out. "Come hard for us. Let him taste how much we please you."

The world exploded and she lost herself to the shattering eruption within. It rose and fell, her climax just ebbing before a second ripped through her. She heard cries of pleasure, the sounds of a body reaching release but she was no longer sure which came from her throat, which were Luke's and which were simply the roaring of her own blood in her ears.

Chapter Three

෨

Anna lay in the comfort of Luke's arms, stretched out on the soft grassy bank. Using his chest for a pillow, she watched Tarris stretched out on Luke's other side, sunning himself like a sleepy tiger. His eyes were closed and a faint smile curled his lips. She hadn't known contentment and peace like this in a long time.

"Annie," Luke's voice sounded thick. "I'm not much of a talking kind of guy but there are some things I need to tell you."

"M'hmm," she moaned and closed her eyes. This was definitely a dream. She'd twice now had the best sex of her life with a man who touched her in ways she couldn't have explained were she stupid enough to try. Said amazing sex-god-man had brought along a gorgeous friend and didn't mind sharing. She was stretched out in his arms feeling the warm sun, smelling the sweet grass and reveling in the lazy delights of after-glow. Now he wanted to talk? Damn was her subconscious was working overtime.

"You need to know two things, up front," his voice sounded serious. She shook off the lazy fatigue and tried to concentrate. "First, I care for you." The words were accompanied by a soft brush of fingers across her cheek. "There's something about you, Annie. I can't explain why just yet but when I'm with you I feel…" His voice trailed off.

"Complete." She offered the word and held her breath.

His voice held a hint of laughter, "Complete. Whole. Yes, my love. That's it exactly."

"I feel that way too," she pressed her lips to his skin as she spoke. Her mind screamed out the words her heart had been repeating since the first time she'd looked into his eyes. *If only you were real.*

His arms tightened for a second then he turned so that he could look down at her. His kiss warmed her body but it only fueled the cold ache of regret that had seized her heart. He wasn't real.

His next words came only after he'd lifted her chin to force her to look into his eyes. "This is going to be hard for you to believe but promise me you'll try." She nodded silently and waited to see what her dream man would say next. "Annie, this is a dream but I'm not. I'm real. Tarris is real. We exist outside your dreams."

She closed her eyes and shook her head. Her mind was certainly good at this game. He was telling her just what she wanted to hear at exactly the right moment. She opened her eyes and looked into his. "I wish you were, my darling. I really wish you were."

"I am. I'm real. My name is Lucas Ursine. I was born in Paris. I graduated from Princeton longer ago than I care to admit, or than you'd believe. I have a degree in architecture but pretty much I spend my time rehabbing old houses in rundown neighborhoods. I love the winter because the cold snowy weather is the perfect time to curl up with someone warm and be lazy. I'm the younger twin. I drive a red pickup truck, I listen to country music when I'm alone but heavy metal when I'm not because it annoys my brother—the king of easy listening."

A soft snorting laugh reminded her they were not alone. "Mark is so going to kick your ass when I tell him."

"Mark is your brother?" Anna was astonished at the complexity of the fantasy. Astonished and a little frightened. Had the disease finally progressed to her mind? She should have a few more years before that happened. Usually the lungs gave out before the dementia took hold.

"Yes." She caught the dark look he flashed to Tarris who stood up. He was mysteriously wearing the buckskin pants from earlier. He walked away from them as if to give them privacy or to avoid Luke's glare, she wasn't sure which.

"If you're real as you say you are, how is it you're in my dream? People can't just pop into other's dreams." *Unless they're incubi.* The incubus could do exactly that. Her eyes flew to Tarris.

"Yes," Luke toyed with a lock of her hair. "I told you the truth. Tarris is a friend of mine. He's an incubus."

"He doesn't look like an incubus, Luke," she started to reason.

"Seen a lot of them have you," he teased.

"No, I've never seen one before," she admitted. But she damned sure knew what they looked like.

"Even if you had, Tarris wouldn't look like what you'd expect. He's never known the hunger and desperation that drives them to the darkness. He's never hunted, never tasted an unwilling person. There are rules he follows and those rules keep him sane and safe. They also keep him from transforming completely." Luke glanced over toward his friend.

Anna looked at the man trying to see him but saw only a subtle shifting, a darkening of his skin for only the briefest of moments.

"Annie?" Luke spoke her name with an anxious tension. "Annie do you believe me? Do you believe I'm real?"

"I don't know," she whispered. "If you're real, why have you only come to me in dreams?"

"The first time I was as surprised as you," his dark brown eyes gazed down at her intently. "This time... Well, I didn't know who you were. I needed Tarris to help me find you."

She watched his face. She wanted to believe him but couldn't. "Prove it to me. If you are real, you'll be there when I wake up."

Luke frowned slightly and turned to look at Tarris who stood watching the water cascading down over the rocks.

"It is possible." Tarris turned the startling blue gaze on her. "I'm with you now in your room, Anna. I'm sitting on the edge of your bed. I can drop you into a dreamless sleep and when you wake, Luke will be there. But once I do, there is no going back. Neither of you can hide who you are from the other. Each will know the other's secrets."

The ominous words chilled Anna but she felt Luke's chest vibrate with laughter. "Shit, you sound more like a fortune cookie every day. Keep talking like that and someone's going to make you an Oracle."

A smile stretched across Tarris' face. He looked at Anna and shrugged. "All right but don't say I didn't warn you."

* * * * *

Luke watched as Tarris walked over and laid his hand on Anna's head. Her eyes closed and she slumped against his chest. For a split second he could feel the weight of her in his arms and then he was jerking awake in the chair in Tarris' room. He stood and looked around him. A bright golden flash of light announced the incubus' arrival.

She's asleep and waiting for you. I don't know how much time you have. It's early afternoon. She won't wake for a telephone or doorbell but if someone disturbs her, she'll wake.

"Then let's go," Luke grabbed his shirt and stepped forward.

Tarris shook his head. *If I take you, how will you get home?*

"I'm sure Annie has a car," Luke rolled his eyes.

She doesn't, the other man stated firmly. *She doesn't drive.*

"Tarris, this isn't New York. People in St. Paul, Minnesota drive."

Not Anna.

Luke frowned at him. "What are you hiding?"

More than your puny Were mind could ever understand if you puzzled it the rest of your days.

110

"You've always been an arrogant little bastard."

Tarris didn't rise to the bait. Mark would have been lunging for him but Tarris just shook his head and gave an annoyingly smug mental chuckle. He crossed to a small desk near a window and scribbled something on a piece of paper. When he handed it to Luke, he realized it was Anna's address. She was only a mile or so away in a small subdivision that had gone up just in the last few years.

"I owe you," Luke jerked Tarris into a quick hug and hurried out the door.

He pulled up to the small bungalow-style house and sat for a minute staring at it. True enough, there was no car in the driveway. But what puzzled him the most was the ramp that extended from the front steps to the paved pathway through the front yard. Luke slid out of the truck and headed up the walkway. He half expected to see Annie come bursting through the door. A smile crept up on him. Would she be excited to see him? Would she throw herself in his arms? Damn, he hoped so.

Reaching the front door, he checked to make sure no one was looking before pressing his palm against the lock in the door knob. The click of the lock tumblers released the bolt and he pushed it open and stepped inside. A beeping led him to her alarm pad and he laid his hand over it. It silenced immediately. Luke looked around the room. Neat and tidy. Okay, he could adjust to neat and tidy. Right now he cared about something else a lot more. He moved cautiously toward the back of the house. Bedrooms were always in the back, right?

The soft smell of her was everywhere in this house but he found her easily enough in the larger of the two bedrooms. The blinds were drawn and he saw her figure stretched out on the bed. The lighting of the room made her face seem pale and drawn. She coughed deeply and shifted in her sleep. The movement pushed back the blanket and he could see her shoulders, the collarbone protruding in a way that shocked him. Her body was thinner than his eyes and hands had told him. She coughed again, a low racking cough that rumbled and the sleeper had to fight for air.

Then he saw it sitting a few steps away from the bed. The black canvas and foam, the metal frame, the large motor on the back—a wheelchair. Next to it, on the nightstand was a rectangular box with dials and buttons. Flexible white tubing hung from it, ending in what looked seemed to be mouthpiece. It looked like something he'd seen on television. One of the human medical shows that had appalled him with its barbarism. Slicing people open, shoving tubes in their bodies. He honestly didn't know how humans survived their own healing practices.

She was ill. His mate was ill. His heart slowed down and suddenly felt heavy, as if the mating stone in his pocket had suddenly settled there. The lovers' stone. It would trap her spirit with his. She'd grow strength from him. It could—damn it, it would—heal her. Luke took a deep breath and approached the bed. He slipped off his jacket and shoes and slid in beside her. She curled onto her side as if subconsciously accommodating his presence. Slipping up behind her he pressed his body to hers and wrapped his arm around her. He held her tightly for a moment, drinking in the feel and scent of her before he spoke.

"Annie," he whispered softly in her ear. "Annie, I'm here."

Her eyes fluttered open slowly. "Luke?"

"Yes, my love." He nuzzled her ear and kissed her cheek.

She smiled softly. "Am I still dreaming or are you really here?" She lifted his hand from where it had lain pressed to her stomach and kissed it. "You feel real."

He smiled. "I am real and I know your secret now, my love."

"Not all of them," she said softly.

"You'll tell me later, then." He buried his face in her sweet smelling hair. "We have a lifetime to tell secrets. For now, rest." He watched, pleased, as she smiled and closed her eyes. She wiggled slightly, pressing back closer against him.

Luke held her this way for nearly an hour before he rose, replaced his shoes, grabbed his jacket and left the bedroom. She'd be hungry when she woke up. He wasn't sure what the hell was happening to him but he had the irrepressible urge to take care of the woman. He was standing in her kitchen, the kettle and a pan of soup heating on the stove. He was cooking. He was cooking for someone else. Luke shook his head in amazement. God Mark would never let it rest if he could see him now. He had no idea what the hell was going on here but he was fairly certain what Sarah would say. The same thing she said when she gently chastised him for teasing Mark. "When you're in love you think of others first."

That goddamned rock was living up to its name. He was in love. He wondered if Annie could accept that. Sarah had told him she'd had trouble believing that Mark could love her so quickly and so devotedly. But it was their nature. Bears clung to and protected what was theirs. They fought brutally and viciously to defend those they loved. And Annie was his. She may not know it yet but she belonged to him. He realized he was grinning and rolled his eyes at himself. Who knew? Who knew this was inside him all along.

He set the table and turned the heat off on the stove before going to wake her. As he passed through the living room something caught his eye. A sparkle of silver and gold glinted from the mantelpiece. He walked to it. In a wooden display case hung a pendent of silver and gold, a large sun with a silver center and golden rays emanating from it. His blood froze in his veins. His eyes pulled away from it and swept the photographs that flanked it. On one side, an old photo of an elderly man and woman, both wearing this design around their necks. To the other side sat a family portrait. A very young Annie stood next to a handsome young man.

Seated in front of them were a woman and a man. It was the man who caused Luke to curse loudly. He too wore the hated symbol of the hunters around his neck.

She was a hunter. His Annie was one of the hunters. "Son of a bitch," he ground out.

He heard the quiet whir of the motor behind him and spun. She sat there looking at him confused before her expression changed to one of terror.

* * * * *

She'd come around the corner to find him standing at the hearth. His broad back, dark hair, oh God, he was real. The man who made her feel as if she'd found everything that was missing in her life was real. Then she heard Luke's curse and was shocked. Shocked until he turned to face her. His features flickered suddenly in her *see'er's* vision.

"No," she cried out weakly. His face morphed before her eyes. The brown eyes glowed a dark gold and one side of his features stretched and pulled out creating a warped and horrifying mask that was half human and half animal. The space behind him shimmered with a corona of light that took the shape of a large hulking animal. A bear.

"You're a Were," she gasped. Her hand hit the lever on her chair and she backed away. She had to get to it. Had to find it.

"And you're a hunter," he snarled. "Isn't fate just fucking lovely? I find my mate and she's hunter." He took a step toward her.

Anna continued to ease backward. "Your what?"

"My mate," his hand pulled something from his pocket. A large red stone glowed in his hand. "So much for happy-ever-after, eh?"

Anna backed until she reached the table beside the sofa. "How can I be your mate?"

"Don't ask me. Ask this," he gestured with the hand that held the stone.

"What is it?"

"My mating stone, the stone that binds my soul to that of my mate. Don't tell me the hunters don't know about them? I thought you were all omniscient," he sneered. "Something you murderers don't know about us, is there?"

The words hit the sore spot inside her. The man her father had killed by mistake, the heartbroken cries of his children as the reporters filmed them at the scene of his death and the sobbing face of his wife as she sat in the courtroom weeping twisted in her mind. She kept her eyes on him and watched his eyes narrow as she pulled open the drawer quickly and pulled out her father's pistol. He looked at her for a moment and then laughed.

"Woman, you better have a lot of bullets in that thing," he stepped closer.

"Stay back," she pointed the gun at his chest. Her hands were shaking as they held tight to the grip. "It's loaded with silver bullets."

He laughed again and continued toward her deliberately. "Then you'd better hit my heart on the first shot, 'cause otherwise it's just going to seriously piss me off."

He closed the space between them and her brain screamed at her to shoot. He stopped in front of her. "Come on, Annie, at this range you can surely hit my heart." She could. She'd been a champion shot when her arms had been strong enough and at the moment his heart wasn't two full feet from the end of the barrel.

She looked into his eyes and pushed past her *see'er's* vision. She saw him, for the first time in the flesh, real. She looked into his eyes and saw not the anger and pain that hovered there but the passion, the adoration, the kindness she'd seen in her dreams.

"Come on, Annie, shoot!"

She couldn't. The gun lowered into her lap and she closed her eyes. She felt his hands take the weapon from her grasp. Somewhere in the back of her mind she wondered if he'd kill her with it. Or would he simply rip out her throat as she'd always been warned.

She heard a click followed by a series of clinking sounds. She looked up at him and watched him empty the bullets one by one onto the polished wood floor, staring hard at her. Empty, he laid the gun back in her lap and crouched down. He still looked angry but there was also confusion etched in the lines of his face. "Why?" he demanded. "Why didn't you shoot me? I'm a Were, Annie. I'm a mindless, merciless killer. Why didn't you shoot me?

She shut her eyes and didn't answer. His hands closed around her shoulders and shook her slightly. "Look at me. Why didn't you shoot? You're a hunter. Why didn't you kill me, or at least try to?"

"I couldn't," she whispered meeting his gaze. His brown eyes were still hard and searching.

"Why? It's who you are."

"No," she shook her head and felt the first tear start to slide down her cheek. "I'm not a hunter. I've never been a hunter. My family but not me. I'm sick. The ancient healers call it *Lunis Pestia*. The moon's curse. It strips our bodies of strength and life. Attacking our lungs, our muscles. Killing us slowly."

"Not good enough. You were raised to hate people like me, why didn't you shoot?" His fingers dug harshly into her skin and she heard a sense of desperation in his voice that matched what was in her heart. "Annie, answer me! The truth."

"Because I love you." She started to cry in earnest now, burying her face in her hands. She heard him groan. Suddenly she was being lifted from her chair. The gun clanked uselessly to the floor and skittered away from them as he cradled her in his arms. A few short steps had them on the sofa. He settled her beside him and pulled her into his embrace. He kissed her so softly it surprised her. His lips moved from hers to brush her damp cheeks.

"Don't cry, Annie. Don't," he brushed away the tears with his fingers and continued to spread gentle kisses over her face. "We'll figure this out. We'll make it work. You're my destined mate, my one love. My soul mate, my darling. We'll make it work."

She touched his cheek, "I'm your mate? How?"

He shook his head with a soft huff of confused mirth. "The lovers' stone chose you for me, sweetheart. That's all I know. It chose you for me and I love you. You are my mate, the only one I can ever have."

She nestled her face against his neck as he held her. "But my disease, Luke, I haven't very long before…you can't tie yourself to someone who is going to die."

"Shh," he pressed his lips to her forehead. "We are all going to die sooner or later. But I promise you it will be much later. Once we mate, our spirits are joined and the power of mine will heal you. There is a reason we live so long, Annie. A reason we are so hard to kill. Our spirits are stronger than you could ever imagine."

He'd heal her. He loved her and he would heal her.

"Annie," he pulled back frowning. "Will you? Will you be my mate? You can say no if the idea of being mated to…" he hesitated, "a Were is…" He paused again. "I know what I am is as repugnant to you as the hunters are to my people. Can you accept me?"

"Can you accept me?" she pressed back. "Can you accept the daughter, the sister of a hunter?"

He looked at her seriously. "As long as you promise not to point that gun at me again, I'm willing to work it out." A slow smile started to curl his lips.

"As long as you promise not to eat anyone I know I'm willing to try too." She gave him a wicked grin in return. He laughed out loud and she felt a large piece of the tension break. Luke met her kiss then and she relaxed into him reveling in the feel of his hands on her body.

Their tongues danced and she had her hands up under his t-shirt and was held against him by his strong arm when she heard it.

"What the hell?" The voice came from the kitchen door. Luke pulled away sharply and stood to face the man who glared at them from just inside the archway between the kitchen and dining room. His expression was stone cold as he stared at the gold and silver sun pendant that hung from Jack's neck.

Chapter Four

ഌ

"Jack," Anna reached up and placed a hand against Luke's. "What are you doing here? Since when don't you knock?"

The two men watched each other carefully. "I came in the back. I need to use the basement to store something."

"Luke," Anna felt her heart pounding wildly in her chest. "This is my brother, Jack. Jack, this is Luke. He's a friend."

"I noticed," the two still refused to break eye contact. "He needs to leave, Anna. I need to talk to you, it's important and private."

"Fine," she tried to control her breathing. God if Jack found out what Luke was...

Luke looked down at her startled. "We can talk in the kitchen. Luke, do you mind waiting here for a minute?" She saw the muscles in his jaw relax slightly and he gave a curt nod. He'd wait but it was clear he was damned unhappy about it. "Jack, get my chair."

"I'll do it," Luke said flatly. He surprised her by picking her up and carrying her to her chair. Jack backed away slightly as they approached.

As he bent to settle her in place she whispered quietly. "He can't tell. He's mind-blind." Luke looked into her eyes for a moment and again nodded.

Anna backed away from Luke and followed Jack into the kitchen. "Who the hell is he?" Jack rounded on her as soon as they were out of sight of the living room.

"How dare you? What are you doing barging into my house? And what was that back there? You could at least have been civil. You know, said 'excuse me' instead of glaring at Luke like some outraged maiden aunt," Anna shot back.

"Who is he, Anna?" Jack demanded.

"My..." she searched for the right words. Future mate would not go over well and neither would lover. "My boyfriend."

"Your boyfriend?" Jack snorted. "Then why haven't you mentioned him before? You seem very well acquainted with him."

"Because I don't exactly make a habit of discussing my sex life with my brother," the words flew out of her mouth and she watched Jack turn bright red. Anna sighed. "What did you want to talk to me about? I know you didn't come here to give me the third degree about Luke."

Jack cast an angry glance at the door as if he could strike out at the man in the other room with it. "I need to store something in your basement for a couple of hours and I need you to take a look at it. Confirm for me what it is."

Anna felt as if ice water had just been injected into her veins. "Well you jumped in with both feet, didn't you?" This was not going to go well. If Luke found out he had...well whatever he had, he would not take it well.

"I sort of got the idea that was the point," Jack slumped against the low kitchen counter. "My *see'er* handed it off to me. I'm supposed to hold it until nightfall, then dispose of it."

"Dispose of what?" The sick dread was starting to reach an overwhelming level.

"They said it's one of the fey, a gnome. But Anna," Jack's voice shook slightly. "I need you to confirm it. Tell me what it is. It doesn't look like a gnome. It looks like a small child."

"Then if I were you I'd be very careful," Luke's voice made them both jump. He was standing in the doorway, dark chocolate eyes shooting daggers at Jack. He turned that glare on Anna. "I thought you said you weren't a hunter."

"I'm not," Anna rushed to reassure him. Justified or not, the harsh look in those eyes frightened her. "I'm not a hunter."

Jack was standing straight now, staring at Luke with an expression that went beyond apprehension. "What do you know of hunters?" He swung his hazel regard to his sister. "What have you told him?"

"Nothing," Anna felt as if she were suddenly drowning in the fear, anger and paranoia that was filling the room. "Both of you calm down. Jack, Luke knows about the hunters. You don't need to know how," she forestalled the question that was poised on his lips. "He knows. Luke, I told you my brother was a hunter. I'm not. Please try to see that this is difficult for me as well." She met his eyes and he nodded.

"I know that," he said softly.

Anna took a deep breath. "Where is it?"

"In the basement. I took it in through the outside entrance and came up the stairs. Anna I don't..." Jack swallowed and glanced at Luke and lowered his voice. "I don't want to make the same mistake Dad made. Will you look at it?"

"Yes," she agreed. Luke stared at her incredulously and she saw the hint of betrayal in his face before it turned to granite.

"And if it is a gnome, will you help him kill it?" his voice was even and dull.

"No one is killing anything in my house," she said firmly to both men. "I said I'd look at it."

Jack reached to lift her out of her chair, clearly intending to carry her down the steps to the basement but Luke stepped up to the chair in a way that was a clear challenge. Her brother backed off reluctantly. Luke lifted her and shouldered past her brother toward the door. "Trust me," she whispered. Luke did not respond.

As soon as her vision cleared the overhang over the stairs she saw him. He was bent over a small iron cage and was opening the door.

"Tarris!"

The word sprang out of her mouth and Luke had to practically jump the last two steps to stay on his feet, holding her to his chest as Jack pushed past him. Her heart nearly stopped when she saw the gun in her brother's hand.

"Get away from that cage," Jack hissed at the blond man.

Luke was carefully lowering her on to the steps. Tarris looked at them for a moment, the blue eyes met hers before he turned, ignoring Jack and swung the door to the cage open.

"I said get away from it." Jack stepped closer with the gun pointed at Tarris' bare back.

Doesn't this guy ever wear a shirt? The errant thought touched her brain lightly.

The tiny creature inside looked more like a small child of about three or four than any dark creature. It was curled on a small nest of rags trying hard not to touch the iron of the cage. Iron was as unnatural and harmful to the fey as silver to the Were, more so in fact. The Were could stand the trace touches of silver and even if shot could fight off its effects if the bullet did not pierce a vital organ. The silver nitrate bullets were another story. Based on the old cop-killers—a type of outlawed human ammunition—they exploded on entry and sprayed the surrounding tissue with liquid silver. It wasn't a death she wanted to think about.

She heard the shot fired before she realized what was happening. Just as the bullet would have ripped through the incubus there was a bright light and Tarris dematerialized long enough for the bullet to pass through him and lodge in the wall behind him. Jack's eyes widened and he didn't see Luke come behind him. Luke's clenched fists swung as hard as if he they held a tennis racket and he was aiming for match point. They struck Jack in the back and sent him flying forward onto his face. A second flash of light and Tarris was standing on Jack's wrist while prying the gun from his hand. He held it dangling from two fingers as if it were a vile piece of trash he was forced to handle. He flung it away from them and moved back toward the cage.

I had a feeling I'd need to watch your back tonight, baby bear. His head shook as he knelt back down before the crate. Anna heard the voice she associated with the incubus fill her mind. She remembered the lore she'd been force-fed as a child. The incubus didn't speak. They were mute in the waking world. Or rather it seemed they spoke other than with voices.

Tarris reached inside and pulled the child from its prison. As soon as it cleared the dangers of the iron box it shimmered in Anna's vision. The child was gone and she saw the wrinkled little face and the pointed little nose of the gnome.

"Put me down," it demanded of its rescuer. "Let me at him." It was snarling and hissing at Jack who was just starting to move. Its tiny pointed shoes were kicking at Tarris viciously.

Stop! You keep kicking me, little friend, and I'm going to take it personally. Tarris sounded amused despite what had transpired.

Jack struggled to rise. Luke's foot came to rest on his back. He stopped and looked up warily. "If you get up, you do it knowing that if you go for my friends again, I won't check my strength." Again the lore floated to Anna's mind. A Were's strength had almost no limit. They could easily kill a human with a single blow.

Anna watched her brother nod and he stood slowly. He turned to look at them. His eyes swung from Luke to Tarris and rested on the creature in his arms. It was no longer hiding its true form. "I should have trusted my gut and killed you."

"Human scum," the little gnarled face was twisted even more hideously with its rage.

Easy little fey, Tarris frowned, *you'll hurt yourself doing that. Do not judge all of a race by the acts of a few. The female would not have harmed you.*

He met Anna's eyes and smiled at her softly. *Would you?* She shook her head.

Jack was staring at the incubus. "What are you?"

"Jack, stop it," Anna spoke up for the first time. "Tarris, I think it's best if you take your friend and go."

Tarris frowned at her and exchanged a prolonged look with Luke she was sure included a conversation from which she had been excluded. Finally Tarris nodded. *Your brother can't hear me, Anna but he is very frightened. Frightened people do stupid things. Keep our Luke safe.* As the light from his departure faded she finally shifted her eyes to her brother.

"What the hell was that and why did it do what you told it to?" His words ground out angrily.

"Tarris does what he chooses," Anna replied. "Life is not about commanding people, Jack. It's not black and white, good and bad. There are no pure heroes and villains. You're too old to believe that anymore."

"What I'm getting too old to believe is that just because I might love someone, they must be good," his eyes were angry. He took a step toward her and Luke stepped between them. Jack glared at him. "What are you?"

Anna held her breath praying Luke wouldn't answer. "I am your sister's mate, or I will be."

"Mate?" Jack repeated the word in a whisper. He shook his head in disbelief. "What does that mean? Humans don't use that word."

"No, they generally don't," Luke leaned against the end of the stair rail and crossed his arms over his chest. God he was arrogant. Cocky, arrogant and so damned sure of himself he made her feel safe even when she was terrified of what was going to happen next.

She closed her eyes at the pained confusion that spread on her brother's face. It was time to stop this. "Luke is a Were, Jack and I've agreed to be his mate."

"His mate? You would whore yourself with the very creatures our family has sought to protect the world from for generations?" Jack took another step toward them and stopped when Luke dropped his feigned indifference and stood up straight.

"You're only alive right now, human, because it would hurt her to watch me kill you." Luke's eyes burned with fury and Anna saw the glow of the bear around him brighten. His face flickered its animal nature and she knew he was pressing the limits of his control to stop his transformation and attack. And he was doing it for her.

"And I'm just supposed to stand here and let it happen? Is that it Anna? I'm just supposed to stand here and let you spit on centuries of tradition?" Jack's voice was eerily quiet.

Anna saw what Luke didn't but only because she knew about it. She knew about the arm bows her father had designed and had made. They were supposed to have been for her. She was the *see'er*. She was supposed to have been the next great hunter. She saw Jack reach up and rub his right arm with his left hand. She knew the motion. Her father had trained her with the weapon. He was shifting the gas firing cartridge into place. When Jack lifted his arm again, a flick of his wrist would send a silver bolt firing straight at Luke.

Anna forced herself to her feet and shoved Luke as hard as she could. Jack's hand came up but instead of dead center aim at the chest of the Were, the small arrow struck his sister's shoulder. Anna screamed in pain and her legs gave out as much from the shock as from the sheer exertion of standing. Luke dropped beside her, saw what had happened and started after Jack with a growl that screamed his blood lust. With her last strength she grabbed his hand and cried, "No!" The cough started deep in her and her body shook with it. She gasped for air and could get none.

As the world grew dark, the last thing she saw was Luke's face as he gathered her up in his arms. She heard him yell as the edges of her vision turned black.

"Tarris!"

When she came to, she felt warm. A dull throb pulsed in her shoulder. A hand was touching her face gently with a damp cloth. She opened her eyes and found herself looking into stormy green-gray eyes that were regarding her with a mixture of pleasure and curiosity. "Good," the voice was musical, soothing. "Finally. I was afraid I was going to lose my sister-in-law before I ever got to meet her."

Anna tried to shift but the pain stopped her. "Easy," the woman tsked and helped her into a sitting position. "You're going to be fine but it will take a while since you're human." The face broke into a smile. "So am I by the way. I'm Sarah. Luke's brother is my mate."

Anna searched her memory. "Mark, Luke's brother is Mark."

"Yes," The woman stood up but returned quickly with a glass filled with cool water. "Here, this will help. Something about the healing dehydrates the body."

As she sipped the water the woman straightened the blankets. The blonde's chatter was an odd combination of reassurance and nervousness. "At least I hope it works the same on humans. Mostly it's my mate's family who find themselves recuperating here." She glanced up at Anna, "You're at the family house. My home and Mark's. He's the *Amar*, the leader of our people. They come to him for help just as Tarris did tonight."

"Your mate healed me?" Anna couldn't imagine such a thing. He couldn't know what she was or he would surely have let her die.

"Yes," Sarah nodded. "As *Amar* he holds the life force of the people in his hands. It's one of the things that came to him as leader. He has an overwhelming responsibility for their lives." When she'd drained the glass, Sarah took it from her fingers and set it on the night stand. "We weren't sure it would work with you, being human and not yet mated to Luke. But there is enough of him inside you, enough of a bond between you, Mark was able to follow it and heal the wound in your shoulder."

"Where is Luke?" Anna couldn't hold the question any longer. A part of her was terrified that something had happened to him. She may have taken the arrow but that wasn't the only weapon Jack had had, she was certain of it.

Sarah hushed her, "Don't worry. When you were hurt he called for Tarris. Tarris can only transport one being at a time. Luke pushed you into his arms, told him to bring you here. I'm sure he's on his way. Let's hope he didn't hit a traffic jam or that's going to be some serious road rage." The woman's chuckle should have made her feel better but it didn't.

"What about my brother?"

"Your brother was the hunter?" Anna nodded and the sweet, pretty face grew harsh and stern. "I'm not sure. Tarris grabbed you and got you here as soon as he could. All he knew was that Luke was holding you, you were bleeding and having trouble breathing and the hunter was on his knees on the floor. Tarris left again as soon as he got you into our hands, I expected him to follow with Luke but he didn't."

A sick fear filled crept in slowly. "You don't think they would have killed him?"

"Your brother?" Sarah shook her head. "I'm pretty sure that's what Tarris went back to prevent. If he went back."

Several minutes passed in silence. She didn't want to speak to the woman, as nice as she seemed. She didn't want to think about what might have happened after Tarris took her out of the basement. She didn't want to think about what it would mean if Luke had killed her brother. She hated Jack right now. But she couldn't deny she still loved him.

The door to the room flew open with a bang and she heard a male voice very similar to Luke's demanding, "Calm down, I told you she's fine for the moment."

Two versions of Luke came through the door. One neatly dressed and looking peeved. The other one wore a t-shirt stained with blood beneath a worn leather jacket. This was the man who bolted to her side and dropped beside the bed. He grabbed for her as Sarah called out, "Easy Luke, be careful."

He seemed to check himself and reached to cup her face. "Are you okay?"

She smiled at him and placed her hand over his. "I'm all right. It hurts but I'm fine."

Luke lifted up to sit beside her on the bed and gently pulled her into his arms. He pressed his face into her hair. "Gods, I was so scared. I'm going to kill Tarris."

"What did Tarris do?" Sarah's voice sounded worried.

"He refused to transport Luke back here. Said he had something more important to do and the drive would calm Luke down and give me time to work before he was in here wreaking havoc." The man Anna quickly realized was Luke's twin, Mark, wore a wry grin.

"More important," grumbled Luke against her cheek before he kissed her quickly. "I'll give him more important."

"Luke," Anna pushed him back. "Where's Jack?"

The dark eyes flared with anger and the curled lip exposed the elongated incisors. "He's fine, Anna. Not because I have any compassion for him. I couldn't give a shit he was horrified by what happened. I couldn't give a shit he was kneeling on the floor with tears on his face because of what he'd done. His remorse means nothing to me and if it had been my choice, he'd be dead."

"Luke!" Sarah cried out. Her mate put his arm around her.

"Sarah, he nearly killed Tarris, Luke and Anna. My brother's right. He deserved to die. And as *Amar* I want to know why he still lives, Brother." Mark's eyes were just as hard and cold as Luke's. "He attacked three members of this family, why does he live?"

Anna breathed a sigh of relief. Jack was alive. The man she loved hadn't killed him. She didn't know what she'd have done if that had happened.

Luke turned to face his brother. "He lives because he is my soul mate's brother. He lives because of what it would do to her if *I* killed him." He turned to Anna and his face was deadly serious. "But no more mercy, Anna. If he comes for this family again, he will die even if I have to be the one who does it."

"The rules of this family are different," Sarah's voice was shaking. "They can be hard for us to accept."

"No, they may be different to you but not to me." Anna folded her hand around Luke's. "I was reared a hunter. My brother will be considered weak by our people if anyone finds out what he did. He could easily be punished. He should have killed me the minute I called out to Tarris. He should have killed me the moment I showed any sympathy to the dark ones. My father would have."

Mark nodded. "We are agreed then. Sarah, let's leave these two alone. I'm sure they want to discuss the weather or something of equal importance." A wicked grin that looked very much like Luke's flashed on the handsome face before he steered his mate out of the door. He paused before closing it behind him. "Luke," he waited for his brother to look at him. "I fixed what I could. It's up to you now. I can't..." He shook his head, the handsome face sad. "I can't."

Chapter Five

ɛͻ

Luke turned back to the woman the lovers' stone had chosen as his mate. Her face was pale and he could see the blue tinge around her lips. Her hands felt cold in his. Mark had told him as he followed him up the stairs to her that he had healed what he could of her shoulder but could not heal the sickness in her. Only mating could do that. She'd lost a lot of blood and there was not enough of a bond yet for him to be able to heal her completely. All he'd been able to do was stop the bleeding and close the wound. It would take time for her body to repair itself.

But the sense Mark had gotten of her illness was far beyond what Luke had realized. As he stood blocking Luke's path, even defying his threats to strike his own brother and, tribunal be damned, his *Amar* if he didn't get out of his way, Mark told him that the disease was virulent and vicious. "Her body is turning against itself. It's genetic, caused by the inbreeding among the hunters. Exactly the sort of thing Grandfather spent centuries warning the purists among our kind of. Exactly what is killing off the angelus as the humans whittle down their numbers and they refuse to breed with other species."

Luke had dismissed this until Mark had yelled after him. "She's going to die Luke and die soon if you don't mate with her." The words had fueled the panic in his chest to an even hotter conflagration. He wouldn't lose her.

He lay down next to her and wrapped his arms around her, holding her close as her head rested on his chest. "Anna, we need to complete the mating soon."

"I know," she whispered back. "This has weakened me, Luke. I know it. My body can't replenish what it's lost. It also can't repair the damage as it normally should. I am, right now, the best I will ever be."

"So we do this now?" Luke looked into her eyes and smiled brightly. "I mean, I know it's a real sacrifice on both our parts but if it's for the greater good, I'll suck it up and do my duty." He leaned down and kissed her, taking great joy in the feel of her in his arms, in the taste of her lips.

"As soon as we can," she agreed. "What will happen? Is there a ceremony? Is it like a human wedding?"

Luke stared at her. He'd expected her to know about the Were matings. She was from the hunters. Did they really understand so little about the creatures they hunted? A piece of his brain cataloged the information to share with Mark. It seemed their nemesis had serious gaps in their understanding, the question was could they use them to their advantage?

"Annie," he watched her eyes, "we don't have weddings. Well, Mark and Sarah did but that was for her family's benefit. Once a couple mates, their family usually holds a celebration and the *Amar* and *Amari* give their blessing to the couple."

"And Mark will give us his blessing," she sounded so certain and relieved.

"I don't know why not, he's mated to a human so he has no grounds to object. The only time in history someone did object formally was when my grandfather mated to my grandmother. She too was human. His brother challenged and they ended up resolving it in the traditional way." Luke grimaced. Sarah had not taken this little bit of information well. "My grandfather was forced to kill his brother to keep his mate."

Anna's eyes left his and she frowned. "But Mark won't object?"

Luke beamed at her. "No, in fact as my closest living relative he has to foot the bill for the party and we are going to blow the roof off." His smile weakened, "But I have to be honest with you, Annie. That's one thing I won't do, lie to you. I objected to Mark mating with Sarah at first. Because she was human. But later..." he hurried the words, "I realized she was probably the best thing that could happen to our family and that my quarrel with Mark had nothing to do with her in reality."

"Would you have killed him?"

Luke sighed. "I don't know. I never got the chance to find out. Sarah stopped us fighting. Said she'd leave, she wouldn't be the source of the bloodshed. It snapped both of us back. I saw her face, she was just standing there looking so heartbroken but so determined. It was then I realized it wasn't about her. We still fought but for the real reasons. At least we did until Tarris intervened."

"I think you're a wee bit in love with her," Anna smiled at him. He looked at her sharply. There was no sense of jealousy or anger. Her smile was teasing and gentle.

"I think we all are," he admitted quietly. "She's like no one I've ever known before. She's perfect for Mark. She made him who he is today, which is a damned good leader." He leaned down and brushed his lips against hers. "But I'd rather not talk about them. I'd rather take my mate."

"You still haven't told me what that means," she chuckled as she ran her fingers over his jaw.

"Simple. We make love," he kissed her. Her soft lips yielded under his as he pressed her back into the pillows. He explored her mouth tasting her breath and feeling the sharp little teeth against his tongue. He nipped her lower lip as he pulled back and went to shrug out of his jacket. Freeing his arms he pulled the lovers' stone from his pocket and set it on the table by the bed. He'd be needing that later.

"Can you do it?" she asked puzzled. "Don't we need Tarris?"

Luke laughed. "Sweetheart there are some things for which my dear friend and lover is handy, however, mating it is best left to you and me. Or did you like his touch so much you'll not want me on my own any longer." He brushed her hair back from her face.

"You mean we'll actually make love?" there was a note of panic in her voice. "Not in a dream?"

Luke frowned. "No, for this I'd rather we were both wide awake. Besides mating has to be in the flesh. Annie? If you don't want this, just say so. If you want to wait, we will. Was it Tarris you wanted?" He was jealous by nature true, but for the first time in his life jealousy of his friend reared its head. The sensation burned and made him feel sick.

She closed her eyes and her breath escaped her in a slow sigh that sank her chest. "No," she looked up at him and her eyes seemed wet and bright. "I want to be your mate. I adore Tarris but it's you I want, Luke. I love you."

Luke kissed her forehead and cheeks, tender loving caresses on her face as he moved back toward her mouth. His mate. He felt a swelling in his chest and in his cock He would finally know the feel of her true flesh holding him, of her soft cries in his waking ears. He moved to her mouth and pushed his tongue between the petal soft lips and began to stroke the outer curve of her breast as he started the acts that would lead to the binding of their spirits.

"I told you he wouldn't wait," A wheezing voice sneered from very near his head making him jump. "Impatient, all the Weres. Would kill his own mate in his lust."

Luke sat up and reached for the intruder only to find his hand stopped, by the grip of another on his wrist.

Easy, Tarris' voice soothed his anger instantly making him feel calm and even more aroused as it cascaded through his mind. *Try not to hurt my little friend. He's come to repay a kindness.*

Luke looked at the small gnome sitting on the pillow. His pointed cap covered a rather pointed head. The same wizened face he'd seen in the darkness of Annie's cellar looked up at him and then over to her.

"And you'd just let him do it, eh? Bet she didn't even tell him he'd kill her by it." The wrinkled face twisted even more. "Sexual reproduction. Makes you all crazy and rash. If you budded like gnomes, you wouldn't be so foolish."

"That's disgusting," Luke grimaced.

"Oh and you about to rut with her blood still upon you isn't? I suppose it's fitting since she'll be dead beneath you before you're done." The little creature stood up. "I'm leaving."

No you're not, Tarris said simply and the little gnome stared at him with contempt but sat back down.

Luke looked down at her face. She wasn't shocked as she sat there leaned against the covers looking pale and wan. She wouldn't meet his eye. "Is it true?"

She nodded and his heart plummeted in a free fall at her words. "I've been warned for some time I'm not strong enough for sex. I can't even stand, Luke."

"Why didn't you tell me?" his anger soared up to fill the empty spot in his chest. "Annie, why didn't you tell me?"

"Because I wanted it. I wanted to know what it was like to touch you, truly to feel you inside me. Before tonight, maybe I'd have had a chance. You said the mating would heal me. Maybe it would have worked fast enough. But not now." A tear slipped down her cheek.

Luke sat back on his heels, numb. If he coupled with her, if they mated she'd die. If they didn't, she'd die, only more slowly. He looked up at Tarris. The tall man at his side laid a hand on his shoulder. His aura and scent wrapped around Luke but it didn't help. He closed his burning eyes. No weakness. He couldn't show weakness but the pain of the reality was ripping through him.

Don't, Tarris' voice was soft and oddly reassuring. *It will be all right. I promise you.*

Luke opened his eyes and looked into the depths of two very different sets of blue eyes. First, Tarris' which seemed to flicker like blue flames, then his Annie's, cool and comforting as the waters of a warm sea. "How? How can it be all right?"

The gnome snorted.

Go on, little friend.

"You're being a fool," the wrinkled old face admonished him. "It's you I owe the favor. You'd throw away a life debt on them. They'd not do so much for you. Why give them this when it only means that you won't…"

Do it! There was a power and finality to those two words.

The gnome grumbled before standing up and leaning close to Anna. Luke watched as he put his gnarled little hand on her chest, just over her heart. She gasped and Luke lunged for the creature afraid for a moment it had hurt her. Then he saw it. The color began to flood back into her skin. She took a full breath and did not begin to cough. He could hear no rattle or wheeze as she drew in several more.

"My debt is paid." The gnome spoke to Tarris and ignored them. "You're a bigger fool than I've ever seen and you don't even have a wretched soul to blame for it. You'll regret this, incubus. But don't come to me when you do, for I'll just laugh in your face." The small creature was gone in an instant, leaving behind only two small indentations in the pillow where its tiny feet had stood.

* * * * *

The air filled her lungs to capacity again and again without pain or triggering the hacking cough she'd lived with for over ten years now. She could no longer feel the pain in her shoulder and her hand flexed on the blankets without stiffness or pain. She looked up at Luke and smiled brightly.

"He healed me," her voice came out as a whisper.

No, he did not, Tarris' hand gripped Luke's shoulder to keep him from grabbing her. *He has merely masked the effects of your illness. It will last only until midnight and that's not as far off as you might think. You will begin to slip back to the way you were. Enough time to complete the mating, if you do not make too much of a production of things.* His hand moved from Luke's shoulder to lift his chin lovingly. *Claim your mate, my friend.* The kiss he placed on the upturned lips was hungry and fierce. The fingers tightened in Luke's hair tilting his head back. She watched the two men lean across her toward each other. An aching need starting to build inside her as the two beautiful males kissed, tongues visible as they caressed each other. Luke rose up on his knees and put an arm around Tarris' neck, pulling him down to sit on the edge of the bed. Tarris lowered himself next to her and allowed Luke to lean over him, forcing back his own neck. She watched, breathing growing more rapid as Luke claimed the inside of Tarris' mouth. His hand sliding over the incubus' chest in a slow tender caress.

The kiss ended and the two sat still, foreheads pressed together, eyes closed. "Enjoy your rest, my dear one," Luke's voice whispered softly against Tarris' face. "Once we are mated, between the four of us in this house, you may never know rest again. You will certainly never know hunger."

You always have to play the Dom. The voice in her head was faintly amused as Tarris pulled away from Luke carefully. The eyes that met hers were sad but there was a hopeful touch to the smile on his lips. He leaned down and placed a chaste kiss on her lips. *Don't waste this time, Anna. Claim him.*

Tarris stood up. She expected him to blink out in a flash as he always did but instead he spun on his heel and walked out the door.

Luke moved to her side. "Midnight. Plenty of time I think."

"Plenty of time for a shower," she grinned. "The fey creature is right. You are rather icky."

"Icky?" Luke lifted an eyebrow before looking down at himself. A crease split his forehead. "Yeah, I am aren't I?"

Anna swung her legs off the bed and stood. Luke grabbed her elbow and held it. She took a step. Then another. And another. "The bathroom is where?"

He indicated a door on the same wall as the head of the bed. That would explain why she hadn't seen it. She smiled wickedly at the man who would soon be her mate. "Race ya." Still feeling odd on her legs, she darted toward the door. He clambered across the bed and met her in the doorway. His arms enfolded her as they backed into the bathroom laughing. His lips crushed themselves to hers as he pressed his body to the length of her. His kiss was powerful and demanding as he cupped one hand behind her head and used the other to start pulling up the nightshirt she had been loaned.

She grabbed the edges of his t-shirt and tugged it over his head. He left her lips only long enough to free himself from it and then returned to the plunder of her mouth. His tongue danced with hers, dueling and teasing as his hands cupped her breasts. She gasped, her head flinging backward as his fingers pinched gently at her nipples, the hard peaks already swollen from need for his touch. His lips moved to her throat and he ran his tongue up the column of flesh making her shudder and shaking the hands that had been wrestling with his jeans. She tugged impatiently at the buttons and he laughed.

"Let me, I'd zap them out of the way but sometimes when I do that I can't find them again and I like this pair." He unfastened them and slipped them off his hips.

"You can do that?" She looked at him wide eyed.

"Annie, I'm feeling better and better about hunters. Of course I can, I can do a lot of things that are going to surprise you." He pulled his pants off and tossed them onto the growing pile. "Come here," he reached for her and she slithered away.

"No way, mister. Not until you're clean." She smiled mischievously at him and pulled open the shower stall door. "Good Lord!" she exclaimed. It was almost like walking into another room, albeit a very small one. There was plenty of room for more than one person, three or four actually. The white marble walls gleamed in the soft recessed light. Stepping inside she turned the gold faucet and adjusted the water. She heard the door close behind her. Luke waited while she found the right temperature then twisted the handle to turn on the shower.

Three showerheads sprayed out jets of delicious hot water to meet in the center where one buffeted Luke's back, one sprayed between them and the third pounded the skin of her neck. She watched him roll his neck and sigh. "That feels good."

She wriggled a bit under the spray letting the water strike the muscles and ease the ache. The stiffness and fatigue were gone. She shouldn't even be standing, let alone have the strength to go on from here. She picked up the large sponge from its shelf and poured out a generous amount of the soap on to it. Moving to Luke she washed his chest and shoulders, removing any traces of her blood. He closed his eyes and seemed to lose himself in the feel of her hands. Down his abdomen she moved with the thick lathering suds. She rubbed circles on his skin with the sponge and traced shapes and patterns in the soap with her fingers.

Squeezing the suds into her hand she worked them into the nest of dark curls that surrounded the base of his shaft. Moving lower, deliberately avoiding contact with his cock, she caressed the soft tender sac. A low moan escaped his lips and his eyes remained closed. One hand reached out to brace itself against the wall. Sliding her hand up, she curled her fingers around the rigid length of him. She stroked the heavy thickness in her hand and felt herself growing wet as she imagined it buried deep inside her. She slid her hand over the sensitive head and back down to the base in a long measured rhythm. She could feel the throb that mirrored her own heartbeat echoed against her palm even as it pounded in the slick flesh between her legs.

She released him and stepped behind him. Her hands moved the soap over his broad shoulders and strong back. He was perfectly proportioned, her lover. Everything about him seemed as if it had been sculpted, carefully created by an artist's hand.

He turned and reached for her, pulling her against him. She felt her breasts press to his chest and slide across the slick soapy surface, as he moved. He swayed slightly, smiling down at her as if he knew exactly what he was doing. As if he knew exactly how delicious the torment of his flesh brushing against her hard nipples felt. His lips found hers and his tongue moved over the delicate skin of her inner lip before he closed it in his teeth and tugged. He pulled the sponge from her hand and stepped away from her.

The warm water slid over her while he used the soap-laden sponge to clean her back. As it moved down to her hips the pressure eased and its rough surface tickled her, making her squirm. Luke reached low and bathed each leg and foot before standing again. His body against her back, she could feel the hardness of him against her buttocks. He brought his hand and the sponge, dripping lather, around to her front. The feel of his chest against her back, his cock pressed against her as his hands massaged her breasts, the texture of the sponge making her want to cry out. Soft gasps of pleasure escaped her even though she bit down on her lower lip.

The calloused tips of his fingers played with her left nipple, pinching slightly as he rubbed it between forefinger and thumb. The sponge moved lower over her stomach until he pushed it between her thighs. She opened willingly for him, taking almost as much joy in the fact that she stood there before him, whole and strong, as from the sensation of the slick sliding against her labia. She heard the soft splat as he dropped the sponge and his hand replaced it, stroking her folds. She leaned her head back against his shoulder and let the feelings in her body take over. Her dream lover was here in the flesh and his hands felt as good, no, better than they ever had.

"My Annie," he murmured in her ear. She felt him reach between them and start to stroke his cock against her.

She pulled away and put her hands on her hips playfully. "Lucas, you must finish your bath. You haven't been properly rinsed off, nor have I." The smile that tugged at her lips in equal parts for the teasing of her man as for the sensation of her breath coming rapidly but without the pain she had long grown used to.

"Rinsed," Luke's dark eyes suddenly shone with something that was exhilaratingly dangerous. "Rinsed. I see."

He moved toward her so quickly she cried out in alarm. He backed her into the wall of the shower near the central showerhead. He grabbed her hands and pinned them over her head. Her surprise gave way to a deep laugh. "Tarris is right. You always have to play the Dom."

The glint in the dark chocolate orbs grew even stronger. "I'll show you Dom." He leaned in and brushed his lips along her neck. The tingle ran all the way to her toes before rebounding upward and making her swollen flesh burn even more for his touch. "And I'll show you a few of those surprises."

Without a word or a hand gesture from him, she felt something cool encircle her wrists. Looking up she saw two gold cuffs that dangled at the end of golden chains affixed to the wall. Her wrists lay cradled against a lining of soft cushioning fabric. Not uncomfortable but a tug at the chains soon revealed she was going nowhere. Before she could protest, he captured her mouth. His hands ran the length of her body, touching her, teasing her, arousing her to the point she was wriggling, rubbing her thighs together to ease the ache of want.

"You want Dom, my Annie, you got it."

Luke stepped back and let the water run over him. He rinsed the soap from his body. Standing there before her watchful gaze he moved his hand down to rinse the soap from the dark curls below his navel and then lower. Long fingers curled around his erection and slid over its length. He looked up and watched her face. She tried to meet his eyes but couldn't keep her gaze from the motion of his hand. She clenched her fist wanting to feel the hot flesh sliding along her palm. Her pussy reacted with a jolt when he started to move his hips to accentuate the motion of his hand. She wanted to feel those hips grind against her. She wanted him thrusting deep inside her, this time for real.

He stopped abruptly, his breathing ragged and labored. He leaned against the wall on his hands for just a moment before he reached up and lifted the showerhead from the wall. He adjusted the spray so that it was a pulsating jet and aimed it at her legs. "Rinsed, I think you said," his voice was low and seductive and her body shivered in response.

The feel of the water as it swept up and down her thighs was wonderful. It massaged as it moved over muscles that had been so long ignored and unused. After a brief shattering blast against the outer flesh of her mons he trailed the spray up her stomach. He avoided her breasts and let the water move between them, up to her shoulders and onto her neck. He moved in close and kissed her throat, his lips moving over the wet surface. As he did he lowered the showerhead and the spray fell against the swelling flesh of her breasts. The soft shuddering shivers that moved through her made her so ready for him only the wetness of the shower could have hidden the dripping evidence of her arousal.

Still nuzzling her neck, he turned the jets on first one nipple then the other, rotating his hand so that the pulse blasted across the hard peak before veering off. Again and again, first one then the other, he tormented her this way for endless minutes. Easing away from her he claimed her tender nipple with his mouth and sucked at it.

He whispered against her, "I don't think you mind me playing Dom, do you?" She shook her head and moaned as he claimed the other with equal fervor. His tongue and teeth tortured her breasts with exquisite delights as she twisted and moaned. Her pussy had begun to ache so badly she was sure she'd die if he didn't fill her soon.

"Turn," he commanded with a soft pinch to one nipple. She found there was just enough give in the chains that held her to allow her to obey.

Luke pushed her thighs apart and she felt the blast of the water against her swollen lips. Her body screamed in pleasure and she was certain she was going to come then and there. He moved the spray back and forth over her outer folds. His hand was caressing her ass, his finger slipping down the crevice and stroking her. Luke pushed his knee between hers and lifted her leg up so her foot rested on the small ledge that ran the circumference of the shower. The shifting opened her lips and when the water again moved to the top of her slit it slammed her hardened clitoris. She cried out loudly and he pulled back on the spray, easing it back down her folds until it pounded against her buttocks.

Luke's hand spread her open and he aimed the jets of water into the crevice. The water pulsated against her anus and she groaned. His hand moved down to join the spray and he pressed his fingertip into the tight opening, slowly working it in, using the spray of the water to relax her and to ease his way. Never had anyone touched her ass or used it to heighten sexual pleasure. But the feel of his thick finger sliding into her was heavenly.

She began to groan loudly as he swept the water back up and circled her clitoris with the jets. Just barely letting them flicker against her, before he eased away. His finger moving in and out of her hole. The feel of the water teased her. She wanted release. She needed release.

"You like that?" he whispered into her ear.

"Yes, oh God yes, Luke." She pushed her hips back against him, driving his hand deeper. She cried out again as she felt a second finger join the penetration of her tightest opening.

"Just wait, my mate. When I again share you with Tarris, what pleasures we'll give you. You'd like that, wouldn't you?" He didn't wait for her to answer. "Both of us taking you, filling you. Does that sound good? Do you want it, my love?"

"Yes," the word erupted from her as both an answer and a plea.

She felt Luke pull out of her anus, then heard him drop the shower head and was certain she was about to feel the enormity of his cock spread her backside. But his thrust, when it came was into her pussy. She screamed his name and nearly came at that moment but he held still inside her as he pushed his thumb back up her ass. His movements were slow and deep, rocking her so her breasts bounced against the wall, the tender swollen nipples feeling the slap of the hard marble with each thrust. And he talked to her. Said things to her that made her weak. Whispers of what he wanted to do to her, of how he would please her in the lifetime before them.

"Come on Annie," his face pressed into the back of her neck. Luke did not hurry his thrusts but reached around to stroke her clit as he filled her. "Come for me. The first of many, my love. Come for me."

His words pushed her to a place where the world shuddered and tossed her off its edge. Her toes curled and her voice cried out. Her hands gripped the chains that held her as her release came.

She felt the restraints disappear and his arms catch her. He held her tight between his body and the wall, his strong arms around her. When her breathing slowed she looked up at him. "Are we mated?"

With a nod to the faucet, he shut the water off magically and grinned at her wickedly. "Not yet. We have to do this again, my love, holding the mating stone between our hands. But I wanted you this way first. I wanted to feel your body in the flesh before I bring us to release together."

He scooped her up and didn't bother to dry her. He carried her to the bed and laid her down. His mouth found the taut nipples and he laved them, licking each tenderly before sucking it into his mouth. His fingers moved down and drew circles around her clitoris, lazy, easy strokes to rebuild her arousal. He broke from teasing her breasts and reached for the red stone that he'd left on the bedside table. "I'll need to get this mounted. We normally do that before mating. After this it can't be cut or shaped so you'll have to keep it the shape it is."

She reached out and touched the stone. It was roughly heart-shaped and when she touched it a vibration burst through her that made her eyes fly open and her mouth form a surprised little O. Luke placed it in her left hand and pressed his hand to hers, tangling their fingers as they clutched it tightly between their palms. They both closed their eyes and gasped for breath. Anna could feel a pulsing through her body that pooled and focused in her warm needy pussy. Luke had been hard already but his length seemed to grow and stiffen even more. Opening her eyes she saw drips of sweat form on his brow that she was certain had no connection to the shower they'd just left.

He moved over her and the contact of his body along hers felt as if a dozen hands had begun to caress her. As much as she loved Luke's teasing foreplay, right now she just wanted him inside her. Before she could say the words, he ground his hips against hers and pushed his cock into her. Anna pulled her legs up and felt him sink even deeper into her body. The stone in their grasp seemed to be pushing her, driving her toward orgasm as surely as the feel of her mate thrusting into her wetness again and again.

He whispered her name over and over as he buried his face in her neck. The world was disappearing around her as the pulsing in her clit swept over her entire body. She felt as if her breathing had stopped, it was unnecessary, unneeded in this shining golden world that was enveloping her and Luke. "I love you," she called against his shoulder as her fingers dug harshly into his back, wanting to pull him inside her completely.

"I love you," he groaned as she felt the entirety of existence explode around her and rush into her body filling her with glorious pleasure as she broke into innumerable pieces. Luke was with her. His body stiffening and a cry escaping him that sounded more like a growling roar. He opened his eyes and fixed them on hers and for that eternity, their bodies erupting with orgasm, she saw his spirit glowing in his eyes. She saw all the way to the center of who he was and the love that swelled inside her made the tears start to fall.

Slowly the force of the stone eased its hold on them and Anna once again felt her heart beat, felt her lungs take air. Luke collapsed on top of her, his breathing more ragged than hers had been during her days of illness and she was suddenly afraid. Afraid of what would happen if she lost him. Afraid of what it would mean to live without him.

Slowly he gathered his strength. He pushed up on one arm, the other's hand still clinging to hers and to the stone between them. He lifted that hand to his lips and kissed it. "Mine." He grinned with a weary playfulness.

"Always the Dom," she shook her head laughing.

He moved off her gingerly and stretched out beside her, pulling her across his chest. "But you are mine, Annie. My mate, my love. You are mine."

"You sound very much like a two-year-old," she teased. "Mine, mine, mine."

"You are mine," he repeated unrepentantly and kissed the top of her head. "But don't forget my dearest love, that I am also yours."

Anna lifted her cheek from his chest and smiled into his eyes. "My mate, my love and my heart. Yes, Luke. You're mine."

His arm held her tightly. Her body ached with misuse. Muscles she'd forgotten she had screamed at the exertion to which they'd been subjected. And only the man in her arms felt better.

Epilogue

ಹಿ

"Luke," Sarah tapped on the door to the small sitting room and peeked in. "Luke, Mark needs you and Anna down at the carriage house." Her voice was tense and held clear evidence she was fighting back fear.

Luke looked quickly at Anna, her fingers toyed with the large stone hanging around her neck wrapped in a golden filigreed nest that held it safe. She rose with him and followed him out of the room. The morning after they mated, just a few days ago, Mark and Sarah had told them they would like them to stay at the house. Mark cited reasons of lineage. Luke was the next adult in line for his position. He would be regent and responsible for caring for Mark and Sarah's boys if anything happened to him. Sarah had spoken of family and of company, of wanting Luke and Anna to share with them and to raise their families together. Luke had accepted tentatively, leaving open the option for them to leave at some point. But Anna could easily see how much the offer had meant to him.

As they covered the distance between the main house and the carriage house, Luke checked his pace for her. She'd been crushed when her weakness had reclaimed her at midnight. But the mating was doing exactly what Luke said it would. It was healing her, strengthening her, just not as miraculously as Tarris' little friend. Tarris had been absent. Only Sarah had seen him in the last few days and she gave vague answers as to his whereabouts, saying only that he was helping some of the fey folk.

Luke opened the back door to the small cottage and led Anna inside. The tiny kitchen into which they stepped also seemed to double as an observation room. Video monitors and electronic consoles littered one half of the room while the other still seemed to have workable appliances. "It's the guard house," Luke explained as he closed the door.

Mark was sitting at the bank of monitors. He waved them over and pointed to the center screen. "Anna, do you know who that is?"

She peered at the image and gasped. "Jack?"

"What the hell is he doing here?" Luke asked.

"So he is your brother?" the dark eyes of the *Amar* fixed on Anna. She nodded.

"The hunter?" Again she nodded.

"The one who nearly killed you and tried to kill Tarris and Luke?"

She swallowed hard. "He didn't hurt me on purpose. But yes, that's my brother, Jack."

She saw the dark-haired man sitting in a straight-back chair before a small metal table in what looked like a scene straight out of a television police show. Two men she didn't know stood behind him obviously making sure he didn't move. He looked as if he'd put up a struggle. His face was bruising and a line of blood dripped from a cut on his cheek. A satchel sat on the table before him.

"Did you go after him?" the words came out of her throat in a croak. Luke's hand closed firmly on her upper arm in warning.

Mark frowned at her. "I'd have been perfectly within my rights if I had, Anna. Don't forget that. He threatened this family and I won't allow anyone to do that." She watched him shift his gaze to Luke. "As it is, he came to us. Rand and Levi found him on the grounds headed for the house." Mark stood and motioned for them to follow.

As she passed through the door Anna's heart sank. How could Jack have been so stupid? What was he doing coming here? Did he think he was rescuing her? She shook her head. No, more likely he was coming to kill her and probably at the order of the hunters.

Mark pushed open the door of the room she'd seen on the screen. When their eyes met, Jack started to stand but the larger of the two men pushed him back down. She could see his hands were cuffed behind his back. The bruising around his eye seemed worse in person. His eyes widened in disbelief as they followed her. "You're walking. Anna? How?"

"Why are you here?" Mark ignored Jack's words and stood over him glaring menacingly. The man she'd seen at her bedside was back, replacing the one she'd watched the last few days chasing and cuddling two young boys and crawling about with them on his back. The day she'd walked in to find a large brown bear toting two small boys on his back to be tucked in, the reality of her new life had hit her hard. She'd asked Luke to show himself to her immediately after. He had, the worry etched across his face. She'd been delighted to find he could speak to her mind in the animal form and they lay on the rug before the hearth in their room with her head on his soft furred belly talking. He was gentler in this form than she'd ever seen him. Her bear reappeared over the next several days as if easing her into accepting him.

"I came for my sister," Jack shot back defiantly.

"Your sister is now my sister and my brother's mate. Somehow I doubt you came offering gifts in celebration of that fact." Mark looked at Luke who shook his head.

"No, I don't think he's going to be throwing us a reception any time soon." Luke's arm tightened around Anna and she could feel his attempt to reassure her. She also read it in Mark's words. He called her his sister, he was telling her she was part of the family and had gained, not just lost, by mating his brother.

"Jack," she stepped forward and looked down at him. "Why are you here?"

He glared at the men around him. "We need to talk in private, Anna."

She saw Luke look at Mark who nodded. A jerk of his head sent Rand and Levi out of the room. He withdrew himself to stand by the door. "This is as private as you get, hunter," Luke said as he sat down on the edge of the table.

"Why are you here," she repeated the words.

"You're walking. Anna I haven't seen you walking in so long..." his voice trailed off and she saw his eyes shine brightly.

"Mating with Luke is healing me, Jack." She rested her hip on the table next to her mate. "Why are you here?"

Jack sighed and his shoulders drooped. "I didn't come to hurt you. I just wanted to be sure you were all right. I knew if you weren't already dead, you would never come back."

"I'm fine, Jack."

"If you didn't come to hurt anyone, why were you so heavily armed?" Mark demanded from the shadows. "The satchel on the table holds weapons."

Anna turned and opened the bag. She started to sort through the items and felt the tears burn her eyes as they sprang free and rolled down her cheeks. Luke was at her side frowning. "Annie?"

"Let him go, Mark." Anna looked at the *Amar*.

"Let him go?" the leader of her mate's people looked at her as if she were mad. "He brought weapons into my home."

She lifted a framed photo of her family. Its silver frame had been replaced by a simple wooden one. "He brought no silver."

"Then he's a fool," Mark snorted.

"I brought my sister her things. She can't go back home, so I brought them to her." Jack's face spoke freely of his dislike of justifying himself before the Weres.

"Why can't she go home?" Luke's frown was frightening.

"Because they know. They had someone watching me on my first 'assignment'. They saw what happened. They heard it.

The cage had a bug, a listening device built in so they could be sure I'd done my duty. They know." Jack's eyes threw the blame for the entire situation on Luke. "If you'd just left her alone she wouldn't have a price on her head."

Mark approached the table and he and Luke ignored the man as they looked at the contents of the bag. The photos, the small wooden box that held the trinkets of her childhood. But at the bottom of the bag. Weapons. Her father's gun. Her father's arm bows.

"Why the weapons?" Mark asked her. "Why would he bring them?"

"Like he said," she answered softly. "They know. They know I've turned traitor and mated to a Were. I'm marked now. The bounty on my head will be higher than any but possibly yours. The *Amar* of the bears may command a higher reward than the traitorous daughter of a hunter. But my head will bring more personal satisfaction."

"You didn't think I'd leave you unable to protect yourself? You were a better mark with those bows than I ever was and you will be again with practice. The bolts are steel. The gun carries standard ammunition." Jack was watching her face carefully.

Anna turned from the table and walked to her brother. She put her arms around him and felt him rest his head against her as he whispered, "I love you, little sister." She kissed his cheek and brushed her hand down his face. He winced slightly as she came too close to the wound on his cheekbone.

"I love you, Anna. But make no mistake, I hate him." He jerked his head at Luke. "Healing or no, he's marked you for death and I hate him." His eyes went to Luke. "Her I protect, but you," his face twisted, "if you and I meet, I'll kill you."

"You can try," Luke said blandly.

Mark walked to the door and rapped on it sharply. When the two men came in he gestured to Jack. "Take him out beyond the gate and leave him. Don't hurt him unless he makes you. But if he ever comes here again, kill him."

Mark left and Luke's arm around her waist pulled her toward the door. Her eyes held Jack's until she was forced to turn.

"Anna," he called after her and she paused. "Dad knows."

She looked back over her shoulder and met the hazel eyes. "Good."

SOUL STONE

ೞ

Dedication

ഌ

For those in my family who have gone on. My great-grandmother whose Romani heritage love-inspired duty to family that held together her wide spread clan. She taught me to love romances, even if she didn't like the ones with "too much sexy stuff". And my grandmother, who would wink and tell me that sometimes the sexy stuff was the best part. Both of them read avidly until arthritis made it painful for them to hold the books and turn the pages. I wish they were here now in the age of the ebook.

Trademarks Acknowledgement

ഌ

The author acknowledges the trademarked status and trademark owners of the following wordmarks mentioned in this work of fiction:

Buffy The Vampire Slayer: Twentieth Century Fox Film Corporation

Diet Coke: Coca-Cola Company

Prologue

ॐ

"Where is Tarris?" Luke Ursine leaned back after making his move. His twin brother, Mark's face was fixed in a frown as he studied the chessboard. "I haven't seen him in almost a month."

Sarah, a short curvy blonde with brilliant green eyes, looked up at the two men letting her eyes fall on Mark, her husband and mate. She said nothing but her expression caused Luke to sit up straight and direct his question to her. "Sarah? Where is Tarris?"

"Around," she gave a noncommittal shrug, gathered up the toddler on her lap and stood. She pressed a button on a small brass box on the wall by the door. In short order a broad older woman appeared and took the boy from her, settling him on one hip. "It's the boys' bedtime I think," she nodded to the nurse who looked after the twins who had been born to her and her mate over a year ago. The woman nodded and approached Luke's mate Anna where she sat on the sofa cuddling the second boy on her lap, she lifted him with one strong arm and settled him on her other hip. With a nod to Sarah she marched out the door.

"Sarah is something wrong?" Anna's dark brow pressed down over her pale blue eyes. Her raven black hair was pulled back into a simple tail.

"Mark?" Sarah's voice held a note of pleading.

"Sarah, it's not ours to tell," his tone was stern and not one his brother was used to hearing him take with his mate but was usually reserved for dealing with the clan, not his family. Becoming *Amar*, leader of their people, was not something Mark had ever wanted but he had done his duty and was surprisingly good at it. The Weres, shapeshifters who lived under his protection, those that were Bear as they were and those who were not but had turned to the family for help, respected him.

"So we just let it happen?" Sarah argued. Her voice startled Luke. As *Amari*, mate to the *Amar*, she never contradicted Mark in front of others, not even him. She might tease him gently but she never openly defied or questioned him.

"It's not our choice," Mark said again and moved his rook.

"So we let Luke find out the hard way? Or do we let Tarris avoid him? You know what that will mean. You know what will happen if he doesn't feed. Why am I the only one who sees this as a problem?" Sarah was nearing desperation and it showed.

Mark sighed. "Fine. Maybe you're right. But Tarris didn't choose to tell them before so I can't help but think he wouldn't want them to know now."

"If you sit there with your head in the sand, Tarris will be the one to pay the price," she said. "Maybe Luke or Anna can help."

"No one can help," Mark said with finality. "The Oracle is trying to find a way but even he…she…whatever, doesn't know if there is one." The clan's oracle was so old that secondary sex traits had faded and few remembered far enough back to know for certain if the seer had once been boar or sow.

"Maybe if you tell us, even if we can't help, we could do something," Anna leaned forward looking intently at Mark.

"Mark," Luke met his brother's eye. "If it's something about Tarris I have a right to know."

Mark nodded, frowning. "A problem has arisen, unexpectedly." Mark's face was hard and though Luke knew he was trying to hide it, the pain was there to see.

"He can't feed from us," Sarah said quietly.

"What?" Luke snapped in surprise.

"Something happened when Sarah and I mated." Mark shifted uncomfortably. "We didn't know it would. We had no idea..."

"Once we mated, Mark..." Sarah hesitated. "He could no longer allow Tarris to join us."

"That's insane. No offense, Sarah, but Mark and I have shared our lives and our dreams with Tarris for as long as we've known him. He's fed off our sexual energies, participated in the most intimate moments of our lives for over a century. He's an incubus but he's not because he's followed the rules. He has only us and you're telling me Mark would deny him? Let him starve?" Luke saw the truth of it in their faces. "But it's only a dream," Luke rationalized, astounded. How could Mark deny Tarris?

"That's the problem." Mark's voice was filled with a dull ache. "In the dream the Bear takes over, Luke. He won't share his mate." Mark's face twisted. "I'd do it in a minute, so would Sarah. But I can't stop it. And awake he can't feed from us. Not like he needs to."

"That's why..." Tarris had surprised Luke with the interest he'd shown in his life since the mating of Mark and Sarah. An interest that had stopped abruptly when Luke and Anna mated just over two months ago.

"Luke, now that you're mated," Sarah said softly. "There isn't..."

"There is no one for him to feed from," Luke's stricken face paled. His heart ached and his brain was twisting trying to find possibilities.

"What happens if he doesn't feed this way?" Anna pressed. "How long can he go without feeding?"

Luke met her eye, "He should already need it. I assumed he was sharing with Mark and Sarah, giving us some time alone."

"Why can't he just find a new partner?" Anna asked.

"He could but that would mean hunting and if he does that he puts himself at terrible risk." Mark answered his face faintly angry. "Besides Anna, what if I told you to just go find another mate?"

She sighed sadly. There was no other mate for any of the four who sat in this room. All had been bound by lovers' stones, a mating more powerful than the norm for the Weres. A mating that was for life and precluded all possibility of finding another. "So what will happen?"

Luke's voice was hollow and cold. "He'll starve. And when the hunger grows it will overwhelm him. It should already be beyond endurance. Tarris is strong. But when he can no longer control it, he'll become what he was born to be. We'll lose him to the hunt."

Tears slipped down Sarah's face as she sat down next to Anna and took her hand. Anna had only been with them since her mating two months before but she was from the hunters, those who tracked and killed the preternatural creatures of the world. "Anna, he'll become a full incubus. Hunted not just by hunters but by our kind as well. They have no soul, no mercy, no kindness. Tarris once made them promise they'd never let that happen to him."

"How could you stop it? If we can't feed him, how will you stop him from becoming one of them?" Anna asked fearfully.

"By killing him," Luke whispered.

"By killing him," Mark agreed.

Chapter One

ဆ

He sat in the overstuffed chair facing the fire. He was hungry. He hadn't planned on this little glitch, none of them had realized it would happen. After all, how many times in the history of things had a Were picked up an orphaned incubus child and taken him home? How often has a creature whose very nature requires him to feed off the sexual energies of others found himself living alongside a family, people who he would love if he were capable of that emotion? But his kind couldn't feel love. All the stories agreed on that point. He had no soul. He was one of a cursed race, a merciless parasite who drained others until he destroyed them. Only glitch in that theory was that Tarris had never harmed anyone and he felt something for his adopted family. He'd sure as hell die for any of them, Mark, Luke, their mates and the children.

In the beginning it had been easy. As a child he fed off the happy, joyful emotions of those around him. This continued as he watched his companions, the boys he was being raised alongside, grow and reach maturity. His body had grown like theirs and no one would believe that more than a few months separated them in birth. But it was long after they'd become sexually mature he realized he too had passed that threshold. Physically he became a man, or at least looked like one, almost twenty-five years before the hunger began.

He remembered the day he sat next to his Weres at the pool. The twins were bickering as usual but in the end the water fight that had them all laughing didn't produce the effect it normally would have. It hadn't fed him. He still felt a deep need inside as if he'd only been allowed to taste his dinner, one or two small bites, before it had been taken away.

A week later it had been Luke, the younger of the twins, who had found him curled in a corner, his body trembling and burning with fever. His skin had started to change, his eyes to darken. He was becoming the demon who humans whispered about in fear. He was becoming the predator who would seek out women and feed from their dreams until sated, until he drove them mad or until he killed them. Luke had taken him to his grandfather who had called the oracle for assistance. The oracle had explained what was happening.

Tarris needed to feed. If he didn't feed in a controlled way he would change, he'd become one of the dark ones, the vampires who fed not on blood but on the desires and dreams of others. Only if they could find a way to control his feeding could they keep him with them.

And so the rules had been made.

Rule 1. Never feed alone.

Rule 2. Never touch unless you are invited to by the female.

Rule 3. Never penetrate a woman in the place reserved for her mate.

Rule 4. Never allow the act to bring you to orgasm.

Rule 5. Never, never must you hunt.

The rules had been created to keep him contained. To keep Tarris fed and happy while stopping him from crossing the line that could make him want more than he could be allowed to have.

Sitting in his chair he watched the flames flicker. He slipped his hand into the pocket of his jeans and pulled out the small oblong stone. It looked like an opal but over one third of its surface was black and dull. He rubbed at it seeking the strange sense of comfort it had always brought him. Tonight it didn't work. Despite the fire, a chill passed through him. The rules. How he hated the rules. How he needed the rules. He'd only broken one and only once. He'd allowed sweet Sarah to pleasure him in a dream the three had shared before their mating. It had been a mistake. Now he knew what he was missing. And he wanted more.

Worse, he could no longer feed off his lovers. Both Weres were mated. No one had realized at the time that it would stop their ability to share their pleasure with him. But it had. He could enter their dreams but in their dreams the men would push him away. He'd learned this the moment Mark mated with Sarah. The animal within him refused to allow him near his mate. In the waking world, Mark had been devastated. In the land of dreams he could not stop himself from turning on Tarris like an enemy. Tarris had not approached Luke. The younger twin had always been the more sexually assertive, the more likely to react to his instincts. He was certain Luke's reaction would be even stronger than Mark's.

Tarris closed his eyes. He tried to remember a time when he was satisfied with the lot he'd been given, satisfied with the role of puppeteer, satisfied to orchestrate the pleasures of others and to drink in their joy and satisfaction. It seemed so long ago.

He'd not actively decided to break the rules. He'd let them terminate him before he'd turn into one of the dark ones. He may not have a soul but one thing living in the Ursine house had given him had been honor. He knew the clean and lighter side of living. He'd not become a monster.

He let his mind drift. He told himself he wasn't doing it. He was only reaching out. He'd been able to take the edge off the past couple of weeks this way. A voyeur watching a young couple, feeling the energies radiate between two soon to be lovers in a club. A siphon, draining off some of the raw sexual arousal of those he watched from the world of shadows. It wouldn't sustain him he knew. The only true food was passion in dreams. But maybe by doing this he could hold off the madness, hold off the day when his own Weres would be forced to destroy him. Or hold out until he found another way.

He felt the touch of the sleeper and backed away. He wasn't a predator. He wasn't supposed to enter alone. But the power of the mind reached out to him as if it had sensed him. It called to him, inviting him in. The hunger raged inside him as he fought it. The moment he turned to the dreamer, the moment he let himself be pulled to the cavalcade of images that passed through the sleeping mind he was lost.

He stood in the doorway of the modest bedroom. The sleeper on the bed was a woman. Her red hair was twisted around her face, strands of it sticking to the damp forehead. The shirt of the men's flannel pajamas that she wore stretched tight across her breasts. Not exactly the seductress. Not precisely the femme fatale. She looked more like a schoolmarm or a librarian. One leg had kicked itself free of the blankets and he noticed she even wore socks to bed. It was early October. No, Red here didn't look like the kind of woman who embraced her sexuality.

Tarris stepped into the room and moved closer to the bed. The woman was moaning slightly and twisting her head. Her fists clenched tight. She fascinated him. She seemed so restricted—closed off so tightly against her own body but the power of the imagination, the dreams that flowed through her had called to him across the distance that had separated them. He could feel the incredible strength of her mind.

The rules repeated in his head.

He hadn't hunted her, he told himself. She had called him to her.

He would not let her please him.

He would not penetrate her.

He would not touch unless she reached for him first.

He would not—Tarris stood watching her, torn as his hunger battled with his conditioning. The emotions, the colors of her mind were so powerful he shook with need. Her soul was laying itself bare for him just as if he'd been a fully mature incubus. He saw all of who she was, all her secrets, dreams and desires. And he loved each and every one.

So yes. Yes, he would. He would feed alone.

He stretched out beside her on the bed and brushed the hair from her face. Her body went slack. He pulled her to him and rested her head on his shoulder. Stroking her face he pressed his cheek to her and closed his eyes.

* * * * *

Her dream changed abruptly. She was no longer trying to climb the steep cliff to keep from plunging to her death. Suddenly she was in a room filled with beautiful scents and colors. Her eyes adjusted and she gasped as she took in the scene. The room was draped with fabric in soft gold and muted browns. The color and the smells were coming from the hundreds of flowers that seemed to be blooming everywhere. Roses, lilies, gladiolas, orchids, peonies, mums and even little sweet-faced pansies created a bower at one end of the room. In the center lay a large bed, tall carved bedposts climbed to the ceiling. Sheer draperies hung from them and brilliant vines of morning glories climbed up the spires.

Looking down at herself she saw the diaphanous white gown that hung from her like an ancient Greek *chiton*, the look complete by delicate golden sandals that laced up her calves. Her reflection in the gilded mirror that hung on one wall showed her hair, a mass of riotous red, hanging loose past her shoulders. Her dark green eyes, bright and clear, stared back at her. They turned from her reflection and swept the room.

She'd never seen its like before and yet it seemed so familiar to her, as if she had been here a million times. She was dreaming. She knew she was dreaming. And more so, though she had never had this dream before, she knew what would happen next. Slowly she turned and faced the bank of tall windows with their French doors that opened out onto an even more impressive garden. She hadn't heard a sound, not even the twittering of birds or the crunch of a blade of grass but she knew he'd be there before she looked.

And he was. His body took up most of the single doorframe. He was tall. She'd never seen a man so tall unless he had on silk shorts and was running up and down a basketball court. He stood backlit by the sun that created a corona around him as it reflected off the blond hair that reached almost to his elbow. It was a soft golden color that cast highlights brighter than the rays of the sun.

This stranger in her dream stepped into the room and walked toward her slowly with the grace of a lion. His bare feet made no sound and she found she could not look away from the blue eyes that watched her. His golden skin stretched across a gorgeously smooth chest. Each muscle defined and calling to her as if trying to tempt her to touch him. Surely this was a dream because no man could really be this beautiful.

"Callista?" He whispered her name softly and she understood the question it held. He was asking her permission to be there, her consent for the dream to proceed. As she watched his eager face, his name appeared in her mind.

"Tarris," she watched as pleasure filled his face. The simple act of speaking his name seemed to please him immensely.

"Please tell me you are not afraid of me, beautiful one." His hand lifted toward her, extended, offering her his touch.

"No," she barely breathed the word but reached out and took the offered hand. He relaxed visibly and his other hand moved up slowly toward her face as if giving her time to move away. His large palm cupped her cheek and he smiled.

"Good." A serious expression filled the searching blue eyes. "Never be afraid of me, my love. Never would I harm you. No matter what, I would never harm you."

"I know," and she did. She saw in him tremendous strength. She saw in him the potential for terrible anger. She saw in him the ability to destroy all that he touched. But yet something inside Callista Marshall knew he would never turn this darker side to her. The absurdity of it teased the edges of her mind. She was so certain who this man was, he was so much more real and defined to her than any real man had ever been.

'Cause he's all in your head, a tiny part of her that seemed almost awake reasoned.

A strange smile flitted in his eyes for a moment before Tarris leaned in and brushed her lips with his own. Her head felt light and fuzzy as if she'd drunk one glass of wine too many with dinner. His hand moved from her cheek to wrap itself in the red curls that defied taming. As he pressed the kiss deeper, she felt his tongue slip out and flicker softly against her lips.

She wrapped her arms around his neck and lifted up on tiptoe to kiss him back. A strong arm pulled her close as his tongue pressed between her parted lips to taste the inside of her mouth. *Definitely a dream because surely no man tasted this wonderful.* His hand splayed across the small of her back as he kissed her passionately. His tongue probing into her, brushing against hers and urging her to take up the duel.

There was something about his scent that caused a physical reaction. The smell of him was pure male, a mixture of the sea, the forest, the sun and the rain with the smell of a man's skin as he cradled you and held you close. Her breasts began to feel constricted by the flowing fabric of her gown, her nipples hardening and pressing up as if pleading for his attention.

His hand slid from her hair and his arm wrapped around her. He pulled her tight against him and she could feel not only the warm hard muscle of his chest pressed against her but the growing evidence of her effect on his body through the thin white pants he wore. As his lips slid from her mouth to her neck she reveled in the power she seemed to have over him. His breathing was quickened and she could feel his heart beating against the palm of her hand as it smoothed over his chest. And when his hands moved over the curve of her hips, molded to their form and pulled her tight against him, the hardness of him pressing into her caused her body to react violently.

A shudder passed through her and the sensations pooled in a single spot in the center of her. A place deep within her that sent shockwaves through her as it began to ready itself for him. His lips, his tongue, his teeth teased her skin as his mouth moved over her throat. The hands that had been kneading the soft flesh of her lower curves moved with a speed that made her cry out.

Tarris swept her up into his arms and carried her to the bed. Laying her on the soft cushions he stretched out beside her. One hand cupped the back of her head and turned it to him so that she could still taste his sweet kiss. The other hand finally sought out the curves of the breasts that had impatiently waited for his touch. She moaned deep in her throat and he swallowed it with his kiss.

His fingers squeezed the full flesh of her breasts with perfect precision, not too hard, not too gently. His thumb stroked at the hard point until she had to pull her mouth away from his so that she could ask for more. He smiled down at her and teased first one nipple then the other, as she pulled his head down to press her own kiss to his neck. His skin tasted… It defied description, so wonderful was the taste of his flesh sliding under her tongue. His fingers pinched and twisted the taut peaks through the thin cloth as she sucked softly at his neck and pulled his mouth to hers. He let her claim his mouth, pushing her tongue into him. Like a sweet honeyed wine, the taste of his mouth played upon her senses even as his tongue danced with hers.

He reached up and removed her hands from his neck. He opened the clasps at her shoulders and pulled the front of her gown down over her breasts. His face darkened as she watched him take in the sight of her. She felt no timidity with him, no sense of self consciousness. The fire in his eyes told her more than any words could of the depth of his desire for her.

The golden head lowered and she watched the long pink tongue sneak out to brush one nipple quickly, just enough to be tormenting. His eyes lifted to hers and he smiled wickedly. Lowering his head over the other nipple he repeated the teasing flicker of his tongue and she moaned, "Tarris, please."

His hand reached up and brushed at her cheek. "Shh, my dearest. I promise I'm only just beginning. Such pleasure I want to give you."

Callie bit her lip and watched, her body arching, pushing her breasts out toward him unconsciously. His smile deepened and he captured one tip in his mouth and sucked hungrily. The flames burst from where his mouth teased her and spread through her body. A tension in the pit of her stomach clenched harder and she closed her eyes, reveling in the feel of his talents on her breasts as he added soft licks and gentle nips to the sucking.

He moved back and forth between her breasts until both ached joyously. He sat up and the green eyes flew open, afraid for a moment he'd pulled away from her. He hadn't. He lifted one foot and slowly unlaced her sandals. He pressed his thumbs into the bottom of her foot and massaged it. A soft kiss to her instep and he moved up, hands stroking her skin, tongue brushing against the back of her knee, before he settled her leg back on the bed and repeated the sequence with her other leg. He moved to kneel between her knees. His large hands pushed up the edges of her gown and caressed the skin of her thighs. Pushing her legs farther apart, he paused and lifted his head to look at her. He was grinning impishly at her and she blushed. She couldn't remember why she had started keeping herself bare, maybe to please a forgotten boyfriend, but she liked the feel of her smooth damp skin when she touched herself. His fingers moved up the inside of her legs until she felt them just brush the soft, wet skin at the juncture of her thighs.

She drew in a ragged breath and watched his beautiful face as he crawled up and lowered himself to lie between her legs. He rested his cheek on her leg and she swore he was breathing in her scent before she felt him kiss the soft skin of her inner thigh. His fingers moved lightly over the crease of her folds. She had the strangest feeling he was examining her closely, memorizing everything about her. He continued to slide his fingers along the outer edge of the lips. His touch made her squirm, it made her want to grab his hand and press it in, anything to make him stop the teasing.

As if he could read her mind he chuckled softly and pressed his fingers into the damp folds. She let escape a small groan as his fingers brushed upward from the edge of her opening to the hard nub of flesh. She gasped and jerked as his fingers brushed over it. He lifted his head to look into her face. The blue eyes were so bright they almost seemed to be flames dancing in the irises. His fingers circled her clit and rubbed at her until she was pressing herself toward him to make him stroke harder, move faster. He moved away from her swollen clit and toyed with her entrance. His head lowered deliberately and again she watched the pink tongue snake out just before he buried his face between her thighs and began the double assault.

His tongue toyed with her clit, his mouth sucked at it gently as his finger pushed inside. Pulling from her warmth he slid two fingers back into her and she cried out as he stroked the spot within her that made her toes curl and her control evaporate. As she started to thrust her hips up to him, he pressed down on them with his free hand. He pulled back slightly and teased her, slowing down the building fire inside her. His tongue continued its attack on her and soon she was whimpering, murmuring to him of the delight he was sending through her, asking for more. Harder. Faster. More.

The tension in her body rose until every muscle was clenched, quivering and waiting on the precipice. The delicious need ravaged her body and she begged him to let her fall. Let her plummet down from the heights to which he was pushing her.

He moaned softly, her name she thought, against her wet swollen flesh. He lifted his head from her, lapping at her with his tongue before his deep voice commanded her.

"You're going to come for me, beautiful one. Let me taste your pleasure." His agile tongue renewed its eager assault and his fingers drove deeper and harder into her flesh.

Reason, thought, awareness was lost beyond the momentary teetering before she felt her body explode into a shimmer of golden light. She screamed out his name as he drained every second of exquisite climax from her shuddering, trembling body.

Only then did he kiss the soft nether lips, withdraw his fingers from her and crawl back to her side. She felt him cocoon her in his arms, her body curled against his chest. "Sleep my beautiful one," he whispered in her ear. And within her dream, Callie fell asleep.

In the warmth and safety of her room, Tarris held her. His body was satisfied. He'd drunk from her and she'd filled him in a way no other lover ever had. But an empty place deep inside him was not satisfied, it wanted more. It wanted what none of his kind should even be able to conceive of let alone want. It wanted what it had tasted between Mark and his mate Sarah. It wanted what it had tasted between Luke and his mate Anna.

And suddenly the rules felt less like a safety net and much more like a chain.

* * * * *

Leaning back in his seat the man smiled. The gray eyes glowed with satisfaction. Finally. He'd finally seen what he'd known he would if he just "looked" long enough. There was no such thing as a tame incubus. As usual the hunter's council was fooling itself. He had never been able to understand why they held such a blind spot where this creature was concerned. These were the very people whose ancestors had sworn a blood oath that had lasted for thousands of years, an oath that was supposed to bind them and their decedents. To break that oath meant death. Yet they'd actually *cautioned* him last month. Told him he was being paranoid. But Adam had known since he'd first been told about the local Weres' pet incubus that this would happen. He couldn't understand why they all ignored the data.

"Look son," the aging leader of the council had actually put his arm around Adam's shoulder, his voice filled with the patronizing stupidity that infuriated the younger *se'er*. "I know what happened. I understand that the incubi are a sensitive subject for you. As *se'ers* we can see the dark ones, sense them and feel their presence and energy. Your history is bound to complicate matters even more. But you have to realize that we have a unique situation here." He'd gone on to explain, while taking great care to be clear that the council held no love for the clan of Bears that led the local Weres, that the incubus was closely guarded and regulated by the Ursine family.

"This one isn't even a mature incubus. Relax my boy, it is the one thing we've found that they agree with us on. They have no love for the cursed race either," the old man had assured him. "They are ruthless on the darker of creatures.

"I thought Weres were cursed. And while we're on the subject how can one cursed race be darker than another," Adam had argued and been dismissed. The Bears would take care of the incubus. He should focus his watching on the blood vampires, the *sanvi*. This pet of theirs was a *psyvi*, a psychic vampire, yes but he was not a full fledged incubus. Adam saw little difference. An incubus was an incubus. It was inevitable that one day the creature would hunt. One day the creature would kill. Or worse.

Paranoid my ass. He thought smugly.

Now he had proof it was beginning. The thing had invaded the dreams of a human woman not directly connected to the Weres. He'd gone outside the protection of his family and fed from the red-haired woman. It wasn't enough to convince the council to give him a kill order but it was enough to cover his ass if someone found out he was going further. It was plenty of justification to find out more about the mysterious redhead. No woman should be left to the clutches of one of those monsters and particularly not a woman whose aura was so brilliant it left him breathless. There was a fire beneath those russet curls. A fire he wasn't about to let any damn incubus extinguish.

Chapter Two

ℬ

Callie looked away from the door of the small restaurant to her watch and sighed. She was late. Or at least she hoped her friend was just late and not standing her up yet again. Since her old college roommate had gotten married two years ago it seemed as if her new family had swallowed her whole. The house she now lived in, one Callie had never seen inside, was huge and surrounded by a large, intimidating fence. In fact it was one of the estate houses that she and Sarah used to joke about, trying to figure out why anyone with enough money for a house like that, who wasn't in local politics, would live in the godforsaken northern tundra of Minnesota. She sure wouldn't. If she had the money that house screamed, she'd be on tropical beach somewhere not caring if she seared her pale skin red because she'd be able to pay several cabana boys to stand over her with an umbrella and apply aloe on a regular basis.

The door to the sandwich shop opened and two tall men stepped inside. Callie's eyes widened as she took in their appearance. They made the Secret Service, the president's personal security force, seem subtle. Both were over six feet tall and seriously monochromatic with black jeans, black boots and black t-shirts. The only difference she could see between them were the chrome frames of one's sunglasses compared to the black of the other. Each had long black hair pulled back tightly into tails and both were absolutely gorgeous. The muscled arms that crossed over their broad chests made her feel a bit fuzzy for a moment, until they swiveled their heads in unison and stared straight at her. Then she felt a sick fear fill her stomach.

"You do know you two make a better door than a window?" came an exasperated voice and Callie watched one of them step quickly forward to avoid falling from the shove that had just been administered to his back. The blonde head came into view and Callie wasn't sure if she was relieved or even more frightened. Sarah. "Go sit over there and try not to get into trouble," she watched her friend point to a table on the far side of the room. One of the men grabbed her wrist only to drop it as if it had burned him. He said something to her in a low voice that made Sarah frown, she looked over towards Callie. "Then I guess today you earn your keep. I mean it, Levi. Go sit down over there." With no more hesitation, the men moved as if following a direct order and sat against the far wall, both turning their chairs so they could keep her table in their direct line of vision.

Sarah hurried toward her. "I sorry I'm late. Frick and Frack over there couldn't agree on where to park the car." She dropped into her seat and slid her purse under the table. "How are you?" The gray-green eyes smiled as brightly as the full, rose-colored lips.

"I'm fine," Callie leaned in. "Are you okay?"

Her friend seemed genuinely startled. "Me? I'm fine, Cal. Couldn't be better. The boys are a handful but thankfully I have some help with them. Mark helps, we have a nurse and my brother-in-law Luke and his new wife Anna are living in the house now." She shook her head and pulled the plastic covered menu from the wire rack on the table. "I haven't been here in so long. I miss the veggie subs. Dinner at our house is definitely carnivorous."

The waitress arrived at that moment and took their orders. Callie watched her eye the other server who had evidently drawn lucky and was taking orders from the two men who had yet to remove their shades. Callie waited until the waitress had gone before continuing.

"Sarah," she wasn't sure where to begin or how to ask the question. "Are you sure everything's all right?"

Her friend's pretty face frowned. "Cal, what's wrong? I told you I was fine." When Callie gave a pointed look at the two men watching them intently, Sarah sighed. "It's nothing to be concerned about. Mark is a bit over-protective these days. He thinks it's better if I have a driver."

"And the other one?" Green eyes, as unalike as the same color could be, met and held. Callie pushed. "Those two look more like bodyguards than drivers." She took a deep breath and asked the question she really didn't want an answer to. "Is Mark involved in something…well…not quite legal?"

Sarah gaped at her for a moment. Then her forehead creased and she seemed to be thinking hard and fast. Callie could almost see the wheels turning. "It's nothing to worry about. Mark's family has a great deal of money, you know that," she added quickly.

"But this looks frighteningly like a mafia movie. I keep expecting Joe Pesci or De Niro to walk in," Callie hissed, aware the two men were watching her with renewed interest.

Sarah started to laugh. "God, your imagination gets more vivid all the time." They quieted as the waitress returned with their orders. When she left, the blonde tried again to reassure her. "Trust me Cal, my life is far from drama free but late night movie of the week it ain't. Mark is an upstanding citizen. He inherited most of his money, what he didn't make investing in the weirdest assortment of ventures from real estate to art to the stock market. I barely understand any of it but I assure you no one ends up sleeping with the fishes and we are not entertaining Columbian drug lords." Sarah took a large bite of the sandwich and sighed contentedly. Once she'd swallowed she continued. "If you knew Mark you'd know he is one of the most gentle and charming souls in the world."

"But I don't know Mark." Callie said flatly. "None of your old friends know him."

"Come on," Sarah protested. "You've met him."

"Met him, Sarah? What? Three times in two years? We used to room together. We worked together. We survived Professor Faust together. Then suddenly you meet this guy, marry him less than three weeks later and disappear." The words she'd been wanting to say for some time flew out of her mouth. She waited for Sarah to get angry. She didn't.

"You're right," her friend conceded. "I have let myself lose touch with some of the people in my life. But not you, Cal. Never you." Sarah toyed with the pickle spear that was dripping green juice onto her potato chips. "My life is just very full right now, my family has grown so much in such a short time. Mark, the boys, Luke and Anna, Tarris..."

The name jolted through Callie like an electric shock. Tarris. The name of the man who had been haunting her dreams for the past week. Five of seven nights the tall blond man had appeared in her dreams. Five nights filled with the most erotic images, the most intense sexual experiences she'd ever known. To hear this name, this unusual name tossed out so casually by her friend nearly caused her to choke despite the fact she'd not yet touched her own food.

"Cal?" Sarah's voice pushed through the haze. "Cal, are *you* all right?"

"Yes," she forced herself to smile. "I'm fine." Her concern for her friend had now taken a backseat to her need to know about the Tarris her friend knew. Had she met him? Had she perhaps been introduced to him at the wedding and forgotten it only to have him appear in her dreams? *Not likely*, she admitted. One did not forget a man like the one who had tormented and wrung the pleasure from her body so violently that she knew she had dark circles under her eyes from lack of rest, though she was spending an inordinate amount of time sleeping. Her mind may have known the encounters were dreams but her body didn't seem to. She'd awakened each morning before dawn feeling weak and sated.

Sarah seemed to be watching her with a new perceptivity that the generally shy and innocent girl had not possessed before her marriage. "Callie, what's wrong? Something's going on here beyond you being angry at me for bailing on you, for letting you down as a friend." The soft hand reached across the table and took hers. "You don't look so great."

"I'm just tired," Callie confessed. She told Sarah she wasn't sleeping well. Told her she was having odd dreams that seemed to be more real than any she'd had and they left her feeling unrested and fatigued.

"What kind of dreams?" Sarah's eyes narrowed and Callie felt her face begin to burn hotly.

"Just dreams," she murmured in response.

"How long have you been having these "just dreams" and are we talking one star player or a host of guest stars?" Sarah's voice sounded oddly concerned despite the casual tone she was trying hard to adopt. Callie looked at her for a moment before answering.

"They're just dreams, Sarah."

"That didn't answer my question," her friend insisted stubbornly.

"Fine," Callie leaned forward, her cheeks blazing so hotly she felt as if her skin were blistering. "Yes, those kinds of dreams and yes, one man."

Sarah's frown heightened Callie's discomfort. Was Sarah upset at her? The humiliation of admitting to having such dreams was bad enough but the feeling that Sarah was somehow judging her negatively for them made it even worse. "Everyone has dreams, Sarah. I'm not some freak you know."

The expression on the blonde's face changed. "Oh Cal, I wasn't suggesting you were. Look, neither of us really ever talked about this kind of stuff but its okay. You're right, everyone has "those kinds of dreams". I'm just asking because you seem so bothered." The hand that was still holding hers squeezed tight and relief flooded through Callie.

She cast a glance to each side and lowered her voice. "It's been about a week now. It's probably just my biological clock and the fact that my little sister just announced she was getting married." Her red curls bobbed as she shook her head. She looked up at the men seated opposite them and couldn't shake the horrifying suspicion they could hear the entire conversation. "I probably just need to take something to help me sleep. My schedule is a bit crazy right now."

Sarah sat back. Callie had the distinct impression she wasn't actually letting the subject go but her friend switched tracks in the conversation. "So how is the thesis going?"

Callie snorted softly. "About how you would expect. It's a lot of digging in old books, going over the transcripts of some of the folklore compiled by Roosevelt's Works Projects Administration during the Great Depression. The correlations between the Appalachian Mountain regions and the Celtic and Gaelic lore are astonishing."

"You're focusing on stone lore, correct?" Sarah asked, her hand going to the large amethyst that hung around her neck. She'd explained to Callie that in Mark's family, the giving of such a stone was equivalent to an engagement ring, yet Callie'd never been able to shake the idea there was something more to it.

"Yes, opals in particular, which thrills the bejeezus out of Faust. You know him. Anything out of the mainstream is a no-no. I've gotten the "No one is going to take you seriously Miss Marshall if you do not take your own field of study seriously," speech about three times now." Callie shook her head. "As if studying the correlations between cultures in a specific area is somehow a radical idea as opposed to focusing on one thread from a single body of lore."

"Since what you're doing crosses departments, anthropology and English, he probably thinks that will mean extra work for him somehow," Sarah shrugged. "That and the fact that he still thinks you're a traitor to the noble world of academia because you went off to get your library degree."

"I know but I had to pay bills. A degree in English doesn't set you up for a lot these days unless you want to teach. No thank you." Callie sighed. "Plus I'm getting it from both sides as usual. Is it any wonder it's taking me forever to finish my degree?" she shook her head. "My branch manager was thrilled when I asked for an extended leave so I could do the field research, to talk firsthand to the Aborigines in Australia and the Romani in Eastern Europe about the lore surrounding opals. I thought he was going to come unglued." Callie rolled her forest green eyes.

"Forget them and tell me about the research. Did you find out anything good?" Sarah asked between bites.

"Yeah, it's a whole separate study in and of itself. I could spend a lifetime and not completely document it. They see them as soul stones or stones with souls. They believe they originated from the places where the gods walked upon the earth for the first time. The iridescent coloring of the stone, particularly the white and black variety gave rise to the idea that the opal could actually trap the soul and hold it. Some cultures also believe that opals act as temporary residences for souls awaiting rebirth." Callie paused to suck a long drink of Diet Coke from her paper cup. "Hence the whole opals are unlucky, the symbol of the evil eye."

An idea she'd had before tickled the edges of her mind. "You know, Sarah, one day I'd like to trace the evolution of the stone lore on this continent. Maybe I could interview Mark about his family's tradition. It's unusual and must have its foundations in stone lore. For example, would they give an opal or do they see it as unlucky?"

She watched as her friend shifted uncomfortably. "I'll mention it to him." From that point, she couldn't help but notice how Sarah steered the conversation onto much safer topics. Topics that didn't involve Mark, his family, the stone around her neck or Callie's research. She talked about the boys and being a mother. She talked about their families, the people they knew and in general kept the conversation light.

Almost an hour after she'd arrived, Callie noticed the two men stand. Sarah didn't miss a beat, she stood and said goodbye promising Callie she'd not let it be so long before they got back together.

"And you'll mention to Mark about the stones?" she pushed.

"Yeah. I'll mention it." Sarah hugged her and joined the two men who flanked her as she walked out. The sight caused a shiver down Callie's spine.

* * * * *

Adam watched the blonde woman leave. He had been hoping for something like this when the tap he'd placed on the redhead's phone revealed that she knew and was in fact old friends, with the Were leader's human mate. What was clear was that the woman who had finally drawn out the Bear's pet incubus had no idea that her friend had married a Were. In fact it sounded as if she had no idea such things as Weres and incubi existed. He gave a soft snort of disgust. Some days he hated the codes of secrecy. If they were allowed to tell the humans just who these monsters really were, they wouldn't be such easy prey for them. He doubted Sarah Ursine would have chosen to be the creature's mate if she had gone into things with her eyes wide open and not helpless to resist the seduction of the magic and persuasion of the creatures.

But then again, that hardly explained the Morrissey bitch. How anyone could turn their back on their family, their race, like as she did when she mated the Bear Luke Ursine, he'd never understand. If his sister had been given the opportunity to defend herself—Adam filled his mouth with the last of the cold coffee in his cup and swallowed hard. He never let Beth get far from his thoughts but that wasn't what he needed to focus on now.

He didn't need to look at the extensive dossier he'd compiled on Callista Marshall. He didn't need it because he'd memorized it.

Name—Callista Reneé Marshall

Born—October 30

Age—thirty years old

Occupation—Librarian, part-time graduate student working on Doctorate in English

He also knew by heart the anecdotal information the file contained. She was quiet, reserved and according to an ex-boyfriend who would never remember their conversation thanks to copious amounts of alcohol, "a repressed, frigid bitch". Adam shook his head as he pulled the book he'd brought from the old battered knapsack. A frigid bitch did not entice an incubus. More likely the man's inept adolescent pawing had been the reason for her lack of enthusiasm. Adam's first look at her had made him suck in a breath. His body told him clearly it had noticed her as it pressed against the fabric of his pants. No, this redhead was a volcano. The cap maybe snowy and lined with sharp edges but underneath there was one hell of a fire. Maybe once he'd saved her from the incubus he could persuade her to show him a bit of that heat.

Adam stood and lifted his bag to his shoulder. In this café in these clothes he looked like a young, underpaid associate professor. From the corner of his eye he could see the attractive Ms. Marshall. He turned and stepped up to her booth. "Excuse me," his voice was hesitant and he hoped lacked anything that might make her feel uneasy. His long hair was pulled back in a loose tail and his worn t-shirt claimed an affiliation to the local university. He pressed with his thoughts for her to see him as unthreatening a presence as possible. And the minute he did his eyes widened in surprise. He hit a wall.

His gifts as a *se'er* were strong, stronger some said than even the man who ruled the hunter's council. All Adam knew was that under normal situations he could convince others to accept impressions he wanted them to have. He could seem much more threatening or much more harmless than he actually was. But when he sent the chosen thought to Ms. Marshall it was reflected back at him. Someone, and he doubted it was the lady before him, had used the minor psychic talents she possessed to form a blockade. From the feel of it, he doubted any but the strongest of telepaths or empaths could reach her. He fought hard to keep the passive expression on his face. The damn incubus was already playing with her mind.

The dark green eyes were looking at him warily and he realized he'd not continued his thought. "Excuse me," he began again, smiling. "I couldn't help but overhear snippets of your conversation." She blushed a deep red and looked down at her hands. Adam slid into the seat across from her. "I am sorry but I think I can help." *Boy could I ever help.* And he'd enjoy it too. No doubt he'd enjoy taking a bite out of that pale skin, see it flush under his touch.

"Help?" her voice was soft in his ears, musical. Her singing voice would display perfect pitch.

"I know a strange man sitting down at your table is a bit scary but I mean you no harm." He extended his hand to her, "My name's Adam. Adam Stanton. I'm an anthropologist of sorts."

Her eyes met his again. The distrust apparent in their jade depths. "Of sorts?"

He grinned. This was the charming little brother look that had always gotten him out of trouble with his mother and let him wheedle his way around his big sister. "I work for a private collector. I specialize in ancient folk lore."

He reached out to her. He wanted to know if he could feel anything that was happening behind those eyes. Again he willed her to trust him. Again he hit the wall.

"That sounds fascinating," she said primly, shouldering the strap on her bag. "But if you'll excuse me. I don't make a habit of talking to people I don't know."

"But how will you know me if you don't talk to me?" He rose with her and stood effectively blocking her path.

"What makes you think I have any interest in knowing you?" Her mouth was set in a tight line. So this was the cold and distant side of her. She could definitely be a frosty little thing when she chose. But Adam had an advantage. He knew that beneath the snow lay a raging fire, one so strong it could draw in an incubus and sustain its interest for over a week.

"Okay," he lifted his right hand, palm out in submission. "But take this. I think you'll find the section I marked very interesting, possibly even helpful." He pushed the book he held in his left hand at her. When she did not reach for it, he took her hand and pressed it into her palm. "Just look at it. I've written down my number and my address. If you want to talk about it, call me. If you decide it is of no use to you, just drop it in the mail."

"Why are you doing this?" the fear in her voice was obvious.

"You might say, in a way, it's my job." Adam smiled at her, turned and walked to the door. Only when he reached it did he look back. Her eyes had followed him. He'd known they would. Giving her a slight nod and walked out.

As he climbed behind the wheel of his car there was no doubt in his mind what Ms. Marshall's bedtime reading would be this night.

* * * * *

Sarah sat in the front seat of the car next to Levi. His brother Laban sat in the back seat. "You heard that conversation didn't you?" she said quietly looking down at her hands, face etched with worry.

"We heard," Levi said simply as he maneuvered the sedan through the city streets.

"Tell me that knowing Tarris has made me jump to a ridiculous conclusion," Sarah turned to watch the side of the older twin's face.

"I could tell you that, *Amari* but I'd be lying," Levi kept his eyes fixed on the traffic ahead of him.

"An incubus?" Sarah spoke the word with dread and fear for the first time in her life.

"That's what it sounds like but it could also simply be a human dream. You would know more about the difference than I," his words were not insulting but a statement of fact. She had known the touch of an incubus before she mated with Mark. A tame incubus, one who had been only gentle and caring and had only come to her with Mark at his side as well. Tarris.

"Tarris could find out," Laban spoke from the backseat. "If you ask him, *Amari,* he would search for you." Sarah filed this away, not answering.

As soon as the car stopped inside the garage Sarah hurried into the house. Just inside the side door she closed her eyes and called for Tarris. He seldom left his room these days and often did not answer the knocks upon his door. But he had never turned her away or failed to speak to her.

I'm here. Do you want me to come to you or will you come to me?

"I'll be right up," she said in a whisper, knowing he heard it in her mind. She hung up her jacket and headed upstairs. She hesitated, starting to knock but in the end didn't because he was expecting her. When she pushed open the door, the usual blast of heat met her. It warmed her to a flush before she could close the door. A fire roared in the fireplace and hot air poured from the vents. A special heating unit had been installed in these rooms he called home. His kind was sensitive to the cold. Where the more sadistic among the hunters would expose the blood feeders they called vampires to the light and watch them die horrifically, they would lock an injured incubus into cold cellars and meat lockers or staked them outside in the brutal Minnesota winters to watch them freeze to death. Even just the autumn chill could be fatal to them.

Tarris sat in front of the fire. As always his chest and feet were bare. His fingers twirled the flat stone he carried with him between them. Over each knuckle the stone flipped to be caught by the next. Sarah smiled at him, her breath catching in her throat as it always did when she looked at him. Mark had once told her Tarris was the most beautiful creature in the world. Somehow that always seemed an understatement. He rose to face her and held out his hand. Sarah moved into his embrace. He hugged her tightly and the genuineness of his affection for her flowed from him without restraint. Tarris was also the most loving and tender of creatures Sarah had ever known. Her heart ached for the situation he was now in.

You are doing it again, sweet Sarah. His voice held a gentle reproach. *You cannot blame yourself for what has happened. Not one of us knew it would be this way. He lifted her chin and looked into her eyes. Do you believe you would not have mated with Mark if you had known? Do you believe Mark would not have mated with you if he had known? Do you believe for a moment that I would have allowed either of you to make that sacrifice? Did I allow Luke or Anna to?*

"No," Sarah shook her head. "You wouldn't have allowed it. But once in a while it's okay not to be so damn unselfish you know."

She heard his chuckle in her head. He pulled her toward the chair and down onto his lap. Sarah was startled. He'd not done this since Luke and Anna's mating. Before that he had often patted her head and cuddled her like an indulgent big brother. There was nothing sexual about his touch, just loving. Once Luke had no longer been there to feed Tarris, Sarah had assumed the contact was unpleasant for the hungry incubus. Now here he was again tucking her head under his chin.

Tell me what has you so concerned. All I can make sense of in this jumbled mind of yours is something to do with a friend and sex.

Sarah smoothed her fingers over his hand where he held her. The stone he'd been playing with was still in his grasp. He let her run her fingers over the surface. Two parts brilliant opalescence, one part black dull glass. Tarris had told her it was his talisman. The way he remembered the youngest of the Ursine brothers, little Jonas who had died before he could make his first transformation into Bear. He told her that it always made him feel better. And every time she touched it, she too felt as if someone were whispering to her that everything would be all right.

She took a deep breath. "Tarris, I'm worried for one of my friends. She just told me that she's been having very vivid dreams. Sexual dreams. They are draining her. She looks tired and worn out." She felt him stiffen slightly beneath her. "Tarris, the way she describes it, well it almost seems like she's describing—"

An incubus.

"Yes," Sarah lifted her head and looked at him. He responded to the worry in her face by brushing his hand over her cheek.

It is probably just a dream, Sarah. Incubi don't often hunt in this area because they have not only the hunters to avoid but this group of Weres as well. I'm sure your friend —

His words stopped abruptly and he stood up depositing her carefully on her feet. He stepped away from her and she could see the tension in the hard and rippling muscles of his back as he lifted his arms and pushed the long golden hair out of his face with both hands. Something was wrong. He'd stopped talking, pushed her away as soon as she started to think about…

"Callie," she said softly. Tarris' arms dropped to his sides and he stood straight and stiff. "You know something about Callie, don't you?"

I know your friend is safe, Sarah. She is not being hunted. No one will harm her.

"But what is happening?" She stepped over to him and put her hand on his shoulder. "Talk to me Tarris. What do you know?"

Don't ask that question, Sarah. Don't ask for answers you don't really want and that I don't really want to give.

Realization swept through her even more fiercely than the heat of the room, which had warmed her body to the point she was perspiring. "It's you isn't it?"

Tarris turned and the electric blue eyes fixed on her face. *Don't ask me questions like that, Sarah.*

"Why?" she smiled at him. "Tarris, Callie is a wonderful woman. If you two have found each other that's incredible, that's happy news."

Tarris' face looked anything but happy. *I am not a Were, Sarah. My kind do not have mates, wives, families.*

"But Tarris," she began only to have him cut her off.

You must not tell Mark. I swear to you no harm will come to your friend. I do not hunt, Sarah and I care for her as much as one like me can. I would never harm her. But promise me you will not tell Mark or Luke.

"But why?" Sarah shook her head. "Why on earth not? They love you. They would be happy for you that you've found someone you care for."

No, sweet Sarah. They would not be happy. It would make the second of the rules that I have broken. It would not make them happy, it would make them hunters and me the prey.

Chapter Three

ﬆ

Callie adjusted the pillows behind her back. She'd shut off her laptop and slipped it into its carrying case. She had to work tomorrow and she was exhausted. If her dream lover didn't leave her to rest soon she'd be worthless. But a tremor of fear mixed with need gnawed away at her. It wasn't normal that just the though of him was making the desire heat up inside her body. She clenched her thighs together shifting as if it would somehow ease the tingling that was growing there. Something was wrong. Why couldn't she shut it off? These dreams were not like any she'd ever had before. In the past few days a part of her brain had learned to tell the difference between what she had come to think of as *her* dreams, times when her brain was acting in simple REM mode and *his* dreams, the times when he appeared and seemed to be orchestrating every move.

She started to reach for the lamp when she saw the book the stranger at the café had given her. She'd brought it into her room and laid it beside the bed thinking she'd glance through it before she mailed it to him with a curt note informing him it was rude to eavesdrop on others' conversations. Even now her face flushed at the thought of exactly what snippets of her conversation with Sarah he might have overheard. She picked up the slim volume and settled back against the pillows.

"The Gehennaht. Almanac of Species"

The title meant little to her. What on Earth was a *Gehennaht*? She ran her fingers over the letters that seemed to have been tooled into the cover. The cover certainly felt like real leather, old leather. Lifting it to her nose she smelled the sharp scent she associated with such bound books and something more, the smell of something oily and heady that she couldn't identify. The young man had said it came from a private collection and that usually meant money. Perhaps whatever was used to polish the shelf that held this book had dripped onto the cover. The book was surely not as old or as valuable as it appeared. Who went around giving strange women books from private collections as some sort of pickup line?

A slip of paper was just visible above the edge of the pages. Tugging it carefully so as not to remove it completely and lose the page, Callie saw a neat, practiced handwriting spell out "Adam Stanton". Sliding her finger between page and marker she opened the book and found, just as he had said, her eavesdropper had written his name, address and a phone number on the paper. Not sure if she was flattered or creeped out entirely, she tucked the paper into another section of the book. Opening the tome for the first time to the page that had been marked, Callie gasped and nearly dropped the book.

Her heart jumped into her throat for a moment but calmed quickly as she shook herself for her silliness. The black and white illustration had leapt off the page at her, its grotesque visage with sharp pointed horns catching her unaware. "Someone forgot to cue the scary music," she muttered to herself, thankful no one had seen her jump like a teenager at a horror film when the monster jumps out of a closet.

The entry was labeled with two names. *Psyvi*, which she didn't understand and incubus-succubus, which she did. So that was an incubus? That was the creature who women couldn't resist and had wild sex with? No thank you! She supposed that someone who had over heard her talking about her dreams to Sarah and who was into the occult might come to the ridiculous conclusion that she was being visited by one of these creatures but the very idea was ludicrous. What next? Vampires? Werewolves?

She scanned the passage out of curiosity. She knew the basics of most of these legends, folklore—the happy little fairies and the creepy bumpy crawly things alike—was her field of study. Callie frowned as she read. Most of this was your usual "ooh scary monster" stuff but some of it was different. They preyed upon humans to feed. Yep, she'd heard that but according to this author the incubi and their female counterparts had crossed some sort of veil to reach this dimension.

When the children of Lilith, as old human legend calls the original species, first crossed from Gehenna into our realm they were torn apart. The first pair were split in two as they crossed the boundary and became two distinct species. One half became the angelus, the beautiful creatures who held all the goodness of the original species and most importantly retained the soul. The angelus — see entry titled The Angelus — have avoided human contact and when they have been seen among humans have long been credited with doing good deeds.

The second creature created by this division became the psyvi, or the incubus-succubus. This creature retained all the evil impulses and impurities of the parent species. They are the embodiment of the seven deadly sins, particularly lust. They have no soul and as such have no conscience. Their lack of soul makes them sterile as well. The female can reproduce only if she steals enough life force from her victims to simulate human existence. This means the death of the human she feeds upon. She will give birth not to a human or even hybrid child but to one of her own kind.

The entry went on to describe the feeding frenzy of the creatures, their obsessive nature and how, if left unchecked, the creatures would drain the victim to insanity or good, old-fashioned death.

Callie's frown returned and a true sense of unease began to slip into her as she read the next passage. According to this version of lore, the creature would not appear as the loathsome monster that had been sketched above in the dreamer's dream. They would appear as the most beautiful of beings. This is the original form for the beast who loses its beauty upon reaching full maturity, after it fully takes a victim for the first time.

Her heart thudded in her chest and the image of her Tarris, her perfect lover, swam before her eyes. *This is foolish,* she told herself. *These creatures don't exist. You're being an idiot.* What wasn't silly was the tightening of her nipples that the thoughts of him produced even wrapped around this silly trepidation that made her lower lip quiver. *Tarris is my imagination. He is not some sexual boogeyman.* Such stories were told to enforce the ideas of chastity and purity, especially among women. She knew they had grown in lore along with the patriarchal societies that sought to warn men of sexually free women and as threats to women who would question the idea that their own sexual needs were shameful. A woman's body in those days was just for her husband's pleasure. She was just supposed to lie back and close her eyes.

She had a sudden feeling as if she were being watched. An urgent wave of fatigue swept over her. Her heart was racing so loudly she could hear her pulse in her ears. Still her mind demanded that she put down the book and sleep. She complied though the adrenalin jolt that she'd just experienced should have kept her tossing and turning. Almost as soon as her head hit her pillow, Callie drifted to sleep.

Tarris stepped out of the shadows of her room. He normally waited until he sensed her sleeping but tonight he couldn't. His conversation with Sarah had pushed him to her. As he'd stood, not quite taking full shape in the darkness of the bathroom that opened into her bedroom, he'd felt her fear and he'd seen the images of what she was reading in her mind. So he had reached out to her and urged her to sleep.

He walked to the edge of her bed and picked up the book she had been reading. Tarris glared at it angrily. He'd seen the name in her mind. Adam Stanton. The man was relentless. He was persistent to the point of obsession. And he was paranoid. Or was he? Was the man who had been a joke among the

Weres and himself, not to mention a goodly number of the hunter's council, for the past few years laughable? Or was he prophetic?

Thinking about what he'd told Sarah, Tarris realized he was about to break more than two of the rules. He'd let a woman pleasure him. He'd fed alone. Was what he was doing now anything less than hunting? Hadn't he sought out Callista, following her energies to her? Hadn't he just urged her into sleep so that he could feed? Hadn't he...hunted? If not, he was about to now.

Glancing at the address on the paper she'd tucked back in the book he closed his eyes and felt for Stanton. The cocky little shit was asleep. Perfect. Callista's room dissolved around him and he found himself in a dark apartment. The moon shone in the window and fell across the face of the man who lay there. Adam Stanton. The man was handsome. His fair skin, his red hair, he was nearly as lovely to look at as the woman who slept dreamlessly a few miles away. But he did seem to be developing a fondness for redheads. Tarris felt a warmth spread through him as he took in the lines of the man's bare chest. He would be a great deal of fun to play with. Well, Stanton wanted an incubus, he was going to get one.

Tarris reached out his hand and brushed the sleeping man's forehead. He sank deeper into the dream he was having. An erotic dream that included Callie. Tarris fought the urge to stop the dream. Instead he sank onto the edge of the bed and entered it. Stanton was nude, his cock stiff and ready for the woman he held tightly. For a moment the incubus considered simply joining the dream. To have this man with his beloved one would certainly keep him well fed and them well sated for the length of their lives. Anna had learned to see beyond her hunter indoctrination, perhaps this man could too.

Then he saw the man's hand reach down and cup the soft mons that in this dream was covered with silken red curls. The man had never seen Callie nude. The momentary sense of satisfaction disappeared with a snap as a jealous fever roared inside Tarris.

His mind seemed to splinter. One half screamed, *No*. He'd never share her with this man. Never allow him to touch her. She was his. The other half drew excitement from the thought of the three of them joined together, touching. That side withered in the face of the fury that clawed at his chest. It was a foreign sensation. Never had he known jealousy. Never had he known such an angry fury to burn inside him. As an empath and a telepath he was too in tune to those around him. He knew their motives and often sympathized with the fear or longing that drove them.

But not now. Now he wanted to crush the man before him and not just physically. How dare he dream of Callista! His redheaded siren was his alone. Tarris approached Stanton and touched his shoulder. Callie faded away and the hunter turned to face Tarris.

Fear flashed in the gray eyes but evaporated when Tarris reached for him and cupped his cheek. "You know I won't hurt you," Tarris said softly. He watched the effect of his voice on the man. Stanton was not a man who sought the touch of another male, yet he reacted to the incubus before him. Tarris had never used this "talent" before, the ability of his race to lull into submission anyone he chose. Inside the man Tarris found the buried curiosity and attraction he'd hidden all his life. Humans. Some of them had such limited and stifled ideas about sexuality. And they ran so deeply that those ideas became fears and those fears controlled them. Tarris pushed the repressed desires to the surface and felt the man relaxed for a moment, then stiffened. Stanton was fighting him. The hunter before him was strong but not strong enough. Tarris pushed back at him with his mind and smiled invitingly. "Come now Adam, we both know what you want."

"I don't want you," the man's body was at ease again, even as his words argued.

Tarris traced the line of the man's jaw and let his fingers lightly trail over the taut throat. The hunter arched his neck to accommodate the touch but his words still denied what his throbbing cock and husky voice were saying to the incubus. "I want Callista Marshall."

Tarris clenched his teeth to hold back his growl. That was not going to happen as long as Tarris drew breath. But this man need not know that, yet. No, this was about proving to the hunter that he was out of his league. One little hunter, no matter how powerful his mind and talents might be, was no match for a century old incubus. And it was about the pleasure he'd exact from the man's reactions. Tarris slowly let his eyes wander over the male form before him. The flesh flushed as Adam realized the thorough inspection his body was undergoing. The man was impressive for a human. His cock was thick and richly veined, hardening even more by the second.

Tarris slid his hand around to cup the back of the man's head. Stanton shuddered. Tarris had a good six inches on him though he was above average for a human. The hunter's hands lay limp at his sides as Tarris pulled him forward and molded the man's body against his own, claiming the willing mouth. Tarris felt the man's cock press against the growing bulge in his own pants.

Forcing Stanton's head back, Tarris caused his lips to part and took full advantage. The part of him that recognized Stanton's appeal as a lover reveled in the taste of the shorter man. When the hunter's hands lifted to rest against Tarris' back a silent cry of victory sounded in the blond man's mind. He'd won. He could have Stanton if he wanted him.

Tarris ran his hand across Stanton's chest and swallowed the trembling groan that resulted. The hunter's hands moved down Tarris's back and over the curve of his tight ass. The fingers massaged the hard muscles and Tarris felt his own excitement grow. Damn this man would bring him hours of pleasure, he would feed him well. Tarris smoothed his fingers over the ripple of the man's abs and playfully brushed the trail of soft hairs that ran down from the navel. Bending into the kiss, Tarris reached down and cupped the hunter's sac, palming it gently before bringing his hand up to curve around his erection. Stanton groaned loudly, gasping and only momentarily breaking the kiss before resubmitting to Tarris' demands for his mouth. Tarris stroked the shorter man's cock and felt him tremble in response. There was no denying the need the man would have fought desperately to repress. A need that in the waking world would have brought him great shame.

Stanton pushed back at Tarris' tongue, his hunger to explore the incubus' mouth growing along with a need to please him. Tarris felt the swell of power inside his chest. Tarris felt the intoxicating sensation of being in control. He reached for Stanton's hand but the moment he touched it, the man moved it to brush over the incubus' hard penis, still hidden inside his pants. Tarris felt the excitement in the hunter as he stroked the curve of the bulge and rubbed his palm against him. Stanton was so eager, so long repressed and more hungry than any incubus for what lay just beyond his reach inside the confines of Tarris' jeans. The incubus knew he could have this man on his knees begging to be allowed to please him, begging to take his cock in his mouth.

As tempting as the hunter was, the strange new presence that seemed to have awakened within him cried out for Callista. It did not eschew the touch of this man or find it unappealing. He simply wasn't Callista. The memory of the hunter's dream, the way his hands had touched the dream version of the woman, the threat he posed to both of them struggled to the forefront of Tarris' attention. The hunter before him, in the waking world, was obsessive in his desire to destroy the incubi. He wanted Callista for his own. There were two ways to end the threat. The emerging voice in his mind urged him to kill the hunter. But the gentle empathic part of his being argued loudly for him to frighten the man. If he scared him enough, he'd turn away. Tarris knew better but couldn't bring himself to not give the man a chance to save his life.

Tarris pulled back from the kiss, his hand still holding firmly to the man's head. Closing his eyes for a moment he pulled the image of the incubus in the book Stanton had given Callie and forced it out through his skin. Black horns sprouted in his hair, his skin blackened and gleaming fangs appeared in the mouth beneath the twisted nose and the flame red eyes. He was every inch the monster, the fully mature incubus.

Stanton's scream was short and changed into a roaring cry of rage. He stared furiously at Tarris. His anger came as much from what Tarris was as from the fact he was helpless, standing nude, crushed against Tarris' body, with the incubus' claws stabbing pinprick wounds into his neck. It was clear to Tarris that the hunter understood that a false move would mean a slash to his throat from those claws. Stanton could die from such a wound as it would manifest itself in the waking world as well.

"Do not interfere with me, little hunter," the pheromones coming from Stanton mixed fear with a powerful shame that his desire had not been dampened by his fear.

"I won't let you have her," the redheaded man said, sounding much braver than the fear and panic Tarris could read in his mind should have allowed.

"I already have her," Tarris said smoothly. Yeah, this new power, one he'd never exercised before, felt good. He liked it. Being in control. His mind laughed. Being the Dom, a joke he'd shared with his Bear Luke when they were lovers. The Bear had always needed to take control. Now Tarris was in control. His free hand drew a line down the other man's lips, over his chin, down his throat, to pause above the pounding heart. "She's mine. Not for a night, not for a week or a moon, but for all time. I will not let her go and you will not interfere again."

"Your kind has taken enough," Stanton growled. "I swore I'd die before I let another woman suffer as you made my sister suffer."

Tarris had read the image in the man's mind when he'd first appeared to him. A beautiful girl with short cropped blonde hair rocking silently in a corner. Her eyes were empty and a small damp spot was on the front of her shirt from a mouth that always drooped open just a bit. The image was horrible even to Tarris. It was one of the reasons he kept to the rules. He'd never do something like this to a human being. But one of his kind had. One of his kind had used this man's sister until her mind broke.

Pity swelled in Tarris' chest but not enough to weaken his resolve. "You will stay away from her. You will not contact Callista again." He drew in a deep breath that ached a little with the pain of the man before him. "I will not harm her. I could never harm her and I have no wish to hurt you, either." He released the hunter and stepped away. "But I will. Remember this night. Remember how easy it was for me to find you, to break your resistance. Think about how easy it was for me to entice you into doing something your narrow-minded little world told you was wrong. Do not make me hurt you, little hunter."

Tarris released the illusion of the monster and stepped away from Stanton. Filling his mind with the image of his beautiful one he slipped out of Stanton's dream and out of his home. He reappeared at the side of Callie's bed. She'd hardly moved since he'd left. Looking down at her, he watched the way her nightshirt cut tight across her breasts. The hardened tips were pressing out at the fabric, two tiny pebbles covered in a soft brushed blue cotton. His palm itched with his desire to feel them under his hand, to stroke them until he heard her moan loudly. Tarris wanted to feel them under his tongue, sucked deep into his mouth as his tongue pressed them tight to the roof of his mouth or clamped firmly between his teeth. Oh, the sounds that would come from her throat when he did that. Sounds that made his cock harden.

And now she knew what he was. She didn't want to believe it. She was trying desperately to cling to what her human reasoning told her and reject him as nothing more than a dream. But he could see it, hear it and feel it. She knew. He had to make a choice. Leave her alone or stop hiding. Walk away from her or face her as what he really was. An incubus. *Psyvi*, the sexual predator that prowled the night. In the end he knew there really was no choice. He could never give her up. He had to face her.

Now that piece of her that was aware she was dreaming was telling her rather forcefully that this was definitely one of *his* dreams. The smells, the sounds, the feel of the heat from the roaring twin bonfires were too real to be one of *her* dreams. But where was he?

She stood at the edge of a large clearing. The open space topped the crest of a large mound and reminded her of a friar's tonsure surrounded by its ring of thick forest. The clearing was filled with people. Twenty or more young men and women danced to a rhythm being beaten out on an old drum while a high reedy sound carried a melody. The dancers passed between the fires in two circles that mixed and blended only to separate again. Spring's first flowers decorated the hair of the women and the men were freshly shaven and all were washed clean of the winter's sweat. Callie watched them move happily. She scanned the crowd looking for him but didn't see his golden form anywhere among the celebrants.

Two young girls separated themselves from the dancers and ran her way. She almost expected to see her sisters. But though both had the same golden strawberry blonde hair of her younger siblings, neither face was familiar. "Come, Callista, it's time," the taller of the pair reached for her hand.

"Are you nervous?" the younger one asked. Her cheeks were flushed from the fire's heat and the excitement of the dance.

"To be chosen as the Spring Maiden," sighed the older. "I hope I'm chosen when I'm of age."

Callie suddenly became aware of the crown of flowers that sat upon her head. Looking down she saw ribbons of small wildflowers twisted with her red hair. Green vines wrapped her wrists and trailed up her arms to wrap around her upper arms forming long living sleeves. Her dress was a simple shift, covered by a white overdress that tied with a blue ribbon. She was barefoot and the grass was cool and soft beneath her feet.

"Come on," her *sister* tugged at her hand. "You can't leave Himself waiting."

"Have you seen him yet?" the younger giggled as they pulled her toward the fires. "He's the handsomest Lord of the Hunt we've ever had."

"Let me guess," Callie rolled her eyes. "Long blond hair, really tall, to-die-for blue eyes?"

"Well if you don't want a chance to polish his horns, I do," remarked the elder girl and the two giggled. Callie groaned. She wasn't sure if the horrible pun was his doing or came from the recesses of her own mind. Either way, whoever was responsible should be thoroughly ashamed.

The dancers stilled as the girls led her through the passage between the two fires. The fires would purify those who walked or danced among the flames, burning away the evils of the winter. As she passed through them, Callie lifted one hand to test the heat. It burned her hand. On her palm was an angry red blotch. One of the girls tugged her and she stumbled forward wincing as she stepped on a stone with her bare feet. Something was off here. Fire in dreams didn't burn you unless you were remembering the pain. Stones didn't bruise your feet in dreams. Again and again his dreams were far too real. Again and again she woke feeling as if she had lived them.

From the fires they led her to a stone altar she hadn't noticed before. On it were several clay jars and baskets, some holding flowers and garlands, some with lids that hid their contents. "You're to wait here," said one of the girls. As her voice faded away so did the sounds of all the others who had been standing in the circle. The crackling of the fire was the only sound she could hear. Then she felt it. She felt him. Turning slowly, she saw that she was alone now except for a long, dark shadow that stood on the other side of the fires. The form was human but not quite. As he stepped from the darkness and into the light of the flames, her breath caught, as it did every time she saw him.

He walked slowly through the path of purification and paused dead center. His blue eyes held hers and the look on his face was somber, almost harsh. Callie let her eyes run over him. He wore soft buckskin pants and was, as always barefoot. His chest was partially covered by a garland of deep green ivy. The golden hair seemed to catch the firelight and trap it, flickering and dancing in a breeze that she could not feel. And on his head, jutting out from the blond strands was an impressive set of twelve point antlers. The Lord of the Hunt had arrived.

The brown horns should have seemed ridiculous but Callie found her heart beating faster and her breathing increasing as she looked at him. He was different in the firelight. He had never come to her like this. In all the fantasies they had enacted over the past week, never had he affected her so deeply. He'd been sexy, yes. Beautiful, yes. Tender, yes. But he had never seemed as primal, as sexual as he did now with his erection stretching the soft skin of his trousers. A layer of perspiration covered his chest and the flesh flushed from the heat of the fire.

Even his walk was different in this dream. He moved as if he were the Forest Lord, the embodiment of the connection between man and the animal world around him. He approached her like a hunter. Like a man stalking a doe he was certain to fell. Callie found herself taking a step back, not in fear but in reaction to the overwhelming sense of deliberation that colored each step he took. The cold stone at her back blocked all retreat and her heart fluttered like a caged bird desperate for freedom. She gripped the rough edge of the altar as she lifted her chin to keep eye contact as he stopped, looming over her.

He didn't speak. In all other dreams he had waited for her to touch first or gently asked permission. It had been charming and had eased any fear she might have felt. But now he simply reached for her, his large hands spanning her waist. He lifted her and sat her on the flat stone surface. For the first time he frightened her. The look of pure desire, pure lust in his face terrified her. She lifted her hands and pressed them to the hard muscles of his chest pushing him back. He did not move away. Instead his fingers closed on the blue ribbon ties of her overdress and tugged at the knot. As the satin pulled loose and the ends were tugged through the eyelets, Callie grabbed at his hands. She tried twice before she finally managed to speak. What came out was not what she had been trying to say. All that escaped was one word. "Sarah."

He froze and looked at her. A door closed somewhere in the eyes that always seemed so open to her, so welcoming. He simply stood there, looking at her. She tried again. "Did I meet you at Sarah's wedding? Is that why you're in my dreams?"

Tarris shook his head slightly. His lips were pressed tightly together and she saw the tick in his jaw. Everything here was too real to be a dream. "You are Sarah's Tarris."

Finally his low voice filled her ears and poured over her. "I am your Tarris. No one else's."

"But you do know her," Callie pressed. The piece of her mind that had gotten good at recognizing when she was living inside this fantasy that she... That he... That someone had created, was crying out the most ridiculous of ideas. This was not a dream. Her lover was not human.

"That's not what you really want to know, is it, Callista? That's not the question you really want to ask." He reached up to brush his fingers across her lips.

She shook her head. "No, it's not possible." The idea was foolish even in a dream but something inside her recognized it and was demanding that she do so as well.

"Ask," he demanded as he lowered his head. His kiss silenced her at the very moment he had demanded she speak. She wondered if, like her, he knew the words must be spoken, longed for asking to be done with but feared it nonetheless. The lips that met hers were hot and sinfully soft. They claimed her mouth in a way no man in the waking world ever had. His tongue pushed past her parted lips and into the depths of her mouth drawing her deeper still into his kiss. His hands pushed the open overdress from her shoulders and began to tug at the ties on the shift. Callie wrapped her arms around his neck and pulled him down to her, pressing back her own kiss. She felt the sharp smooth line of his teeth on the underside of her tongue as she slid it against his in the warm wetness of his mouth. Honey, spiced honey. The man whose hands were sliding her remaining garment from her shoulders tasted like no other.

The mild coolness of the air was instantly replaced by the heat of his hands as he cupped her breasts and squeezed them gently. Callie no longer cared about the question of reality or dream as she pulled her arms from the arm holes letting it pool around her hips. Incubus or fantasy she really didn't care when his hands touched her. And it seemed he had forgotten her questioning as well.

The vines on her arms dragged across the bare skin of his shoulders and he drew in a sudden, harsh breath. A wicked smile broke on his lips as he pulled back from the kiss. "That works both ways, my darling one," his arms pulled her to his chest and the garland of ivy brushed her breasts, the edges of the leaves pricking into her nipples slightly. She tried to wriggle loose and only succeeded in making herself gasp with the sensation of the greenery, warmed by his skin, teasing across her flesh.

Tarris eased her to lie back. Her legs hung off the edges of the stone, the curve of her ass just barely catching the edge as he leaned over her. The garland again brushed her skin as it swayed against her stomach. He stood almost still, almost. The slight swaying of his shoulders caused the leaves to brush against her, sending tickling tremors through her that were making her nipples swell and harden. Slowly he moved upward, placing one knee on the surface of the altar. His movement was slow and deliberately tantalizing. The slow drag and sway of the garland brushed over the swell of her breasts. Left and then right he dipped his shoulders letting the leaves brush her nipples. Callie bit her lip and almost succeeded in stifling a moan of pleasure.

His laugh was low and devilish. "I think someone likes that." His gentle dominance play over the past week was becoming bolder and bolder as he took delight in making her squirm and wiggle. But never had it been as commanding and powerful as it was tonight. It was as if someone had removed a shackle from him and he was free to take charge of the situation in a way he'd not been before. In the way he was meant to.

His head lowered, careful of the large rack he still wore as the Lord of the Hunt. He kissed her neck, letting the wonderful tickling continue as his tongue and teeth toyed with the pale column of flesh. Callie felt the wetness grow between her thighs. The spiraling of desire was beginning to center there and she knew it would soon grow into a vortex that was beyond her control. It always did with this man. Somehow Tarris pulled from her a range of passions she'd not known she possessed. And he was doing it again.

Tarris lifted and removed the vines from his neck. "As much as that seems to excite you, my dearest, I want nothing separating our skins." He immediately began to trail his kisses down her throat to the rise of her breasts. He tongued the flesh at the side of each mound making her breathing become more rapid. Centering his weight on one hand, he used the other to tease her left breast. His mouth claimed the right. A hard sucking was followed by a sharp nip that sent a blast of pleasure straight to her pussy.

Callie reached up and smoothed the long blond hair back, a bit anxious about the antlers that moved near her face. When her hands brushed the horns that stood out on his head, Tarris gasped and his head shot up in surprise. His gaze was so intense it felt like flames, two perfect blue flames, burning into her. Slowly, keeping her eyes locked to his, she stroked the smooth, bony surface that jutted from his wild mane and he shuddered. "I think someone likes that," she quipped. The smile that broke the heat of his regard blazed like a sun.

He opened his lips and she put her hand over his mouth, "If you say one word about being horny, I'll slap you."

His laugh was low in his throat and nearly as seductive as his touch. "As the Spring Maiden wishes, so shall it be." He lowered his head and began to tease her breasts. Nuzzling them gently, he raked the smooth surface of the protrusion that would have been a figurative sign of his virility had he not chosen to make them a literal part of his being, across her skin and joined her in a low ragged groan as they rubbed against her nipples.

His lips brushed her stomach, his horns caressed her breasts and his hand slipped down her side to find the curve of her hip. Callie wrapped her legs around his waist and used him to anchor herself as she lifted for him. He knew she craved his touch on her ass and was always eager to comply. He pushed the fabric of her shift up until it was a soft band of fabric around her waist. When he did cup her ass, his fingers were rougher than in the past, his touch was firmer, his squeezing teetering on the line between pleasure and pain. Pulling her up against him he ground the bulge of his straining cock against her wet lips. The press of the hard ridge covered by the soft, pliable leather against her clit made her cry out with surprise and delight.

He looked at her with an expression she was beginning to recognize. It wasn't that he was predictable but simply that there was a particularly hungry look in his eyes just before he…

Pulling from her embrace he dropped to his knees between her thighs. Callie tried to push herself up but his hands slid under her ass and pulled it even closer to the edge. He paused for a moment, looking like a wild primitive being, kneeling at the altar of a favored goddess. Then, as if he were even more impatient than she, as if he enjoyed this act even more than she, he eagerly buried his face in her pussy. His talented and agile tongue began to circle her clit. Her wetness flowed and she could hear the soft sound as he lapped up her juices. Each stroke of his tongue on her clit caused her to jerk slightly, gasps coming from her.

Sliding his tongue along the folds of skin, he explored every inch of her bare pink flesh. His hands kneaded her cheeks and his tongue moved down to find her entrance. It flickered at the edges and she lifted her knees to her chest. "Lay your legs over my shoulders, beautiful one," his voice rumbled against her sensitive skin and her clit vibrated sending the spirals of need and pleasure tightening so fiercely they were almost a pain. A sweet delicious pain that only he could ease.

She complied and in doing so, brushed the smooth antlers causing him to jerk his head back and gasp. Deliberately she rubbed the inside of her thigh against the protrusion. She wasn't supposed to find the feel of horns erotic, was she? It was so damn hot but so taboo. He swallowed several breaths before meeting her eyes and solving her dilemma. "These were fun but I think it's time they were gone. Because if you keep rubbing them like that something's going to happen I don't think either of us is ready for." The impressive rack disappeared.

She didn't understand him. What could she possibly not be ready for? What could he possibly not be ready for? From the way her pussy was oozing and the way his breath was coming in ragged pants, it seemed to her they were both ready for anything. Bracing her weight on his shoulders, he lowered his mouth to her again. He licked the damp slit with broad firm strokes before plunging his tongue into her opening. She moaned as he penetrated her pussy more deeply than she had thought was possible. Returning to flick across her clit, he slid a finger into her wetness and withdrew it slowly. Then entered her again. Then withdrew slowly.

It was torment. Callie tried to push herself toward him but had no way to brace herself. Pressing up with her legs moved her closer to his mouth but away from the long, thick digit that teased her. When she felt a second finger slide into her pussy she gave a cry of frustration as he spread her wider but did not hurry his pace. As he worked her slowly, she could feel the evidence of her need drip down from her lips and tickle the crease of her ass.

Suddenly the fingers were gone from inside her and she called out to him, "Tarris, please. I need it. I need you."

She felt him smile as he kissed her swollen nether lips, his tongue flickering out to toy with them. His breath was hot and shot darts of pure, raging want through her body as it blew across her damp flesh. "I can see that. But I can also see that you need more. More than I've given you until tonight."

Something inside her burst into flames and melted at the sound of the words spoken into that most tender of places on her body. Until now his mouth and his hands had delivered to her wondrous pleasures. He had allowed her to stroke his magnificent cock but he had not let her taste it, had not let her feel it deep inside her. *Until tonight,* his words had shaken her. Her body had already learned more about pleasure than it had ever known and now he was promising her more.

All she could do was gasp his name. He rose, supporting her hips in his hands. "Slide up a bit, beautiful one."

The stone beneath her should have been rough to the point of being painful. It wasn't. As she moved, its rough surface only teased her skin, the scraping just enough to make the nerve endings come to life and scream their need for more of his touch. Scream for more of the indescribable pleasure he flooded through her body whenever he appeared to disturb her sleep. She eased her way, wiggling back up until her ass once again rested on the very edge.

"I think it's time we found out how much you trust me," he whispered the words softly but Callie shivered at the hard edge underneath. He let her legs fall loose and leaned over her gently taking hold of each wrist. "I'm not sure you should, you know," he leaned closer to her, his sweet breath warming the side of her face, fluttering past her ear. He pushed her wrists up even with her head and held them tightly. "Not too tightly now," he said softly.

Callie's heart started to pound as fear added itself to her desire. She was about to ask what she was doing too tightly when she felt the movement. The vines that had encased her wrists and arms tightened their hold and began to grow. They tangled with the ivy that was growing around the altar and wove themselves seamlessly into one thick, solid, living cord. Tarris let go. She tugged at the restraints, starting to panic. She couldn't move her arms.

Tarris' hands cupped her cheeks and forced her eyes to his. "Callista," his voice was firm. "My beautiful one," his eyes were soft and kind. A smile hovered on his full lips. "I told you the first night we met you would never have reason to fear me." One hand caressed her face and moved down her neck. He rose up onto the altar and rested on a knee to one side of her. Bending low he pressed a soft kiss to her throat. His fingers continued their journey downward to her breast where he cupped it and let his thumb brush across her hard nipple. She shuddered at the sensation and felt the tip contract, puckering tighter under his touch. His tongue laved a path from her jaw to the soft pulse point behind her ear. Pressing his weight onto the knee on the altar, he pressed his thigh, now miraculously bare, against her folds. His hard cock brushed her stomach as he moved. The tremor that passed though her wove itself as tightly into her center as the vines had woven into her restraints. It wrapped around the core of need for him, and twisted, increasing the burning ache that was already gnawing at her. His hand and thigh rhythmically pulsing against her made her blood sing in her ears. No man had ever made her feel this way.

No man.

As if he'd heard the thought, she felt him stiffen. Her clit throbbed as he lifted his head and looked into her eyes. The impossible blue irises were now tiny flames dancing in his eyes. She couldn't look away from him. Her mouth parted and she panted as she flexed her abdominal muscles trying press back against his thigh.

"Yes." He said the word softly and she saw him change slightly in her vision. His skin seemed to become iridescent and when he drew back his lips, his teeth were sharper than she'd noticed before. His ears seemed to grow upward, coming to soft points. "Yes, Callista. I am."

He was an incubus. The man who was turning her body into a mass of need aching for fulfillment was the impossible. He was an incubus. Not the terrifying monster in the illustrations of the book she'd been given or even in the lore she'd seen previously. His skin was beautiful and the ears more than a little cute. His teeth gave him a dangerous look that did the impossible. It made her wetter. She was dripping in earnest now and the juices from her pussy were sliding between her cheeks, dampening her ass.

"This is my form. Not the monster you were told of. I will never become that. I would die before I would become that creature." He lowered his face and his lips brushed hers tenderly. His fingers rolled her nipple between thumb and forefinger. She whimpered softly, closing her eyes and groaned as he squeezed harder. His thigh rubbed slowly against the damp folds. "Look at me, Callista." She opened her eyes and watched the blue flames dance. "I would die before

I'd harm you," his voice carried all the weight of a solemnly declared vow.

She started to reach for his face and felt the vines tighten. She wanted to touch him, to stroke his face and tell him it was okay. The books were wrong, the myths were wrong. This man who held her body quivering on the edge of delight was no monster. What he was, she didn't quite understand, but he was no dark and evil creature. Unable to sooth the wariness from his face with her hands she whispered his name and lifted her head to press her lips to his.

He accepted her kiss. When she pulled back, uncertain, he watched her face intently. "You are strong, beautiful one. So strong. I should be able to hear your thoughts loudly, clearly but sometimes they are only whispers."

"They are not whispers, my darling, they are screams. They are screaming for you to stop tormenting me. Take me, Tarris. I need you." The flames in his eyes leapt as if they had suddenly exploded. He crushed her mouth beneath his and swept his tongue into her mouth. Exploring every inch of her, he plunged his tongue in as his hand moved down to touch her pussy. He pushed into the crevice and found her clit. His gentle squeeze made stars explode behind her eyes and she would have begged him for release but for his lips swallowing her cries.

Suddenly he pulled away from her and slid between her thighs. Callie wiggled trying to bring his hard shaft into contact with her clit. When he stood again between her thighs she nearly screamed in frustration. "Bad things can happen to men who tease," she growled.

Tarris grinned at her. She saw his hand grasp his cock and begin to rub the length in slow, deliberate movements. "My, my but aren't we eager," he smiled brightly at her and brought the rounded head into contact with her wet lips. She saw him suck in a harsh breath. Tormentingly slowly he began to rub the sensitive head against her wetness. She could just lift her head enough to see the glistening tip of his cock as he pushed past her lips, bathing his entire length in her cream. His breathing was labored and his skin seemed to glow even brighter in her eyes. She felt him press his cock to the entrance of her channel and then stop. Just when she thought he would thrust into her she heard him mutter a harsh word that could only be an oath, though she didn't understand the language.

"Tarris," she cried out as he pulled back. The swirl of desire he'd built in her needed to be released. She felt she would go mad if he didn't let her come. A passage from the book she'd seen danced in her mind. This was how the incubi drove their victims to insanity. The prolonged desire, the need unfulfilled while they drank of the growing energies. Some women broke mentally from the overwhelming lust that claimed their bodies.

"Shh," Tarris soothed her. His left hand reached up to caress her clit, slow strokes that held her arousal at its present intolerable level.

"I want you inside me," she begged. "Please Tarris. Tonight, inside me." The look on his face was pained. She didn't understand why he held back.

"I will be inside you. I promise you. Tonight I will be inside you. You must trust me. There are...rules." His fingers eased down to the weeping opening of her pussy and plunged inside. When he withdrew his fingers they were so moist with her cream that they dripped. He lifted her leg back up so it rested against his shoulder, pushing it up and lifting her ass. At his nod she placed the other leg up to match. Her ass was now open to him and he ran his wet fingers down her crevice to find her anus. He rubbed the wetness from her pussy over the opening causing the torturous need that was making her pussy throb to grow beyond all endurance.

He moved his hand from her and she let forth a strangled cry of protest. She watched him reach for one of the clay jars that rested in a basket on the altar. Lifting the lid he revealed a thick clear oil. She couldn't identify the scent but it wove around her seductively. Dipping his fingers in and coating them with the thick liquid, he brought his hand back to her ass and stroked her opening and then slowly pushed his finger into the tight hole.

Callista gasped. He'd fingered her ass in earlier dreams but from the harsh, hungry look on his face she knew what was coming. She couldn't stop the hesitation and worry that filled her face. His touch felt good but she knew enough about her body and sex to know that the initial entry could be somewhat painful. Especially when the man was built like Tarris. Admittedly she'd not seen all that many naked men in her time but never had she seen a man as large as the one who now held her at his mercy.

He shook his head at her. "This is a dream, Callista. In this dream there will be no pain." He slid a second finger into her ass and she cried out at the sensation. It stretched her but it did not hurt. "With my kind there can be no disease, no chance of conception and no pain," a wicked glint shone in his eyes. "Unless of course you would find that pleasurable? You do enjoy when I…" He snapped his teeth together, "Bite."

"Tarris," she panted. "More. I want more."

He chuckled softly and removed his fingers from her. She watched him, reach for the jar again but could not see where his hand went. Her legs hid him from her view but she could see the tight frown compress his brow. When he slowly slipped his cock past the ring of muscle and into her ass she understood immediately he'd been coating it too with the lubricant. She felt a mild stinging that was almost pleasurable as her nipples contracted and her clit swelled even more. When she looked at his face, something more than physical pleasure roared through her body. His eyes were closed and a look of pure delight was etched upon his features. He opened his eyes suddenly and caught her gaze. He eased in farther until he was fully buried inside her. In the waking world this would have taken a good deal more time for her body to accept his size into her. But here in the dream he controlled, the pleasure grasped the small amount of pain and rolled it inside it until they became one.

Slowly he moved, pulling back and thrusting forward again and again. The pressure built inside her. Her body felt like it was filled with lava, red-hot liquid rock building and pushing at her core demanding to be set free. When his fingers found her clit and began to rub the sensitive nub in time to his quickening thrusts she lost all ability to reason and think about what was happening. She could only feel.

He leaned in harder, her legs pressing back against her body as he rode her ass. His own cries grew in volume and became almost feral. He no longer spoke in any language she understood. His words were harsh and guttural, as if they ripped painfully from his throat yet she knew they were filled with his need to express the beauty of the feeling that was flooding both their bodies.

"Now, Tarris. Now," she cried as the pressure within her reached the limits of what she believed she could withstand. "I want to come now."

His eyes opened and fixed on hers. His fingers squeezed her clit roughly and he plunged himself repeatedly into her ass with a speed and power that could have crossed the wondrous line between pleasure and pain had they been in the flesh. It was one of the glorious things about being with this man. He could make her feel things her body said were impossible. As a strangled cry left his lips and his body stiffened, she could feel his release flooding into her. The molten rock pushed from beneath her skin and erupted. She screamed in ecstasy, her hands straining at the vines, her body trying to double in on itself as the orgasms, one after another, raged through her.

When thought entered her brain again, she realized the scene around them had changed. She was in her room once more and she was awake. Beside her, his golden mane of hair spread out on the pillow and a sheen of perspiration covering his face and chest, was her dream lover. Her incubus was sound asleep.

Tarris lay next to her, his face peaceful. She leaned up on an elbow and examined him. A smile spread her lips as she saw him with her eyes for the first time. His skin still seemed to shimmer in the moonlight but not nearly as much as it had in her dream. His ears still had adorable little points that she longed to touch and lick.

Reaching out she lightly touched his lips. He twitched slightly but gave no other response. Feeling a delightful sleepy satisfaction, Callie lazily traced the line of his pectorals, circling his nipples that stood stiffly at attention. She wondered if it would please him to have her lick them and nip at them in the real world as it did in her dreams. Her hand moved over his abs and down to the waistband of his pants. In the waking world he wore heavy jeans. She smoothed her hand over his hipbone and down toward his thigh. They were so beautifully sculpted in her dreams she was dying to know if he really looked and felt that good.

Her fingers hit a hard lump in his pocket and she frowned, wondering what sort of talisman he might carry. Too distracted by the warmth emanating from his skin and the soft sounds of his breathing to consider it long, she moved her hand down over his thigh. The muscles contracted slightly at her touch and the glorious hard feel of him awakened her need. She felt her inner muscles contract tightly and the pleasant shudder moved over her flesh making her feel damp and causing her to long to feel his shaft sliding inside her in this waking world. Would he feel as good? Would he feel even better driving inside her as she looked up at him moving over her, watching the sunlight form a corona around that golden mane?

Her wicked fingers acted of their own accord as they moved up his inner thigh and stroked over the bulge that pushed his zipper out. Cupping her hand around him, she was rewarded with a soft moan from his lips and a definite shift beneath the denim fabric. But still he slept and her own weariness hit her like a wave claiming the shore at high tide. It pulled her down to him and urged her to surrender.

Callie lay down and smiled as he shifted and sighed in his sleep. His powerful arm pulled her close and she laid her head upon his chest. She was pleasantly surprised to hear his heart beating beneath his breastbone. Lying there, breathing in his scent she could almost forget he wasn't human. Slowly, lulled by the sound of his heart and the rhythm of his breathing Callie drifted off to sleep.

Chapter Four

ഔ

Her feet were damp and freezing, her upper body burned with cold so fierce it nearly made her immobile. The only relief from the bitterness was the warm arm wrapped around her shoulders. Half lifting her, it propelled her forward through slick, cold grass and down an embankment. She was thrust into a small indentation in the side of the hill. It was not a cave but a dug out section of the earth that let her slide in only a few feet. A smaller body was pushed in beside her. Instinctively she pulled it against her chest and curled around it both for heat and to protect it. The sandy blond head fitted under her chin. Her mind knew the boy she held was about fifteen but very small for his age. And she knew she was not much older.

Arguing. Two people were arguing. She felt the dread and fear in her chest as she heard their words.

"You can't stop me, Mark," one dark-haired boy shoved the other one away from him. "I won't leave her to die."

"Luke, don't be stupid. Mom said to stay with Tarris and Jonas. She said to protect them," the other boy tried to grab his twin again. "They're both too young. If the hunters find them they can't defend themselves." The first boy struck the other, hard and twisted out of his grasp to run back up and out of sight over the hill. His twin cursed softly, the sound of it odd from his young lips. He crowded into the small dugout and knelt face to face with her. His hands rubbed her arms and shoulders trying to warm her. The nearness of the young boy pressed between them helped but the cold was still brutal.

"Take my shirt," the older boy she recognized as Sarah's husband Mark wiggled out of his pajama shirt and wrapped it

214

around her shoulders. She closed her eyes and let go of the younger boy long enough to slide freezing limbs into the shirt. Suddenly, socks still warm from the body of the boy who was now bare but for his pants were thrust on her feet.

The sound of gunshots split the night and screams followed. Animalistic screams, sounds no human throat could make. The older boy's eyes closed, his face was pale with fear and pain. He opened his eyes and met hers. "I have to go after him," the voice barely croaked out the words.

"No, you can't leave, Mark," the small boy in her arms answered him. "Mom said to stay here until she came for us. We're too young. None of us can change yet."

"Jonas, I have to go. I have to find Luke," the brown eyes still held her gaze. "Tarris, watch him. Keep him safe. I'll find Luke and be back."

"And Mom?" Jonas asked, his voice almost a whisper.

She knew in her heart what the older boy knew. Their mother was probably already dead. They would be lucky if Luke survived. They would be lucky if any of them survived.

Nothing more was said as the older boy stooped and hurried back into the night. She listened for what seemed like forever as the shots and yelling got closer and closer. The boy moved from her grasp to sit beside her. His shoulder pushed against hers and his arm wrapped around her.

"We need a fire but they'll kill us if they find us. Only if they don't go soon you'll freeze," the small voice stated the obvious. Her eyes felt heavy from the cold. It was sucking any energy she had out of her body. She wanted to comfort young Jonas but her arms were so leaden that they wouldn't move and her mouth felt as if it were filled with cotton. Just when she could barely keep her eyes open, a shadow crossed the doorway blocking the meager moonlight. Looking up she expected to see Mark, Luke or one of the adults from the Bear clan.

In the door crouched a man, his humanity swirling about him like a mist. Around his neck hung the silver and gold sun that was the mark of the hunters. She wasn't sure why she knew this but the knowledge of what this man was and that he was a deadly enemy filled her mind. In his hand he held an old gun, something you'd find in a museum or Wild West exhibit. It was pointed at them, no, pointed at Jonas. She heard the click of metal as the man prepared to shoot. She threw herself to the side to cover the smaller boy. She heard the gun fire and knew she was going to die.

Her fear heaved and before she knew it, she began to shimmer and glow. Her body was breaking apart. The bullet burned as it touched her flesh. She screamed in anguish and disbelief as it passed through her, leaving only a slight sting behind and ripped into the body of the boy. A second shot was fired and again passed through her into the boy. He whimpered and began to convulse, dropping from her arms onto the floor as the silver from the bullet poisoned and destroyed his body.

She heard the grunt of the hunter and the sound of a thud behind her. Either someone had killed the hunter or he was engaged with another. It didn't matter. What mattered was Jonas, lying there. She rose to her knees willing her body to become solid. Jonas' hand clutched up at her, passing into her form, reaching for her heart. His eyes grew wide and dark with the death that tried to claim him. She saw the wisp of soul light that lifted from his form. He was dying.

The soul light tried to pull free but seemed to be anchored where Jonas' hand had passed through her chest. The light stretched and tugged before breaking. As it swirled into a ball and shot through the sod above their heads it caused a shower of dirt and small stones to fall on the boy. She felt her body coalesce and heard Jonas' last breath. Solid again she grabbed at him and pulled him to her. She felt tears sting her eyes and heard low, husky cries escape her throat. Suddenly hands pulled at her shoulders until they held both her and the boy.

When the hands finally pried her away and more hands lifted the frail and broken body, she sat there on her knees rocking. It was Mark and his errant twin, Luke, who held her. Mark and Luke who cried their tears onto her shoulders as she held them in return, the blood on Luke's face and shirt barely registering. Adult hands lifted them all to their feet. As she rose, the moonlight filtered past their bodies and struck something on the ground. She stared at it, rooted to the spot. An elderly woman walked Mark away, while an elderly man swept the injured Luke into his arms and carried him away. An even older figure stood at her side.

"Pick it up," the voice was flat and shaking with pain and rage. She looked up into the face and saw instantly she was not the focus of either emotion. "Pick it up," the stranger repeated, more gently this time. She leaned down and picked up the stone. Two thirds of it shone as if it were an opal. One third was black and dull as smoky glass. The rock was flat and smooth, oblong and curved slightly inward at the point the colors changed. "Never lose it. Keep it with you always," the Oracle rested his hand on her shoulder, his compassion, sadness and fury radiating from that single touch. But she only faintly recognized the gesture. The stone in her hand held her focus. As it lay in her palm it began to warm her. It warmed her hand, then her arm, then her whole body.

More than that. It whispered to her. She couldn't understand the words but the feelings it drove into her heart were absolutely clear. Forgiveness and hope.

Callie jerked upright. Tarris was still by her side but his sleep was no longer peaceful. He tossed his head, sweat beading on his forehead and upper lip. His hands were fisted in the covers and his body jolted almost violently. It was then she knew what had happened. After so many nights of finding Tarris in her dreams, she had been pulled into his. Into his nightmare. Into his memory.

She reached out to caress his face. Before she even made contact a hand shot up and grabbed her wrist. The blue eyes flashed open and stared at her unseeingly for long seconds. Then he released her hand and the same glowing she'd experienced in her dream seemed to take his body and he was gone.

Terrified, Callie climbed out of bed and grabbed the phone on her beside table. She dialed the number and waited. What had happened to him? In her dream it had happened when he'd been shot. Was he hurt? Oh God, what if he was somehow hurt? Finally a male voice answered. "Ursine residence. May I help you?"

"I need to speak to Sarah Ursine," Callie took slow deep breaths trying to calm down her heart. It was beating so loudly she could barely hear the voice on the line.

"I'm sorry, Mrs. Ursine is not available at the moment. May I take a message?" The voice was calm, even bored.

"This is important. Please tell her Callie Marshall is on the phone. She'll talk to me." Or at least Callie hoped she would.

"I'm sorry, Ms. Marshall but Mrs. Ursine is having breakfast with the family and we do not interrupt breakfast for phone calls." The bored voice was gone and replaced by a clipped tone that sounded angry.

Well, that was too bad. She was not playing this game anymore. It had taken six left messages the last time she'd tried to call Sarah. Now was not the time to mess with her.

"Listen, whatever you are, you march your stiff-necked little ass in there and you tell Mrs. Ursine that Callie is on the phone and she needs to talk to her about Tarris. Now!"

* * * * *

"Calm down and quit pacing. You're making me seasick," the ancient voice croaked a bit before the Oracle cleared his throat. "And sit down. You're not helping my morning headache."

Tarris pushed his hair away from his face impatiently and folded his large frame into the chair opposite the old one. He knew the gender of the wise man before him, though no one else did. As an incubus his senses had immediately cataloged the man as male. But since no one had ever asked him and since the Oracle seemed to enjoy keeping the younger members of the clan guessing, Tarris had held his tongue.

What happened? Tarris asked the question for the third time since he'd materialized in the Oracle's small cottage. The home was located on the large Ursine holdings and was surrounded by more protections and spells than most Weres knew. No one approached that the Oracle didn't know. And only two could breach his protections, Tarris and the *Amar*. Tarris because he'd learned the old man's magic inside and out and had found the holes in it and Mark because, as *Amar*, he was inherently exempt. An *Amar* could afford no places in his clan he could not go or control.

"Near as I can tell your little human turned the tables on you," the solemn look was belied by the faint laugh present in the Oracle's voice.

No kidding, Tarris snorted impatiently. *How?*

"Calm yourself for a minute and you'll figure it out. You're a bright boy." The Oracle looked away from him to pour a cup of tea.

I was still linked to her when I fell asleep, Tarris realized. He felt more than a bit foolish. He'd not had the heart to let go of Callista completely and had sunk into a satisfied sleep while still connected to her. In truth, he needed the connection, needed it desperately. He'd become increasingly aware of a dull, empty ache inside him whenever he was separated from his redheaded siren. A dull, empty ache that drew his attention from whatever he was doing and back to how much he needed to be with her. No matter how sated his appetite was, his entire body seemed to call out for her and a certain part that had never troubled him in the waking world — a specific part of him that in the past only rose to full attention in his dreams — was exceedingly vociferous.

As much as he needed to feel her with him, he'd panicked upon waking and come straight to the one person who didn't flinch from discussing his people with him. He'd come straight to the one person who always seemed to understand his pain and stress. The one person he constantly ran to as a boy and a man, when the strain of playing peacemaker between Mark and Luke grew too much. The Oracle.

"Yes, that would be my best guess too," the old man nodded. "But you, boy, have a bigger problem."

Tarris frowned, *What?*

"The rules, Tarris. How many of them have you broken now?" The eyes were wickedly sharp and pierced through him.

Three. Tarris rubbed the back of his neck with a tired hand. He could feel Callista, couldn't help but reach for her with a part of his being. She was confused and hurt. Not to mention more than a little angry. That didn't bode well.

"Four," the Oracle picked up his cup and sipped.

Blond brows came together over the blue eyes. *Three,* he insisted.

"Four," the Oracle repeated and ticked off each violation on his fingers. "You've allowed yourself to receive pleasure. You've touched without permission..." Tarris started to interrupt but a sharp look from the older man stopped him. "You've fed alone and you've hunted."

Now he knew why Mark often bemoaned the annoying nature of telepaths. The old man had no telepathic abilities but had learned long ago to read the subtle signs of change in the young incubus. It had been he, after all, who had divined the rules that kept Tarris safe. Or had.

Four, Tarris conceded. *Do you allow anyone privacy old man? Have you been watching me?*

"Don't be foolish," the Oracle leaned back in his chair, sipped again and sighed contentedly. "Of course I have been watching you." At Tarris' indignant glare the old man actually chuckled. "I'm an oracle, boy. You know, all knowing, all seeing, yadda-yadda-yadda and so forth," he waved his hand impatiently. "That's what oracles do. We watch. We are the busybodies of the Universe."

The incubus' angry silence did nothing to rattle the serenity of the Oracle's demeanor. "You're walking a dangerous line, Tarris. We've never been completely sure that these precautions would work at all. If you keep flaunting them, you may just destroy yourself."

What am I supposed to do? Just walk away from her? Give her up? The very idea of turning away from Callista bored a hole inside him that burned like fire. He couldn't let her go. She was in his head even now, inside him and linked to him in a way he didn't understand. It had never happened before with any female he'd known. Of course they'd always belonged to someone else. Callista Marshall belonged to him.

"Interesting," the Oracle muttered and looked off over Tarris' shoulder. "Very interesting."

What is interesting?

"What is interesting is that you don't speak of feeding. You didn't say, "What am I supposed to do? Starve?" You spoke about her. Giving *her* up." The wrinkled face was still turned aside, watching out the window.

That's what's very interesting? Tarris shifted uncomfortably. The old man didn't miss anything.

"No, that's what's interesting. What's *very* interesting is that Luke and the *Amar* are coming across the grounds at a run. Oh wait, Luke has stopped him. They're arguing. Pointing at this house… Yes, I'd say this is definitely about you."

Tarris rose and turned toward the window. The twins were having a heated conversation that came to an abrupt halt when Mark resumed his pace toward the Oracle's house. *I think it's time…*

"That you were going? Yes, I agree." The Oracle rose. "Stay out of the way a bit. Let me talk to them. This is fear. They love you."

I know they do, Tarris fixed a destination in his mind and began to dissolve. *That's why they're afraid.*

* * * * *

"So, Tarris is an incubus. What does that make Mark?" Callie tossed the words at Sarah as she closed the door behind her. Her friend had come rushing over after Callie had told her on the phone she knew about Tarris and needed to talk to her.

"Calm down, Callie. The first thing to remember is that Tarris would never hurt you. He wouldn't hurt anyone. I know him. It's not in him no matter what anyone may say," Sarah sank onto the old overstuffed couch. The sight was so familiar to her it caused the loneliness of the last two years to swell in Callie's chest. She and Sarah had been nearly inseparable through their early twenties. Even after college, at least twice a week they could be found curled up on this sofa laughing, sipping wine, weeping at the latest romantic movie or drooling over its hero. Hell, Sarah'd held her hair the first time she'd had imbibed too much their freshman year and she had made sure Sarah didn't fall on her ass when she'd gotten tipsy while wearing the four inch heels she'd though made her look slimmer. They'd only made her fall down, a lot. Looking at her friend now, the only thing Callie felt was lonely and betrayed.

"I repeat Sarah, what does this make Mark? Is he an incubus too?" Callie leaned her forearms on the back of the Queen Anne chair opposite the couch.

"No," Sarah looked down at her hands. "Tarris is the only one of his kind that I know. Fully grown incubi aren't exactly welcome to dinner at our house. As to Mark, you're not going to find this easy to believe…"

"Are you kidding?" Callie's voice shot up an octave. "I've just spent the last several nights being visited by an incubus, one I find out one of my dearest friends knows well. Yesterday some weirdo gives me a book about creepy, monster creatures. Then after one hell of a dream…" she paused and swallowed hard as her body started to react to the memory of her night with Tarris, "I wake up and literally find the man of my dreams in my bed. But we're not done. Then I get pulled into a dream that gives me a damn good look at your husband as a young man and something called a hunter while some little kid dies in my arms. I wake up and watch my own personal incubus dissolve into a shower of gold light. What the hell could you possibly tell me that I wouldn't believe?"

Sarah grimaced and let out the breath she'd been holding. "Riiight. Cal, you can't tell anyone what you know. First of all you must understand that. It's the reason I didn't tell you or my family any of this in the first place. I won't risk Mark, my children or my new family for anyone. If you can't handle this, walk away and keep your mouth shut. I'll do my best to make Mark believe you'll keep the secret."

"Do your best?" Callie felt a wave of apprehension slide over her. "And what would he do if I refuse to keep this a secret?"

"Let's cross that bridge when we come to it. Come sit here." Sarah refused to meet her eye but waited until Callie had joined her on the sofa. She drew a small frame from her bag and held it almost reverently in her hands. "Cal, Mark and his family are Weres, shapeshifters. They can transform into bears." The blonde shook her head. "It's more than that. On a very basic level they are bears.

"Here, this is a portrait of Mark. Tarris painted this when he was still a boy. It was a gift for Giselle, Luke and Mark's grandmother. In her heart she was Tarris' grandmother too." She held out the miniature for Callie to examine. "She left it to me when she died just a few months after her mate. She missed him so much I think she was almost relieved when her time came."

Callista took the frame in her hands and looked at the image. At first it was hard to understand what she was seeing. It was beautiful in a horrible, terrifying way. The image was so small, so delicately created. It wasn't a picture of the Mark she'd seen at the wedding or the handful of times she'd met them for dinner. Or it wasn't completely Mark. One half of the face was human but the other half morphed into that of a large brown bear. Callie felt her hands start to shake. "Tarris painted this?" She had no idea why it was important but it was the only coherent thought she could articulate at the moment.

"Yes, Cal. Tarris is quite a gifted artist. He paints wonderfully but Mark says he's also a wonderful sculptor, that he was at his happiest covered in clay and creating. Only he doesn't do it anymore. He doesn't paint. He doesn't do any of it anymore." Sarah's voice was heavy with her sadness. "He was taking lessons with the youngest of the boys for a while. Mark said the boy was also talented and that it was one of the things that Tarris and Jonas shared only with each other. The last thing Tarris had been working on was a bust of Jonas. He destroyed it the night the boy died."

Of course he did, Callie thought. He blamed himself for the boy's death. Tarris stopped creating when Jonas died. It was his penance. The wholeness of what Sarah was saying to her began to overwhelm her. No matter how hard her rational mind struggled, she couldn't make herself believe that what she was hearing was anything but the truth.

Several seconds ticked by. Sarah reached over and took Callie's hands in hers. "Cal, do you hear me? Do you understand this? It's real. Tarris is an incubus, not a monster but not human. Mark Ursine, my husband and the father of my children, is a Bear. A full grown, growling, padding on four paws Bear."

A half choked hysterical laugh bubbled out of Callie as she pushed herself off the couch and stepped away from

Sarah. "Mark *Ursine* is a Bear. Of course he is. What else would he be?" Suddenly she couldn't stop laughing. It wasn't the joyful kind of laugh that lifted your spirits and sent endorphins rushing through your body but the angry painful laughter that hurt your chest and made your stomach turn. The kind of laughter you just wanted to stop but no part of you seemed in control enough until the laughing turned to tears.

Sarah rose and wrapped her arms around Callie's shoulders as she led her to the couch. Dropping down onto the soft sofa, she let Sarah pull her over so their heads touched. Her friend kept a soft soothing rhythm as she rocked Callie and rubbed her shoulder. "It's a lot, I know."

"A lot?" Callie choked out between the tears. "A lot?"

"I know how you feel," Sarah began.

"No you don't." Callie shook her head and tried to pull away.

Sarah's hands grabbed her shoulders, gentleness gone and shook her slightly. "Yes. I. Do." The misty green-gray eyes were filled with compassion and with not a little bit of pain. "If anyone knows how you're feeling, Callie, it would be me."

Callie sniffed loudly and tried to nod. She was right. If anyone understood what it was like to find out the man in your life wasn't really the *man* in your life, it was Sarah. "So you're in love with a Bear?"

"Yes," Sarah's smile turned gentle. "I am. And my Bear loves me too." She patted Callie's cheek and pushed away the strands of red that clung to the wet skin. "And my boys will one day be Bears as well. My life isn't what I thought it would be, Callie, but it's wonderful. You just have to be able to see past what we've been told, what we've believed to be impossible."

A loud, staccato clapping sound came from the doorway that led to the back of the house. Both women gasped as they turned in their seats to see two men standing there. One man was tall with dark hair and hazel eyes. He was holding a gun that was pointed way from them but held in front of him so as to be all too visible. The other, the one clapping, Callie recognized. His auburn hair was pulled back from his face as it had been the day in the café. His gray eyes watched her with a jarring cold amusement. She felt Sarah stiffen at her side and heard her sharp intake of breath.

"How did you get in here?" Callie demanded as she rose to her feet.

"Ground level windows, Ms. Marshall. You really should have an alarm system," his eyes flickered to the white panel by the door. "Or at least remember to arm it when you're at home."

Sarah rose and stepped in front of her. Callie glanced at her and saw the telltale sign of nervousness as she twisted the gold bangle on her wrist. But no other sign of fear or anxiety was visible. Callie was impressed. But the anger in her friend's voice was far less contained than any other emotion. "Leave her out of this." Sarah stepped toward them. "She's one of those innocents you purport to protect with your barbarism. Leave her alone and I'll go with you quietly."

"You flatter yourself, woman." The redheaded man ground out, his lips twisting into a bitter snarl. "I have no interest in you. You've chosen your own destruction. I don't hunt Weres and their whores."

Swallowing hard, her face furious, Sarah spit her words back at him. "Then what do you want?"

"He wants me," Callie whispered. She'd barely let her gaze flicker from the man's face. "He's the one who gave me the book."

"What book?" Sarah demanded.

"The one that should have served as a warning. But we both know it was unheeded." His face relaxed as he spoke until he finally smiled. It was as if he suddenly knew something she didn't. Something he found greatly humorous.

"I told you on the phone about the guy who stopped me in the café, this is him." Callie looked the man over. The other one held the gun but it was clear who was the bigger threat. "Stanton... Adam Stanton," she lifted her chin and drew in a deep breath. "That's your name. Why are you so interested in my life, Mr. Stanton?"

"I'm trying to save your life," his words were smooth and were framed in a calm detachment. "Barring that, I intend to make sure you are the last victim. The pet incubus has finally come hunting, my sweet, and this time the prey is ready to turn the tables."

"God do you know how stupid that sounds? I think someone has seen too many Buffy episodes." Sarah's hand shot out and grabbed her wrist. She didn't need the warning. She knew better than to even breathe the name of the man it was now so clear they'd come to destroy. Stanton shifted, pushing away from the doorframe he'd been leaning on and the movement swung a glint of silver and gold into view. A gold and silver sun. A cold sweat started to form in the center of Callie's back and threatened to drip down her spine. She'd seen that symbol before, seen it on the chest of the man who had shot the child in her dream. If their kind would kill a child, they would certainly kill her. And Tarris.

"Let's get going," the taller man grumbled irritably. "Talking is a waste of time and stupid. Her mate or one of his goons could be here any minute." He rubbed at the back of his head as if soothing an old but not forgotten wound. "Believe me, Stanton, the last thing you want is to go up against the Bears. They'll chew your throat open and I won't hang around to say I told you so."

"I'm in charge, Morrissey, don't you forget that. You're still treading dangerous ground where the council is concerned." Stanton glared at his companion.

"Morrissey?" Sarah breathed the word. "Jack Morrissey?"

Neither man spoke but Stanton watched the other man, eyeing him critically as if waiting for something. Sarah spoke again, "Jack, if my husband or Luke find out you were part of this…" she let her voice trail off.

"Shut up, woman" Stanton took a quick step toward Sarah his hand lifting as if he'd strike her. Everyone, Stanton included was stunned when Jack put himself between the women and his fellow hunter.

"No," the steel of his voice scraped at Callie's ears. "You will not touch her. We protect humans, we don't harm them."

Stanton recovered quickly. "Who said I was going to harm a hair on her animal loving little head?" He turned his gaze to Callie. "Come along now, Ms. Marshall. The four of us are going to take a ride."

Before she could respond the other hunter shook his head. "Mrs. Ursine stays put. I won't let you risk my sister for your vendetta. An incubus I'll hunt with you. An incubus I'll kill. They have no soul. But the Bears we leave alone."

"Your sister chose her path," Stanton reminded him, his mask almost slipping as the volume of his voice rose. "She deserves to die."

Jack ignored him and turned to face the women. "She was supposed to be alone." He spoke the words to Sarah. "If I'd known you would be here, I'd not have come. I keep my word, Mrs. Ursine. Tell your husband and my sister's mate that. There is no need for her to pay for what has happened. You're free to leave."

Callie's head spun. This man's sister was married — no, mated — to one of the Bears? She'd accepted all of this as reality hours before but the reminders of how real it all was just kept coming.

"Mr. Morrissey, Luke loves your sister. He'd never harm her. He'd die before he let anyone else, including his brother, hurt her in any way." Sarah frowned at the man. "Surely you know that. You saw how hard he fought for her life when you accidentally shot her. You've seen how being with him has healed her. Luke loves her."

Callie saw no give on the man's face, no measure given or taken. She saw only a flush of embarrassment and regret, no doubt at the reminder he'd shot his sister. It was clear he didn't believe Sarah and his worry that his sister would pay for his involvement was so powerful it swirled about him in such a way Callie fancied she could almost see it as a mist, a glow about his body.

"Look, I don't give a damn what she tells her *mate*," Stanton spat the word as if it tasted vile upon his tongue. His eyes locked on Callie's. "Let's go, Ms. Marshall. I made no promise not to hurt your little friend here. Frankly, I don't give a shit about making the big, bad Bears mad nor do I care if they end up killing Mr. I-Keep-My-Word here's sister because they are pissed. I care about one thing and one thing only."

He stepped forward and grabbed her wrist. "I care about killing one nasty little monster and I care about doing it as quickly as possible." He leaned down over her, his face so close his nose almost touched hers. "I only need you alive long enough to act as bait. Beyond that you are at my grace and leisure and I will kill you if you push me too far. Are we clear?" When she didn't answer him but stared defiantly back up into his face, he roared the words at her, his hot breath stealing her air as his voice slammed into her eardrums. "Are we clear?"

"Yes," she clenched her hands into tight fists. She'd be damned if she'd let him see her afraid. She felt something then, a feather light touch in her mind that grew to an insistent push. She pushed back, not quite knowing how but she pushed.

"Impressive," Stanton drew back, keeping his hold on her arm. "I'm no longer sure this little shielding of yours is the work of our incubus. It's too deeply rooted too strong. I'd say a search of your ancestry would be quite intriguing, Ms. Marshall."

Tugging her arm, he dragged her to the doorway that led to her back hall. "Now be a good girl. You wouldn't want my friend here to have to shoot anyone who tried to be a hero, now would you?" Callie shook her head. Stanton opened the door and paused. "Oh, Mrs. Ursine, since we are leaving you alive, would you be so good as to grant me a favor? You will tell your little incubus that I have his latest toy. If he wants her, he'll have to come and get her." Sarah gave no indication she had heard but stared straight ahead. She didn't even look at Callie as she was pulled through the door. It snapped closed and she was propelled down the stairs on the back of the house and into a waiting van. It was broad daylight, the middle of the day. And yet no one seemed to see anything. No one looked out their window or stepped out into their backyards. It wasn't until she was dumped unceremoniously into the back of the van that she began to shake. As Stanton began to secure her hands with a set of dark metal cuffs, she let the first tear of fear escape.

His finger beneath her chin lifted her gaze to his. She was stunned to see how gentle it was. "Don't worry, Callie. I'm not going to hurt you."

"Then why did you threaten the people I care about? Why are you cuffing me?" God, she hoped it wasn't some sex game. Tarris had tied her hands or restricted them more than once and it had made her wet and hungry for his touch. But the last thing she wanted was to be helpless before this man.

"I have to restrain you, dear. You're not thinking right. I don't want you to do something that will make my friend up there, or me, have to harm you. I don't want to hurt you or anyone else. All that bluster back there, it was for your friend's benefit. She's mixed up with some bad creatures, Callie. It's too late to help her but I can still save you."

She opened her mouth to tell him she didn't need saving but he shh'd her softly. His hand caressed the skin of her cheek tenderly. The cold gray eyes were soft and welcoming. "I know it doesn't seem like it now. That's his hold on you working, sweet one. We'll break it. Don't worry. When he's dead, then you'll understand just how much he's hurt you."

Then gently, so very softly and tenderly, he brushed her lips with his. He leaned in, his forehead against hers, as his hand slid to cup the back of her head. "When this is all over know I won't hold you any blame, sweetest. Know you'll find only understanding and acceptance with me. I will wipe away what this monster has done to you. You'll see, Callie. You'll see."

He kissed her again, more intently, before pulling away and buckling her into her seat. "I'll take care of you, Callie. I'll take care of everything."

Chapter Five

Tarris paced his room. It was the first place the Bears would have looked for him and it wasn't likely they would be back for a second check soon. Besides under normal circumstances they'd expect him to be able to hear them before they arrived. Luke tended to broadcast so loudly that he could be heard across the compound when he was agitated. And the more intimate connection he had shared with the brothers until their mating had made his brain hypersensitive to them. He should have plenty of warning they were coming.

Normal circumstances. Things were far from normal. Stopping his movement, Tarris leaned against the back of a chair and rubbed his hands over his face. The confusing torrent of emotions and thoughts that raged through him were almost entirely his own. And that was the problem. His thoughts had never been this quiet. He could hear Mark and Sarah's twin sons, Nicky and Jake, down the hall arguing over nap time with their nanny. He could even hear the woman's tired thoughts that Sarah's human ideas of discipline might be fine for a human child but they were not so effective when the youngsters in question were also small bear cubs. He had faint impressions of the two Bears Mark had assigned to Sarah for safety and Callista's jumbled emotions were a faint echo in his mind. But that was it.

He hadn't heard Luke as they came across the lawn to the Oracle's home. Mark could still his thoughts and be calm, becoming a peaceful oasis in Tarris' mind but not Luke. He should have heard the younger twin's thoughts shouting at them from the house if his face had been any measure of his anger. And he should have felt them both as they grew closer. The Oracle definitely shouldn't have known before him that they were coming. It had been slipping away for some time now, this connection, no matter how badly he wanted to deny it. He was slowly losing the sense of them in his mind and in his heart. He'd excused it initially, passing it off to the matings as first Mark, then Luke, faded from him. As the two people who had been closer to him than any his entire life slipped away. Now, he hated to admit it they were no stronger in him than anyone else.

And it would have made sense except for one thing. Everything else was graying for him as well. He couldn't read Callista as he should have been able to. Sarah had surprised him on one or two occasions lately when he'd been deep in thought. That should never have happened. Luke's mate Anna was one thing as she had some training as a daughter of the hunters but not Sarah. She was as unspoiled a human as you could find. And as a human she should have no shielding from him. She was, by all rights, prey.

Tarris closed his eyes and reached out for Sarah. She wasn't in the house. He frowned. Why was Sarah not here when Levi and Laban were? The two were charged with her safety and they took that charge seriously. And they'd damn well better because if anything happened to her Mark was the least of their worries. He and Luke would kill them before Mark got to them. You did not mess with Sarah Ursine. There was something vulnerable and completely beguiling about her, something he also saw in Callista. It was their untainted humanity. Anna could defend herself. She was an even match for most of them now that her mating to Luke had healed her. Tarris held no doubts any member of the family would kill or die to protect Anna but Sarah... All the gods and divinities in existence couldn't protect the person who hurt her.

Tarris pushed outward trying to find her. When he did, the fear, anger and hatred that he found in her shocked him. What had she gotten herself into? Focusing on her he shifted himself through space as if walking through a door that only he could see. The folds of the space-time continuum opened for him until he could see the glowing golden door that was his destination. Walking through it, he found himself in Callista's living room. It was empty except for Sarah who was sitting on the arm of a chair. Her hands covered her face and she was shaking.

He crossed to her quickly. *Sarah?* His mind reached out to hers, catching it with his mental caress. She turned just as he opened his arms to enfold her. He could hear both their hearts beating wildly.

Where is Callista? Why are you here? Why are you upset? Why is Callista afraid? What the hell has happened? These and a dozen other thoughts ripped from his mind before he could stop them.

The projected thoughts slammed at the young woman before him and he felt her jerk in his arms. He tightened his grip as much to stop himself from shaking her and demanding answers to the questions he'd been unable to hold back, as to hold her upright. Her hands came up against his chest and pushed him back.

"The hunters," she gulped the words. "Tarris, calm down, I can't think." There was a glazed look in her eyes that told him she was close to being overwhelmed. He took a deep breath and forced himself to calm down. He was projecting more than his spinning thoughts. He was bombarding her with his emotions as well. Being a telepath and an empath worked both ways. He'd had to learn hard lessons as a boy about retaining control so he didn't send without thinking.

Callista is afraid, Sarah. You're afraid. What's happened?

"You don't know?" she stared at him in astonishment. "You can't read it from Callista's mind? Or mine?"

Clamping his jaw down tightly and trying to suppress the frustration and irritation at her delay, Tarris shook his head. *I can't see it clearly, Sarah. I can't reach Callista and you're thinking too many things at once.*

"That's happened before," Sarah was watching him with an expression that would have concerned him if he weren't already so damn busy being worried about Callista.

Sarah...

"The day I talked to you first about Callie. You couldn't read my thoughts clearly then either. Since when can't you read my thoughts better than I can, Tarris?" The suspicion that filled her voice stabbed at him harshly.

Sarah, I don't have time for this. He told himself to relax. He was only heightening her anxiety. He was the one who was supposed to give peace, to bring comfort. He'd done it so often his entire life. It was ingrained in him. He was the peacemaker, he was the mediator and it was he who diffused situations. He swallowed hard and tried to give Sarah a reassuring half smile. *What's happened?*

But the young woman who had never shown any fear of him before pushed him away hard and stepped back. "Tarris? Your teeth. Tarris what's happened to your teeth?"

He lifted his hand to his lips and felt the sharp points that hung down lower than the rest of his teeth. His incisors had started to grow. He'd never let them manifest their length except when he had intentionally frightened the man, Stanton, last night and when he'd shown his true self to Callista. As a rule he'd never let them show, he wasn't letting them show now. They were just there.

And last night. Last night he'd intentionally used his powers on a human. He'd intentionally seduced and then frightened the man. Because of his jealousy. Because of his need to claim the woman, to claim Callista as his. Oh God, was this it? Was this finally what he'd feared his entire life? He tried to think, to catalogue what was happening while struggling to control the desire to grab Sarah and force her to answer his questions. Callista was his. She was in trouble, he knew it and yet this woman was stalling. She was keeping him from her. For one terrifying fraction of a second it didn't matter that this was sweet Sarah. She was in his way.

"Tarris?" Her voice stopped the flash of fury that had started to broil in his chest. He met her eyes and saw the pity and the fear that blended in their foggy green depths. "Is it…" she couldn't even make herself finish the thought that was screaming from inside her mind and pounding at the inside of his own. It was happening. He'd broken the rules and now it was happening.

I don't know. And he didn't. The shadow of transformation he'd felt when he was younger, before anyone realized his feeding needs had changed, had been only a burning hunger and the pains of starvation. Other than a darkening of his skin and a shift of his eyes from their normal blue to red, nothing about him had changed. *Sarah, I have to find Callista. I have to find her.*

He could hear most of Sarah's thoughts and she knew he could. He felt her deliberately sift through what she knew of him, her fear he would hurt her and her fear the hunters would hurt his beloved. He now knew everything he needed to know. Stanton had taken Callista. He even knew where he'd taken her even though Sarah didn't know that she knew. He could almost hear Stanton's voice inside Sarah's memory. "You will tell your little incubus that I have his latest toy. If he wants her, he'll have to come and get her."

Tell Mark I'll meet him as soon as I'm done. I'll find Callista and then once I know she's safe, I'll find him and Luke. Tarris started to focus his mind on his destination. "Come and get her." He not only expected Tarris to know where she was but wanted him to know. The arrogant fool had taken her to his house.

"Tarris?" Sarah seemed to thrust aside her hesitation and stepped toward him.

Just tell him Sarah. Tell him I won't run. I'm still in control of myself. I won't run. He closed his eyes and saw the path to the hunter's door. He may not survive the day but he damn sure would make certain that his darling one was safe from that asshole before it was over. The step he took toward Sarah, who was grabbing for her cell phone, moved him not in her direction but across the barrier he knew so well and into the last moments he would have with Callista.

* * * * *

Sarah knew she'd been taken. Sarah would tell her big bad Were-Bear husband and they'd come and get her. Just as long as Sarah didn't tell Tarris. *Surely Sarah's smart enough to know she'd be sending him straight into the jaws of the trap*, Callie worried. Stanton had called her bait and that was exactly what she felt like at the moment. A worm, skewered on a hook, dangling in the water and waiting for the fish to bite. She wasn't afraid as much as annoyed. Stanton had attached the dark metal cuffs to a metal hook hanging from the ceiling. She'd nearly fainted when he and that big baboon had pushed her down the stairs into the basement. And when they had opened the door to this strange little room and she'd seen the chain hanging there it had taken both of them to lift her and carry her into place. She honestly couldn't say she was sure this wasn't sexual. Stanton's breathing had certainly gotten shallower as he'd fastened the ring on the cuffs to the hook. And she was positive he'd touched more than was necessary as he adjusted her footing, saying he wanted her to be as comfortable as possible. Yeah, rubbing her crotch was definitely not part of helping her be more comfortable.

Before she'd met Tarris such an incident would have left her humiliated instead of angry. Then again, before Tarris had begun whispering to her of her beauty and desirability, she probably would have convinced herself she was imagining things. But she was absolutely sure she wasn't. Heavy breathing and the kiss in the van aside, there had been no mistaking the feel of the man's hard cock against her ass as he'd stood behind her to fasten the restraints.

The metal on her wrists was cold and just starting to chafe. Even if they were dreams, Tarris had only used soft things like scarves and the vines to tie her hands in place. It had been incredibly erotic. Maybe they should try something a bit more serious. The flicker of the image of being chained up in a spooky little dungeon room with Tarris in black leather and playing the Dom role sent a shiver through her body. Damn that could be fun. Maybe once this was over she should tie him up. Then maybe she'd get that lovely instrument of his exactly where she wanted it. His avoidance of taking her pussy was driving her to distraction.

Damn! She had to stop this train of thought too much drifting in that direction could make her wetter than hell. Tarris didn't put her here, she reminded herself. That deluded asshole Stanton had. And while that was a nice bod and a handsome face, crazy was never going to part her from her panties.

Callie opened and closed her jaw. Her cheek hurt from where Stanton had struck her as she fought them. He'd later apologized and again told her how it was all necessary. Told her she wasn't in her right mind. Told her that he'd forgive her when it was all over, when she finally understood what was happening. The scary part was that for a few minutes there in the van, until they'd dragged her through the garage and into this room, she'd almost begun to think she must be crazy. Shapeshifters, incubi, men with guns and chains who hunted creatures that her brain still tried to convince her couldn't really exist? Maybe this was all some bizarre dream or worse. But her heart was outraged by the idea. Tarris was no dream, no symptom of insanity. He was real. She'd touched him. She knew him. Even more, though it seemed impossible, she loved him. And she had loved him almost from the first when she'd believed him the subconscious manifestation of everything she'd wanted in a man. Even when he'd just been a dream, she'd loved him.

And if he loved her, if he came for her, he'd die. Or that's what Stanton had said. He's told her that incubi became obsessive about their prey. He'd called her prey.

Stanton said that Tarris would do anything to get her back, that incubi had been known to kill the husband or lover of the woman on whom they'd fixated. Or they had called in the more dangerous succubae to keep them away from their targets. Succubae didn't just take a man's mind, they actually stole the life force so they could reproduce. He told her that Tarris had already come to him in a dream and threatened him. All of this, he recited calmly as if it were conclusive proof of the inhumanity of the one creature who to her seemed more humane than most people she met.

And this crazed hunter was going to kill him. Looking around she couldn't see how. She knew from her dream, the dream in which she had been Tarris, that they couldn't kill him with the gun the large hunter Jack carried. Stanton didn't even seem to have a weapon. But he'd been so sure that he could kill Tarris. She didn't see how. If he could do that invisible, golden sparkly thing of his, he could surely get in and out without a problem.

The room she was in was about the size of the Special Collections room at the library which meant it couldn't be much over ten feet by fifteen feet. The hook that secured her hands over her head was at one end of the room. It had a small amount of give and if she pulled down on it she could lean back enough to feel the cold of the wall behind her. From what little she remembered of the outside of the room as she'd struggled against her captors, it had looked like a large closet. Inside it looked more like a walk-in freezer you'd see in restaurant kitchens. There were three vents on one side of the room blowing cool air and two large narrow ones just inside the door. These larger ones ran the entire width of the room and the one closest to the door was pouring cold air. The force of the blower acted almost as a shield of air, keeping cool air in and cold air out even when the heavy metal door was open.

The temperature was cold. Callie watched the digital display over the door as it flashed the number thirty. She'd not been in here long enough yet for it to hurt her and she hoped the men didn't plan on leaving her here long enough for it to. Her hands and feet were freezing. Stanton had released her wrists long enough to thrust her arms into a down filled jacket. But her struggles forced him to leave the zipper open. Her body was standing in the direct line of one of the smaller vents and the gooseflesh had begun to form on her neck. Worst of all was the fact that the overhead restraint was forcing her chest out while pushing the jacket back, allowing the frigid air to strike directly against her breasts. They ached slightly and her nipples were rock hard. Each movement of her shoulders, each fidget of her body, rubbed them along the inside of her t-shirt. She'd not planned to be trussed up like a Thanksgiving turkey and strung up like 'gator bait this morning when she'd thrown on her yoga pants and the 10,000 Maniacs t-shirt she'd had since high school. The jerk hadn't even let her grab shoes.

Yes, it was cold and she knew from her dream the cold affected him but she still didn't see how this bit of a chill could hurt him. Still, as romantic as the idea of his flashing in and rescuing her was, Stanton seemed so smug that she would rather not risk it. Again, she hoped Sarah was smart enough not to tell Tarris. If he knew, he'd come for her. There was not a doubt in her mind. Nor in Stanton's it seemed.

She saw the golden shimmer a second before she saw him take shape before her. His scent struck her nostrils as his beauty flared in her eyes. She had to admit she'd been eager for this moment in a way, she'd just imagined it happening a lot differently. She thought the first time they'd actually be face to face and fully awake would be more exciting for good reasons. She'd imagined he'd move toward her with that lovely predator's lope and sweep her into his arms. Her mind had always likened him to a lion and he never looked more like one than he did now. His expression fierce, his eyes blazing and his hair caught by the cold current, he was more beautiful in the flesh than he'd ever been in her dreams. And then, as he became fully solid in her presence, he gasped, doubling over as a shudder racked his body.

"Tarris," the word came out as a worried whisper. He straightened up, a pained expression on his face. His movements were less than graceful as he closed the few steps between them. When he reached up to unfasten her restraints his hands were trembling.

Damn!

The cold hit like a sledge hammer to the gut. His breath was ripped from his lungs and his body screamed in pain. He'd not expected the cold. He should have, fool that he was. He hadn't realized he was walking into a freezer. Still he should have known this wouldn't be easy. Stanton wasn't stupid. If he'd been prepared he would have entered more slowly. As a child he'd been easily devastated by even the slightest chill. Though it had been mid-October, the night Jonas died was the coldest in his memory and not just because a piece of his heart had seemed to freeze. If he had a heart. Most of his life he'd believed he didn't, had believed he didn't have the capacity to love as he saw those around him. But the strange new feelings moving through him where Callista was concerned…well, maybe they weren't love but they seemed pretty close to what he knew of the emotion.

The cold pushed all other thoughts away. He could be in these temperatures for brief periods of time if he was prepared for them. He'd done it before, like the night he'd stopped Luke and Mark from tearing each other apart over Mark's challenge to become *Amar*. He'd manifested outside in late February. There'd been snow on the ground and he'd actually been without a shirt. But he'd known it was coming. Had held his breath and stepped slowly through the dimensional doorway. His slowness that night had cost Sarah and their grandmother Giselle a scare and Luke a nasty scratch on his back that had pained him for several days before his rapid healing had eliminated any trace of it. Unlike the hole from the silver bullet he'd earned trying to save his mother that long ago night of death that had claimed one and almost two, of the woman's sons. That scar Luke would carry for life.

Tarris met Callista's frightened jade green eyes and gave her a small nod that he hoped she took as reassurance. The cold was pulling even more of his ability to read what was happening from his mind. He forced his fingers to work and unfastened the cuffs from the chain that kept her suspended. It was lead. He tried to pull the cuffs from her but his strength was slipping pretty fast. He managed to pop the link on the chain that held them together leaving her with two thick, unstylish iron bracelets. Iron and lead? Surely Stanton wasn't such a fool he thought the metals would stop him. He wasn't fey to be burned by iron or angelus, the über beautiful winged creatures humans mistook for divine beings that could be easily poisoned by lead. For the record, there was nothing divine about the haughty pains in the ass. They were the other half of the incubi. The lore had followed them into this world and woven itself into the fabric of many cultures. When the children of Lilith had been torn in half upon entering this dimension, it had created the angelus and the incubus.

Tarris shook his head. His mind seemed to be floating incoherently from thought to thought. He needed to focus, not let his mind ping about like a bb pellet in a metal shed. Her hands free, Callie wrapped her arms around his neck and held him tightly. The heat from her body was welcome and he pulled her close, feeling slightly guilty when he turned her so she blocked most of the direct air blowing at them from the side vent. Pulling away gently he brushed the tears that had started to over flow her eyes and placed his hand on her lips when they opened to speak.

Don't say it. Think it, loudly.

He watched her brow furrow. He heard nothing. His empathy was still working and he knew she was trying hard to "think at him" but the cold had turned the soft whisper of her voice into silence. He couldn't hear her at all. He shook his head. *I can't hear you. You'll have to whisper. Softly, Callista, very softly.*

"Stanton, he's outside the door. He's not alone, he has someone else with him. The guy has a gun." Her voice was faint, barely audible over the blowing of the vent fans.

He nodded. I can't shift us out of here, he explained quickly. *The cold is draining me fast. We'll have to use the door and we'll have to hurry. Stay behind me.*

"No," she shook her head, her eyes darting to the empty window in the door. "If you're too weak to do the shifting thing, then you could be shot. Put me in front. A shield. They won't shoot if I'm in front."

Tarris reached for the minds of the men outside the door. He heard the one musing over his sister's safety. Anna's brother, Jack. That was interesting but not particularly helpful. He'd already shot at Tarris once and failed. Did he realize this time it might work? Would he risk Callista? Tarris didn't think so. But he knew without searching Adam Stanton's mind that he would. In his arrogance he'd be sure he could save her in time, or he'd consider her a casualty of war.

No. Behind me. Just do it, Callista. He frowned harshly at her when he saw her open her mouth to object. Glaring at him, she nodded. *It will only take a moment and I'll be able to get both of us out of here. But if it looks like they're going to shoot, my love, drop to the ground.* He saw awareness flicker in her eyes and knew she was thinking of how the bullet had passed through him in the memory he'd shared with her.

Callie tucked behind him, Tarris started toward the door. They reached the line of horizontal vents and Tarris was dreading passing under the powerful curtain of frigid air. But before they reached it he heard a slight click and then icy fire began to rain down on him.

From the first vent poured a shower of carbon dioxide pellets, or dry ice. He couldn't stop the scream that roared out of him as the small cylindrical bits of hell struck his head and slid down the collar of his shirt. He jerked backwards, knocking Callista to the ground as he frantically brushed the glacial nodules from his hair. Everywhere they touched felt like hot metal searing into his flesh. Several bits slid down the opening of his shirt and were burning like coals against the skin they touched. He heard the vents roar to life around him and the air inside began to drop in temperature dramatically. He fell to his knees and tried to pull the shirt from his body.

Small hands were suddenly there pushing his away and tugging at the front, ripping the buttons away and dragging the shirt from him. The pellets fell away and the fire stopped, leaving trails of angry welts that ended with blisters where the pellets had rested against his skin for even a few seconds on his chest, neck, back and arms. His body shuddered violently and he felt as if his skin were turning to ice.

"Oh God, oh God," he heard her voice as he felt the fabric of the jacket she'd been wearing wrap around him. He didn't fight her when she pulled him against her and began to rub his skin. The friction sent waves of pain shooting through him but the warmth of her touch and the heat she was generating were too needed for him to complain.

A second click sounded and a voice he'd learned to hate filled the room. "Nice try, incubus. You didn't really think I'd just let you walk out of here, did you?"

He turned his head enough to see the face of the red-headed man in the window of the door. His voice was coming over an intercom and the triumph was obvious. "You took the bait and sprang the trap. Now all I have to do is wait. And we both know who will win that little contest, don't we?"

"Stop this. You're killing him." Callie's voice was filled with a fury that would have made him hesitate had it been directed at him. He felt her arms under his as she tried to get him to stand. Didn't she understand? He couldn't. The temperature was dropping fast and the shower of dry ice had shocked his system so much he couldn't fight it. Hell he could barely think as the frigid air bombarded him.

"That is rather the point, my darling," Stanton cooed softly. "Soon he will be dead and you'll be free. I'd say another five minutes or so of this cold and he'll be finished. I know it's unpleasant, Callie but it's for the best. Put your jacket back on, there are gloves in the pocket and try to keep warm, the temperature is going to drop a bit more."

The obscenity Callie flung at the man brought Tarris' head up to look at her despite the fact that all he wanted to do was lay down, curl in a ball and go to sleep. The woman had quite a vocabulary. But more, the man's possessive tone caused something to spring to life inside Tarris' gut. A fire. A flame was raging inside him at the thought of this asshole ever touching Callista. Never. He tried to pull himself up to his feet with her help. If he could just get out of this room, just for a few seconds, he'd shift them both.

Stanton's voice came over the speaker, it wasn't smug as much as it was hard and filled with irritation. "I wouldn't do that, Callie, unless you want to make this an even more unpleasant death for him and painful for you. He triggered the first sensor when he tried to walk out of there. That released the dry ice. If you trigger the sensor a second time, it won't be more fog pellets, you'll get a shower of liquid nitrogen. Do you really want to watch him melt before your eyes? Not to mention it would blind you at the very least but more likely kill you too."

Tarris pulled away from her. *Don't.* He flung the word out as hard as he could. *I won't let you hurt yourself.*

She turned her emerald gaze to him. "Tarris? Did you say something?"

Hell, he should have known. He was no longer strong enough to reach her. He heard Stanton again. "Aw, how noble. He doesn't want you to try again, Callie. He doesn't want you to get hurt." The sneer in his voice matched the one on his face that was just visible to Tarris as his vision began to dim. He'd not been strong enough to reach Callie but had been strong enough to reach the hunter. "It's bullshit, darling. He just doesn't want to die that painfully."

He couldn't stay upright any longer. He lowered himself to the icy floor and curled into a ball. Callie was beside him rooting in the pockets of the jacket that was wrapped around his shoulders. She shoved the small tight gloves onto his hands and then lay down beside him. She curled against him, wrapping him tightly in her arms. She wriggled until her breasts were pressed against his chest, the rock hard little nipples pushing against his skin. How wonderful it had been to love her. How wonderful it had been to feel her and to share the lovely heat and passion of her body. She held the edges of the jacket tight trying to stretch it around them. Trying to trap the heat of her body against his. She didn't have much but she was giving him what she had.

"Don't you dare die," she whispered and he felt the wetness on her face. He wanted to tell her not to cry, that her tears would only make her face colder. He wanted to tell her he wasn't worth her tears. He wanted to tell her that it didn't matter in the long run, he couldn't be with her anymore. He'd crossed the line, turned into the thing he hated. He would die today one way or the other. He was stunned to find a single drop of wetness on his own cheek. He didn't regret dying, just that he'd not managed to get her safe before it happened.

There was a faint shout from outside the room, a gunshot and then silence. Tarris pulled Callie closer, his arms weakening around her. He could no longer read the minds outside the door. He struggled to stay awake, to stay with Callista as long as he could. He lost the battle as he heard the door to the freezer creak open.

Chapter Six

附

The blower on the fans shut off abruptly. Callie looked up at the door. She wasn't afraid, she was furious. When Jack appeared in the doorway, she grabbed Tarris tighter. His breathing was becoming slow and shallow. His skin was so very cold and his lips had started to take on a bluish tinge. And he looked different. He appeared almost as he had when he slept in her bed. His ears came to slight points but there were now small dark horns poking through his golden hair and his incisors were visible—just the tips—beneath his upper lip. It didn't matter. He was still beautiful. He was still her Tarris.

"Stay away from him," she growled softly, the ferocity in her voice surprising even her. The hunter simply pushed the door open farther and a very old figure swept into the room with much more agility than she could believe possible. She sat up, hunching herself over Tarris' body, a living shield from whatever these people meant to do to him. "I won't let you hurt him."

The old one stopped. The face that was wizened beyond anything she'd ever seen before seemed surprised. The eyes narrowed for a moment before it spoke. "I'd never dream of hurting him. I've known him and loved him, almost his entire life. But if we don't get him out of here quickly he will die. I take it you would agree that would be a bad thing." He approached her much more slowly than before. Kneeling beside them, the gray eyes looked her over first, before they turned to Tarris. He said nothing but turned to the hunter. "Help me," he took one of Tarris' arms, stood and started to pull him.

Jack approached quickly but when he reached for Tarris' hand, Callie knocked his hand away. "Don't touch him," she shouted. She grabbed the arm that lay still at Tarris' side and helped the old man start to pull him to the door.

"You know, Oracle, it's really going to hurt him if you pull him over that pile of dry ice by the door," the hunter spoke with a quiet irritation.

The Oracle stopped and caught Callie's eye. The last thing she wanted was to hurt Tarris more. "Now we can waste time looking for a broom to sweep them up, child, or we can trust Jack to carry him out for us." Callie glared at the hunter but nodded. The large man lifted Tarris up and slung him awkwardly over one shoulder.

Callie cleared the freezer just seconds after Tarris' body. Her only thoughts were on him so she was stunned when a familiar voice called out, "Bring him over here." She turned to see Sarah piling what seemed to be rather old tattered pieces of cloth into a nest on the floor. Jack obliged and Callie joined Sarah in positioning Tarris on the rags. "Sorry, they're not quite clean but they were all I could find." Sarah placed a heavy, moth-eaten quilt over the incubus before she turned to hug Callie. "He'll be okay."

"He has to be," Callie said softly as she dropped to her knees beside him. The Oracle was there already, pushing back the blanket Sarah had just put in place.

"Let me get rid of those," the hunter was at her side and quickly unlocked and removed the iron cuffs. He moved away quickly as if he sensed she was fighting the urge to strike out at him. Tarris had almost died, might still die and he was at least partially responsible.

"Where is it?" the old one muttered and began patting down Tarris' lower body. "Why didn't he use it, the fool?" The gnarled hand slid from Tarris' right front pocket to his rear pocket. Without thinking Callie helped him roll Tarris slightly so he could continue his search. When the hands brushed over the left front pocket of Tarris' jeans, the face relaxed and the

Oracle gave a muttered exclamation Callie didn't understand. She didn't need to. The relief was clear. He seemed to be fingering the same lump Callie had felt that morning when she explored Tarris' body. "I can't get it, you pull it out, dear, your hands are smaller and nimbler than mine."

Callie slipped her hand into the tight pocket and her fingers closed around the flat, smooth object. Pulling it out she stared at it in awe. It was the stone she'd picked up as Tarris in his dream. The almost-opal stone glittered and glowed except where it looked more like black glass. The incandescent light floated and shifted as if it were alive. A faint vibration rolled through her. Her skin warmed up and she felt the flush of excitement sweep through her and settle deep in the center of her stomach. From there it flowed down and she felt the vibrations tease her as if someone had just pressed a slowly vibrating egg against her clitoris. Her fingers clutched convulsively around it and her body jerked. She heard the Oracle laugh softly. "That's what I thought." Embarrassed, she held the stone up to the Oracle who smiled at her a bit too brightly for the situation. "Don't give it to me, girl, put it on his chest."

Callie laid the stone in the center of Tarris' bare chest. She took his hand and pulled it into her lap and held it between her own. With him lying like this she could see the damage the dry ice pellets had done to his skin. She didn't want to think about what the liquid nitrogen would have done. Turning, she searched for Stanton, remembering him for the first time. He was standing against one wall, blood trickling from his nose and scowling. His eyes tried to pierce through her as if he could burn her with his gaze. Standing out of arm and leg range was the dark-haired woman Callie had met only twice before. Sarah's sister-in-law Anna Ursine held a rifle pointed at Adam Stanton's chest. The same rifle her brother had been holding earlier. Seeing them close together now, though their coloring was disparate, their features were quite similar.

Callie turned her eye to the hunter that no one seemed to be guarding. Jack Morrissey simply shrugged. "I know when I'm beat."

"Besides, he loves his little sister," Anna's lips were twisted into a smirk. "Not to mention he knows I'll kick his ass if he tries me. Then there's what Mark and Luke would do to him if he hurt Sarah or me." She paused and shifted her attention from Stanton just long enough to lock on Callie's gaze for a split second. Turning back to the man who was so angry he was shaking, she continued. "And we would have made him hurt us before we let either of them injure Tarris."

"I'm sorry it took so long," Sarah apologized from beside her. "I called Anna as soon as you left the house. She was with the Oracle. I thought if we could find you, that she could reason with her brother."

The snort of laughter that escaped Anna wasn't exactly pleasant. "According to Luke, no one reasons with a Morrissey." Callie saw the hunter's lips twitch slightly at his sister's words.

"Laugh now, Morrissey," Stanton snarled. Evidently he'd seen the faint up curl as well. "You've signed your death warrant."

"Tell me something I don't know," Jack's voice sounded bored.

Callie felt the cold hand in her lap move. She swung her head back to Tarris. His skin was flushing and as she clutched tighter at his hand she noticed it was warmer now. His lips were back to the soft dusted rose and his breathing was deeper. She started when his eyes snapped open and he tried to move.

"Don't," she shushed him and pushed him back. The bright blue eyes found her face and he seemed to relax. She couldn't hear him in her mind but from the smile on the faces around her she knew he had spoken. "I can't hear you," she whispered softly.

Tarris moved his gaze to the Oracle who nodded. "I'm not surprised. Unless I miss my guess, it is all fading away from you and it will continue to do so. You will be less and less able to hear us and we you."

"Which explains why none of you knew we were coming." A voice spoke from the shadows of the basement stairs. Two tall men, identical men, stepped off the wooden stairs and into the room. One of them walked directly to Anna and Jack. He stood staring at the hunter, his hand resting on the shoulder of the woman with the rifle. Callie had seen the two together only twice before and one of those times in a dream. She had forgotten exactly how identical the two were. Behind them stepped the two men who had been with Sarah in the café. Another set of twins.

"Since the gang's all here and the last thing we want is to discuss family matters in front of those who aren't family, I'd suggest someone gets rid of the hunter. Levi. Laban." The man who still stood at the base of the stairs spoke with such quiet force that had the other not gone directly to Anna, she still would have known this was Mark, the *Amar*. His power and authority wrapped around him indelibly.

Anna blanched slightly and Sarah turned away from them at those words, making a huge production out of helping Tarris sit up and arranging the old quilt around his shoulders. The two men were at Stanton's side in a flash. Levi had one hand twisting Stanton's hand up behind his back and one arm wrapped around the hunter's throat. Anna turned away. Surprisingly, so did Jack. Sarah grabbed her shoulders and turned her toward Tarris who was sitting, leaning against the wall with his eyes closed. "You don't need to see this," she whispered.

"No one needs to see anything," Luke spoke quietly and took the rifle from Anna. He handed it to Laban and nodded toward the door. Levi pushed Stanton into the storage room and Laban followed closing the door. There was no sound in the room for several seconds except Mark's footsteps as he crossed the room to wrap a shaking Sarah in his arms.

"He would never have stopped," he whispered into her hair as he held her to his chest. His eyes were watching Callie. "He would have kept coming. Even the hunter's council knows he was obsessed. He, they, had been warned what would happen if he came after our family. Even if Tarris were to…" the *Amar's* voice faltered. He lifted his eyes to the far wall. When he resumed his tone was cold and even, "Even if Tarris were to die, he'd never stop hunting you, Ms. Marshall." His eyes moved down to hers and she saw his plea for understanding in their depths, though it never touched his voice. "He would never have stopped hunting you."

The door to the freezer opened slowly and the two Bears emerged. There was no hint of what might have transpired on their faces. One of them reached up and pulled the power lever on the side and the light in the little window went out. The two turned to Mark and gave a slight bow before walking up the stairs and out of the room. Far from a decrease in the tensions, she felt them spike upwards. Mark and Luke exchanged a guarded look. Mark nodded and turned toward Tarris.

The hand she was still holding lifted from her grip and touched her cheek. The sadness and regret in the blue eyes made her ache. He too seemed to plead for her understanding. The voice that spoke was that of the Oracle. "No matter what you've seen, know that this family would never harm you, child. Sarah's friendship aside, for Tarris' sake we will always protect and love you."

She turned to look at the gray eyes and saw a pain there that didn't fit with what was happening around her. Tarris looked at her a moment and then leaned forward, brushing her lips in a soft kiss. His palm cupping her cheek, his lips opened, forming soundless words that looked a lot like "I'm sorry." His eyes held hers and she felt the Oracle rise at her side. Leaning in, Tarris rested his forehead against hers. She could smell his warm and sweet breath on her face and she closed her eyes.

"Isn't this the happy ever after part?" she whispered. "The bad guy is defeated and everyone smiles and slaps high-fives?"

Tarris' head shook from side-to-side. His answer was clearly, no. He lifted his head from hers and looked down at the stone in his hand.

"I'm sorry, Ms. Marshall," Luke was still standing beside his mate, his arm was wrapped around her as if he offered her comfort while looking like it was he who needed to be comforted.

Mark was still holding Sarah. She was crying now into the front of his shirt. "I'm afraid the danger, the villain if you will, still exists."

"What?" she stared at them and watched all eyes in the room settle on Tarris. Tarris a bad guy? Tarris a villain? She swung her gaze back to him but he wouldn't meet her eyes. He simply nodded and his eyelids fluttered shut. Then suddenly the golden light took him and he was gone.

"Tarris," she felt the scream tear from her throat.

Mark pushed Sarah away gently and nodded to Luke. The younger twin was holding onto his mate tightly and it was several seconds before he seemed able to let her go. They turned and started to walk toward the stairs.

"Mark," Sarah called his name. Her mate's step halted for a moment but then he continued up the stairs without looking back.

"Don't make this harder on them, Sarah." Anna was staring at her hands, hands that were shaking. "It's going to kill a piece of Luke to do this. I can't believe it will hurt Mark less."

Silence hung heavier than before. Callie forced herself to her feet. "Do what?" she demanded. "What are they going to do?"

"What they have to," Anna brushed angrily at a tear that was sliding down her cheek.

"Sarah?" Callie turned warily to her friend.

"They promised him long ago they wouldn't let him fully become an incubus. It's happening Sarah. He broke the rules and it's happening. He's maturing and now Mark and Luke have to keep that promise."

"You mean…they're going to kill him?" the words were loud and shrill as they bounced off the small room.

"Well, they will if you three stand here talking," the Oracle had almost been forgotten. All three turned to stare at him. "I suggest we get going. The way Anna drives, with a short cut I know, I think we may get back ahead of them. Or at least right behind them."

"Let's go," Callie started toward the door. Sarah moved more hesitantly but started after her.

"Don't," Anna called to them.

"Don't?" Callie spun around to face her. How dare she try to stop her? "Don't stop them from killing the man I love? The only man I've ever loved? The gentlest and kindest person I've ever known? If the situations were reversed, would you let them kill Luke?"

"I don't know," the voice was hard. "You don't understand Callie. You don't understand what's happening here. He doesn't want to become one of the dark ones. You can't understand what it means, the total loss of all conscience, of all control. To become a hungry demon who cares only about feeding on others."

"You sound like Stanton," Callie waved her hand dismissively. "You don't know Tarris or you wouldn't say these things."

"I do know Tarris. I love Tarris. Not as you do but I do love him. We all do. The two men who just walked out of here love Tarris more and longer than any souls on this planet. And I'll be damned if I let you say otherwise for a moment. You don't understand what Tarris is afraid of. If he turns, Callie, he could kill all of us easily. He knows our minds and he could slip in where no other incubus could. He could wipe us all out, systematically driving us insane or draining enough from us to kill us." Anna's face was flushed bright red and more tears hovered on her eyelids.

"I don't care," Callie spat at her. "I won't let you kill him."

Anna caught her arm and held her. The woman was stronger than she looked. "Don't do this to them, to Tarris. He forced the promise from them. He'd rather die than become fully mature. He doesn't want to be a full-fledged incubus."

"And he won't be," the Oracle sighed. "Not in the way you think. Not in the way Mark and Luke think. He's not maturing Anna. He's changing, yes but not in the way he's always feared."

The dark-haired woman stared unblinking at the Oracle. "You're sure?"

The old one nodded, "I'd bet my life on it."

Anna seemed to crumple and fold in on herself. Callie actually found herself clutching at the hand that had held her vice-like.

"Anna?" Sarah's concerned voice was hesitant.

Anna reached up to touch Callie's hand. "Let's go stop them." She turned to look at her brother. "Jack?"

He shook his head. "I'll clean up here."

"You can't stay," Anna protested.

"I know. I won't."

"Come with us," his sister insisted.

He shook his head. "I'll be fine. Go save your friend."

* * * * *

He could run. He knew them both well enough to stay a step ahead of them, at least for a while yet. At least until he lost all reason. It wouldn't be long now before they arrived.

Tarris stood in the middle of what had long ago been converted from a small dugout cave to a full scale bunker. The walls had been expanded out, the floor cut downward and the hill over his head heavily landscaped. The entire place had been turned into a large concrete room. The family could evacuate the young, the old and the sick here in case of an attack and those inside could last for days until someone could get them. It was a far cry from the cold dirt floor he'd once huddled on. There were fold up bunks hanging from each wall and a small propane stove for cooking and heating. Two soft couches pulled out to form beds if needed and gave the place the look of a family room.

It didn't matter how much the former *Amar* tried to eradicate the memory of that night from this place, it never left. This was the place no one knew he came to. When he couldn't turn to the Oracle or didn't want to explain himself, he'd come here. Sometimes he just needed to be close to Jonas. It would sound crazy to the others he knew but this place held something of youngest Ursine. Tarris dreamed about him in this place. Sometimes he felt as if he were with him. He wasn't, of course. The spirit that had been the individual Jonas had moved on. The soul that had given life to that spirit would have been reborn. Perhaps in one of the younger Bears, perhaps even in Nicky or Jake.

But none of that mattered. What mattered is that soon Mark and Luke would arrive to fulfill the promise they made him long ago. The night the Oracle had explained the rules. Rules everyone prayed would work. Rules everyone was afraid would fail. The rules hadn't failed. He had. And now he would force the two men he loved beyond all else to kill him. Here in this place where he should have died, here they had agreed he would die.

A swoosh announced the arrival of his executioners. The air seal popped slightly as the door swung back into place. Slowly he turned around and faced them. Tarris looked at the two men. Their faces would seem so alike to someone who didn't know them. To Tarris there was no way to confuse them. Luke's face was flushed and his eyes the raw red of a man who was forcing himself not to allow his emotions to overflow. He'd always been the more passionate of the two. The small scar above Luke's right eye always gave him away. It was the result of a stone shot at him from a slingshot Mark had made in retaliation for Luke's nearly skewering him with an arrow during archery lessons. Mark's face was pale. His eyes were dull and empty. Little Marky, he'd have to remind Luke to call him that more often. The name drove the Bear crazy. It was good for him, he was always so tightly controlled.

None of them spoke for a moment. As hard as this was for him, he couldn't help but feel nearly overwhelmed by the emotions that he felt from them. He shrugged off the quilt he still wore. The bunker had been cold when he'd arrived. Crossing the room he wrapped his arms around Luke and pulled him close. For once Luke didn't try to reverse the hold, to take control. He simply pressed his face into Tarris' neck and held on to him tightly. Turning his head and reaching out his hand he invited Mark into the embrace. Mark wrapped his arms around them both and they stood, almost as they had the night Jonas died until the adults had pulled them apart. Luke shuddered and slid his hand into Tarris' hair. He pulled his head down and kissed him. Tarris swallowed the pain, the guilt and the anger that filled the kiss. Luke released him and he turned his head to Mark. Mark leaned in gently. His kiss was soft and tender. The kisses were so indicative of the two Bears. Luke the one who needed to feel in control and Mark, who often longed not to be in control but to be able to give to others sweetly and gently.

Tarris pulled away. He put a few steps between them before he sent his thoughts to them. He could see them straining to hear him. He wasn't sure why it was happening but the loss of his telepathy was increasing rapidly.

It's time.

Mark nodded and walked to a large door near the back of the room and with a key from his pocket removed the padlock. Inside it would look very similar to the room Tarris had just left. It was the frozen storage room for the bunker. There were few ways to kill an incubus. A few gifted humans, those known as mages, had managed to do it by disrupting the incubus at a cellular level with spells and bursts of magical energy. But those reports were rare. Besides, it sounded a hell of a lot more painful than freezing to death. And it since he'd already almost done it once, this should go quicker, right?

Mark pulled open the door. "We'll stay with you," he whispered. Tarris knew he was waiting for him to pass through the door on his own. He walked toward it and shivered at the blast of cold air. He paused again, his hand sliding into his pocket. He pulled out the stone. He held it in his palm for a moment, feeling its heat and the sensations that moved through him. A soft voice seemed to come from the stone. A voice that at first pleaded, then demanded that he not do this. *Don't go coward on me now,* he chided the voice.

Suddenly the stone began to heat up. It began to burn in the palm of his hand. Tarris swore as he jerked his hand and the stone fell to the floor. A swoosh of sound shocked them all. Tarris felt his heart contract when he saw Callie push past Sarah, Anna and the Oracle to run to him.

"No," she grabbed at his arms. She pulled him close and held him, then turned and placed herself between him and the twins. "I won't let you do this to him."

Mark was staring angrily at the new arrivals. "Sarah," his voice was brittle and strained. "Don't interfere." The blazing brown eyes turned to the Oracle. "Honored one or not, you had no right to tell them we would be here. I am your *Amar* and yet you disobey me?"

"Mark," Sarah moved toward him and placed her hand on his arm. "I love you. You are the *Amar* and as such we all honor you. But darling, just this once, shut up."

Tarris stared at the small blonde in amazement. Luke looked as if he'd fall down. But Mark…if the situation hadn't been so damn serious Tarris would have been rolling on the floor laughing at the look on Mark's face. "Did you just tell me to…," he began to sputter at her, his face a portrait of stunned disbelief.

"Yes, dear, I told you to shut up. You know I'd never do it in front of anyone important," Her voice became almost conciliatory.

"Excuse me?" the Oracle and Luke chorused together, the former amused and the latter indignant.

"Luke!" Mark's voice was sharp. He turned to look at Tarris. The incubus nodded and turned Callie to face him. He looked into her eyes. He thought the words and heard Mark repeat them.

Go. You don't understand what you're doing. I'm dangerous, Callista. Dangerous to everyone I love and I won't live that way.

"You're not," she shook her head. He sighed in frustration. This had been bad enough before. But this emotional scene with her wasn't helping. That part of him that had become possessive of her was growing in strength with every minute that passed. It roared at him to pull her to him, to claim her as his own and to leave those who would try to stop him behind.

Again he met Mark's eye. He tightened his thoughts to the *Amar* and hoped it would be enough for him to hear. Mark nodded slightly in acknowledgement. Tarris was just more than five steps from the entrance to the freezer. Mark still held the lock in his hand. If he pushed Callista away, he could make it inside and Mark would lock the door. No one could stop it. He didn't want to think of how it would hurt Callista but it would hurt her more to watch him become the monster that was growing inside his chest. It clawed at him as if seeking freedom and he wasn't sure how much longer he could stop it.

"Now would be a good time, child," he heard the Oracle mutter. At first he thought the man had heard his words to Mark and was telling him to proceed but then he noticed the Oracle was looking up at the ceiling.

Either way he was right. Now was the time. Tarris pushed Callie away toward Sarah who caught her, both stumbling backward. He turned to bolt into the room when he realized his legs wouldn't move. A golden mist had begun to swirl up around him. It rose up from the stone he had dropped and was wrapping itself around his legs.

"Any time now," the Oracle muttered again and Tarris turned his head to look at the old man. He was the only person in the room besides Tarris who wasn't staring in shock at the mist. "Ah, late as always, boy."

Tarris followed the Oracle's gaze to his left and saw a translucent shadow moving toward them. The distortion it caused made it clearly visible despite its being fog-like. It had a roughly humanoid shape. "What the hell?" Luke put voice to the thoughts of everyone around them. Him included.

When it hovered just a yard from where Tarris stood, two tendrils of the gold mist reached out. One stretched to the door to the freezer that still stood open and pushed it shut before quickly retracting. The second moved toward the form that now seemed more like a void, an absence of matter than a shadow. It was shaping itself into the figure of a slight man. When the gold mist touched it, it began to fill the emptiness within it. Swirling upward it expanded to occupy the space of the void, filling nearly two thirds of it.

"Oracle?" Mark's voice was edged in the one thing he'd been trained all his life not to show. Fear.

"It's all right, *Amar*. There is nothing here that would harm any of us," the old one assured him. And he was right, Tarris realized. The emotions coming from the shape and there were powerful emotions emanating from it, were happy, loving and tender. Once all the mist had flowed into the shape, still leaving the lower third of it an empty milky color, it began to clarify its shape. The face started to form and arms lifted from the body as hands and fingers became clearly defined. When the face turned to Tarris he gasped, his gut feeling as if someone had reached in an icy hand and was twisting his organs.

The face was that of a young man in his mid-teens. His sandy hair floated about his face as if he existed under water. An impish smile twisted his lips. Tarris heard Callista gasp. She would recognize this face. Luke's moan followed and the sound tore at Tarris' heart. But he couldn't look away from the apparition before him.

"Jonas?" the soft sound of wonderment came from Mark. He started to step forward and stopped when the face looked at him. The young man nodded.

"About time, you were always late for everything but dinner," the Oracle snorted seeming completely unimpressed by the sudden appearance of the young ghost before them. "You were even born late."

The soft laugh tore through Tarris leaving a trail of pain and guilt. One that lasted until the blue eyes once again fixed on him.

"I can hear you, you know." Jonas spoke softly to him. "I hear you every day, every time you speak to me. I'll help them to hear you now."

Tarris looked at Callie. *Even Callista.* The answer didn't come from the figure of the young Bear. It came from the woman.

"Yes, even me," she walked toward him and placed her hand on his arm. Tarris felt her touch like a jolt of electricity running through his body. It sprang to life in a way that it wasn't supposed to. He wasn't supposed to react this powerfully to anyone outside a dream. He tried to distract himself by focusing on Jonas. Hell, if he couldn't distract himself with the appearance of his long dead foster brother, he was in deep trouble.

"Ask me why I'm here, Tarris," Jonas' eyes sparkled.

"Oh get on with it already," the Oracle muttered.

Jonas turned to wink at the old man. "You're no fun, you know?" He turned back to Tarris. "He's right though, I haven't much time. I can only hold my soul and spirit together briefly. Tarris, you are not maturing in the way you think. You're not turning into a fully adult incubus. It has nothing to do with a bunch of stupid rules." The boy gestured to the stone on the floor. "Pick it up."

Tarris did and when he looked at it in the palm of his hand it was no longer his strange opal. The entire stone was the same smoky black glass that had marked its flawed end. Lifting his eyes to Jonas he shook his head.

I don't understand.

"Now there's an understatement," Jonas rolled his eyes. "I thought you'd figure it out. I've been watching you, thinking you'd recognize it when it happened to you. You'd watched it happen to Mark and Luke. Sure you're a bit long in the tooth for it but you were always so smart."

"Jonas," the Oracle warned with a frown.

Recognize what? Tarris could almost forget he was dealing with a spirit. This Jonas was just as infuriatingly flighty as the real one. The boy's mind had always astonished and delighted him with its leaps in logic and reason. Now, on the receiving end of one of his riddles, Tarris found himself just as irritated as he'd been over a century ago.

"Our little boy is becoming a man," snorted Jonas.

Tarris grimaced at the joke. *That's exactly what I'm trying to stop, Jonas. I won't become a "man".*

"Nope and you're not going to become an incubus either."

"Jonas," Luke interjected, his voice sounding odd speaking the name of the brother whose death had tormented them all with grief and guilt. "Jonas, he is an incubus."

"Not entirely," the boy insisted.

Jonas, Tarris sighed. Callie's hand smoothed over his back and he felt the comfort and reassurance she was trying to offer him. He smiled at her faintly before returning to the apparition. *Jonas, enough riddles. Just tell me what the hell is going on. I have a suicide to commit.* Callie's hand froze and her nails dug into his arm where she still held it.

The ghost frowned. "I can't just blurt it out. It's not allowed. You have to ask me the right questions. Not why I'm here but why I'm not..." he trailed off biting his lip.

Tarris looked into the blue eyes. Bringing together his soul and spirit. Jonas had said he could only bring them together for a short time. His spirit yes, that was him. It was the part of Jonas that lived on. But his soul?

Jonas, why hasn't your soul been reborn?

Relief flooded the young face. He floated closer to where Tarris stood and reached out his hand. The palm that pressed to Tarris' chest was without warmth, without coldness. It was a faint tickling along his skin and nothing more.

"It already has been." He stared into Tarris' eyes and the truth crept slowly from to the other. "Incubi have no souls," Jonas continued. "But you do. A piece of one, anyway."

The night you died...

"When I reached for you. I didn't want to leave you alone. A piece of my soul clung to you and wouldn't let go. It broke off and stayed with you. That's why you've never transformed into an adult incubus. You never could as long as you had a soul."

"And the rest of your soul?" Callie was staring at the stone in Tarris' hand.

The young man smiled and nodded. "Yes. A smart one you've got there, brother."

"A soul stone?" awed she reached out and stroked the black glass. "But those are supposed to be opals."

"This was an opal, or at least mostly one until I called what was unclaimed of the soul from it." Jonas was grinning at her as if he was delighted to have someone who understood.

"When you leave it will return to the stone?" The academic in Callie's voice made Tarris smile. Good gods the woman was unusual.

"Not if I can help it," Jonas said. "But it's up to Tarris."

To take your soul? I already caused your death, Jonas. How can I take your soul?

Luke and Mark started to protest but the young spirit cut them off. "No. The hunter caused my death. You tried to protect me." The blue eyes moved his brothers. "You both blame yourselves and when the pain gets too much you blame each other. I know that. I've heard you too calling out for forgiveness. There is nothing to forgive. Mark, you saved Luke. If you hadn't found him and pulled him away, back to this place, he'd have died. Luke, you tried to save mother. You fought like a full grown Bear instead of the cub we all were. There is nothing to forgive."

He turned back to Tarris, "I am not my soul. It is that piece of the divine which gave me my life. When I died, it chose to stay with you. So brother of my heart, will you claim the rest of what belongs to you? All that belongs to you," he looked meaningfully at Callie. "You weren't maturing as an incubus, Tarris. Your Were's soul had finally found what it had been looking for. It had finally found its mate."

The words were too much. Tarris felt his head spinning wildly. His mate? That was why he'd felt so possessive? So jealous? Just like Mark. Just like Luke.

"Mate?" Callie looked up at the ghost.

"I know this must seem like a lot for a human to absorb," Jonas began.

But Callie cut him off. "I'm sure the shock of this day will catch up with me at some point. Incubi, hunters, Weres, ghosts… But at the moment my brain is a bit numb. I doubt I'd bat an eye if the Easter Bunny had came hopping through pulling the Tooth Fairy in Santa's sleigh behind him. Hell, the Easter Bunny is probably a Were with lots of stock in the candy industry."

Luke, Anna and Jonas laughed loudly. Mark was shaking with a silent chuckle. Sarah smiled at her. "It's a bit much to absorb. This group forgets that from time to time."

"Only because you've adapted so well," Mark murmured as he held Sarah closer.

Tarris watched Callie look down at the black stone in her hand. Whatever magic Jonas was working he could hear her joy. But he could also hear her doubt.

"Will you claim it?" Jonas repeated, his voice starting to sound a bit strained. "I haven't much time, Tarris. You have to decide quickly."

Callista? he looked at her, waiting.

"You're not really asking *me* are you?" she frowned at him. "This is about you. If the soul lets you have a normal life, why wouldn't you take it?"

He swallowed hard, his regard never wavering, *That's not what I'm asking. Of course I'm accepting the soul. What I need to know, while you can still hear me in your head, is will you accept me?*

She stared at him astonished. "How can you doubt that I want you? My question is do you want that? Us to be married, mated."

I want it. But I want you to want it too. It can wait until you're ready. For now, Callista, all I want is to know that you want me. That you want to be with me.

Her answer was a kiss, one that made his need for her flare to life. She held his face in her hands as she nipped gently at his lips. Pulling back she smiled. "Of course I do. I just need to know what you want, how you feel. Being with you, just you, is all I've ever wanted. Even before I knew you were real, you were the only man who ever made me feel as you do." She shook her head, a sad smile on her lips. "Imagine how insane I thought I was. That the only man I knew I could ever love was only a figment of my imagination?"

She loved him? She loved the incubus? The dark demon? The monster? She wanted the man who was always second, who was always the extra player in the game? He looked into her eyes and saw her honesty and sincerity. He didn't need telepathy to know she was telling the truth. It had been a cruel joke of fate that he couldn't hear her as clearly as he could everyone else. He'd felt her passion he'd felt her affection but even now he wasn't sure. He thought he recognized the same emotion that he felt between Mark and Sarah, between Luke and Anna. But it seemed so much…more.

She softly stroked his jawline and placed a tender kiss on each cheek. "I love you, Tarris."

He felt the desire burning in him. He wanted her. He wanted to be with her forever. *Then will you be my mate? Will you let me love you all the days of our lives?*

He heard a soft sob escape her voice and started to panic. Did she not want to be with him? But she said…

"Yes, Tarris. All the days of our lives," she wrapped her arms around his neck and her lips claimed his boldly. Joy spread through him like he'd never known. He held her for a moment until Jonas intruded.

"Tarris, I'm running out of time."

Tarris turned to Jonas and nodded wordlessly.

"I'll need your help for this beautiful one," his use of Tarris' endearment startled her. "Take the stone and old it over Tarris' breast bone."

Callie scooped the stone out of Tarris' hand and laid it flat against his chest, holding it with her palm.

"This won't hurt you a bit. Just do us both a favor and don't drop it," Jonas laughed. He turned to his family. "This is goodbye. I've been waiting for this day before I moved on. But it's my time too. This soul will be fully reborn into our dear Tarris and I will move on to the next...well, the next wherever." The boyish grin widened. "I love you all. You've chosen your mates well and I see nothing but happiness for you all." He turned to Callie. "Take care of him," he inclined his head toward Tarris. "Make him start painting again, will you? Play with a bit of clay from time to time?"

"I'll try," she nodded.

He winked at Tarris. "No more fun without fuss for you, old man. You may not be subject to human disease but once you have your full soul, you'll want to...well, do things I'm not supposed to know about in the flesh. You might want to get Mark to have "the talk" with you before then. I wouldn't trust Luke. He told me you could get a girl pregnant by drinking out of the same straw." His laugh rang out less loudly. His form seemed to undulate for a moment before he turned to the Oracle.

"No advice from the likes of you, child," the old one shook his head. "Besides, I'll be seeing you soon."

Jonas did not dispute this comment but simply bowed from the neck. The blue eyes closed and the last words he spoke were to Callie and Tarris as the gold mist started to retreat from his body. "Put your arms around her. Don't let go of each other. Hold on 'til the stone tells you to let go. And Tarris, Callie, this will mate you. So be sure."

The mist sped out of the shadow that had been Jonas and rose up around her and Tarris, hiding them from the others. When they were completely surrounded by the column of shimmering gold, a wisp moved inward and closed around her hand, pressing it even harder against Tarris' chest. A second wrapped around his wrists where they crossed at her back and spun themselves into ropes trapping his arms in place. They weren't touching in the front. An inch of space separated their bodies.

Then it began. The sensation rolled through them both with a fury. Callista felt her body come alive as it did whenever Tarris touched her. He seemed to be touching her everywhere at once. Tendrils shot from the swirling mass and wound around their necks. Callie felt the sweet touch of Tarris' lips on her throat. His sigh told her he too was being caressed by the mist. The whirlwind moved in tighter and Tarris let out a soft cry of pleasure. A second later Callie too was panting and gasping as she felt hands cup her breasts and stroke her nipples. The walls of their tiny chamber closed even more, pushing them together. When his erection pressed into her she cried out. His arms lifted her and she wrapped her legs around him. She no longer remembered Jonas' admonishment not to let go. She'd realized he had been joking. There was no way she could let go. Her hand was cemented to his chest by the thin topaz rope.

Tarris slid his hands down to her ass and pushed her against the straining bulge in his pants. Callie pushed forward, her legs tightening as she forced him in tighter. Her free hand wrapped around his neck and she used it to balance herself as she tried desperately to grind her pussy against him. No one could see them and she doubted it would have mattered if they could have. All that did matter was the throbbing of her clit as it swelled and vibrated with the need to find release.

A band of light pressed between them and encircled her around her breasts. The feeling of her nipples being sucked, nipped and tugged at roared through her making her whimper. She wanted him. Her pussy was wet aching. She wanted him inside her. She wanted to feel him thrust into her. His hands dug into her ass as he ground himself against her. Low tones that sounded more like notes of music escaped his clenched jaw.

Her body felt over-stimulated, every neuron screaming pleasure into her brain but not enough to bring her the release she craved. She pressed her face into his neck and felt tears burning her eyes. Her need for him was so desperate that she was going to cry. Two more tendrils of light swept in towards them, pushing between them. The golden fingers curved around both of their groins and the fire that exploded in her was more than she feared her mind could handle without breaking.

She felt Tarris trembling as the light stroked his erection where it thrust so tight against the denim she thought he could conceivably split a seam. The light passed through her fleece pants and the silk panties beneath them. It pressed into her dripping folds, spreading her pussy like huge amber cock. She gasped and tightened her arm around Tarris' neck. He turned his cheek into her face and rested it against her temple. His breathing was ragged. She had no idea why they were still standing or why her hand hadn't moved except that the golden mist didn't want them to.

The thrusting light, the scent of Tarris' skin and the golden hands that toyed with her breasts, plucking her nipples and squeezing them roughly pushed her to the brink of orgasm. But it was the soft whisper in the back of her mind that finally pushed her over the edge.

Callista, my darling, I love you.

She screamed then, the vortex of pleasure spun her faster and faster, forcing wave after wave of orgasm through her body until she hit overload and could feel no more. The edges of her vision grew black just as the onslaught eased into a gentle soothing sensation. But not for Tarris, she could feel him shaking, his body almost convulsing as suddenly the column of gold rushed in on them and poured through her hand, through the stone and into his chest. Tarris threw back his head and the sound that came from him was almost a song. The way the cry of a whale or the roar of a lion was a song. Primitive and beautiful.

She clung to him, holding him. Her body still ached to find climax. She lifted her head from his shoulder and realized that their protective shield was gone. The Bears and their mates stood several yards away, watching with wide eyes. The bright azure eyes of Luke's mate the widest.

Callie unwound her legs from Tarris' waist and settled herself back on her feet. She met his eyes and saw that they no longer seemed to glow. They were a vivid, bright blue but they no longer seemed to dance as if they were tiny flames. The stone between her palm and his chest was warm. It still sent small pulses of pleasure through her hand to the core of her but they had gentled. Tarris' hand covered hers and eased it away from his chest. The opal was restored. What's more, it was whole. It shone from his chest, embedded in the skin. No dark areas, no missing pieces. It and he were whole.

Callie touched it again gently and felt him shudder. "Does it hurt?"

He smiled ruefully and shook his head. "How does it feel?" she asked, forgetting for a moment that he couldn't answer her. His grin turned sad and he shook his head. "You can't talk to me anymore can you?" Another shake. "Can you hear me at all?" He touched his hand to his ears and nodded, then to his forehead and shook his head. There was a sharp stab of pain in his eyes. And worry. "It's okay," she whispered, moving in closer to brush her kiss against his lips. "We'll figure it out."

"Tarris?" Sarah's worried voice was filled not only with her concern but with her affection for him. "Are you all right?"

He turned and nodded to her. "You can't speak to us either, can you?" Again Tarris shook his head.

"There was bound to be some compromise when you blended the two natures," the Oracle spoke calmly.

Mark frowned at the old man. "You knew this was happening?"

"Of course I knew," the Oracle shook his head in disgust. "I'm the Oracle. It's my job to know. Do you think they just drew my name out of a hat and said...Oh goodie, you get to be the Oracle? Younglings!"

"Then why didn't you tell us?" Luke demanded. "We could have killed him," he choked. "We would have killed him."

"Jonas would never have allowed it," the ancient one scoffed. "As long as Tarris had that stone with him, he was connected to Jonas. And when you lot told me of the agreement, made me witness to your vows, I knew your brother would never allow you to harm him."

"Still..." Mark began.

"He wasn't sure," Callie frowned at them. "That's why you didn't tell them. You weren't sure."

"Oh, you're going to be fun to have around," the old man sniffed, avoiding the harsh glares of the Bears. "Fine. I wasn't sure. I thought it was better if everyone involved was a bit careful."

Chapter Seven

෨

Careful? Tarris thought. He struggled to keep the smile off his face. Careful?

"Tarris?" Anna's voice was quiet and her face pale. He turned to her. She was a *se'er*. Just like Stanton she was able to see the true form of those who weren't human. Those her hunter family called the dark ones. Her first look at Luke had been quite a shock for both of them. He wondered what she saw now. She stepped toward him cautiously. She reached for his face and touched it. Her wary eyes examined him carefully.

"Anna? What's wrong? " Luke asked with concern.

"I've never seen anything like it," she whispered.

"What do you see, girl," the Oracle asked with interest.

"He casts a Bear's shadow but in my eye he has horns and pointed ears," she smiled. "He should be terrifying, a horrible mutation but he's not. He's beautiful."

"Then he'll be able to transform?" Mark asked curiously. Tarris detected a note of concern and grinned. Luke laughed out loud and Mark flushed slightly.

"Afraid he'll be able to kick your ass again, brother?" Luke snorted. He addressed the humans, "Before Mark transformed for the first time, Tarris could always best him physically."

"He dumps you on your ass regularly, so I don't see why you're laughing." Mark glared at his twin.

"What I want to know is if they're mated?" Sarah said softly from Mark's side. "Callie's hand was over the stone as it touched Tarris' skin. Are they mated?"

"Yes," the Oracle assured them. "When the soul that is now Tarris'—that has been Tarris' for some time—passed through Callista, it joined them together."

"And the stone in Tarris' chest?" Sarah asked staring at the swirling, flickering lights that were settling a bit now as the stone began to look more and more like a natural opal.

"Yes," the Oracle nodded. "From the way it has always soothed Tarris, the reaction Callista has when she touches it," this last brought a flush to the face of the woman at Tarris' side, "I'd say yes, it is their mating stone."

"Only Tarris gets to wear it like a girl," Luke chuckled. Tarris shot him a nasty look and was pleased when Luke yelped as Anna elbowed him hard in the stomach.

His head was starting to hurt. There was so much noise and yet, so much quiet. There was no one in his head with him. Their feelings he could still sense. His empathy was still in place. But he had no idea what caused those feelings or what they were thinking. It stirred a sick feeling in his stomach and Luke's comment had touched a nerve. Not that he was afraid of some stupid gender role reversals, hell that was crap. He'd always been strong enough to let others be strong when they needed to and still take command when it was necessary.

What made him ill was the loss of control. The loss of the ability to know what was happening. The inability to communicate with those he loved. He couldn't even speak the name of his new…mate? Everything had changed and changed suddenly. The being who shouldn't have wanted anything to do with love and family and mates had gone from desperate craving what he believed he couldn't have and wasn't supposed to want, to having it. But at a price. He loved Callista, he didn't regret anything he'd have to give up to have her but he felt helpless and alone. Two things that had overwhelmed him in those moments before Jonas died. Now he was trapped in them. He had to get out of this place. He had to…

Callie's hand slipped into his and squeezed. He looked down into eyes filled with concern and caring. He wasn't alone, exactly. As isolated as he felt in his head, he wasn't alone, yet he was. It made no sense and he couldn't even talk it out with her. Gods, he wanted to be back in his room, away from the eyes of others, away from the questions he had no answers to. Tarris saw her nod slightly. He didn't know if he could do it. Had this been taken from him? He reached out and saw the doorway. Holding her hand firmly he stepped toward the door.

"You always were a rude little shit," Luke's voice was the last thing he heard before he pulled Callie with him through the opening and into a place where they were alone.

Suddenly the air was twenty degrees warmer. The vent was pouring warm air from the ceiling and a fire blazed in the grate. He saw Callie open her eyes and look around the room. They were in his room in the house. They were alone. Now he just had to find a way to talk to her.

Callie turned to him and wrapped her arms around his chest. He held her tightly, feeling her body mold itself to his. Though she was taller than Sarah or Anna, she still tucked up under his chin. Suddenly so much of what had churned inside him under the eyes of the others dissipated and he felt himself relax. This was how it should be. He and Callista. He loved his family and yes, he was certain that was the feeling that filled him where they were concerned. He loved them but watching their blank faces, the emptiness behind their eyes and words was more than he could handle.

"Wow," she whispered softly.

Tarris had no idea if this was a good wow, or a bad wow. Positive and negative emotions were swirling inside her. But it didn't seem as bad as the deafness he had with the others. *Probably because I've always had trouble hearing her*, he mused. Perhaps that would turn out to be a good thing. He'd already had to learn to watch her face and eyes, to fill in the blanks left by the muffled thoughts he'd always read from her.

"This has been one hell of a day." She pulled back and tilted her head up to look at him. "Are things always like this in your world?"

He smiled softly and shook his head. He swept his arm outward indicating the room and then tapped his chest hoping she'd understand. "You're saying you spend your time here, mostly." He nodded. "I understand. I'm a bit of a homebody myself." Her hand came up to touch the stone. It should have seemed odd to him but he felt no weight or discomfort from it being there. It was as if it had always been a part of his body and had just now claimed its rightful place. Sort of the way he felt about Callista. He did feel a ripple of sensation shoot through him and cause a tightening in his groin. When she stroked the stone, the desire he'd felt in their dreams awakened.

"And now I'm your mate?" she was still stroking his chest, fingers fanning out from the stone and moving over his skin.

He sighed and nodded again. How was he supposed to say the things he wanted to say to her? How was he supposed to tell her what he felt? This sucked. His head was full of the words he wanted to say, words that told her how beautiful she was, how undeserving of her love he felt and how much of him she held in her power. But there was no way to do it.

"Tarris," Callie was watching his face. "You spoke to me in dreams, why can't you speak now? Is it that different?"

It was true he'd spoken in dreams but never in the real world. Could it be that different? He opened his lips to form the words but no sound came out. He pushed air through his throat trying to force the words to come. A soft sound came from his throat but he couldn't quite shape it into words. He knew how to form the words with his lips but there must be more to it than that.

She sighed. "It's okay. We'll figure it out. You can make sounds so it must be possible for you to talk. Maybe a speech therapist could help. Whatever it takes we'll work it out." She grinned at him. "You could carry around a notepad for a while." She hesitated, "You can write can't you?"

He let her go quickly and moved over to the desk. Hitting a key on the keyboard of the computer woke it from hibernation mode. His fingers flew over the keys and he beckoned her with his hand. She moved around to stand beside him and read the screen, *Yes, I can write and read.*

"Thank God," she laughed wearily. "Imagine a librarian mated to a man who was illiterate. I'd have to keep you locked in our bedroom, chained to the bed."

He knew she was teasing him. He sensed no shame in her at their mating. He loved her humor. It had been so seductive to him during the time they spent in dreams. Not just loving physically but loving with their souls and minds. They talked and touched and laughed. He hoped fervently that it would be the same way in the flesh.

Eager to find out, Tarris wrapped his arms around her and lifted her. He carried her over to the bed and stopped. Setting her on her feet, he unwound her arms from his neck. He kissed her, his tongue pushing past her soft lips to slide against the warm sweetness of her mouth. His cock shifted and grew harder as her hands answered him as urgently as her lips. The sensation surprised him and he gasped. Her palms smoothed down the small of his back and cupped his ass, squeezing it. He tilted her head back and plunged his tongue deeper, he wanted to climb inside her and never leave. He wanted every length of him pushing inside her, filling her with him until she never doubted that this was where they belonged. Together, two wholes becoming even stronger by their joining.

Her nails raked up his back before her hands came to rest on his shoulders. Her kiss, her eager tongue, offering the reassurance he no longer received from her mind. But at the moment all he could think was that he needed to have her shirt gone. He pulled it over her head quickly and she reached down to push her pants down over her hips. She kicked them away as he turned back to her. His breath caught in his throat. When she moved to press against him, her hands reaching for his waistband, he stopped her.

All he could do was stare at her. She was so beautiful and the inferno the sight of her was causing, the heat that was infusing him, settled in his groin and made him ache. He'd never felt this in the confines of his own flesh. He'd never felt the actual sensation of sex and need and desire in his own body. They were overwhelming and a bit frightening. But good. So good.

"Tarris?" Callie's eyes were wide and her lower lip trembled. He pulled her close to him and held her. Her breasts pressed against his chest and he could feel the hard nipples. He kissed her again, silencing whatever she was about to say. Her hands opened the fly on his jeans and she pushed them down over his hips. The briefs followed as he released her long enough to shove them down and kick away the last of the cloth confines. The heat of her body as he felt it pressed against his swept through him. His swollen shaft prodded into the soft flesh of her stomach as he plundered the soft mouth. She pushed back at this tongue with her own. Her own passion just as inflamed as his.

She left his lips to trail her kiss across his collarbone. What had been good in dreams had been better in dreams with her. But what had been better in dreams with her, was beyond words in the flesh. Her sharp teeth nipped at his skin as he moved his hands up to caress her breasts. Her soft moan was stifled by his shoulder but his hissed into the air. Her breasts, the weight of them in his hands, the feeling of the supple flesh, the raised texture of the areola, the hard tip, he'd not expected it to feel so much more wonderful.

Callie heard the rush of pleasure escape his lips and looked up at him. There was a confused, almost wondrous look on his face as he cupped her breast, his thumb brushing over the skin. Desire began to swirl at her core and the tingling sensation darted directly from her nipple to her clit. She needed him inside her. The sensations of the golden mist earlier had been overwhelming but they had not eased the need that had filled her for some time. She was perpetually ready for him, needing to feel the length of him inside her. And his length was just as impressive, just as beautiful as it had been in her dreams.

She slid her hand across his chest and she saw him smile. He gently pressed her nipple between his finger and thumb and she squirmed, pressing her thighs together trying to ease the need that was making her want to grab him, push him down onto that bed and ride him until he made her come. It wasn't exactly working as he rolled the hardened flesh, one after the other. She heard his name pass from her with the gasp of air that escaped her lungs. His smile widened.

Two could play at this game. She moved her hands down over abs that made her want to lick honey from them and then farther to the soft nest of blond curls. Her fingers curled around the base of his cock and he jumped back from her, his eyes wide and his breathing much faster.

"Did I hurt you?" she worried. He shook his head and a look of unadulterated frustration claimed his face. He ran a hand through his hair and from the jerking half gestures of his hand she knew he was trying to find a way to tell her something. "Do you want to go back to the computer?" she asked helpfully.

He shook his head violently. His hands trembling as he reached up and tapped his own chest. Great, they were going to play charades. All she wanted was to make love with him and she was going to have to play charades first. Her irritation must have passed to him because he reached for her hand, his face a plea for her patience.

"I get *you*, what about you," she sighed, moving closer to him and running her hands over his chest. "Tell me what about you." He seemed to think for a moment, or perhaps he was distracted when she leaned down and flicked her tongue across his tiny nipple. He grabbed her face and pulled it to his, his expression failing to be stern. Tarris guided her hand to touch his ever hardening cock. He drew a ragged breath and shook his head. "You don't want me to touch your...well, touch you there?" Callie looked astonished.

Tarris let out a sharp exasperated grunt. He drew a deep breath then closed his eyes, his head drooping as if he were asleep. His hand suddenly reached down and cupped her bare mons and stroked it. He peeked at her with one eye and nodded. Then he opened his eyes, his face alert his body tall and stiff, then pushed his finger deeper into her folds, making her bite her lower lip and shook his head. The nerves were showing on his face, his gaze hesitant and uncertain.

Confusion suddenly gave way to understanding. "You're nervous," she started to giggle. "We've never done this when we were awake and you're nervous." It was laughable. She'd been eager for it all this time and here he was apprehensive. Tarris was watching her with an odd expression. He nodded then started to slowly shake his head while pointing to his own chest.

"Oh my God," Callie realized what he was saying. "You've never...when awake you've never..."

The shy smile that accompanied his nod was so stunning that she almost forgot the point. "Tarris, you've never been touched nor had sex when you were awake?" He shrugged. His hand moved over his chest lightly and he leaned in and quickly kissed her. His hands lifted in a gesture that meant, "That's all." He'd been caressed, he'd kissed but everything else that he'd experienced had been in the realm of dreams. She thought back to the book Stanton had given her, loath to bring even the thought of him into this. But it had clearly said that the incubus was only functional in dreams. It felt arousal, it felt desire only in the confines of the dreams.

But Tarris wasn't just an incubus any longer and the hard shaft of flesh that stood as a beautiful testament to his excitement was proof that he was definitely functional. Callie tried to stop the grin on her face that was flushing red despite her best efforts. She hung her head and her shoulders shook with embarrassed laughter. "Oh my God, you're a virgin."

The indignant grunt from the man who held her showed her he didn't like the comment at all. His response was tip her head back and proceed to show her he knew exactly what he was doing. And damn did he! His kiss swept every corner of her mouth making her even wetter for him. His hands slid down, one cupping her ass and the other slipping back between her folds. His fingers teased the damp and sensitive flesh as he continued to feast on her lips. She didn't need telepathy to know the thought in his head. *I'll show you virgin.*

She felt him push her back toward the bed. When it bumped against her legs he pushed down on her shoulders and she sat. He dropped to his knees, pushing her legs apart as he did. She leaned back on her hands and watched his face. It was almost as if it was the first time again. The hungry look that seemed to be studying her. Tarris lowered his head and ran his tongue up over her slit. She sucked in a sharp breath at the feeling. This had definitely lost nothing in the translation between dreams and reality. His smile and the pleased look on his face showed he echoed her thoughts.

His tongue pushed at the bare, tender wet flesh and parted it. He ran broad strokes up the inner lips and teased a path over the top of her clit. The sensation of his tongue stroking her was doing the unbelievable, the impossible. It was making her wetter. The probing invader moved down until he found the opening and dipped inside. Callie fell back and moaned. The hard velvet of his tongue plunged into her, tasting her, drinking her in as it flicked against her inner walls. He withdrew his tongue, used it to deliver sharp, hard flicks to her engorged clit. The need was overwhelming and he was pushing her. He was going to make her come fast. First one, then a second thick finger pushed into her pussy, curling against the most explosive of spots within her as they drew in and out of her. He tongue continued to assault her clit.

Callie bucked her hips up to him, trying to make him lick her harder, trying to push his fingers in deeper. But he resisted, he kept her right there, on the verge until she pushed herself up and grabbed a handful of his hair. "Tarris," she groaned between pants. "Now, make me come. Now."

His laughed triumphantly as he pressed his fingers harder, the rhythm of his strokes becoming faster. His tongue showed no mercy to the hard nodule as he rhythmically licked it and sucked at it. Callie cried out as he gave to her. Her head tossing back and forth on the mattress, hands clenching the comforter she suddenly felt a burst of vibration against her swollen clit. Tarris hummed deeply in his throat, the sound piercing her tender flesh and sending her cascading over the edge. He drew out her pleasure as long as he could, not stopping the ministration of his mouth and hands until she'd swung upward once again and the second orgasm had racked her body.

Only then did he raise his head from her. Only then did he stand and slip his arms under her. He lifted her and repositioned her against one of the pillows. She felt his body slide in beside her and cradle her against his flesh. He held her for a moment as her breath returned to her body. Her hand moved over his chest. So beautiful was her Tarris, so giving. It was time someone gave back.

Her hand brushed the stone over his breast bone and something happened. Callie opened her eyes. She should have been tired, drained but the pulsing stone that danced beneath her fingers sent a jolt of desire through her. She heard Tarris moan slightly as she traced it. Stroking the stone seemed to make its effect even stronger, for both of them. His blue eyes met hers as she sat up.

Yes, it was time someone gave back.

"Tarris," she whispered. She lifted up and kissed him deeply. His tongue met hers and the wet velvet dance continued for several moments. She pulled back reluctantly. She looked at him and then at the headboard. The wooden slats of the large bed seemed to have been made for a bit of naughty fun. She had nothing to tie him with and didn't want to leave the bed long enough to find something.

Rolling over him, she straddled his waist. She felt him suck in a deep breath as his cock came into direct contact with the moist flesh that would soon bring him even more pleasure. "You're going to be a very good little virgin," she said firmly. He lifted a brow at her, clearly annoyed. She took his hand and lifted it over his head. She formed his fingers around one of the slats. "Don't let go," she ordered. He was clearly amused at her sudden bossiness and willingly complied when she placed his other hand in the same position.

"Here's the deal, my innocent one," she began only to be interrupted by a disapproving snort from the man below her. "Behave," she admonished firmly. "As I was saying, here's the deal. If you let go, I stop. Move your hands from those posts and I'll stop whatever I'm doing, get dressed and go home. Got it?"

He opened his lips wordlessly, obviously wanting to argue. "I'll take your silence as agreement," she teased and his eyes narrowed at her. He wasn't angry, he was as curious as hell and enjoying this game. But he wasn't going to make it too easy.

She started with a soft kiss to his lips. Leaning over his body, his hard shaft sliding against her lower lips, she slid her tongue against his. His hands tightened on the headboard. Callie moved to his jaw and licked and kissed her way to his ear. She let her tongue slide over the outer curve and felt the shuddering breath that he expelled. Moving her lips to his neck, she caressed the tightly corded skin with her lips. As she teased the flesh, her hands reached up and lightly brushed the skin on his inner arms. She tasted the gooseflesh her touch had stirred in him. His soft groan vibrated deliciously against her lips.

Down farther her fingers brushed, soothing over his shoulders, then across his chest. She followed with her mouth, awakening his flesh with her teeth and tongue. She caressed the stone over his heart and he moaned loudly. She felt the current that flowed from her hand directly to her core, making her squirm against him, rubbing her pussy against his hardness. Lower she moved, her tongue pausing to tease his taut nipples. His grip tightened on the headboard and the action caused his muscles to contract under her lips.

Lower she moved, tracing the lines of his abs with fingers and lips. Lower still, she moved pushing between his thighs as he had often lain between hers. She pointedly ignored his swollen cock and spread kisses up his inner thighs. When she reached the soft sac that lay against him, she cupped it gently and began to explore it with her mouth. His ragged panting turned into low, delighted moans as she relentlessly teased the tender flesh, sucking it into her mouth, licking it and tracing patterns on the sweet skin with her tongue.

His legs jerked as she teased him. Looking up she saw his eyes on her. The intensity of his gaze nearly undid her. It was so needful, so hungry and so full of love. Shifting to her knees, Callie took the rounded head of his penis into her mouth. Tarris let loose a strangled cry and bucked his hips up toward her involuntarily. She'd been ready for that and pulled back before he could push himself deeper than she could take him. He filled her mouth and teased her throat. She sucked him firmly and his head twisted from side to side, pure pleasure etched on his face. She loved the feel of him sliding against her tongue. Just as in her dreams he wasn't salty but sweet, as small droplets of his cum rose for her to taste.

She didn't have to guess at the depth of the effect of the sensations. His body suddenly stiffened under her and the same beautiful, wordless song that had ripped from him early sounded again as she felt him burst inside her mouth. She sucked harder, greedily drinking in the honey-sweet taste of him. As his body relaxed she licked the tender head of his cock and gently kissed it.

She wasn't finished with him. So far his reactions, though more intense, had been just as they had been in her dreams. She'd bet that this included the speed at which he was always ready for her. Moving up again, she straddled his hips. His cock rested against her pussy and she leaned forward to kiss him.

His arms wrapped around her and he returned her kiss with a heat that showed he was far from sated. Lifting her face slightly, she brushed his lips with hers as she whispered. "Does this mean you want more?"

A soft soundless laugh tickled her face as he tucked a hand under her chin and lifted her eyes to his. No words were necessary when she saw the hunger burning in the blue depths. His point was driven home by the sudden slip of his hand over her ass to cup her curves. Pushing herself up, Callie reached down to stroke him. She pressed his cock against her wet slit and rocked her hips. His hardness rubbed against her clit sending shivers of delight through them both.

His hands slid over her stomach to cradle her breasts. He squeezed them gently and moved his thumb over the nipples in tantalizing circles. She drew in a deep breath and continued to move against him, writhing rhythmically against his cock until the burning need for him grew so hot she could no longer deny herself.

Their eyes locked to one another, she lifted and guided him into place. Easing down with deliberate slowness she allowed just the tip of his erection to slide inside her. It was cruel torture she was exacting upon herself but it was worth it to watch the expression on his face as he got his first taste of the warm wetness that would envelope him. His jaw clenched and his hands moved down to grip her hips. For moment she thought she saw a flicker of the jumping blue flames in his eyes.

She took a deep breath and with one single fluid movement lowered her body to capture his full length. The loud cry of pure pleasure that the action pulled from him turned into a dual cry when she reached out and placed her hand on the opal over his breastbone. The shockwave hit her body and narrowed with excruciating intensity as it assaulted the most sensitive portions of her body. Tarris' hands, lips and tongue seemed to be everywhere at once. Sucking her hard nipples, stroking her flesh, toying with her ass, licking at her hypersensitive clit.

She rocked harder against him as he thrust upward to meet her. His eyes were closed and she watched the light shift and twist on the planes of his face as his brow furrowed and his jaw snapped together and clenched. A growling sound came from low in his throat. She tried to concentrate, to focus on him. The beauty of his face and body as he trembled in ecstasy drove straight into her heart and filled her with her own sense of delight. She was pleasing him as surely as he pleased her.

His fingers tugged at the stiff peaks of her breasts and she had to push them away. She wanted to watch his face, to see him come for her before she gave in, before she surrendered to the swirling need that was pulling her under, grabbing at her and demanding she yield to it.

Tarris lifted his hands and grabbed at the headboard, the muscles on his forearms thrown into dramatic relief as he strained against the wood, his thrusts increasing with her in the escalating tempo she was demanding of him. His hands squeezed the slats so tightly that his fingers grew pale and white. She saw his arms start to tremble.

His eyes opened and met hers. The blue fire danced in their depths. It leapt as if it could escape the confines of the orbs and flicker along her body. She was moving over him, her pussy throbbing its demand for release, the rest of her body in agreement. Suddenly his head flew back and an erotic, primal cry was forced through his lips. Callie felt his climax explode inside her. The sensations that raged through him pummeled her senses and combined with the feral beauty of the man beneath her in full release. The power that demanded her pleasure suddenly robbed her of all awareness except the waves of orgasm that slammed into her body.

Her breathing seemed to stop and the screams that came from her throat barely registered as her body rushed in on itself only to erupt again and again until she collapsed on top of him.

How much time passed she didn't know and it didn't matter. Eventually she became aware of the hand that stroked her hair and the arms that held her to the wall of muscle beneath her. She heard a soft shushing sound and a quiet hum. Slowly she realized she was no longer awake. The feeling of being inside one of his dreams gained her attention and she lifted her head. Her heart fluttered with joy as she realized he could still enter into her dreams. They could still have these immensely private times where no one else could intrude. Where the limitations of the real world could be negated. The edges of her vision were a bit fuzzy as she watched his expression. His face was sleepy and the smile on his face was smug. But his eyes. The light dancing in his eyes gave away the happiness inside him.

"Not bad for a virgin, eh?" he chuckled.

"No," she agreed and tucked her head back up under his chin, inhaling his delicious scent. How long he held her before he too drifted to sleep she didn't know. But this time as their dreams tangled and wove together, there were no nightmares, no hunters, no guilt and no loss.

There was only peace. Peace and love.

Epilogue
Nine Months Later...

℘

"Callista, you know your father and I love you," her mother stood beside the small gray sedan. She'd stopped by to visit that afternoon as she did every couple of weeks. Callie looked forward to the lunches despite the fact that they could be a bit trying. Especially the ones her mother made without one of her sisters tagging along. Since Callie and Tarris had moved from the main house two months ago, her sisters seemed to lose interest. Callie figured it had to do with the decreased opportunity to ogle Levi and Laban whose presence was deliberately obvious when "outsiders" were in the main house. She and Tarris now lived in the small cottage that had belonged to the Oracle. True to his own prophecy that day in the bunker, he'd followed Jonas only a few weeks later. He'd died peacefully in his sleep, a ready smile on his face.

She waited for her mother to continue, though by now she'd heard this particular litany enough she could recite it. "We know you love Tarris and it's obvious how much he dotes on you," her mother continued, patting an errant strand of her graying hair back into its tight chignon. The woman's tailored gray suit was as conservatively put together as her meticulous makeup.

Callie held back her sigh. *Here it comes.*

"My darling we think it a fine and noble thing the way you love him despite his *handicap*," she whispered the last word as if it were a terrible secret she was revealing. "We've even learned to accept the fact that Tarris is an artist and think it's wonderful that his brothers are so supportive. Allowing him to live here and helping out with things..." the woman paused.

Callie bit her tongue hard. She'd never change her parents' impression of Tarris as some bohemian artist who lived off his brothers. She and the others had nudged him not so gently to return to his art. Luke was even planning to build him a studio here at their new home. It was not something her family warmed to readily. It had gotten particularly bad since her mother had arrived to find Luke, an architect by trade and passion, overseeing the installation of the new heating system for the house. The look she'd given her daughter when Callie explained that Tarris was in his studio up at the main house painting had been infuriating. She was tempted to grab their bank book and shove it in her mother's face when she got like this. The balance would surely have caused the woman a small coronary. Tarris had lived more than a century and was no fool about money. He'd left "comfortable" behind and long ago moved into "Damn!"

"Your father is adjusting to the fact that the two of you are living..." Callie heard her bite back the words "in sin" before finishing, "together."

"So quickly?" Callie muttered, "We've only been living together nine months."

Her mother glared at her harshly. "Callista Marshall, you will watch your tone."

"I'm sorry, Mom," she replied. "You were saying..." *You're always saying. Over and over again you're saying.*

"My dear what your father and I don't understand is why you and Tarris don't just get married."

"Tarris' family does things a bit differently, Mom. They don't go for large formal weddings." Callie knew the response before it escaped the older woman's lips.

"Nonsense. I was at Sarah's wedding." Her mother pulled her keys from her purse.

288

"That was more for Sarah's family." She cringed as soon as the words left her lips.

"And your family is less deserving of consideration?" The sharp eyes narrowed.

"That's not what I meant, Mom," she tried to smooth the situation over but knew it was hopeless.

"It's just that at your age…" her mother let that hang for several seconds. Yes, at thirty years old she was way over the hill in her mother's eyes. It was probably why her parents tolerated her living in sin. At least she'd finally captured herself a man. "Well, you would think that the two of you would come to your senses. You are not children playing house. It's time to accept some grownup responsibilities."

"Mom, Tarris is a grown up," Callie's face flushed hotly.

"I'm not just talking about him. You had a perfectly respectable job at the library that you gave up to do this research thing of yours. You've already said you don't want to be a professor, so I fail to see why you would waste time and money…"

"Mom, you're going to be late." Callie pointed out. If there was one thing that got her father worked up more than Callie's current living arrangements it was someone being late for an appointment, particularly if it was he who was left waiting.

"Promise me you'll think about it," the older woman pressed as she unlocked her door and slid behind the wheel.

"I promise," Callie replied flatly. She waved as her mother pulled way. Her gray mother. Gray hair, gray suit, gray eye shadow, gray car… The woman was all gray. Callie turned back to walk into the house and the front window caught her eye. Swirls of brightly colored glass formed an impossible pattern around the edges of the window. Vines, leaves and brightly colored birds and flowers decorated the edges of the large pane. Tarris. He'd painted this window for her before they'd moved in.

Stepping inside she saw the bright contrasts of color and the hand-painted borders that edged the small entry way and continued down the narrow hall to the back of the house. She followed the intricate Celtic knot design. Turning left would have led her to their room. Truth be told she'd like to lie down but a sudden impulse made her turn right.

Tarris was still experimenting and adjusting to the idea of food he could actually touch. She'd taken great delight in introducing him to foods she thought he'd enjoy. He was true to Bear form in loving meat but she'd also discovered he had quite a sweet tooth. Sarah told her it was a trait all the Ursine men shared. No chocolate was the rule for Sarah's twins but the adult males enjoyed it in moderation. Callie shook her head at the thought. Only men could be moderate about chocolate.

Callie opened the refrigerator door and checked its contents. Yep, she had all the ingredients she needed. Tonight she'd introduce Tarris to Pavlova. The airy, light, almost marshmallow base with the layers of fruit on top. He'd love it. Though he'd explained to her in their dreams that he had known about things having taste, in fact he said when he fed as an incubus each person had a different flavor. But each new dish she could find to introduce him to was met with excitement and a wicked sense of adventure. Though he'd shied from them at first, he had quickly warmed up to the idea of spicy foods such as Indian or Thai cuisines. Now he was game for almost anything she tossed at him. Except Brussels sprouts. Those he hated.

Each night he'd tell her exactly what he liked and didn't like. And not only in the area of food. And each night he told her how much he loved her. His musical voice wrapping around her and warming her.

But only in their dreams. He'd been going to rather intensive therapy with a speech therapist who had flown in from London. The need for such therapy wasn't common among Weres and it had taken a good deal of networking on

Mark's part to locate one. The man turned out not to be a Were but a half fey. The fey dealt more with such issues among their Halflings. Telepathy, which most fey possessed to some degree, might be handy but it didn't work well on its own for anyone wanting to mix in the human world. Learning to speak was vital. Callie'd still not heard Tarris speak a word but he assured her in her dreams that it was going well.

* * * * *

As dessert chilled in the refrigerator and the lasagna baked and bubbled in the oven, Callie sat down in the living room and leaned her head against the back of the soft chair. It seemed as if only seconds had passed when a hand was shaking her. Opening her eyes, she looked into the smiling blue orbs of her mate. He stood before her in the soft white pants he'd worn the first time she'd seen him, though that had been in a dream. The white shirt he'd worn to his appointment with the speech therapist that afternoon was unbuttoned and hung from his shoulders. She was surprised he'd not removed it yet. He stood there watching her with interest. One eyebrow was raised half in amusement and half in concern.

Are you all right? Tarris signed to her. She'd brought him a book on sign language and he'd poured through it rapidly. Some of their waking communication consisted of standard signs and some of gestures they had settled into using by mutual understanding and agreement. He used one now. *Your mother?* His hands were held vertical with his finger spread wide. He passed the fingers through the spaces between the fingers on the other hand, moving his hand back and forth. It was the sign for gray. To them it was the sign that meant Callie's mother.

"Yes. But it's fine. She is how she is." Callie sighed. She seemed sigh a lot where her family was concerned.

Was she angry? Tarris drew his hand together like a claw in front of his face.

"No, just disappointed," a smile started at the corner of her mouth. "You know how she gets. It's the same thing every time she gets on that roll of hers and doesn't stop. Every visit she asks the same question..." Callie paused. She made it a point not to raise the question of marriage with Tarris. It wasn't really a part of his world and to him they were married in every way that mattered. She was his mate. He didn't understand how some human ceremony could validate, or the lack of it invalidate, the joining of two souls. Such a thing was personal.

Ah, he nodded his understanding. *Maybe she has a point.*

Callie stared at him in shock. "She has a point?"

Maybe, palms up he shifted them up and down as if balancing scales. A mischievous smile tugged at his lips until he could no longer deny it. Slowly he knelt before her. His hand reached out and touched her face, his palm pressed to her cheek.

He held her gaze, his grin slowly slipping into an earnest and tender expression that caused her heart to feel as if it had skipped a beat.

"Callista."

Stunned, Callie stared wordlessly at him. Had she really just heard him? Heard him speak?

"I love you."

A shuddering sigh that was almost a sob shook her body and she reached to grab him. He'd spoken. He'd spoken her name and for the first time her ears had heard him say the words, "I love you." His cheek was pressed against her breasts and his arms wrapped tightly around her waist as she buried her face in his hair. It wasn't his previous melodic voice, though the hint that it one day would be again was evident but no sound had ever been so glorious.

"Oh Tarris," she whispered. She'd begun to worry despite the reassurances he and the speech therapist had been giving her.

He held her for a long moment before he pushed her away. He took her face in his hands and gave her a deep, lingering kiss. When he finally leaned back, he took her hands in his. "Will you marry me?"

The tears that had been clinging to her lashes spilled over onto her face. "But you don't really want…"

He shook his head and stopped her words. Letting go of her hands, he reverted to signing. *I want you. I was confused by why this was important but now I think I understand.*

Callie looked at him sharply. He'd been at the main house the entire afternoon for his therapy. Sarah. He must have talked to her. Callie held her tongue and waited for him to continue. When he did, he confirmed her suspicions.

Sarah explained. To you and me, we are one. I belong to you and you to me. To my family we are mates, no questions asked. But to your family and your world we are not. Sarah said it would be as if you and I were lovers but not mated. There would be no clear message to others that you accepted me and wanted to be with me. All the days of our lives.

"Tarris, lots of humans don't get married and they're happy." She tried to fight back her growing excitement. No matter how she denied it to herself, him and her family, she wanted it. And no amount of telling herself she was being silly, that she was being incredibly unenlightened and old-fashioned would change things in her heart. There was a little bit of gray inside her too.

Callista, he used the sign he'd adopted for her name. His right hand formed a "c" and it touched his lips briefly in a gentle kiss. It was absolutely adorable if she thought about it. *This isn't just about you. I understand now and it bothers me. Do you think I want human men thinking I don't claim you?*

She saw the possessive surge register in his face. She'd always felt this from him so she was not as shocked as his family tended to be when the Bear in him reared its head.

"Callista," he formed the word slowly and carefully. His hand reached into his pocket and pulled out a small dark blue box. When he opened it, she saw the diamond solitaire that sat in the velvet lining. It was large without being excessive. Her parents would never be able to criticize it, though they would probably assume Mark paid for it. Her pride burned more than a little. He waited as she examined it, the tears again starting to fill her eyes. The simple clean cut of the stone fitted him. It fitted their life together.

"Will you marry me?" The effort that went into the words made them all the sweeter in her ears.

"Yes, Tarris," She replied simply and the tears began to flow again. "I love you."

His smile was dazzling as he slid the ring on her finger. His brow furrowed and he concentrated on his words again. "I love you. All the days of our lives."

Also by Elyssa Edwards

ഔ

Seeing Me

About the Author

ഔ

Elyssa Edwards' life has sometimes felt more like fiction than reality. She is currently living her own happily-ever-after with her darling one, whom she calls Precious, mostly because it causes a good deal of gnashing of teeth.

Elyssa welcomes comments from readers. You can find her website and email address on her author bio page at www.ellorascave.com.

Tell Us What You Think

We appreciate hearing reader opinions about our books. You can email us at Comments@EllorasCave.com.

Why an electronic book?

We live in the Information Age—an exciting time in the history of human civilization, in which technology rules supreme and continues to progress in leaps and bounds every minute of every day. For a multitude of reasons, more and more avid literary fans are opting to purchase e-books instead of paper books. The question from those not yet initiated into the world of electronic reading is simply: *Why?*

1. ***Price.*** An electronic title at Ellora's Cave Publishing and Cerridwen Press runs anywhere from 40% to 75% less than the cover price of the exact same title in paperback format. Why? Basic mathematics and cost. It is less expensive to publish an e-book (no paper and printing, no warehousing and shipping) than it is to publish a paperback, so the savings are passed along to the consumer.

2. ***Space.*** Running out of room in your house for your books? That is one worry you will never have with electronic books. For a low one-time cost, you can purchase a handheld device specifically designed for e-reading. Many e-readers have large, convenient screens for viewing. Better yet, hundreds of titles can be stored within your new library—on a single microchip. There are a variety of e-readers from different manufacturers. You can also read e-books on your PC or laptop computer. (Please note that Ellora's Cave does not endorse any specific brands.

You can check our websites at www.ellorascave.com or www.cerridwenpress.com for information we make available to new consumers.)

3. *Mobility.* Because your new e-library consists of only a microchip within a small, easily transportable e-reader, your entire cache of books can be taken with you wherever you go.

4. *Personal Viewing Preferences.* Are the words you are currently reading too small? Too large? Too… ANNOYING? Paperback books cannot be modified according to personal preferences, but e-books can.

5. *Instant Gratification.* Is it the middle of the night and all the bookstores near you are closed? Are you tired of waiting days, sometimes weeks, for bookstores to ship the novels you bought? Ellora's Cave Publishing sells instantaneous downloads twenty-four hours a day, seven days a week, every day of the year. Our webstore is never closed. Our e-book delivery system is 100% automated, meaning your order is filled as soon as you pay for it.

Those are a few of the top reasons why electronic books are replacing paperbacks for many avid readers.

As always, Ellora's Cave and Cerridwen Press welcome your questions and comments. We invite you to email us at Comments@ellorascave.com or write to us directly at Ellora's Cave Publishing Inc., 1056 Home Avenue, Akron, OH 44310-3502.

COMING TO A BOOKSTORE NEAR YOU!

ELLORA'S CAVE

Bestselling Authors Tour

UPDATES AVAILABLE AT

WWW.ELLORASCAVE.COM

erridwen, the Celtic Goddess of wisdom, was the muse who brought inspiration to storytellers and those in the creative arts. Cerridwen Press encompasses the best and most innovative stories in all genres of today's fiction. Visit our site and discover the newest titles by talented authors who still get inspired - much like the ancient storytellers did, once upon a time.

Cerridwen Press
www.cerridwenpress.com